Bilston
Moun
Bilsto
Tel: (

2 ſ

0

V   OL'S
I   HECY

3.

SHAUN HUTSON

WARHOL'S PROPHECY

LONDON NEW YORK SYDNEY TORONTO

This edition published 1999
by BCA
by arrangement with Macmillan
an imprint of Macmillan Publishers Ltd
CN 4306

Typeset by SetSystems Ltd, Saffron Walden, Essex

Printed and bound in Germany by
Graphischer Grossbetrieb Pössneck GmbH

*Dedicated to
Bill Hicks.
From the heart.
Genius never dies.*

Acknowledgements

In view of the fact that I nearly got lynched by several readers because there were no acknowledgements in the last novel (are you lot only buying them for *that* bit? I suspect you are . . .) you will hereby find that omission rectified. It won't happen again, I promise.

I would, as usual, like to thank a very large and disparate (in some cases, desperate) group of people and places for help, inspiration and sanity-saving connected with the writing of this novel.

Many thanks to my new publishers for their support and belief. Extra special thanks to Peter Lavery for his expertise and his scribblings (OK, so I rubbed most of them out, it's the thought that counts . . .). Thanks also to Matt Smith (for the ideas and for making me extra work . . . Cheers, Matt, I'll do the same for you some day). Just joking fellas, thanks. Many thanks to the sales team of Macmillan. In fact, to all of you.

Special thanks to Dee, Zena, Jo Bolsom, Sanctuary Music, Iron Maiden, Wally (if it's Thursday it must be Madrid) Grove. Thanks to Martin 'Gooner' Phillips, who suffered, as I did, last September. To Terri, Rachel and Rebecca. To Ian Austin (congratulations again . . .). Thanks to Nicki Stinson (dinner's ready!).

Very special thanks to James Whale, Linda Bartley and Ash.

To Jack Taylor, Tom Sharp, Amin Saleh, Lewis Bloch, Damian and Christina Pulle. To Stephen Luckman, too.

Thanks also to Maurice for the hot dogs and the insults . . .

ACKNOWLEDGEMENTS

Special thanks also to Hailey Owen. To Caroline at Platinum Services. To Factotum.

A special thank you to Rob Jones at Central TV. Always a pleasure to work with you, Rob, even if that bloody bulldog *did* smell . . .

To a mate of mine who didn't want to be named, so I'll just say, thanks R.H.

Indirect thanks to Martin Scorsese, Sam Peckinpah and Walt Disney (just making sure you're still paying attention – the last one was a joke . . .). Also to Metallica, Queensrÿche and Ozzy Osbourne. Thanks also to whoever makes those elasticated bandages for when your calf muscles disintegrate . . .

Thanks to the Rhiga Royal Hotel in New York and still to Margaret in Lindy's in Times Square.

As ever, thank you to Liverpool Football Club. The mighty Reds. The *only* Reds. To all those in the Paisley Lounge and beyond. Many thanks to Steve 'The Residents for ever' Lucas and Paul 'mastermind' Garner. Thanks to Aaron 'cultured' Reynolds for sharing the driving and the anger and the jokes and the tea at Keele. By the way, up yours Sky Sports. I hope you're happy to see your efforts to ruin our game are continuing as planned. Football belongs on a Saturday afternoon. Leave it there. Swivel, you bastards.

I try to say thanks to my mum and dad in every book but, as usual, it never seems enough. Probably because it isn't.

Extra special thanks to my wife, Belinda, for absolutely everything. The only woman I know who is prepared to accept me for the man I can only apologize for being. And, of course, to the other girl in my life, who doesn't really care that Dad shouts at the TV when the football's on, laughs when he drives too fast on the way back from nursery, or sings along to the CD. And who forgives him when he can't quite manage to do *all* the *South Park* voices at seven in the morning. I speak, of course, of my precious, beautiful daughter. OK, I own up, it *was* my idea to buy that black outfit for Barbie . . .

ACKNOWLEDGEMENTS

And to you, my readers. You're always there and I thank you. I hope you always will be. It's a long road sometimes, but we've still got a hell of a journey left. There's a lot of fighting to be done yet.

Let's go.

Shaun Hutson

Everyone will be famous for fifteen minutes
Andy Warhol

10030 CIELO DRIVE, LOS ANGELES, CALIFORNIA

There was blood everywhere.

Deep red pools of it. Bright splashes. Droplets here and there.

The room, the house, was filled with that vile, coppery odour.

The whole place smelled of death.

And she knew *she* was next.

These people, whoever or whatever they were, had come into her house with the express purpose of murdering them: herself and her guests.

They had entered the house with ease.

Four women, one man.

And within they had found two men and two women.

The three others were dead now.

She alone remained alive. But only until *they* decided otherwise.

The intruders had brought pain and death with them.

Knives . . . guns . . . ropes.

Death.

She was eight-and-a-half-months pregnant. She didn't want to die. All she wanted to do was have her baby: her perfect, unborn child. She pleaded with them to let her live. Pleaded with the women in particular. Trying to appeal to some semblance of maternal feeling that might be hidden beneath their blood-drenched clothes and drug-blanked expressions.

But there would be no reprieve.

They had come with a purpose decreed by their leader, and that purpose was about to reach its conclusion.

'You're going to die . . .'

One of the woman had told her that already.

'Look, bitch! I don't care if you're going to have a baby. You'd better be ready.'

Sweet Jesus, why did death have to come at all? But not this way. *NOT THIS WAY!*

If there was a God, she prayed for him to intervene.

Prayed for him to save her and her unborn baby.

Her perfect child. Her legacy. Her love . . .

One of them held her arms tightly behind her back.

Another of the women held her legs.

She tried to struggle free as she saw the man approaching with the knife.

She screamed.

For herself.

For her child.

He struck, and the blade sheared through her left breast.

Please God, help me. Please . . .

He stabbed again.

And again.

And again.

She was beginning to lose consciousness.

Stabbing . . . sixteen times.

Death.

8 August 1969

Look down on me, you will see a fool. Look up at me, you will see your Lord. Look straight at me, you will see yourself.

Charles Manson

You're coming home, there's blood on the walls.
When Charlie and the Family make house calls . . .

Ozzy Osbourne

Looks like Warhol wasn't wrong,
fame fifteen minutes long.
Everyone's using, everybody's making the sale.

Queensrÿche

I wanna be somebody, be somebody too.
I wanna be somebody, be somebody soon.

W.A.S.P

1

HER CHILD WAS dead.

That one thought had forced itself into Hailey Gibson's mind, and stuck there like a needle pushed under a fingernail.

No matter how hard she tried to tell herself that it could not be, that agonizing, tortuous idea remained. And, as the seconds passed, so did the conviction. A malignant, cancerous thought that gnawed at her reason.

Hailey spun round, looking to her right and left . . . behind her . . . in front of her. Her eyes constantly searching the mass of shoppers for any sign of her little daughter.

My child is dead . . .

She shook her head, as if to silence the voice inside her own mind.

She and Becky had entered the HMV store only moments earlier.

Moments, or hours?

Becky had been close by her side. Like any other five-year-old, smiling, laughing, dancing a little jig to the music that blasted from the shop's sound system.

Like any other five-year-old.

It was busy inside the store, as usual. A group of youths was gathered around one part of the 'Rock and Pop' section, laughing loudly, comparing possible purchases. Elsewhere, others had been scanning the rack of calendars displayed, two boys no older than fourteen taking their time over a *Baywatch* collection.

Becky herself had wandered a short way towards them, her eye probably caught by one calendar devoted to the latest pop sensations. Twelve monthly pictures of more one-hit wonders, Hailey had thought.

Business as usual.

Then, Becky was gone.

My child is dead.

Hailey had felt a grip of panic almost immediately, but that grip was tightening now. Like a noose around her neck, it was forcing her to breathe more deeply, to fill her lungs, because now it felt as if her head was swelling. As if she couldn't get enough breath. She could feel her heart hammering against her ribs, so hard it threatened to shatter them – and all the time she looked around. And around.

Dead!

She couldn't see the little red coat that Becky was wearing

(*you nearly said* had been *wearing. You already half believe she's dead, don't you?*)

despite the fact that it normally stood out like a beacon, even in crowds.

Jesus, how far could Becky have gone?

Where could she have gone?

Hailey looked around the shop again, towards the games area, towards the T-shirt racks, and the cassettes. She hurried in that direction, pushing past a woman who was picking slowly through the bargain bins. The woman muttered something under her breath as Hailey shoved her aside, but Hailey didn't hear her words. They didn't matter; nothing did, other than finding her daughter.

Two men in their thirties were playing on one of the Playstation consoles, shouting and cheering their progress on a football game displayed. Hailey passed them. She passed two youths checking through the other games on the shelves, complaining about the prices of them.

No sign of Becky.

Hailey walked to the far end of the aisle, her pace hurried, eyes constantly darting from side to side.

Please God, let me see that red coat.

Past yet more computer games. Past the huge video screen that dominated one end of the store's lower floor. Back through T-shirts and 'Easy Listening'.

Becky might have gone upstairs.

Hailey made her way towards the escalator, which carried her up to the first floor containing the Video Department. She stood still on the moving stairway until it had reached halfway, then could stand it no longer, so began hurrying up its metal steps, the heels of her ankle boots clacking loudly as she climbed.

The Video Department wasn't as crowded as the lower floor. So if Becky was up here, she should be relatively easy to spot, Hailey told herself, searching for any shred of comfort in her despair.

On three walls there were monitors showing the same selected video, but Hailey had no time to guess what it was. The images of Al Pacino flickered around her unnoticed.

On the screens he was shouting, but his rantings were silent, the film's dialogue drowned by music drifting from other speakers.

Hailey hurried around the video racks.

Al Pacino continued to scream silently.

No sign of Becky.

Hailey hurried back towards the Down escalator, taking the steps practically two at a time.

She stood, panting, at the bottom.

Now what?

If Becky wasn't inside the store, then she could truly be anywhere – hopelessly and irretrievably lost.

Dead?

Hailey tried to think. Tried to think where her daughter might have gone.

If Becky realized that she had become separated from her

mother, which by now she must have, how would she react? After the initial panic, what would she do? Where would *she* search? Would she stand obediently outside the store, just waiting for Hailey? Would she ask someone to take her to the store manager, to convince the staff to put out a message over the tannoy for . . .

(*she's five years old, for Christ's sake! Get real. Get a fucking grip*)

Get a fucking grip.

Outside the HMV store the sight that confronted Hailey was even more daunting. The wide concourses separating the rows of shops were swarming with people. At least inside the store she had a chance of finding her daughter. If she could be sure that the little girl had stayed within the confines of HMV, Hailey could continue her relentless, desperate circuit of the display racks. Just walk and walk until she finally found Becky somewhere between Metallica and Texas. But if Becky had left the store, then it was hopeless.

Hopeless.

Pointless.

My child is dead.

Perhaps Becky had retraced their steps. Perhaps she had remembered which shops they'd been in before entering HMV, and was – even as Hailey stood helplessly outside the main entrance of the store – trailing vainly around Dorothy Perkins or Next or WHSmith.

Or not.

If you can't think straight yourself, how do you expect your five-year-old to?

Hailey tried to remember what her instructions to Becky had been, should she ever become lost in a crowded shopping centre. Surely at some time, when the child was younger, she had been told what to do. That was what responsible parents did, wasn't it? They took their offspring to one side, and calmly and clearly told them what to do and how to behave in any emergency.

Didn't they?

And while their kids were behaving calmly and collectedly,

the parents sat around and waited for them to return safely. That was what happened, wasn't it?

Hailey tried to swallow, but felt as if someone had filled her throat with chalk.

She scanned the mass of shoppers.

So many faces.

So many expressions.

Hailey wondered how many, passing her by, looked with puzzlement at her own tortured features. Not that she cared. She just wanted to scream Becky's name. That if she bellowed her daughter's name aloud, it would be heard in every corner of this vast shopping complex and that, as if by magic, the child would appear at her side.

Shout? Scream? Run back and forth? Retrace your steps?

She had no idea what to do.

Hailey felt like a child.

The thought of what Becky herself must be going through now only intensified that agony.

Please God, let me see that red coat.

Her voice cracking, Hailey spoke her daughter's name.

She spoke it again, slightly louder this time.

Then again, with growing volume. She was close to shouting it now. And then, after that? Shrieking uncontrollably?

Hailey knew that she was close to breakdown. Tears of panic and fear were just seconds away. Becky was probably already sobbing somewhere else, running helplessly back and forth, calling for her mum, unable to find her in that vast amoebic flow of faceless shoppers.

My child is dead.

Hailey felt the first hot tear cut its way down her cheek, burning the skin as fiercely as if it was acid. She realized there was only one thing she could do now. And she had to do it before it was too late.

Then she saw the red coat.

2

THE CHILD WAS standing alone, looking towards the entrance of a café.

She had her back to Hailey, who had already set off towards the little blonde figure, sometimes politely weaving in and out of knots of shoppers, sometimes barging straight through them in her haste to reach the child.

Red coat!

That was the one thing she saw: the beacon drawing her like a moth to a flame.

God, she loved that coat: that beautiful, incandescent piece of craftsmanship that was about to reunite her with her daughter. The daughter she had feared was dead! And how ridiculous that thought now seemed. How could she be dead? She'd been momentarily lost. For a moment of terror and extreme anxiety admittedly, but only a moment.

Hailey was mere feet away from the child now.

The child who was standing stock-still outside the café entrance.

That must have been the instructions Becky had been given. The instructions that Hailey herself, as a responsible parent, had at one time or another given her.

'If you ever get lost, stand outside a café and wait for Mum.'

God, it was simple. So wonderfully, transparently simple.

And Becky was doing as she'd been told, and everything was all right in the whole twisted, stinking world, and there was nothing else now but to sweep her daughter up in her arms and hug her and kiss her, and they would both cry with relief and then they would laugh.

And then . . .

And then?

The child turned around.

The little girl was older than Becky by a year or two.

She stared with bewilderment at Hailey, who had already dropped to one knee close by, looking into her face – searching that alien face, that strange, unfamiliar visage.

The child took a step back, as if shocked by the sudden approach of this insane-looking woman. The kind of woman her *own* mother had always warned her to keep away from.

Hailey gazed into the child's eyes.

Frightened eyes?

The little girl took another couple of paces back. Hailey straightened up and advanced towards her, as if reluctant to believe that this red-coated figure was not her daughter after all. The child suddenly turned and ran into the café, and Hailey could see her pushing her way through the maze of tables towards two women inside. The child was now pointing out towards Hailey, that one index finger fixing her almost accusingly. Hailey could see the women's lips moving, could see their expressions darken as they stared angrily back at her. She turned and walked away from the café entrance, tears now flowing freely down her cheeks.

Becky . . .

The sight of that red coat had raised her hopes. The identity of its wearer had shattered them. And now she felt a sense of crushing despair unlike anything she had ever felt in her life before. Fear, anxiety, hopelessness and thousands of other emotions swirled around inside her mind, and that unthinkable, monstrous thought resurfaced with renewed venom.

My child is dead.

Hailey trudged robotically through the shopping centre, eyes occasionally flitting right or left, but there was no longer conviction in the thought that she might yet catch a glimpse of her missing daughter. And now other thoughts began to intrude with equally unwanted force.

Perhaps Becky hadn't just wandered off on her own in the crowds. What if she had been snatched?

Whoever had taken her could have been trailing them all morning, waiting for a split second when they became separated. You couldn't keep your eyes on your kid every second of the day, could you?

Justifying yourself now?

No one could – especially not in a crowded shopping centre. You could hold their hands, you could keep an arm around their shoulders if possible, but at some point there would be a break in contact, and in that split second it would happen. Once you were physically separated, the child could be snatched. Whisked away into the crowd, their screams muffled by a strong, determined hand across the mouth. And who else would interfere? Who would do anything more than look on with bemused or irate disinterest? And, while those blank looks registered their indifference, the child could be bundled effortlessly out of the centre and into a waiting car.

Jesus, it was all so easy. So clear.

Hailey had read about it – of parents whose children had been abducted

(*no, don't even think about words like 'abducted'. They carry the same terror as 'malignant' and 'terminal'*)

from their very sides. Parents who, hours, days, weeks or months later, were called to the local police station or hospital to identify their dead child.

Hailey no longer bothered to wipe the tears from her cheeks.

Whoever had snatched Becky might not even have needed to wait until mother and daughter had reached the shopping centre. The kidnapper could have already been watching that morning as Hailey reversed the Astra out of the garage. He could have followed them the five or so miles to the mall, parked close by, then tailed them into the building, his eyes never leaving Becky. Just waiting for the right moment.

And now?

Was Becky already dead?

Hailey continued her trance-like journey through the shopping centre, every child she passed seemingly smiling as it clutched its parents' hands. Laughing even.

All around her so much joy.

Inside her, pain such as she had never experienced.

But it could grow far, far worse, couldn't it?

She passed another mother, Hailey guessed in her early twenties, perhaps twenty-one or twenty-two: six or seven years younger than Hailey herself. The woman had two children with her, one in a buggy. The other was aged about three, and he was crying while his mother shouted angrily at him to stop, that he couldn't have any sweets yet. That she'd break his toys if he didn't shut up.

Something like that.

What did it matter what the words were?

Hailey wanted to grab that woman, to tell her she shouldn't shout at her child, because she could lose him all too easily. Lose him for ever, as Hailey had done with her *own* child.

The thought that Becky was already dead or else in the clutches of some child-molesting psychopath was so strong now that Hailey had virtually accepted it as fact. She could imagine *no* other possibility.

All that was left was pain.

Up ahead, she spotted the place she'd been heading for.

3

THE INFORMATION CENTRE was usually busy, but to Hailey it seemed even more crowded this day. Visitors, both frequent and infrequent, could go there to obtain free maps of the large shopping complex. It was also where wheelchairs could be hired, or small buggies for young children. There were several children in there now. The atmosphere inside was one of amiable chaos, a little like the entire precinct itself.

There were two women working behind the small counter, dealing with various queries and enquiries, each managing to retain the fixed smile of those in public service.

Hailey found herself queuing behind a woman in her seventies who was balancing unsteadily on two crutches and glancing around sniffily at the other occupants of the information room, and indeed at most of those passing by outside. She turned and looked appraisingly at Hailey, who was more intent on getting past her to attract the attention of one of the two officials behind the counter.

'Excuse me,' said Hailey, wiping away her tears.

The old woman glared at her disdainfully. 'I'm next,' she said, moving closer to the counter.

'Look, I'm sorry, but this is an emergency,' Hailey told her.

'I've been waiting for ten minutes already. They're not very fast here, are they?' the woman sneered audibly.

Again Hailey moved slightly forward.

'You must wait your turn,' the old woman snapped, scowling at Hailey full in the face through eyes milky with cataracts.

14

This time Hailey ignored her and pushed towards the counter, where one of the two women glanced first at her, then at the old woman, who looked as if she was about to strike Hailey with one of her crutches.

'I was first,' the old woman said angrily.

'My child is missing,' pleaded Hailey. 'Please put out an announcement.' She wiped away more tears.

The official, whose badge proclaimed CHRISTINE, looked at her companion then back at Hailey.

'Would you like to come through?' she offered, gesturing Hailey towards a door at the end of the counter.

'I shall report this,' the old woman shrieked, as Hailey disappeared into a small office beyond.

Christine Palmer closed the door behind them, and motioned for Hailey to sit down.

She pulled a pad and pen towards her and took a seat opposite Hailey, studying her briefly, taking a mental note of the swollen, puffy eyes and red cheeks. The shoulder-length brown hair looked unkempt, and her mascara was smudged around one eye. She offered Hailey a tissue, which she gratefully accepted.

'What's your child's name?' Christine asked with a practised tone that implied she had asked the same question hundreds of times before, when dealing with hundreds of equally distraught parents.

Hailey told her – adding Becky's age as an afterthought.

'And what's she wearing?'

'A red knee-length coat, white sweatshirt and black leggings with stars on the seams.' She blew her nose.

Christine wrote dutifully.

'Can I have *your* name, please?'

Again Hailey told her.

'And age?'

'What's the point of that?' Hailey snapped.

'Some kids remember things like that instead of their addresses. They remember strange things.' The woman smiled efficiently. 'Every little helps.'

'Twenty-nine,' Hailey said. 'Just get an announcement read out, will you, please?'

'Where did you lose her?'

'I didn't lose her: she wandered off,' Hailey retorted. 'It wasn't my fault.'

'I didn't say it was. I just asked.'

'One minute she was beside me, the next she was gone. It wasn't my fault.'

Shifting blame? Justifying yourself? Tut-tut.

There was a second of silence.

Then Hailey explained to Christine what had happened, and where – watching as she finished scribbling it all down on her pad. Then the woman nodded and got to her feet.

'I'll get this read out,' she reassured Hailey.

'Someone *will* find her, won't they?' Hailey said quietly, as if expecting the other woman to respond to a question that couldn't possibly be answered with any certainty.

'Let me get this read out first,' Christine Palmer said, and disappeared momentarily, leaving Hailey alone in the small room.

The walls were painted a dull yellow, and adorned with a number of leaflets advertising attractions within the shopping centre itself – including, Hailey noticed, a crèche.

If you'd put Becky safely in there, she'd still be OK.

But, for the most part, Hailey absorbed very little. Or, at least, what she did see didn't register. She could still think of nothing but Becky. How could she not?

The door opened a moment later and Christine Palmer re-entered.

'They've made an announcement,' she said.

'Now what?'

'All you can do is wait, Mrs Gibson.'

Hailey ran a hand through her hair and exhaled almost painfully. She noticed that Christine Palmer was carrying two steaming styrofoam cups. The older woman sat down and pushed one towards Hailey.

'Coffee,' Christine explained. 'Out of a machine, but it's better than nothing.' Her tone was apologetic.

'Shouldn't it be *tea* and sympathy?' said Hailey, annoyed at herself for the acidity of her tone. She sighed and accepted the coffee with a wan smile.

'This happens here fifteen or twenty times a day,' Christine said, sipping her own coffee. 'Missing kids, I mean.'

I don't care about the others!

'I can't believe I let it happen,' said Hailey.

'You can't keep your eyes on them every second.'

'I've been trying to tell myself that,' Hailey continued, fiddling around in her handbag for her Silk Cut. She pulled one from the packet and lit it, ignoring the NO SMOKING sign on the wall behind her.

'They usually turn up within about twenty minutes,' Christine reassured her.

'How?'

'Either someone recognizes the description and brings them here, or they make their own way once they've heard the announcement. The older ones at any rate.'

'Someone *brings* them in!' Hailey said incredulously. 'You mean any bloody stranger?'

Christine watched her impassively.

'Look, I've got kids of my own. I know how you feel,' she said.

'Do you?' Hailey snapped. 'My daughter is *lost* out there somewhere. Do you know what *that* feels like?'

'Were you on your own when she went missing?'

'What do you mean?'

'Were you with a friend or boyfriend or husband who might have seen something? Perhaps . . .'

'My husband's at work,' Hailey said, cutting her short. 'There was no one with me.'

'Would you like to call him?'

Hailey shook her head.

'No sense in *two* of us worrying, is there?'

'What does he do?'

'He's a partner in a local removal and haulage firm.'

'How long have you been married?'

'Six years.'

'Any other kids?'

Hailey smiled. 'I appreciate the consoling small talk,' she said quietly. 'Is it part of the job? To keep the distraught parents' minds occupied?'

'That's some of it.' Christine smiled. 'And I *am* nosy too.'

Hailey took a drag of her cigarette, then a sip of coffee.

'We got married in Barbados,' she said, as if content to speak of something else – something other than the disappearance of her daughter. As if that act alone would help her forget the pain she was feeling.

'That's romantic,' Christine offered.

'Rob said he never could have got married over here. All the messing about before the wedding day, and then the ceremony itself, he said it was too much. We might as well spend the money on a good holiday and get married at the same time.' She chuckled. 'We had a little do for some friends when we got back, but that was it.'

'Did you get married on the beach?' Christine asked with genuine interest.

'No, in a church. Just the two of us, and a couple of locals they hauled in to be witnesses. Then we went back to the hotel for photos.'

Hailey looked at her watch. 'How long now since the announcement was read out?'

'About five minutes.'

'It feels like hours.'

Christine reached across the table and gently touched her hand.

'You can go back to work if you like,' Hailey said. '*I'm* not going anywhere, am I?'

Again she glanced at her watch.

It felt as if time had stopped, and she wondered if it would ever begin again.

4

Hours . . . Minutes . . . Seconds . . .

Hailey had lost track of time and its meaning. All its divisions seemed to have blurred into one. Every small movement of her watch seemed to take an eternity. She eventually checked her own timepiece against the clock on the wall behind her.

How long had she been sitting here now?

An hour. Two hours? Longer?

Thirty-seven minutes.

She swallowed hard and looked over at the phone on the desk.

No sense phoning Rob.

Not yet.

She looked at her watch again, as if by doing so she would cause it to speed up – cause time to accelerate.

Where is Becky?

Hailey could hear sounds of organized chaos from the information office outside. Occasionally she heard children's voices. More than once she had been tempted to run to the door and look out, in the vain hope that one of those voices belonged to Becky. She could picture the scenario in her mind: she would hear the voice, rush out to see her daughter, they would fall into each other's arms, cry, hug each other, and all the pain would turn to joy. Then they would happily head for home.

And the other *scenario?*

The policeman would enter the office quietly and officiously, with Christine Palmer behind him, and he would apologize for

20

what had happened to Becky, and he would ask Hailey if she could come with him to the hospital to identify the body of a little girl in a red coat, wearing a white sweatshirt and black leggings. A body that they'd found in an abandoned car no more than five minutes' drive from the city centre.

Hailey tried to drive this particular chain of events from her mind, but it stuck there stubbornly. What initially had been fear was turning into icy conviction.

Thirty-eight minutes.

She was also beginning to wonder why she was the only parent in this room. If, as Christine Palmer had assured her, fifteen or twenty children went missing every day in this shopping centre, why had she not been joined by other devastated parents? Was hers to be the only lost child today? Was she to suffer alone?

She lit up another cigarette, took a couple of drags, then stubbed it out in her empty styrofoam cup.

Jesus Christ, she felt so helpless. She wanted someone to put an arm around her and tell her everything was going to be all right.

Rob, perhaps?

She feared it might be the comforting arm of a policewoman instead.

Hailey looked up as the door to the small office opened and Christine Palmer peered round.

She was smiling.

Hailey saw a small shape push past her.

Heard a word shouted.

'Mum!'

Dear God, what a joyous sound.

Becky swept into the room and crashed into Hailey, who had already dropped to one knee, throwing her arms around her daughter and lifting her into the air, tears flowing freely down her cheeks. She held onto her child so tightly it seemed she must break her in half. Hailey didn't want to let go of her again, *ever*.

Becky was smiling, kissing her mother and, by the look of it, altogether less concerned about her recent predicament than Hailey had been. She looked hard at her daughter, checking her face as if searching for any tell-tale signs of injury. She didn't even see puffy, red eyes – no sign of tears. No indication that Becky had been as distraught as Hailey through this ordeal.

'Are you OK?' Hailey smoothed a hand through her daughter's hair.

'Yes, Mum,' Becky said, her blue eyes like sapphires lit from behind by incandescent light.

Hailey hugged her again, for brief seconds fearing that she was imagining all this. She looked into her daughter's face once again, then touched both her cheeks with her shaking hands.

'Where did you get to?' Hailey said finally, a slight edge to her voice, her concern now almost overridden by anger. 'Why did you walk away from me? I've told you before never to leave me when we're out in a crowd.'

'I went to look for a CD for Dad,' Becky said apologetically. 'I could still see you from where I was. Then some men stood in front, and I couldn't see you. You ran away.'

'Because I thought I'd lost you,' Hailey snapped. 'I was *looking* for you.'

Again she hugged her daughter. 'Are you sure you're all right?' she persisted. 'No one touched you, did they? Where have you been all this time?'

'Adam found me,' said Becky, turning. Now, for the first time, Hailey noticed that there was someone else at the door.

She straightened up, still holding Becky as if frightened to release her.

The newcomers moved sheepishly into the room, nervous of intruding on this reunion. One wore the dark blue uniform of a security guard.

'That's Adam,' said Becky, jabbing her small index finger in the direction of the other man by the doorway.

'Adam Walker,' he said, smiling.

'My name's Stuart Jenkins,' the uniformed man told her. 'I'm with Security here.' There was an officiousness to his tone.

'Where did you find her?' asked Hailey.

'By the fountain outside,' Walker said. 'She was looking at the fish – weren't you?' He winked at Becky, who smiled coyly.

'What were you doing by the fountain?' Hailey demanded of her daughter. 'That's nowhere *near* where we got separated.'

'Mr Walker actually prevented an accident,' Jenkins offered. 'Your daughter wandered outside onto the road. If it hadn't been for Mr Walker's intervention . . .' He allowed the sentence to trail off.

'What were you doing out on the road?' Hailey rasped, gripping her daughter by the arm. 'You could have been killed.'

'I was looking for the car,' Becky said, tears welling. 'I thought I'd wait for you there.'

Walker cut the child short. 'You've got her back, that's all that matters,' he said, still smiling that infectious smile.

He took a step back.

'I'll leave you alone now,' he said, retreating. 'Unless there's anything else I can do to help. Do you need a lift home or anything? You must be a bit shaken up after what's happened.'

'We'll be OK. Thanks for offering, though.'

'Goodbye, then, Becky,' he said, waving to her. 'It was a pleasure to meet you.' He bowed exaggeratedly. 'Although I wish it had been in happier circumstances.'

Becky sniffed back a tear and managed a smile.

''Bye, Adam,' said the little girl, waving back at him.

'Thanks again, Mr Walker,' Hailey offered.

'Adam,' he insisted. 'It was my pleasure, Hailey.'

She looked surprised that he knew her name.

Noticing this, he pointed at Becky.

'You can't have any secrets when you've got a five-year-old, can you?'

And he was gone.

Jenkins followed him out of the room.

'Are we going home now, Mum?' Becky wanted to know.

Hailey looked at her and kissed her on the forehead.

'What do *you* think?' She smiled.

16 WARDLE BROOK AVENUE, HATTERSLEY, GREATER MANCHESTER

It was too cold to be out at this time of night. Standing waiting for the door to be opened. What was the big deal anyway? Why the secrecy?

Mind you, Ian was always like that. But Ian knew what was what. Clever man, Ian.

He'd lent him books and recommended others for reading. Part of an education, he had joked.

It was Ian who answered the door now. He looked smart for such a late hour: waistcoat and cufflinks. He looked as if he was on his way out somewhere, not on his way to bed.

He ushered his visitor inside, said something about those miniature bottles of alcohol he'd been promising to show. Then he disappeared for a moment.

The scream came from the sitting room.

Then a voice he recognized.

'Help him. Help him.'

He dashed into the sitting room, stopping dead at the threshold.

The room was in virtual darkness. Thick shadows, cast by the lamp on top of the TV set, carpeted the small room.

On the floor next to the couch a figure lay on its stomach.

It was screaming.

Ian was standing astride it.

Hitting it with something.

Great savage blows across the back of the skull, and the figure continued to writhe and scream.

He realized that the figure was a youth barely older than himself. Or wasn't it real?

No, this had to be some kind of joke, didn't it?

Ian was playing a joke on him.

The figure *had* to be a life-size model the way it jerked about with each fresh impact.

Each fresh impact on the skull.

With the axe.

The weapon was wielded with expert ferocity. And now he saw blood spurting, and he knew for sure that this was no joke.

He looked at Ian, who continued striking with the axe. He heard words like *'bastard'* and *'cunt'* shouted with each blow.

Fourteen blows.

And there was blood everywhere.

On the carpet. On the sofa. The walls. The fireplace.

It would have to be cleaned up.

Perhaps the woman watching would do that, he thought. The woman with the platinum-blonde hair, who stood gazing raptly at the scene of carnage before her. She was patting her two dogs, who had been in the room the whole time – but he had only just noticed them.

The woman paused for a moment, as if waiting for orders, then she wandered into the kitchen and he heard the sound of running water.

Ian told him to go and help. Help to clean the place up. Myra couldn't be expected to do it all on her own, could she?

And, when they'd finished, she'd make them all a cup of tea.

Good old Myra.

As he stepped across the blood-slicked carpet, he almost trod in something.

Something reddish-grey in colour.

Something with the consistency of jelly.

It took him only a second to realize it was a sliver of brain.
He thought he was going to be sick.

6 October 1965

Do you see the terror in her eyes, Ian?
Myra Hindley

God save Myra Hindley, God save Ian Brady,
Even though he's horrible and she ain't what
you call a lady . . .
The Sex Pistols

Preparation

THE BLADE WAS no more than three inches long.

Fashioned from a single piece of iron, it was triangular in shape, rough-sharpened on both sides and needle-sharp at the tip.

The makeshift handle had been formed by driving the sharpened metal into a piece of thick wood. That wood had then been repeatedly wrapped in masking tape.

The whole lethal weapon was less than six inches in length.

'And how the fuck did you get that out of the machine shop?' asked Paul Doolan, looking at the blade.

David Layton didn't answer.

He sat silently on the edge of his bunk, gazing down almost lovingly at the knife that rested on his pillow.

'If the screws flip this fucking cell, we're both in the shit,' said Doolan. 'If they find that, we'll . . .'

'They're not going to find it,' snapped Layton irritably. 'The fucking thing won't be here long enough for that. Besides, if we don't give the fucking twirls reason to flip us, then they won't, will they? This'll be gone by tomorrow.'

'When you doing it?' Doolan wanted to know.

Layton shrugged.

'When the time's right,' he said quietly.

'Who is this geezer anyway? Why does Brycey want him cut?'

'It's family business, so I hear. This Morton bloke, the one who Brycey wants cut, they stick him in here for receiving, or something like that. Only it turns out, while he's been in the real world, he's been shafting Brycey's cousin, hasn't he?'

'And Brycey didn't know that?'

Layton shook his head.

'One of the most powerful gang bosses in East London, and this Morton geezer is cutting a slice off his fucking cousin,' he chuckled.

'So Morton didn't know who this bird was?'

'No, not a clue. 'Course, the fact that she's only seventeen didn't exactly please Brycey, did it? I mean, from what I've heard, she's a right little slag anyway. Could suck a golf ball through a fucking garden hose, that type.'

Both men laughed.

'More pricks than a second-hand dartboard,' Doolan added.

'Yeah – and the rest,' Layton continued.

'So Brycey wants you to do him up?'

'What was I going to say? If Geoff Bryce asks you to do something, you fucking do it, don't you?'

'With less than a month to parole?'

'What would you have done? Told him to go fuck himself?'

'No, of course not. But I haven't got less than a month to jam roll, have I?'

'Look, if I do this job for Brycey, I walk out of here with a few bob in my pocket. If I don't do it, I don't walk. Besides, I couldn't give a fuck. I don't know this Morton bloke, so what do I care?'

David Layton slid the blade beneath his pillow and lay back on his bunk.

He lay on his side, gazing across at the opposite wall of the cell: at the array of photos showing naked women in every manner of pose. He'd stuck most of the pictures up there himself, Blu-tacked to the discoloured stonework.

On the bunk above him, Paul Doolan was flipping slowly through the daily paper, occasionally reading sections aloud.

He was thirty-two, four years older than Layton. Both men had spent the majority of their lives in and out of various institutions. Layton himself had begun with a remand home at thirteen and then, as theft had become receiving stolen goods, then possession of cocaine, and finally several charges of assault and grievous bodily harm, he had graduated to a series of prisons.

This cell in Wandsworth was his latest.

A three stretch for glassing some fucking ponce inside a nightclub in Hackney. It had left the victim with one hundred and twenty-six stitches in his face, and Layton with another listing on his record. He had once joked that he had more form than Red Rum.

Prison life didn't bother him. Why should it? He knew the system here inside out. He knew how to work it to his advantage. Lots of men folded inside. Not David Layton: he had blossomed.

'So,' said Doolan, leaning over to look down at his cellmate. 'How did you get that blade out of the machine shop? You didn't tell me. You couldn't have crutched something like that.'

'Does it matter?' said Layton.

'Just curious.'

'Well, you know what curiosity does, don't you? And not just to cats.'

Doolan grinned.

'Why's the blade so dirty?' he wanted to know.

'I covered it in shit. When I cut Morton, that will infect the wounds. They'll turn bad. The cunt might even end up with blood poisoning, with any luck. If he does, Brycey might bung me a bonus.' He grinned crookedly.

Beneath the pillow, he closed his hand around the weapon.

5

'WELL, I HAPPEN to think it matters quite a lot,' snapped Robert Gibson into the mouthpiece of the receiver. 'I'll explain why, and I'll try to keep it simple for you. Our company is called BG TRUCKS, right. Every day, lorries and removal vans go all over the country with that logo painted on the side of them – like a mobile advert, right? You've just sent us headed notepaper that says BEE GEE TRUCKS, which makes us sound as if we only do removals for that pop group who did the soundtrack to *Saturday Night Fever*. It's a spelling error, understand?'

The person at the other end was having difficulty.

'BG TRUCKS is different to BEE GEE TRUCKS,' Rob said, spelling out the disparity. 'Are we clear now?'

The voice at the other end still couldn't see the problem.

'I'll make it very simple,' Rob continued. 'If this headed notepaper isn't replaced, then you get no money. N-O. No. Know what I mean? Or should I say k-n-o-w what I mean?' He hung up.

'Dickhead,' Rob snarled at the phone, then he leant back in his seat and stretched his arms, feeling the beginnings of a headache gnawing at the base of his skull.

The responsibilities of management, he mused.

Eight years earlier he wouldn't have needed to deal with such petty concerns. Eight years ago, his only concern with the haulage business was in *driving* trucks, not working out where they should be at what times of each day, for fifty-two weeks of the year. His and his partner's decision to start up their own business had been

31

vindicated by its success, and so far they had encountered few problems. Business had been plentiful to the point that they'd had to employ two more drivers the previous year, and there was certainly no sign of that business drying up. And why should it? They provided a good service for their customers, and at cheaper rates than most of their competitors.

At thirty-four, Robert Gibson could, if he wished, consider his life to be a success. A thriving business, an expensive house and a loving family. Life didn't get much better, did it?

He exhaled deeply.

Did it?

He looked across his desk.

A photo of his daughter smiled back at him. It had been taken at her birthday party just nine months earlier.

Hailey had taken it. The two of them there together, laughing happily.

The perfect dad.

He smiled, then his thoughts were interrupted as his office door opened.

'Every time I walk into this bloody office you're staring at that photo,' said Frank Burnside.

'Do you blame me?' Rob asked.

Burnside shook his head. 'No, I don't. She's a beautiful kid. It's a good job she got her looks from her mother and not you.'

'Ha-bloody-ha. What do you want?'

'You know those two other vans we were after? I spoke to the boss at the garage, and he now wants five grand each for them.'

'Tell him to fuck off. No, better still, give me his number and *I'll* tell him to fuck off. Three and a half each, we said. He agreed it.'

'Well, he's changed his mind.'

'Then we'll change our supplier, sod him. Come to think of it, Frank, don't ring him. Put it in writing. That makes it more official. Just don't put it on any of this new notepaper.' He grimaced.

'I'll get ... um ... her to type up a letter,' Burnside said, hooking a thumb over his shoulder.

'Sandy, you mean. You *can* use her name in front of me, you know. She *is* our secretary after all. Don't try being tactful now, Frank. It's a bit late for that.'

'Yeah, well, if you want *my* advice—'

'I don't.'

'If you were going to have an affair, then why have it with someone who works for us, Rob? For Christ's sake, talk about shitting on your own doorstep. I mean to say, that's why *her* bloody marriage broke up, isn't it? She was always knocking around with other blokes, and her old man finally gave her the push. You weren't the first, you know.'

'Give it a rest, Frank. OK, so she's divorced. So she's been around a bit. If it's a problem, it's *my* problem.'

'Not entirely, Rob. If it affects the running of this firm, then it's my problem too.'

'And did it? No, I tell you what, Frank. You stick to worrying about your fucking cholesterol, let me worry about Sandy. That's all over now anyway, you know that.'

'Does Hailey know it?'

'Jesus, what is this? *Woman's Hour?* Stick to running this business, Frank. Forget the Agony Aunt routine. Any problems I've got with Hailey, *I'll* sort them out.'

'It might seem like I'm sticking my oar in but, if it does, I'm doing it because I care about both of you. I mean we're mates, not just business partners, aren't we? If I had any problems with Maggie, I'd talk to *you* about them'

'Hailey and I are OK, right? We're working things out. I didn't exactly sit down and consider the pros and cons before I had that affair with Sandy. I didn't think about any of the consequences, because I didn't expect to get caught. But I *did*, and that's the end of it. Now, if there's nothing else, why don't you give Sandy a shout and we can tell her what to put in this letter?'

Burnside paused a moment, then opened the office door again.

'Sandy,' he called, 'have you got a minute, please?'

The two men locked stares, Burnside finally looking away, stepping to one side to allow their secretary access to the room.

Sandra Bennett smiled at both men as she entered, the smile a little more muted as she looked at Rob.

He ran swiftly appraising eyes over her: the slim legs and narrow hips, the shoulder-length ash-blonde hair. Narrow, finely chiselled features, and those eyes – inviting.

An invitation you couldn't turn down, Rob pondered, shifting in his seat.

She was wearing a black jacket and skirt. Simple. Efficient.

She sat down opposite Rob and crossed her legs, smoothing a crease from her skirt, aware that he was studying her. There was still a part of her that welcomed that gaze, and all that might lie behind it.

'Take a letter, Miss Bennett,' said Burnside, grinning.

'Frank, you're not usually *this* formal.' She smiled.

'We need to be this time,' Rob said. He explained to her what was going on with the vans they wanted to buy, watching as she made notes on her pad, stopping occasionally to look at him, unsettling him by the length of one or two of those glances.

Burnside was chipping in with his own ideas but, when Sandy looked up at them after each flurry of scribbling, it was Rob's gaze that she caught and held.

Finally she got to her feet, and tapped the notepad with her pen.

'I'll sort it out,' she said, smiling.

And she was gone.

'Give them hell, Sandy,' Burnside chuckled after her.

'What else can I do for you, Frank?' Rob wanted to know, looking up at his partner still standing in the doorway.

Burnside appeared vague.

'You're still here,' Rob continued. 'So is there something else?'

'Just be careful, Rob,' said the older man. 'Like I said, I know it's none of my business, but . . .'

Rob cut him short. 'That's right,' he said flatly.

'If it's any consolation, I can understand *why* you did it. I mean, she's a good-looking girl, I don't deny that, and—'

'Spare me the shoulder to cry on, Frank. I said it's over, and it is.' He got to his feet, crossing to the door, holding it open for his partner, who hesitated a minute then left. Rob closed the door, but lingered next to it.

Through the glass wall that formed the front of his office, he could clearly see Sandy sitting at her desk, fingers flashing quickly across the keyboard of her VDU.

Waiting for her to turn round and look at you?

'It's over,' he said under his breath.

He wondered if these words of reassurance were for his own benefit.

It was a moment or two before he went back and sat down again.

6

'I GOT LOST today, Dad.'

Becky said the words almost gleefully, smiling happily first at Rob then at Hailey.

They had eaten dinner in the kitchen, as they always did; the room that had once been the dining room having been transformed, about a year ago, into a study, and what had once been the study having been redecorated to turn it into a playroom for Becky. What the hell: they only ever used the dining room once or twice a year, when their parents visited and Hailey cooked for more than just the three of them. They weren't exactly dinner-party types. The room was wasted, Rob had said. So for the last eleven months they had eaten every meal in the kitchen. Some had been consumed in an atmosphere close to despair, especially in the last six months, but the meal this particular evening had been an enjoyable one. Not just because of Hailey's culinary skill, but also because they had all laughed and joked. The conversation had flowed easily, Rob had looked a little more relaxed than usual, and Hailey had been grateful for the change in his character.

Both of them had tried hard to keep their true feelings hidden from Becky, ever since the discovery of Rob's affair, and, most of the time, they had been successful.

Of course, Becky wasn't stupid and, especially when Rob's indiscretion had first come to light, she had been only too quick to spot a difference in her parents. Puzzled when her father, in particular, snapped at her so vehemently for apparently trivial things, there had been tears. But on the whole the emotional upheaval that both Hailey and Rob had been – and were still – going through was well disguised.

At first, Rob didn't react to his daughter's last words. He merely sipped his glass of mineral water, lost in his own thoughts.

'Dad, I said I got lost,' Becky repeated, unsure whether her father had heard her.

'Where?' he said finally, a slight edge to his voice.

Becky began to tell him.

'Or should I say how?'

He was looking straight at Hailey now.

'I didn't want to worry you,' she said. 'Everything was all right in the end.'

'Well, that's OK then, isn't it?' he said. She wasn't slow to catch the note of sarcasm in his voice.

No, it was something even stronger.

Disdain?

Anger?

'A man found me,' Becky continued. 'He was really nice, wasn't he, Mum?'

Hailey smiled and nodded, aware of Rob's eyes boring into her.

'Well, that's fine then, sweetheart,' he said, getting to his feet and kissing the top of Becky's head.

He carried his plate across to the sink, then returned and collected those of Hailey and his daughter. As he looked across at Hailey, she saw his eyes narrow slightly.

'Can I watch a video before I go to bed, Dad?' Becky wanted to know.

'Just half an hour,' Hailey offered.

Becky scrambled down from the table and disappeared through into the sitting room, leaving Hailey and Rob to clear the table and wash up.

'Don't start, Rob,' Hailey said, filling the sink with hot water.

'Start about what?' he snapped. 'Our daughter getting lost

when *you* were supposed to be looking after her. Why should I? I mean, she's fine, isn't she? Why should I start?'

'If you knew how I felt, waiting for her to be found, you might be a bit more sympathetic.' She handed him a clean, dripping plate.

He didn't answer, merely continued drying crockery as she passed them to him.

'Don't give me the silent treatment, Rob,' Hailey muttered. 'If you've got something to say, then say it.'

'Perhaps I should wait and do my talking tonight. That's what those bloody sessions are for, isn't it?'

She shot him an angry glance.

'I didn't force you to come, Rob. And if you want to stop going, then that's up to you too. I thought we needed help. I hoped you understood that. I thought you *wanted* to do something to help our relationship. After all, it was you who fucked it all up in the first place.'

'Yeah, I know. And if *I* hadn't had an affair, we wouldn't be going to Marriage Guidance, would we?'

Again she caught that heavy scorn in his voice.

'It's called Relate,' she told him.

'What difference does the name make? It does the same job, doesn't it?'

'And what job's that? What job do you think it's *supposed* to do, Rob?'

He shook his head. 'I'm going to sit with Becky,' he said, throwing the tea towel onto the worktop. 'Perhaps she needs someone to keep an eye on her.'

He was out of the kitchen before Hailey could reply.

*

She heard his footsteps on the stairs.

Despite the fact that the television was on, the volume was low and Hailey wasn't really paying much attention to the programme. It was a soap opera – *wasn't it always?* She merely gazed blankly at the screen, listening as Rob made his way down the stairs, then into the kitchen. A moment later he wandered into the sitting room and sat down in the chair on the other side of the room, his gaze straying first to the TV and then to the daily paper lying on the coffee table close to him. He picked it up and flipped it around to the sports pages.

'Did you read her a story?' Hailey asked.

'She was tired anyway,' Rob answered. 'It didn't take long for her to drop off. Not surprising really, is it? I mean, she's had a lot of excitement today – if that's what you want to call it.'

He continued looking at the paper.

'Oh, for Christ's sake, Rob, drop it, will you?' Hailey said wearily.

He lowered the paper.

'Drop it? Our daughter gets lost in one of the biggest shopping centres in the country, and you say "Drop it." What the hell were you doing?'

'I knew this was coming. You think it's *my* fault, don't you?'

'Do you have any idea what could have happened to her?'

'I spent nearly an hour thinking about nothing else.'

'You weren't going to tell me, were you?'

'No. Because I knew you'd react like *this*.'

'How do you *expect* me to react?'

'With a little bit of understanding. I went through hell this afternoon until they found her.'

'And you just decided *not* to tell me?'

'Don't start lecturing me about deceit, Rob. You're not really in a position to do that, are you?'

He raised his hands. 'Change the record, Hailey,' he said irritably.

She glared at him.

She was about to speak again when she heard the two-tone door-chime. Flashing him one final, angry glance, she got to her feet and headed for the door, from habit peering through the spyhole before she opened it.

As she waited on the doorstep, Caroline Hacket rubbed her hands together.

'It's getting colder,' she commented as Hailey let her in.

Caroline slipped off her long grey coat to reveal a dark sweatshirt and jeans beneath. She draped the coat over the bannister and turned to Hailey, seeing how pale and drawn she looked.

'Are you OK?' she wanted to know.

Hailey nodded. 'Becky's fast asleep,' she said, reaching for her own coat that hung on the rack behind her. 'We'll be back by nine.'

Caroline touched her friend's arm and nodded. She turned as Rob appeared in the doorway to the sitting room.

'How's things in the world of big business, Rob?' Caroline asked, smiling.

'Not bad,' he said, forcing a return smile that appeared more like a leer. He pulled on a jacket and dug in his pocket for the car keys. He then wandered outside, and a couple of minutes later Hailey heard the engine of the Audi throb into life.

'You know where everything is, don't you?' said Hailey.

'I should do by now,' Caroline told her. 'Go on. Everything will be fine. I'll see you later.'

Hailey closed the door behind her and headed towards the passenger side of the waiting Audi.

'*Everything will be fine.*'

How badly she wanted to believe that.

7

THE ROOM WAS small. No more than fifteen feet square. Sparsely furnished. It contained little except three chairs, a filing cabinet and a small coffee table. The walls were plain, their banality not even enlivened by a photograph or a painting.

The consultation room reminded Rob of a cell.

Cigarette smoke hung in the air like a curtain of dirty gauze, and the ashtray on the table next to a box of Kleenex was already full. Hailey and Rob were both smoking, watched with something approaching disapproval by the woman who sat in the room with them.

Marie Anderson was in her early forties: a small woman with the kind of outrageously rosy cheeks that made her look like a badly painted doll. She looked from Hailey to Rob, and then back again. For three weeks they had been attending these Relate sessions. For three weeks she had listened to their pain and their anger spilling out into this small room. And what she had heard from them she had heard a hundred times before, from a hundred different couples.

Words like 'Betrayal', 'Infidelity', 'Anger', 'Revenge' . . .

'Hatred'.

Marie often wondered if her role was merely that of referee to these bouts of emotional pugilism. She had voiced her concerns about that to some of her colleagues, but found they saw their own roles as something similar. They were there to guide, to cajole, to interpret; they were not there to solve problems. They could not wave magic wands and reassemble marriages shattered by infidelity or a hundred other kinds of indiscretion.

The thing that Marie had found most difficult when she first began as a Relate counsellor was distancing herself from the personal problems of those she advised. It had been difficult then to merely lock up the office and walk home after every evening's emotional upheavals. As time went on, Marie had found it all a little more bearable, but every now and then she was more deeply touched than she should be by the plight of a particular couple or individual. She wondered if even *that* would wear off in time. Was it ever possible to become immune to pain? And, if so, how long did it take?

Hailey stared at Marie, as if willing her to force an answer from Rob. Wanting her to *make* him reply to the question she had asked him a moment ago.

He took another drag on his cigarette, and blew out a stream of smoke to join the grey haze already filling the confined space.

'Can you see why Hailey is still so upset, Rob?' Marie said finally, her voice soft. 'She's still concerned that your affair might begin again.'

'I can understand it, but it won't happen,' he said.

'As long as she works with you, the temptation's always there,' Hailey intervened.

'So what do you want me to do: sack her?' he demanded.

'If that's what it takes.'

'That's not fair.'

'Not fair,' Hailey snorted. 'She had an affair with you. It could happen *again*. No wonder her husband divorced her.'

'I told you, I won't *let* it happen again.'

'Crap. If she comes on to you, you'll fuck her. I know you, Rob. You're weak.'

'If the only way to reassure Hailey that you wouldn't have another affair with this woman was to get rid of her, would you be willing to do that, Rob?' Marie wanted to know.

He took another drag and tilted his head back, a headache crawling around his skull.

'Look, if I sack Sandy and get another secretary, Hailey will start thinking I'm having an affair with *her*.'

'It depends what *she* looks like,' Hailey said acidly.

'Do *you* think Rob would do this again, Hailey?' Marie asked.

'I know what he's like, especially with attractive women. He likes to be surrounded by them. It boosts his ego.'

'Oh, come on,' Rob muttered.

'It's true,' Hailey continued. 'If you did hire another secretary, you'd make sure she was good-looking. Don't deny it.'

'All right, it's true. If two women came for the job, both with the same qualifications, and one was pretty and the other looked like the back of a fucking bus, I'd hire the good-looking one. Satisfied?'

'Is that the reason you first got to know Hailey?' Marie asked. 'Because she's good-looking?'

He nodded. 'But it wasn't *just* that. It was her sense of humour, her attitude, the way she made me laugh. It just helped that she was the sexiest thing I'd ever seen.'

'And is she still?' Marie asked.

He nodded.

'Does she still make you laugh? Do you still like her attitude and her sense of humour?' the counsellor continued.

'Of course I do. I *never* intended to leave her for Sandy. I would never leave her for anyone else.'

'So why did you fuck that slag, then?' rasped Hailey.

'Because I *could*,' he snapped. 'I don't know what else to say. How many times do I have to tell you?'

'That isn't a good enough reason,' Hailey persisted. 'There must have been more to it.'

'Did you feel that there was something missing from your relationship with Hailey?' Marie enquired.

'No,' he said. 'Look, you could strap me into an electric chair now and ask me why I did it, and I still couldn't tell you. You'd have to throw the switch. I never fell out of love with you – ' he looked towards Hailey – 'I never fell *in* love with Sandy. I was never going to leave you. I never wanted to.'

'Did *she* want you to?' Hailey demanded.

'She knew exactly where she stood. She knew there was no future in it.'

'Yeah, I bet she did,' Hailey hissed. 'She knew you were married, so why the hell couldn't she leave you alone, find someone single? Or did she keep nagging away at you because she knew you'd give in? Did *she* know you were weak, too?'

Rob shot her an angry glance.

'I know what I did was wrong,' he replied furiously. 'How many fucking times do I have to say sorry? If I said it every minute of every day, every day for the rest of my life, it wouldn't alter what's happened, would it?'

'Do you wish you *could* change what happened, Rob?' Marie interjected.

He nodded.

'Don't say it if you don't mean it,' Hailey muttered.

'Yeah, I wish I could change what happened,' Rob said. 'I wish things could just be the way they were between us before all this shit.'

'Shit that *you* started,' Hailey reminded him.

Again he glared at her.

'That's what makes me sick,' Hailey continued. 'You were the one who had the affair, and yet *you're* the one who's angry. Why?'

'Because I want things between us to go back to the way they were. I hate this arguing, sniping all the time. Every time we have an argument you throw it back in my fucking face.'

'What do you expect?'

'Is that true, Rob?' Marie wanted to know. 'Are you angry? There certainly seems to be a lot of aggression inside you. Who is it directed at? Hailey?'

'It should be directed at *her*,' Hailey spat. 'At that fucking whore.'

'It's not just her fault: it takes two to tango.'

'See, you're doing it again. You always defend her.'

'I'm not defending her. I'm just trying to tell you what I feel, what I believe. I went after *her*.'

'Then she should have told *you* to clear off, since she knew you were married. But she wouldn't do that, would she? Being chatted up by the boss, being taken out for lunch, being taken away for weekends. Why should she give all that up? God, she must have thought you were her dream come true.'

'I don't know what she thought. I don't *care* what she thought.'

'Do you think your marriage is worth saving, Rob?' Marie asked.

'Obviously, or I wouldn't be here,' he told her.

'I've told you before, you have to accept that there's been a lot of pain and that things won't go back to normal overnight. They'll probably *never* go back to the way they were before this happened. Your relationship will grow stronger if you let it; it'll just have a different shape.'

'Yeah, a fucking pear-shape,' Rob murmured, stubbing out his cigarette.

'How long did you expect it to take before things got better between you?' Marie asked.

Rob shook his head.

'I hadn't thought about it,' he confessed. 'Some days things are fine: we manage to get through a whole day and night without all this shit being raked up. And on other days it just goes on and on.'

'At least you're off at work,' Hailey snapped. 'I'm stuck at home with the time to think about it, time to wonder if you're chatting up that bloody tart while you're there together in the office, wondering what you're saying to her.'

'Then stop thinking about it.'

'Oh, for God's sake . . .' Hailey shook her head despairingly.

She saw Marie glance at the wall clock behind them.

Time up.

They'd been there for their allotted hour.

Doesn't time fly when you're having fun?

Hailey was first to get to her feet, running a hand through her brown hair and exhaling deeply.

They made an appointment for the same time the following week, said their goodbyes, then headed out to the small car park where the Audi was waiting.

As Hailey clambered into the passenger seat, she thought how cold it had grown. How chilly the night air was.

She looked briefly at Rob as he started the engine.

As he did, the cassette burst into life too, the lyrics echoing inside the car.

'. . . *Will you be there, am I the one who waits for you, or are you unforgiven too?* . . .'

They didn't speak during the drive home.

8

THE SILENCE WAS oppressive.

Broken only by the steady click-click of Hailey's high heels on the polished floor of the corridor, it seemed to surround her like a blanket.

She walked slowly, eyes fixed ahead, not glancing left or right, concerned only with the door at the far end of the corridor. It was dark wood polished so vigorously it practically shone.

Hailey paused at the door and wondered whether or not she should knock.

As she waited, she turned and looked behind her.

The corridor was empty.

It was filled only with that deafening silence.

She shifted slowly from one foot to the other, embarrassed by the noise her heels made on the floor. She raised herself up onto her toes to minimize the tattoo they clattered out. She tapped gently on the door, then walked in without invitation.

The room was barely twenty feet square and, if anything, the silence here was even more palpable than out in the corridor.

Red velvet curtains were draped across the far wall, and between them was suspended a large wooden cross. On either side of it two candles burned, their flames unmoved by the slightest breeze.

There were two tables inside the room, the occupant of each covered by a heavy black cloth.

Hailey tried to suck in a breath, but the air seemed as static as it was noiseless. At least her heels made no sound on the thick carpet as she moved towards the first of the tables.

She thrust out a hand and gripped the edge of the dark cloth, preparing to ease it back, but also afraid to.

She closed her eyes so tightly that white stars danced behind her lids, and she tried again to breathe deeply.

Hailey lifted the cloth . . .

Becky's body seemed a mass of dark blue, violet and yellow bruises. Hardly an inch of flesh seemed to have escaped the massive onslaught – not even her face. The skin around her eyes was so swollen that the orbs seemed to have sunk down into the skull itself. Those few areas of her body that weren't discoloured looked as white as milk.

Two jagged cuts bisected her throat: hacked so deeply into the flesh that her head was practically severed. The two savage gashes joined to form one bloodied chasm that, to Hailey's tortured gaze, looked like another mouth smiling obscenely up at her.

She wanted to scream, wanted to cry out, but it was as if her emotions were as paralysed as her larynx. All she could do was stare helplessly at Becky's body. She wanted so much to touch it. To hold it one last time. Embrace it. Kiss those ragged, torn lips, to say sorry.

Sorry for letting her get lost in the crowded shopping centre.

Sorry that she couldn't help her now.

Hailey felt a solitary tear run down her cheek.

She turned towards the second table, pulling the cloth away with more certainty.

There were two bodies on this one.

Unblemished. Uninjured.

Both naked.

They were locked together in an embrace, pressed urgently against each other.

As one, their heads turned towards her and they smiled.

Her husband and Sandy Bennett.

Both naked. Both smiling.

From behind her she heard movement and she turned to see that Becky had sat up.

She was pointing at the entwined figures opposite – and laughing.

But she was laughing through that gaping rent in her throat.

It was then that Hailey finally began to scream.

9

PROPELLED FROM HER nightmare with ferocious speed, Hailey sat bolt upright, breathing in gasps.

She looked around her, at details of the room.

It took a second or two for her to realize that there was no velvet draped across one wall, no thick carpet. No tables bearing the bodies of her daughter or of her husband and his lover.

Instead she saw the luminous red digits of the radio alarm, the bedside lamps, the outline of built-in wardrobes across the room.

Normality.

She swallowed hard and let out a deep breath, the last residue of the nightmare fading slowly.

Rob rolled over and saw her sitting up, eyes staring wide, unkempt hair plastered across one cheek.

'Are you OK?' he asked, reaching out to touch her arm.

She nodded.

'Bad dream?' His voice was thick with sleep.

She lay down and felt him snake one arm around her shoulder, drawing her towards him.

Hailey slid a hand across his chest, running her fingers across his flesh.

'Did *she* have bad dreams?' she asked.

Rob sighed.

'Not now, Hailey. Please.'

'*Did* she?'

'Sometimes. Does it matter?'

'And did you comfort *her* like this?'

'Why is it so important for you to know?'

'I want everything clear in my own mind. I *need* to know.'

'We've been over these things so many times before. Why torture yourself by coming back to it again and again? It's over: I told you that. Christ, I can't even remember half of what happened between us.'

'Was she good in bed? You must remember that.'

He rolled onto his side to face her, kissing her gently on the forehead.

'How many times, Hailey?' he said evenly. 'How many times do I have to tell you before you've heard enough?'

'*Was* she good?' Hailey persisted.

'I'm not an expert.'

'Did she do things I wouldn't? Did she dress up for you? Did she act out your little fantasies?'

'She didn't do *anything* that *you* haven't done.'

'Did she come when you fucked her?'

He drew in a weary breath.

'*Tell* me, Rob,' Hailey insisted.

'Yes,' he said flatly. 'You've asked me that before and I've *told* you before.'

'Did you go down on her?'

'Jesus Christ, let it go, Hailey. Please.' There was a hint of irritation creeping into his tone, but she ignored it.

'*Tell* me,' she implored.

'Yes.'

'I bet she enjoyed that, didn't she? Mind you, she's probably had plenty of other blokes do it to her before. I bet she's slept with loads of men. I wonder if the others were married too.'

He gritted his teeth and pulled her closer to him.

Hailey looked into his eyes. Her own were clouded with tears.

'Why did you do it, Rob?' she whispered. 'You knew how much I loved you. I would have gone to the ends of the earth for you. Why did you want to hurt me?'

'I *didn't* want to hurt you.' He stroked her hair. 'Go back to sleep,' he soothed.

Hailey gripped him firmly by one wrist, sliding his hand down her flat belly towards her tightly curled mound of pubic hair. She parted her thighs and pushed his index finger between her moist lips, allowing him to feel the slippery warmth there. Then she raised his compliant hand to his face and pushed his index finger between his lips, allowing him to taste her.

With her other hand she enveloped his stiffening penis and squeezed gently, kneading the flesh and muscle.

'Not now, babe,' he said softly. 'It's late.'

'You wouldn't have refused *her*, would you?' she said, rolling away from him.

Rob opened his mouth to speak, but then merely shifted onto his side, his back to her.

Within moments she heard his low breathing again. Low, even breathing.

Contented?

Hailey lay on her back, staring at the ceiling. A single tear rolled from one eye.

It was a long time before she slept again.

Retribution

THE AIR INSIDE the recreation room was thick with cigarette smoke.

It was a large room that could comfortably house more than a hundred men at a time. And on this particular evening it seemed to David Layton that even more bodies were crammed into it.

That was fine with him. More men, more noise, more cover.

'Dave.'

He heard his name, but didn't react.

'Oi, Layton.'

Still he didn't respond. Merely sat there, his eyes scanning the room and its occupants.

There were more than a dozen tables set up throughout the room, groups of men huddled around them: talking, playing cards, or other games the prison provided.

Two men were attempting to play chess with six of the pieces missing. Scraps of rubbish had been used to replace them. A balled-up piece of chewing-gum foil had just taken a bishop, and was moving in to put a matchbox in check.

A heated game of dominoes was in progress at another table; the men gathered around it were shouting enthusiastically as it progressed.

On the far side of the room stood a small television.

Several rows of plastic chairs had been set up in front of it, and a number of men sat watching the flickering screen.

Layton could see that one of those men was Peter Morton. Early twenties, tall, almost gangling. He had, Layton noted, large ears that stuck out almost at right angles to his head.

He was sitting undisturbed, watching the television, puffing content-edly on a roll-up, occasionally leaning to one side to mutter something to the man sitting next to him.

Layton reached down and touched the hilt of the blade that he had earlier stuck in his boot. It was hidden by the blue prison overalls he wore.

'Are you going to show those fucking cards, or what?' a voice close to Layton said.

Finally he looked up, as if stirred from his musings by the tone of the voice.

There was a powerfully built black youth sitting opposite him, gesturing towards the cards he held.

'Sorry, Midnight,' said Layton, 'I was miles away.'

Paul Doolan glanced at his cellmate, then over at Morton, perhaps able to understand his companion's distraction.

'Seventeen,' said Layton, laying his cards on the table.

'Gutted,' chuckled Midnight, snatching at the cards. 'I pay nineteens.'

The other men around the table added a chorus of groans.

'That's two hundred thousand you owe me,' said Midnight, scrib-bling something down on the pad next to him. He prepared to deal again.

'Fuck it,' said Layton. 'I've had enough.' He got to his feet, watched by his companions. 'I think I'll watch some telly.'

Paul Doolan nodded slowly and inspected his cards as they were dealt.

Layton wandered through the recreation room, past the other tables. Past the three uniformed warders gathered close to the door to watch the inmates. Two other guards paced unhurriedly back and forth from one end of the room to the other. One, an older man with grey hair and a pitted complexion, was standing close to the pool table in the far corner of the room, watching the game under way.

Layton fixed his eyes on the back of Peter Morton's head and sat down in the row of plastic seats behind him, crossing his legs.

He could feel the knife pressing against his ankle.

Paul Doolan glanced across at his cellmate, and saw that he had taken up his chosen position.

It was then that he overturned the table.

Cards, chairs and men all overbalanced. The cards flying into the air, men and chairs tumbling like building bricks.

'Fucking cheat,' shouted Doolan at the top of his voice, lunging at Midnight, who raised his hands into a boxer's stance.

All hell broke loose.

All eyes had turned towards the noisy eruption.

Peter Morton spun round in his chair to see what had caused the disruption.

For fleeting seconds he and Layton locked stares, and Morton briefly wondered why this man was staring at him so intently.

He didn't even see the knife.

Layton struck quickly and expertly.

The first blow caught Morton across the left cheek and laid it open to the bone. A gout of blood spurted from the wound, almost spattering Layton.

He lashed out again with the knife, this time catching his prey on the nose.

The tip was sliced off effortlessly by the razor-sharp blade, and an even more violent eruption of crimson spouted from this fresh wound.

By this time Morton was screaming, but his shrieks of pain were drowned by the din still coming from the other side of the recreation room.

The third cut severed most of Morton's right ear, slicing through flesh and cartilage easily. The lump of flesh fell to the floor and lay there in the puddles of blood that had already formed.

Morton kept trying to escape, but he only managed to fall backwards over the plastic chairs.

Layton was on him again in a second.

As Morton lifted a hand to protect his face from the slashing metal, the razor-sharp weapon sheared through the tip of his right middle finger. It cut effortlessly through the pad of his finger and the nail, driving as deep as the first knuckle.

Layton drew the blade swiftly across the stricken man's right cheek, then grabbed his bottom lip and hacked it off with one savage swipe.

The bulging, scarlet tissue fell to the floor and lay there like a bloodied, fleshy slug.

'Next time it'll be your fucking balls,' snarled Layton and walked away, dropping the knife on the floor, kicking it across the room.

Morton was still screaming, gurgling as blood ran down his throat.

He lay alone, writhing in agony, clutching his face, surrounded by overturned chairs. The floor splattered with his blood and pieces of his ravaged face.

Layton looked back impassively at the disfigured, howling man.

Job done.

10

She didn't hear the phone at first.

Hailey pushed a second load of clothes into the washing machine, stood up and listened, trying to pick out the ringing above the sound of the radio.

At first she wasn't even sure it *was* the phone.

Another couple of rings and she crossed to it, lifting the receiver, then reaching across to lower the radio volume.

'Hello,' she said, wiping one palm on her jeans.

There was a second of silence at the other end, then a voice she didn't recognize.

'Is that Mrs Gibson?' the voice wanted to know.

'Yes,' she said, smiling.

'I hope it's the *right* Mrs Gibson.'

'Who *is* this?'

'You probably don't remember me,' the voice said hesitantly. 'You had a lot on your mind and . . . I, well, my name's Walker. Adam Walker. Your little girl got lost yesterday and I was the one who . . .'

'You found her,' Hailey said, grinning now. 'Mr Walker, if I'd forgotten your name, I'm sorry.'

'Adam,' he insisted. 'Please call me Adam.'

'Adam.'

'How is Becky?'

Hailey was a little taken aback.

'She's fine, thanks,' she said.

'Look, if I've called at the wrong time . . . if I'm disturbing you . . .' He allowed the sentence to trail off.

'No. I'm sorry if I sound a bit vague. You just caught me by surprise, that's all.'

'I got your number from directory enquiries, I hope you don't mind.'

'No, not at all.'

'It's just that Becky told me your address yesterday and I remembered it, so I rang them and they gave me your number.'

'You must have a good memory.'

'If that's a compliment, I'll take it.' She heard him chuckle. 'She's a beautiful girl. You're very lucky. I'm just glad I could help.'

'You'll never know how grateful I am, Mr Walker.'

'Adam. I think I can guess how grateful.'

'No you can't, believe me. Not unless you've got kids of your own.'

There was a second's silence.

'I haven't,' he told her. 'I had a nephew about the same age as Becky. He died in an accident a couple of years ago. Hit-and-run driver.'

'I'm sorry.'

'We were very close. That's how I can imagine what you were going through. He was lost when it happened. He wandered away from my sister in a crowded street. Stepped straight into the road. A little like Becky. I'm just glad I could do something *this* time.' His tone suddenly lightened. 'Anyway, I didn't call to tell you *my* life story, Mrs Gibson.'

'Hailey,' she insisted.

He repeated it.

'Becky's here if you'd like to speak to her,' Hailey told him.

What the hell are you doing?

'I don't want to disturb her,' he said.

'I'm sure she'd like to talk to you. She seemed quite taken with you.'

You feel sorry for him, don't you?

'If it's no bother, I'd like to,' Walker said.

Hailey told him to hang on a minute, then she returned with her daughter from the sitting room, where Becky had been watching cartoons, and handed her the receiver.

Hailey saw the delight on Becky's face as she spoke to Walker, watching her nod and giggle as he chatted.

'Tomorrow,' Becky said, and Hailey could only wonder at the question he'd asked.

'I hope so,' she continued, still mesmerized by that invisible voice.

Finally she said her goodbyes, handed the receiver back to Hailey, and disappeared back into the sitting room.

'You *did* make an impression, didn't you?' said Hailey, smiling again.

'I aim to please,' Walker replied.

'Look, if you want to call again, then feel free,' she said.

Oh, come on, get a grip.

'I won't bother you again. I just wanted to make sure you were *both* OK,' Walker told her. 'I hope it didn't upset your husband too much either.'

'I might not be married,' she said, chuckling. 'I could be a single parent. Do I *look* married?'

Are you flirting with him now?

'I saw your wedding ring,' he told her.

'Divorcee?' she offered.

It was Walker's turn to laugh.

Hailey thought what a wonderfully infectious sound it was.

'I'll leave you in peace now,' he said, evidently still amused. 'I'm glad everything is all right.'

'I really appreciate you calling, Adam. And I mean it: you can ring again anytime. I'm sure Becky would like to speak to you.'

'Just Becky?' he mused.

Hailey felt her cheeks colour.

You're behaving like some stupid teenager.

'Take care, Hailey,' he said.

'And you,' she murmured.

'See you.'

And he was gone.

Hailey hung up, still smiling at the phone, then turned up the radio again.

Once more the room was filled with music.

11

'HAILEY, I DIDN'T plan this,' said Rob, almost apologetically. 'I only found out this afternoon.'

'Do you *have* to go?' she demanded.

'It's a very important trade fair, and it's only for two days,' he told her. 'If it's any consolation, I'm not too overjoyed about it myself. It is Manchester, after all. I mean, no one spends two days in fucking Manchester unless they have to, do they?'

'Why can't Frank go?'

'Someone has to run the business, and Frank's better in the office. He hates this kind of thing.'

She watched as he dropped socks, underpants and T-shirts into his small suitcase. His suits he folded carefully, placing them in position before resting some shirts on top of them.

'You always were better at socializing, weren't you, Rob?' she said, a slight edge to her voice.

He looked at her for a moment, then continued packing.

'It's got to be done. I've got to go. That's all there is to it,' Rob told her.

'And what if I don't want you to go?'

'Oh, come on, Hailey. Don't be bloody ridiculous.'

'I'm serious.'

'OK,' he snapped irritably. 'I won't go. I'll stay in the office. Sod the trade fair. To hell with all the contacts I can make. Fuck the extra business I could get for the firm. Happy now?'

She watched him struggling to fold a shirt, and stepped in front of him to complete the task.

'This is for *our* benefit, not just mine,' he reminded her. 'If I can get some extra business, then it means more work, and more work means more money. More money means we all live better. You, me, and especially Becky.'

'I don't need a lecture in economics, Rob. That's not the problem.'

'Then what *is*, for Christ's sake?'

'This will be the first time you've been away from home since your

(affair. Go on say it. It's only a word)

little game with that slag. I assume she arranged it all, this trip, seeing as she's your secretary. Did she book your hotel, too?'

'Don't start, Hailey. You know bloody well she did. It's her job.'

'And what kind of room did she book? A double? Just in case she fancies nipping up to see you while you're there?'

'Look, if you think that's going to happen, then ring the office while I'm gone and talk to her. Talk to Frank. Get him to tell you where she is. Ring me. Ring the fucking hotel: it's the Piccadilly. I'll leave you the number. I'll call you every night. You can get the manager to check on me if you like, make sure I haven't got any women in my room.' He glared at her. 'Do whatever you have to do, Hailey. I've got to go to this fucking show, and that's all there is to it.'

'Well, it'll give you some peace and quiet for a couple of days, won't it? Two days of not having to answer my questions.'

'I'm sure you'll have some more when I get back.'

'Did she say she wished she was coming with you?'

He merely shook his head wearily.

'Where else did you take her? London? Reading? Leeds? God, that *was* romantic, wasn't it? Manchester not classy enough for her?'

He dropped the last of his things into the suitcase and snapped it shut.

'I'll call tonight and speak to Becky before she goes to bed,' he said quietly.

Hailey nodded.

'I just want you to see *my* side of this, Rob,' she told him.

He held her gaze for a moment. 'I'll call you before I go to bed tonight,' he said. 'The fair doesn't start until the morning.'

'What will you do tonight?'

He shrugged. 'Have a meal in the hotel. Go to the pictures. What *do* you do in Manchester when you're on your own?' He smiled wanly.

'As long as you *are* alone,' she insisted.

'Hailey, I—'

She cut him short.

'I mean it, Rob,' she said quietly. 'If I find out she's with you, or she's meeting you there . . .'

She allowed the sentence to trail off.

'I'd better go,' he said, picking up the suitcase. 'If I leave now, I can be there before five.'

She followed him downstairs, watched as he gathered his jacket and a coat from the rack in the hall.

'See you in a couple of days,' he said, smiling.

He leant forward to kiss her, his lips brushing hers – gently at first, then more insistently.

She stood in the doorway, watching as he loaded the suitcase into the car boot, then slid behind the wheel and started the engine of the Audi.

He swung the vehicle out onto the road.

She waved.

He didn't look back.

*

Hailey couldn't sleep.

Despite the fact that her eyelids felt so heavy, that her body was crying out for rest, she could not drift off into that oblivion she wanted.

She sat up in bed, glanced first at the radio alarm, then at her own watch: 1.43 a.m.

Rob had rung her over two hours ago from his hotel in Manchester.

He'd eaten a meal, been to see a film.

Blah, blah, blah . . .

She had tried her best to sound amiable, managed to resist asking him if he was really alone.

Thirty minutes later she'd run the Picadilly and asked the receptionist if there had been any messages for *Mrs* Gibson in room 422. The receptionist had checked: as far as she was aware, Mr Gibson was alone. Hailey had thanked her and hung up.

Very clever.

Hailey felt satisfied that Sandy Bennett wasn't at the hotel.

She would check again the following night.

Happy now?

She ran a hand through her hair, catching a brief glimpse of her naked image in the mirror on the wardrobe door opposite.

For interminable seconds she stared at it, studying her own features as if she was seeing them for the first time.

The narrow face and the pointed chin, the finely chiselled cheekbones.

She allowed the sheet to slip down to reveal her firm breasts, her flat stomach.

Hailey rose up on her knees, still watching the figure of the woman in the mirror. She allowed her gaze to rove, to trace the curve of her hips, the small triangle of downy hair between her thighs. She touched one index finger to her slim legs, and felt how smooth her skin was.

What was so wrong with this body?

Her image stared back.

She sank down onto her heels again, then lay down, covering

herself with the sheet, pulling it tightly around her neck like a cocoon.

Still sleep eluded her.

There was a portable TV in the room, but she decided not to switch it on in case it woke Becky. There were books on the cabinets on both sides of the bed. Rob was reading a biography of Michelle Pfeiffer. It was propped on top of another hardback, about the class system in Britain.

On her own side of the bed there were a couple of thrillers, neither of which tempted her.

Inside the bedside cabinet was her Walkman and a handful of tapes, and for a second she considered trying to drift off to sleep with the aid of music. In the end that idea didn't appeal either.

She wondered what Rob was doing.

Sleeping soundly, she guessed. He never had trouble sleeping alone – or in strange beds.

Well, he'd had more practice, hadn't he?

She reached out a hand towards his side of the bed, longing to feel him there.

For the first time in months, as she thought about him

(*and the affair*)

she was filled not just with anger but also with a feeling of incredible sadness. It felt as if she was in mourning.

She wondered how much longer the feeling would last.

Weeks?

Months?

Years?

As the first tears began to flow, she turned her head into the pillow.

CASA CASUARINA, OCEAN DRIVE, MIAMI, FLORIDA

The bullets felt heavy in his hand.

The young man in the white shirt and grey shorts fed the .40-calibre rounds into the magazine, and watched: eyes alert for the one he sought.

He would not be difficult to spot.

The target's routine was so predictable it was almost robotic.

Every morning around 8.30, the man with the silver-grey hair would exit through the ornate wrought-iron gates of the mansion. He would then walk a few blocks at a leisurely pace, enjoying the magnificent weather, occasionally nodding greetings to those he recognized.

Then he would return, to be swallowed up again by the palatial grandeur of the residence he loved.

So predictable.

The young man studied the huge villa – seeing others walk past its stone steps.

Some would look up towards the Mediterranean-style gates. Others merely passed by.

The young man watched as patiently as a bird-watcher waiting to get a glimpse of some incredibly rare species.

He hefted the pistol in his hand, feeling its weight. The coldness of the steel was a marked contrast to the warmth he felt on his bare flesh.

The sun in Miami that morning was warm, even at such an early hour. It hung in the sky like a burnished talisman, suspended in a cloudless firmament.

The young man took off his dark glasses for a moment, wincing up at the sun.

He didn't look at his watch. He hardly needed to. The man he waited for seemed to have his own built-in timing device. His morning stroll was like a ritual.

The young man knew: he had watched him perform it enough times.

When he saw the grey-headed figure approaching the gates, his expression didn't change. He merely watched as the older man mounted the steps, newly purchased magazines gripped in one hand.

He began to pull open the ornate gates.

The young man strode towards him, his heart thudding harder against his ribs.

The time had come.

He pulled the pistol from his shorts and raised it so that the barrel was practically touching the back of the grey-haired man's head.

In the stillness of the wakening day, the sound of the first shot was thunderous.

The bullet erupted from the muzzle of the pistol and – from point-blank range – drilled its way through bone and brain. A geyser of blood erupted from the wound, some of it spattering the young man himself, who barely blinked.

He fired again.

Another thunderous discharge.

More blood.

The grey-haired man fell forward, crashing face down onto the stone steps. Blood from his head wounds began to cascade down them like a viscous waterfall.

The young man stood there for precious seconds, staring at the body, then he turned and hurried away, aware that someone was already hurtling down the main path from the palazzo, shouting at him.

On the steps themselves, a spreading pool of blood stained the stonework around the bullet-blasted head of Gianni Versace.

14 July 1997

People don't know me. They think they do, but they don't.

Andrew Cunanan

People always turn away, from the eyes of a stranger.
Afraid to know what lies behind the stare . . .

Queensrÿche

12

She had heard the doorbell, but hadn't yet been able to reach the door in time to open it.

Hailey muttered to herself as she padded across the hall towards the scattered letters lying on the mat. She picked up the correspondence quickly and scanned the addressees, then she opened the door itself.

The postman was already making his way down the street, but once he heard her door open he waved back cheerily to her.

The package in the porch stood almost two feet tall: wrapped in shiny red paper, topped by an enormous silver bow.

There seemed to be no label on it, and for a moment she wondered if it had been delivered to the wrong house. But, as she bent to retrieve it, she spotted a small tag attached to the bottom.

MISS R. GIBSON, it announced. Then their address.

Hailey picked up the parcel, surprised at how light it was.

Becky had already wandered out into the hall to see what was happening. She was dressed in her school uniform, ready for her first day back after half-term.

'What is it, Mum?' she said, looking at the large package.

'You'd better open it and find out,' Hailey told her. 'It's addressed to you.'

Becky's eyes widened in delight, a huge smile spreading across her face.

They took the package back into the kitchen, Hailey looking

on with a combination of curiosity and delight as her daughter pulled open the immaculately wrapped parcel.

She wondered where Rob had ordered it from.

Would flowers for her follow later that morning?

Nice touch. Away for a couple of days, so send a present. Good psychology.

'Mum, look,' Becky said delightedly, as she pulled the last of the wrapping paper free.

The teddy bear was about eighteen inches tall with big blue eyes and an inviting stitched-on smile. It wore a school-cap and a little knitted scarf.

'He's lovely, darling,' said Hailey, smiling.

Even cleverer, Rob: the teddy was wearing the same colours as Becky's school uniform.

As Becky lifted the bear to cuddle it, Hailey noticed the label hanging around its neck. She reached across and flipped open the small card.

TO BECKY.
MAKE SURE HE DOES HIS HOMEWORK.
LOVE, ADAM.

Adam?

Hailey frowned slightly as she read the label again.

'I'm going to put him in my bedroom,' Becky said.

'Later, darling,' said Hailey. 'We've got to go now, or you'll be late for school.' She sat the bear on the kitchen table. 'He'll be here when you get home.'

Becky shrugged, then scurried into the hall to fetch her coat.

Hailey looked at the bear.

Then at the label.

LOVE, ADAM.

This bear couldn't have been cheap.

What a lovely thought.

She picked up her car keys, seeing her reflection momentarily in the big blue eyes of the bear.

A lovely thought.

Hailey shepherded her daughter out of the house, after ensuring she had all the necessary paraphernalia for her return to school. Then she followed her out, pulling her own jacket around her shoulders.

As she reached the end of the path, the phone in the hall began to ring, but she decided to leave it for the answering machine.

The caller left no message.

13

'Don't say much, do you?' Hailey chuckled as she passed the teddy bear on the table, wiping her hands on a tea-towel.

The toy sat where she had left it, blank stare fixed on her as she moved about the kitchen.

Every now and then she would stop and glance at the label.

LOVE, ADAM.

She picked up her mug of coffee and stood looking at the smiling bear for another moment.

She was still standing in the middle of the kitchen when the phone rang.

Hailey answered it. 'Hello,' she said.

'Sorry to bother you,' said the voice, and she recognized it immediately.

'Adam. I was just looking at the teddy bear.'

'She got it. Great.' He sounded genuinely excited.

'It was a lovely thought. You shouldn't have.'

'I saw it in a shop window the other day, and I just thought, why not? I hope you don't mind.'

'Of course not. Becky loves it. It must have cost you a fortune, though. You're very kind.'

'I just wanted to give her a surprise.'

'You certainly did *that*. And in her school colours too. How did you manage that?'

'She told me which school she went to that day I found her. I got a friend to knit the scarf and hat.'

'Well, like I said, it was a very nice thought, and she loves it.'

'Is she OK? She goes back to school today, doesn't she? Like most of the schools around this area do, don't they?'

'I've not long got back from dropping her off, as a matter of fact.'

'Well, I won't keep you talking. You must have things to do.'

'No, it's OK. Listen, I never did get around to really thanking you for finding Becky that day.'

'You had other things on your mind.'

'I know, but I still haven't told you how grateful I am. I was just wondering if you fancied having lunch. On me, of course – as a thank you.'

'Hailey, that would be great, but you don't have to. I didn't do this to be thanked.'

'I know that. Look, let me buy you lunch – that's all. It's no big deal. I owe you that.'

'You don't owe me anything.'

'Is that a no?'

'Definitely not,' he laughed. 'Throw some dates at me.'

'What about tomorrow?' she offered.

After all, my husband is away at the moment.

'I'd love to. Where shall we meet?'

'Are you sure it isn't interfering with your work, or anything?'

'I'm self-employed. I'll give myself the day off.'

'Do you know a restaurant called Tivoli's? Well, it's not really a restaurant, more a glorified snack bar, but the food's good.'

'I know it.'

'How about outside there at one o'clock?'

'One o'clock tomorrow. I'll look forward to it.'

'Me too. See you then. And thanks again for the teddy bear.' She smiled broadly.

'See you tomorrow,' he said, and hung up.

Hailey replaced the handset and looked across at the stuffed toy.

It was still smiling.

14

SHE WAS NERVOUS.

No matter how she looked at it, this fluttering in her stomach was caused by nerves.

Hailey checked her watch: 1.02 p.m.

Perhaps he wasn't coming.

Been stood up, have you?

She peered through the window into Tivoli's, wondering if Walker had perhaps arrived, not spotted her, and gone inside to wait.

It was busy inside. It usually was at this time of the day. But there were still plenty of tables. It was only self-service, nothing flash. But the food was good and it was pleasantly unpretentious.

But Walker wasn't inside.

He's not coming.

She looked at her watch again.

He *couldn't* have missed her if he'd walked past. There were only two doors in and out of the place and they were so close together he couldn't have slipped by unnoticed.

She felt a little foolish. Like a teenager on her first date who feared she was going to be ignored.

First date? You're having lunch with the bloke, for Christ's sake. That's all – isn't it?

She turned and checked inside again, glancing at her reflection in the window. Her hair was freshly washed that morning. She was dressed in a black skirt and jacket, and a white blouse. Hailey looked down to check that her black suede shoes weren't scuffed, muttering to herself when she saw a mark on the toe of one. She knelt quickly to wipe it away with her finger.

As she straightened up, she felt a hand on her shoulder.

'Jesus,' she said, startled, and spun round.

Adam Walker stood grinning at her.

'I'm sorry,' he said apologetically. 'I didn't mean to scare you.'

It was her turn to smile.

They looked at each other for a moment, then cracked up laughing.

As he stood close to her, Hailey could smell the scent of his leather jacket. He wore it over a denim shirt, with a pair of black jeans.

Very nice.

'Sorry I'm late, I had trouble parking the car,' he told her.

'I didn't even realize you *were* late,' she lied.

They walked together into Tivoli's, chose their food and drink, and sat down at a table in one corner.

'You should have let me get this,' Walker told her.

'It's hardly the Ritz, is it? And I did say this was the least I could do,' she said.

She glanced at him briefly, then began eating.

'I like the suit,' he told her. 'It's Louis Feraud, isn't it?'

She smiled. 'How do you know that?' Hailey wanted to know.

'It's very striking.' He looked at her and held her gaze. 'I tend to remember things that catch my eye.'

'I thought maybe you were in the fashion business or something,' Hailey said. 'Most blokes wouldn't know Louis Feraud from Louis Armstrong.'

'Come on, do I look like I work in the fashion business? I haven't got a ponytail for a start.'

They both laughed.

'So what business *are* you in?' she enquired. 'You said over the phone you were self-employed.'

'I'm an artist,' he replied. 'Graphic design – that kind of thing.'

'Who are you working for at the moment? If you don't mind me asking.'

'A record company, designing album covers. I've done a lot of that. Book covers, too.'

'I'm impressed.'

'Don't be – not until you've seen them, anyway.' He smiled again.

Hailey looked at him across the table, running appraising eyes over him. Early thirties she guessed, good-looking. She dropped her gaze as he looked up, as if she felt guilty for staring at him so intently.

Why are you feeling guilty?

'Did you go to college or university to learn design,' she wanted to know.

He shook his head.

'You can't *learn* to draw – well, other than the mechanics of it. You either can or you can't. It's like anything creative: it's a gift. That's my theory anyway.' He leant forward and whispered this conspiratorially.

'So how did you find work in the beginning?' Hailey enquired.

He shrugged. 'I spent some time in London, and I just walked around publishers and record companies and showed them my portfolio. As simple as that.'

'You must have had a lot of confidence in your own ability.'

'I was just an arrogant bastard.' He smiled. 'I couldn't see how they'd be able to turn me away.'

He laughed and the sound was infectious.

'Have you always lived here?' Hailey continued. 'Apparently there used to be some beautiful little villages in this part of Buckinghamshire. Until they all got swallowed up by the New Town.'

Walker sat back in his seat, looking thoughtful.

'What's wrong?' she wanted to know.

'I've done nothing but talk about myself ever since we sat down,' he said.

'I'm interested. You did find my daughter, didn't you? I *want* to know about you.'

'All right, let's get the boring details out of the way, then. What do you want to know? But I'll warn you *now*, there's a lot less to me than meets the eye.' Again that smile. Again she found herself looking deeply into his eyes.

'What about family?' she asked.

'One brother, one sister.'

'Do they live around here, too?'

'No.'

'You said on the phone that your nephew was killed in a hit-and-run.'

'My sister's boy,' he said, cutting her short. 'That was why, that morning, when I saw Becky out in the road, I *had* to do something to help her. That brought back all those memories of what had happened to my nephew.' He smiled thinly. 'Go on – next question.'

'Now you're making me feel like I'm interrogating you,' she protested. 'I'm curious, that's all.'

'Go on, then.'

'Are your parents still alive?'

'My father is. I don't know about my mother. She left home when I was eight. Ran off with another man.'

'I'm sorry.'

'I'm not, and I'm not surprised either. I think my father *drove* her out. He was a vicar. Ironic, I suppose. He's up in his pulpit every Sunday preaching about adultery, and then his own wife fucks off with somebody else.' He looked at her. 'Excuse my language.'

'Don't worry about it,' she told him. 'Do you still see him now?'

'When I can. Most of the time it's a wasted trip. He can't even remember who I am, usually. Alzheimer's. He's in a nursing home just outside the city. We talk about as much now as we did when I was growing up.' He tapped the table top gently with the flat of his hand. 'Right, that's enough about me. I want to know something about you.'

'Like what?' She smiled.

'Whatever you want to tell me.'

'Well, you know I'm married with a little girl.'

'Happily married?'

He was smiling.

'Sometimes,' she told him, her own smile now a little strained.

'What does your husband do?'

She told him. Told him about the wedding. About Becky.

Are you going to tell him about Rob's affair? Tell him how angry you still are?

'What did you do before you had Becky?' he asked.

'I worked for a local company director, as his PA,' she informed him.

'Which company?'

'SuperSounds, it's just outside the city.'

'I know it. They make guitars, don't they?'

She nodded.

'I was PA to Jim Marsh, the owner.'

'Did you enjoy it?'

'I loved it. It was long hours though, and there was quite a bit of travelling involved. Whenever he went to trade shows, I had to go with him.'

'Anywhere exciting?'

'Tokyo, New York, LA, Milan. Shall I stop there?' She grinned.

'Quite a globetrotter. Did it bother your husband that you were away so much?'

'A little bit.

(*tell him the truth, Rob hated it*)

But he was very tied up with his own business, so it wasn't too bad, and I didn't travel *that* often. Jim still stays in touch.'

'Do you miss it?'

'I miss the job sometimes, not the travelling so much.' She looked down at her half-eaten meal. 'I think Rob was pleased when I gave up.'

'Would you go back?'

'I couldn't – not now we've got Becky. Jim's called a few times and asked me. He even offered to pay for a nanny, but I couldn't leave Becky.'

'And your husband wouldn't like it?'

She shook her head.

'What was it like working for a famous man?' Walker persisted.

'I wouldn't call Jim Marsh famous,' Hailey replied with a mock grimace.

'He's successful. People know him. They've heard his name. He's made his mark on the world and I admire him for that. I admire *anyone* who does that. Life's short. I certainly don't want to die without anybody knowing I was here in the first place.'

'Is fame important to you, then?'

He looked directly into her eyes.

'Have you ever wanted something so badly you'd kill for it?' he said flatly.

15

FOR A SECOND she looked at him blankly, studying those features set in a determined expression.

Then that familiar grin spread across his face once again, and Hailey too found herself smiling.

'Yes, I admit it, I'd love to be famous,' he said, chuckling. 'The adoration, the money, people following me around telling me I was great. Others running up and asking for my autograph. I reckon I could cope with that.'

She laughed.

'You conceited sod,' she said.

'What's conceited about it?' he wanted to know. 'When they put me in a bloody box and bury me, I want someone to know I've *been* here. And it'll happen. I know it will. After all, Andy Warhol once said that everyone would be famous for fifteen minutes, didn't he? I just hope to Christ he was right.'

'So, you're looking forward to your fifteen minutes, are you, Adam?'

He nodded.

'I'm not joking, Hailey,' he insisted.

As she looked at him she didn't doubt his sincerity. In some ways he reminded her of Rob: that same single-mindedness and drive.

Rob? Why think about him now? Guilt pricking you, is it?

She pushed the thought aside.

'What does your girlfriend think about it?' she wanted to know.

'No girlfriend,' he said.

'I find that hard to believe.'

'There's a compliment in there somewhere, isn't there?'

'Isn't there anyone, then?'

'Not at the moment,' he told her. 'Work comes first. You should know that, Hailey. You've been around men like Jim Marsh. They don't let relationships get in the way of their careers. He's been married a couple of times, hasn't he?'

'Twice.'

'Has he ever tried it on with *you*?'

She looked at him for a moment, taken aback slightly by the question.

'He knew I was married,' she said.

'What difference does *that* make?'

'Perhaps I wasn't his type.'

'Did it bother your husband that you went away abroad with Marsh?'

She shrugged.

Are you going to tell him the truth? Tell him how Rob practically accused you of having an affair after a trip to Madrid?

'He understood it was part of the job,' she lied.

Lying comes quite easy, doesn't it?

'*I'd* have been jealous,' said Walker.

She smiled sheepishly, feeling her cheeks colour slightly.

'Does your husband know you're having lunch with me?' Walker persisted.

Again they locked stares.

'It's only lunch, Adam,' she told him.

'A thank you.'

Was that a hint of sarcasm in his tone?

'I meant what I said,' she insisted. 'I appreciate what you did that day, finding Becky. *And* what you've done for her since.'

'So he doesn't know?'

She shook her head. 'He's away for a couple of days on business.'

Walker nodded sagely. 'Does it bother you when he goes away?' he enquired.

'Sometimes,' she confessed.

'Is he ambitious?'

'I suppose he is.'

'Is that why you married him?'

'There was a little more to it than that.' She smiled.

'But did his ambition make him attractive to you?'

'Yes, it did. He used to say that if he wanted something he'd get it, and most of the time he did.'

'I admire him for that.'

'It's a haulage firm he runs, not British Rail.'

'He still made something of himself,' Walker insisted. 'And so did you. Working for a man like Jim Marsh must have been quite prestigious.'

'I suppose you're right.'

'Why did you give up that kind of life, Hailey?'

'I told you, I gave it up when I had Becky.'

'But why would you *want* to give it up just to have a child?'

'We both wanted a child. My biological clock was ticking, I suppose.' She smiled.

'At twenty-four? You could have carried on working for another ten years, and then had a baby. But you gave it all up for your child. I respect that kind of devotion; I just don't understand it.'

She looked at him blankly.

'It might happen to you one day,' she said finally. 'If you fall in love, you might find that even your career isn't so important, and—'

'Never,' he said, cutting her short. 'If you could turn back the clock, would you have a child later in life?'

'I don't know, Adam. I wouldn't give up Becky for anything now.'

'No, but *then*. Were you happy when you found out you were

pregnant, when you realized you were going to have to give up work?'

'I didn't mind,' she said defensively.

What the hell was he driving at? Had he touched a nerve in her?

'You were prepared to give up everything you had to play happy families?'

Tell him the truth.

The knot of muscles at the side of her jaw pulsed.

She was aware of his eyes boring into her. But, when she looked at him, she saw compassion in his gaze.

'I *didn't* want a child then,' she said flatly.

Why are you telling him this? You've known this man for less than two hours.

She looked back deeply into his eyes, as if seeking reassurance for her confession, wondering why she wanted to tell him. Surprised at how easy it had been.

'Rob wanted a child,' she continued, her tone subdued. 'He had his heart set on it. *I* wanted to carry on working. I loved that job, and it paid well too. I thought that I could be a help to Rob if I was independent, not relying on him for money all the time.' She exhaled wearily. 'We even spoke about an abortion. Well, *I* mentioned it. Rob didn't want that.'

Walker didn't speak, merely sat gazing at Hailey as she continued.

'As the pregnancy became more advanced, it got to the stage where it was too late for an abortion. By that time I'd come to terms with it.'

'But you weren't happy?'

'I would have waited until *I* was ready. I suppose some people would say that I gave in to Rob. He always wanted me to give up my job working for Jim, and the pregnancy gave him an excuse.'

She shrugged. 'But I wouldn't change things now,' she said, none too convincingly. 'I love Becky more than anything in the world.' She swallowed hard. 'I suppose you think I'm stupid.'

He reached out across the table and, very slowly, drew one index finger across the back of her right hand.

She caught the digit and squeezed gently, holding it for a second, looking again into his eyes.

'You're not stupid,' he told her.

'If I'd been as determined as you, I wouldn't have given up my job, would I?' She smiled.

'It takes a lot of strength to be so single-minded, to want something so badly that everything else becomes secondary. Not everyone *has* that strength. Not everyone *should* have that strength. It took just as much courage for you to give up your job.'

'Like I said, I love Becky more than anything else in the world.'

'*Anything?*'

'What do you mean?'

'Do you love her more than your husband?'

Hailey shook her head and smiled.

'Adam, what kind of question is that?' she said.

'I was curious, that's all.'

'It's a different *kind* of love. It's unconditional: both ways. Perhaps it's easier to love a child than another adult, because the child doesn't expect anything of you. All they want is for you to be there when they need you.'

'And what does Rob want from you?'

She looked down at the table, her eyes focused on a small puddle of spilled milk.

'Sometimes I'm not sure what he wants,' she said finally.

'You know he loves you, though?'

She nodded.

'What about you?' she wanted to know. 'You must have loved someone at sometime.' Hailey wanted *him* to talk for a change. She was beginning to feel she had already said too much to him, and yet it was so easy to talk in front of this man – this stranger. She felt as if she'd known him all her life. No detail of her life seemed too intimate to share with him.

Even Rob's affair?

'There've been women,' he told her.

'Lots?' she said, smiling.

'I don't keep score.'

'And you're telling me you never loved *one* of them?'

'Career first,' he reminded her.

She grinned.

'I'll make it, Hailey,' Walker continued.

'I don't doubt that, Adam. Not for a minute.'

Only when she looked down did she realize she was still holding his hand.

And it felt right.

Despite everything she knew.

It felt right.

16

HAILEY STOOD BENEATH the shower spray, eyes closed, the jets of water stinging her skin. She adjusted the temperature slightly, reached for the soap and began smoothing it over her body.

She'd arrived home less than twenty minutes ago and headed straight upstairs for a shower. She had another hour before having to pick up Becky from school.

There had been a couple of messages on the answerphone, but she'd decided to leave them until afterwards.

Now she stood beneath the spray, an image of Adam Walker imprinted on her mind.

Their parting had been awkward, almost clumsy. Both of them standing outside Tivoli's looking at each other, wondering what to do next. How to conclude their meeting. Hailey had wondered for brief, ridiculous seconds if she should shake hands with him.

Finally she had leant forward and kissed him gently on the cheek, thanking him for meeting her for lunch.

He had seemed a little reluctant to leave her then, offering to walk her back to her car. She had declined.

She'd kissed him again on the cheek, then turned and walked away, though wanting to look back in his direction. Even now she wondered why she hadn't.

Frightened he wouldn't have been still looking at you?

Because she knew that was what she wanted.

She had wanted to turn and see him looking longingly after her.

She had *wanted* him to be attracted to her, wanted him to desire her.

Wanted him to want *her*.

As she wanted him?

As she soaped her breasts she felt her nipples stiffen and she worked the soap into the hard buds, her other hand gliding down her belly into the wet curls of her pubic mound. Then beyond to the warm moisture between her thighs.

She tried for a moment to push his image from her mind, but then decided not to. She wanted that sight in her subconscious. Wanted to think of him looking at her. To think of him *touching* her.

Her breathing became deeper as her index finger began to gently stroke around her clitoris. She stepped back so that the jets of water struck her hips and upper thighs, their stinging sensation pleasing, adding to the pleasure she was already feeling from the movement of her fingers.

What are you doing?

Her eyes snapped open and she pulled her hand away from her swollen labia, as if ashamed of the sensations she felt there.

What are you doing?

She switched off the shower and stood motionless in the cubicle, droplets of water still falling from the shower head, plopping into puddles on the tiles beneath her feet.

Hailey listened to her own harsh breathing for a moment longer, then stepped out of the shower, grabbed a towel and dried herself hurriedly.

She pulled on jeans and a T-shirt, stepped into trainers and hurried downstairs.

As Hailey walked into the kitchen, her breathing was now slowing slightly. Her heart was still thudding against her ribs, and she felt that warmth between her legs as insistent as unconsummated desire.

She took a glass from the draining board, spun a tap and filled it. Swallowed the contents. Drank another glass.

Get a grip.

She wandered out into the hall to check the messages on the answerphone.

One from her mother: would Hailey call her back?

Another from Caroline Hacket: call her when she got a minute.

Hailey looked at her watch. Time to pick up Becky.

She sucked in one last breath, held it, then let it out slowly, satisfied that she had regained control.

Ten minutes to drive to the school. Becky would be kept waiting otherwise.

Hailey walked out, shutting the front door behind her.

Inside the house, the phone began to ring again.

ASPEN, COLORADO

The girl had been dead for two days.

He'd hidden her body well — concealed it in the boot of an abandoned car.

As he walked back through the woods towards the vehicle, he could picture her in his mind, picture her in life.

Late teens. Pretty. Her long dark hair parted in the middle. He'd asked her name. He always asked their names, but as he approached he could not recall it.

That didn't matter.

All that mattered was that she was still where he had left her. She was still waiting for him.

In life she had sought his company eagerly. He was a good-looking man: he knew that (enough women had told him so). And he used his looks and his charm for his own ends. He sometimes thought how ridiculously easy it was, how simple it had been, to lure so many of these women into his clutches.

How many had there been so far? Twenty? Even more?

Figures, like names, sometimes slipped his mind.

God, how they loved his charm.

He smiled to himself as he drew nearer to the abandoned car.

He paused for a moment, then opened the boot.

She was naked. Just as he'd left her.

He reached out and touched one of her breasts.

It was cold. The skin waxen.

And it still bore his bite marks. Especially around one nipple. The delicate bud had almost been severed by his frenzied chewing.

She had screamed loudly when he had bitten her there. She had struggled, those struggles intensifying when he flipped her over and sank his teeth into her buttocks, so deep that blood flowed.

He'd strangled her, to shut her up as much as anything.

She'd taken longer than the others to die, and he'd looked into her bulging eyes as he'd squeezed the life from her, gradually seeing those throbbing orbs glaze over.

Her eyes were still open now and he looked deeply into them, seeing his own reflection in the dead blackness of her dilated pupils.

He'd severed her head shortly after her death.

That same head he now picked up by its long hair, staring again into those eyes.

He could feel his erection pressing urgently against his trousers and, with his free hand, he pulled his swollen penis free. He clamped one fist around his shaft and began to rub, gazing raptly into those blind eyes, his excitement building.

There was a strong smell emanating from both body and head. Even forty-eight hours could produce a fair amount of deterioration in a corpse, and her wounds were already infected. One, on her stomach, was suppurating.

He continued to masturbate, his climax drawing closer.

He was grunting loudly now, enjoying the pleasure of it. Just as he had enjoyed it while she had been still alive. When he had forced himself into her anus, pushing her head into the earth to silence her screams.

But now he paused, releasing his penis, using both hands to force open her jaws.

There was a loud snap as one of the rigored joints cracked, but he managed to achieve his objective with relative ease.

Her tongue was blackened and swollen. Her lips bloodless lines on her bruised and bloated face.

The stench of putrefaction seemed to billow from that gaping mouth like an invisible, reeking cloud.

He began masturbating again, holding the severed head close to the tip of his throbbing penis.

His orgasm gripped him, and he watched as several thick spurts of ejaculate spattered the face and mouth of his trophy, some of it entering that gaping, dead maw. He lifted the head so that it was inches from his face and he saw his seed on that blackened tongue.

He smiled, his breathing gradually slowing.

Finally he threw the head back into the car boot and slammed it shut, turning to walk back to his own vehicle.

The wind was growing stronger and he pulled up his collar.

Still, it was comfortably warm inside his own car. And only a short drive to the small diner he'd passed an hour or so earlier. He would stop there and get some lunch. He was hungry.

9 May 1976

We serial killers are your sons, we are your husbands, we are everywhere. And there will be more of your children dead tomorrow.

Ted Bundy

Look inside, open your eyes.
I'm you. Sad, but true.
Metallica

17

Rob Gibson sat at the end of the bed, flicking channels. Jabbing the remote control towards the TV as if it was a weapon.

News, soaps, some American chat show.

The same old shit.

He located MTV and left it on: at least the music was fairly decent. Well, until some trendy moron announced that they'd be looking through the Dance Chart. Rob groaned and switched the set off.

It had been a long day. However, it had been profitable, which was all that mattered. He'd ring Frank Burnside first thing in the morning to tell him the good news: that he'd secured contracts with three major firms in the North. Rob was meeting two other reps for dinner that night, to discuss more plans for BG Trucks. They were supposed to meet him downstairs in the bar of the Piccadilly at 8.30.

He checked his watch.

Christ, it was already 7.30 now.

He might just have time for a quick bath and a few minutes to himself before the day's business spilled over into the evening's arrangements.

While the bath was running, he selected another suit from the wardrobe, and laid it out on the bed beside a fresh shirt and tie.

Rob switched on the radio and was relieved to find some listenable music there. He began to relax a little, wandering into the bathroom every now and then to check on the bath level.

The trade fair had proved even more of a success than he'd hoped. He was looking forward to telling Frank Burnside about the successful deals. Hopefully he'd have another in the bag after this meeting tonight.

Like most business deals, it required a certain amount of practised bullshit. Rob had to pretend to care about his would-be client's private interests, about their families, about where they were going for their holidays.

The usual bollocks.

But he was gifted in the art of duplicity. More so than his partner.

Rob smiled.

Frank Burnside had a habit of looking bored after about ten minutes, whereas Rob himself could maintain an aura of feigned enthusiasm for as long as it took to close the deal.

He wasn't looking forward to the forthcoming session. Both his potential clients had mentioned that they liked a drink – Rob's interpretation being that they intended staying in the bar all night getting pissed, and running it up on *his* room bill. That didn't bother him too much, but he wasn't a great drinker himself, and didn't relish the idea of getting smashed when he had another heavy day ahead of him tomorrow.

Still, he mused, needs must when there's a fucking great contract at the end of it. So he'd smile, he'd laugh in all the right places, he'd even pretend he *gave* a shit when one of the clients announced that he was a Manchester United supporter. When *normally* his inclination would be to spit in the bastard's beer.

Such was business.

He checked the bath again and began to undress.

The knock on the bedroom door startled him.

'Shit,' he murmured.

He'd obviously forgotten to put out the DO NOT DISTURB sign.

The maid was about to come in and draw his curtains, turn down his bed, and do whatever else she had to do.

He wrapped a towel around his hips and opened the door.

Sandra Bennett smiled in at him.

18

'WHAT THE HELL are *you* doing here?' Rob stood motionless, staring at her.

'*That*'s a nice greeting after I've come all this way,' she said. 'Aren't you even going to ask me in?'

He exhaled and stepped aside, allowing her inside the room.

She was carrying a small overnight bag, which she dropped on the end of the bed beside his suit.

Rob slammed the door closed, and stood looking at her.

Navy blue trouser suit. Black ankle boots.

She ran a hand through her blonde hair.

'What are you playing at, Sandy?' he said. 'Why are you here?'

'It looks like you were expecting me,' she said, smiling, nodding towards the towel around his hips.

He took a step towards her.

'I'm serious,' he snapped. 'This isn't a fucking game.'

'What's the problem, Rob?'

'Number one, I've got a meeting with clients in less than an hour. Number two – you. *You're* the problem.'

'I had to come.'

'Why, for Christ's sake? It's all over between us, you know that.'

'We never talked about it – about us.'

'There is no *us*. There never was, and there can't be. I thought you understood that.'

'Why not? That was one of the things we never discussed. It just finished between us, no explanations.'

'My wife found out. What more fucking explanation do you need?'

'I just wanted to talk to you. Perhaps you're right, it's over – but we've never had the chance to talk about our feelings.'

'Jesus, I don't believe you, Sandy. What do you think's going to happen if Hailey finds out you're here?'

'She won't.'

'Just like she wasn't ever going to find out we were having an affair in the first place?'

'She wouldn't have found out if you'd been more careful. If she hadn't found that receipt from our trip to Leeds.'

'So now you're blaming me? You knew there was no future in it anyway.'

'So you say.'

'Yes, that's what I say, because it's true. Aren't you listening to me? If she finds out you're here she'll throw me out, and I dread to think what she'll do to *you*.'

'I don't want her to find out either. The last thing I want is some crazy, jealous wife on my doorstep. Look, Rob, I came here because I wanted to see you, to talk to you. I know it'll probably be the last time we'll be together. Just let me say goodbye, that's all.'

'I've got to go,' he said, looking at his watch. 'I've got to meet clients.'

'So what do I do? Are you going to throw me out? I can't get home now. The last return train went half an hour ago.'

He stood with his hands on his hips, his breath coming in short gasps.

'How long will your meeting be?' she wanted to know.

'Fuck knows,' he rasped. 'I could be down there until the early hours of the bloody morning.'

'I'll wait up here for you.'

'Sandy—'

'Please, Rob, I only want to talk.'

He spun away from her.

'Fuck it. Wait here, then. Watch the TV, order some room service, do what you want. We'll talk when I get back.'

He began to dress.

'You might as well have a bath,' he told her. 'There's one waiting in there.' He hooked a thumb in the direction of the bathroom.

She smiled as she saw him disappear into the bathroom. He emerged a moment later, hair combed, smelling of aftershave.

'Don't answer that phone if it rings,' he said, jabbing a finger towards the bedside cabinet. 'I'll see you later.'

And he was gone.

Sandy Bennett's smile widened and she began to unpack her overnight bag.

19

'When is Dad coming home?'

Hailey looked at her daughter with an expression of bemusement, as if she'd just asked her to explain the Theory of Relativity or the Origins of the Universe.

She lowered the book she'd been reading to Becky, and blinked hard.

The child was sitting up in bed.

'He'll be home tomorrow night,' said Hailey. 'Why?'

The little girl slid down beneath the sheets and pulled them up around her neck.

'Dad does all the different voices when he reads my stories,' Becky explained.

'And I *don't*?' said Hailey, feigning annoyance. 'My stories not good enough for you, eh? Right, that's OK.'

Becky began to giggle.

'I know when I'm not wanted,' Hailey continued, tickling her daughter, smiling as the little girl wriggled.

Finally she sat back in the chair beside Becky's bed, running a hand through her daughter's hair.

Becky was still smiling, clutching a battered old stuffed dog.

'Are you going to go to sleep now?' Hailey asked.

Becky nodded and leant over to kiss her.

She waited until Hailey was on her feet, then rolled onto her side.

'Mum, do you still love Dad?'

The question took Hailey by surprise. She turned and took a step back towards the bed, kneeling beside it, looking into her daughter's face.

'What makes you say that, darling?' she wanted to know.

'You *do* still love him, don't you?'

'Of course I do. I'll always love your dad.'

'And he loves you?'

'Yes. Why do you ask?'

'I've heard you and Dad shouting sometimes. I thought you didn't love each other any more.'

Hailey gripped her hand and squeezed.

'People disagree about things sometimes, Becky, that's all,' she said reassuringly.

'Do they shout when that happens?'

'Sometimes. They *shouldn't*, but they do.'

'Dad hasn't gone away because you've both been shouting, has he?'

'No, darling. He's working, that's all.'

'And he *is* coming back?'

'Of course he is.'

Hailey began to stroke her daughter's hair again. She felt tears welling up inside, but fought them back.

It was less than five minutes before Becky drifted off to sleep. She shifted beneath the covers and rolled onto her back. Hailey kissed her gently on the forehead and cheek.

'I love you,' she whispered. 'Sleep tight.'

She walked out of the room, pausing against the closed door for a second as if to recover her composure.

'*I've heard you and Dad shouting.*'

Hailey made her way downstairs and into the kitchen, where she turned on the kettle.

'*Do you still love Dad?*'

Hailey was surprised at how quickly her own tears began to flow.

20

Fuck!

That was what Rob thought.

Fuck!

That one word stuck in his mind.

Fuck the meeting. Fuck the clients. Fuck the hotel, and fuck this lift.

It rose slowly and he leant back against one of the walls, his head spinning.

He'd had too much to drink; he knew he had. He felt a little sick and also angry with himself for letting alcohol get the better of him.

He glanced at his watch as the lift continued to rise towards the designated floor.

The meeting had been a success: he'd done what he had to do. He'd laughed and smiled in all the right places. He'd raised bullshit to an art form as he secured a deal with the two reps he'd spent the evening with.

12.46 a.m.

He'd been in that bar downstairs for over three hours, but at least it had been a successful three hours.

He'd phoned Hailey from a payphone at about 10.30 and told her to go to bed, that his clients were likely to keep him drinking for Christ only knew how much longer.

She'd told him she loved him.

He'd replied in kind.

Lousy bastard.

Fuck it, what she didn't know wouldn't hurt her, would it?

The lift bumped to a halt and he got out, fumbling in his jacket pocket for his key as he wandered down the corridor towards his room.

Sandy would be waiting for him.

He'd thought about her once or twice during the evening, wondering what she was doing at that moment up in his room.

He paused outside 422 for a second, before he pushed his key into the lock.

Rob could hear no sound from inside. Perhaps she was asleep.

He opened the door and stepped in, locking the door behind him.

The two bedside lamps were lit, but apart from that the room was in darkness. Even the TV was off.

Sandy Bennett was sprawled on the bed, wearing just a long grey T-shirt and a pair of white knickers. He could see them clearly as she stretched her slender legs. Her eyes snapped open as he stood at the end of the bed gazing down at her.

'Sorry, I must have dozed off,' she said sleepily.

He noticed the tray with its plates of half-eaten food beside the bed.

'Was it a good meeting?' she wanted to know, sitting up and running a hand through her hair.

He pulled off his jacket and draped it over a chair.

'I got what I wanted,' he told her.

'You always do, don't you, Rob?' she said.

'Yeah,' he grunted, smiling.

He began unbuttoning his shirt.

'I see you made yourself at home,' he observed, nodding towards the room-service tray.

'You told me to.'

'And you always do what I tell you, don't you?'

He fumbled with one of his buttons and she slid off the bed and crossed to him, trying to help.

'I can manage,' he told her, and she smelled the drink on him.

'Are you drunk?' she said, a thin smile touching her lips.

'Not drunk enough.'

She stood close to him, looking into his eyes, searching for some sign of reciprocated longing there.

He could feel the warmth of her body, smell her delicate scent. His breathing grew heavier.

'You said you came here to talk,' he said finally. 'So talk.'

'What happened between us . . .' she began.

'Is over,' he reminded her, interrupting.

'Because you *want* it to be?'

'Because it *has* to be.'

'Why?'

'Oh, come on, Sandy, don't start that shit all over again. You *know* why. I'm married. I've got a kid.'

'You were already married with a kid when we started seeing each other.'

'All right, it's over because it *has* to be over – because we got caught. Got it? You knew the rules when we started.'

'Whose rules? Yours?'

'No. *The* rules. I never told you my wife didn't understand me. I never said I wasn't happy at home.'

'Then why did you want to screw me?'

'Because you're very good-looking. Because I fancied you. Because I'm a fucking man. Because I *could*. What do you want to hear?'

'I knew you'd never leave Hailey. I didn't want you to. And I played by your rules, but that doesn't mean I can't still get hurt. It doesn't mean I can't still miss you. Don't hate me for it, Rob.'

'I don't hate you,' he said, his tone softening.

Again she took a step towards him, holding one of his hands, draping it around her shoulder and pushing herself against him.

She leant forward and allowed her lips to brush against his, lightly at first but then more urgently. He responded, his tongue snaking into the warm wetness of her mouth. They remained locked together like that for what seemed an eternity.

She gripped his right hand, gently stroked his index finger and guided it between her legs. When she withdrew it a second later it was glistening. She pushed it towards his mouth and smeared the transparent moistness across his bottom lip – then pushed it into his mouth, letting him taste her.

They were both breathing heavily now.

Rob kissed her even more passionately, then pushed her back onto the bed, climbing alongside her, feeling her hands scrabbling at his trousers. Expertly she undid them and tugged them free, smiling as she saw his erection straining against his underpants.

She eased them over his hips. Over his bulging manhood. Then she lowered her mouth to his stiffness and enveloped its swollen tip.

He grunted as he felt her free hand massage his shaft, her tongue still playing over his glans.

Sandy stood up on the bed and pulled off first her T-shirt, then her panties, which she dropped onto his chest.

For long seconds she stood there, allowing him to look up at her body, at her plump vaginal lips and the dewy moisture on her downy pubic hair. Then she sank down and straddled him, guiding his erection towards her moist warmth. She teased the tip around the hardened bud of her clitoris, closing her own eyes as the pleasure intensified. Then she moved forward slightly, allowing him to penetrate her. Wanting to feel his stiffness inside her.

With a deep sigh of delight, she began to ride his erection, shuddering as she felt his hands cupping her breasts, thumbing the nipples that already stuck out stiffly from the puckered flesh around them.

She looked down at him: his eyes screwed tight, his face contorted with pleasure.

Sandy was smiling even before the first unmistakable feelings of orgasm began to spread gloriously from her pelvis and belly, and up through her body.

She continued her rhythmic movements, aware that Rob too was close to his climax, enjoying the increased pressure of his hands on her breasts as he squeezed harder.

Sandy gripped his shoulders as the first wave of intense pleasure surged through her, and she gasped his name in the midst of it.

Rob thrust his hips up, as if to penetrate her even more deeply, and he too grunted as he filled her with his semen.

They were lost in that wonderful moment – in the sensations that enveloped them.

His eyes were still closed as Sandy smiled down at him.

21

At first Rob Gibson thought he was dreaming.

That the ringing phone was the residue of some dream.

Its strident sound continued, piercing his sleepy haze.

He blinked hard, and realized that this wasn't a figment of his imagination.

It was 2.18 a.m.

'Jesus,' he murmured, sitting up.

Beside him, the naked form of Sandy Bennett stirred slightly.

Rob had to lean across her to reach the phone and, as he did so, she tried to snake her arms around him. He pulled free from her and swung himself out of the bed, wandering around to the other side of it and slumping in a chair.

He took a couple of deep breaths before lifting the receiver.

Some fucking arsehole calling the wrong room?

'Hello,' he croaked, clearing his throat.

'It's me.'

He recognized Hailey's voice immediately.

Lying on her side no more than two feet from him, Sandy looked sleepily at him, allowing the sheet to slip away and reveal her breasts.

Rob glared at her, convinced that he could see the beginnings of a smile creasing the corners of her mouth.

'What's wrong?' Rob wanted to know, waving a hand to signal Sandy to keep quiet.

'I couldn't sleep,' Hailey told him.

He exhaled deeply.

'I was thinking about you,' she continued. 'Sorry I woke you.'

'It's OK, babe,' he said, still glancing at Sandy, who had now eased the sheet even further down and rolled onto her back.

Rob shifted uncomfortably in his chair.

'Becky's missing you,' Hailey said.

'And what about you? Are you missing me, too?'

Sandy Bennett stretched, kicking the sheet right off, to reveal her body totally. She raised both knees and pressed them together, then allowed her legs to fall apart. Permitted one hand to glide between them.

Feeling a stirring in his groin, Rob looked away.

'I just wanted to hear your voice,' Hailey murmured.

'Try to sleep, Hailey,' he said softly.

There was a long silence.

He saw Sandy's right hand moving gently between her legs, her breathing becoming a little harsher.

Again he tried to look away.

'What time will you be home tomorrow?' Hailey said at last. 'So I can tell Becky.'

'I don't know. It depends what time this finishes. About tea-time I suppose. If I'm lucky with the traffic, too.'

'What have you been doing tonight?' she wanted to know.

Sandy had now slipped her other hand between her legs too. Her heels were digging into the mattress.

'Did you have a meeting tonight?' Hailey persisted.

I've been fucking my mistress. No big deal.

Rob stroked his chin and lowered his gaze.

'Yes, I had a meeting,' he said. 'It went well.'

'I'll let you go back to sleep now.'

He swallowed hard.

'I love you,' Hailey said quietly.

Sandy turned onto her side so that she was looking directly at him, her hands still moving expertly between her legs.

'I said I love you,' Hailey repeated.

His eyes were fixed on Sandy.

'I love you too,' he said and hung up.

'How touching,' Sandy said, her voice wavering.

'What is your fucking game, Sandy?' Rob snapped. 'Do you think you're being funny?'

He stood watching her as she rolled onto her back once again.

'Come back to bed,' she said breathlessly.

He stood close to her and she could see his erection.

'Come on,' she gasped, fingers still moving frantically.

'You're a fucking bitch,' he said angrily.

'Maybe – but I'm not the one who just told my other half that I love them. What does that make *you*?'

Her breathing was ragged, her fingers moving more urgently.

'Come on, Rob,' she panted, reaching out one hand towards his stiffness.

He felt her moisture on his shaft as she enveloped it in her slender fingers.

He climbed onto the bed and she hooked her legs around the small of his back.

'This is just for old time's sake, isn't it?' she said, her voice dissolving into a loud moan as he penetrated her.

Rob grabbed both of her hands and squeezed hard, his own hands balled into fists as he thrust roughly into her.

Fucking bitch.

She arched her back.

'What does that make you?'

His own breathing was now laboured.

He closed his eyes.

Expectation

PAUL DOOLAN PUT down the copy of Mayfair and sat up as he heard the key turn in his cell door.

Muffled voices outside, then David Layton stepped in. The door slammed behind him.

For long seconds the two men looked at each other, then Layton suddenly punched the air, his teeth gritted in a triumphant snarl.

'Yes!' he shouted.

'You got it?' Doolan said, also grinning.

'Cunts approved it, didn't they? I'm out of here in three weeks.'

He sat down at the small table and pulled his tobacco tin from his overalls. He flipped it open and began making a roll-up.

'Parole?' mused Doolan. 'You lucky bastard.' He rolled over onto his side on the top bunk and looked down at his companion. 'What are you going to do when you get out?'

Layton shrugged. 'I haven't thought about it,' he confessed. 'You know you don't think about the future inside, do you?'

'I think about getting out of here all the time.'

'Well, if you hadn't got caught for that fucking Securicor van job you wouldn't be in here now, would you?'

'It wasn't my fault. I told them I'd never handled a shooter before.'

'Good job you hadn't. Otherwise you might have killed that fucking guard instead of just shooting the cunt in the leg.'

'Yeah, well, next time I'll get it right.'

Layton lit his roll-up and sucked on it.

'Have you seen Brycey since you did the job on Morton?' Doolan wanted to know.

'One of his boys had a word with me. They said he was pleased: said I did a good job. One of them works in the infirmary where they took Morton. He saw the damage. They said I could see Brycey when I got out, see about a job with his firm.'

'Are you going to do that?'

'I don't know. I don't want to work for somebody. I'd rather be on my own: nobody breathing down my neck.'

'You want to go straight?' Doolan chuckled.

Layton merely spat a piece of tobacco in the direction of his cell-mate.

'By the way,' he said after a moment, 'they've put me on kitchen duties until I get out.'

Doolan's smile faded.

'You jammy cunt,' he said disdainfully.

'They said my behaviour here has been excellent.'

'It's a good job they didn't know about what happened to Morton.'

Layton smiled crookedly.

'Yeah, well they don't know and they're not going to find out, are they?' he hissed, glaring at his cellmate.

'You think I'd grass you up?' Doolan said, offended by the implication.

'No, I know you've got too much sense for that.'

'Anyway, it won't be that fucking easy working in the kitchen. That bastard Gorton runs it. Scotch cunt. You'd better watch him.'

Layton drew slowly on his roll-up.

22

HAILEY GIBSON PUSHED open the front door and staggered in with three bags of shopping. She almost dropped one it was so heavy, but she managed to retain her grip on its handle until she reached the kitchen, where she set all three bags down on the worktop.

Caroline Hacket followed her, also carrying three bags. She heaved them up alongside Hailey's and wiped her hands on her jeans, blowing out her cheeks with the effort of carrying such weighty loads.

Hailey looked at her friend and started laughing.

'What now?' Caroline asked innocently.

'I can't believe how you were flirting with that poor lad on the checkout,' Hailey told her, filling the kettle. 'He couldn't have been more than about eighteen.'

'He was old *enough*,' chuckled Caroline. 'He had big hands, too. And you know what they say about big hands.'

'I thought that was big feet,' Hailey said, starting to unpack the shopping.

'Whatever – it probably works the same way.'

'You could see he was embarrassed.'

'He was enjoying it.'

'Until you started stroking that courgette, and asking if that would make it any bigger. I think that was when he asked to be relieved from duty.' Hailey burst out laughing again.

'I don't know why I bothered. It was *you* he fancied anyway,' Caroline said. 'He couldn't take his eyes off you.'

Hailey tossed her head exaggeratedly.

'And me a happily married woman,' she said, a note of scorn in her voice.

'How *are* things at the moment?' Caroline wanted to know.

Hailey shrugged.

'We keep going,' she said a little sadly. 'It isn't easy, and we usually have a row most nights, but we're trying, Caroline.'

'Is *Rob* trying?'

'He *wants* it to work as much as *I* do. I'm sure of that. He wouldn't have agreed to come to the Relate sessions otherwise.'

'I hope you're right, Hailey.'

'What's that supposed to mean?'

'It just seems to be you who's doing all the work. *You* fixed up the meetings with Relate. *You* had to talk him into going. Tell me to mind my own business if you like, but he doesn't seem to be very sorry for what he did.'

'I can't expect him to walk around in a hair-shirt for the rest of his life.'

'Perhaps you should have done what *I* did when I found out *my* old man was messing around behind my back.'

'Which one?'

'Very funny. *Either* of them. You should have kicked him out.'

'It's not as easy as that, Caroline.'

'It is when they shit on you from a great height.'

'You didn't have kids.'

'Don't use Becky as an excuse. What Rob did was wrong. He betrayed *her* as much as he betrayed you. You should have told him to get on his bike for her sake, too.'

'Becky doesn't know what happened, and if I have my way she never will.'

'That still doesn't excuse what he did.'

'I know that, I'm not making excuses for him; I'm giving him another chance. Is there anything so wrong about that?'

'Leopards don't change their spots.'

'Maybe not, but perhaps some of them can learn a lesson.'

'*You* should have an affair.'

Hailey looked at her blankly.

'That would teach him: give him a taste of his own medicine. See how he likes that.'

'Are you serious?'

'Why not? He doesn't have to find out about it, but at least *you'd* know you were getting some revenge.'

'It's not about revenge, Caroline. It's about saving my marriage.'

'*You* didn't wreck it in the first place.'

'So, I go out and fuck some bloke and that makes everything all right, does it?'

'No, but it evens the score.'

Hailey shook her head and smiled wanly.

'Come on,' Caroline said, taking a step closer to her friend. 'Don't tell me you haven't thought about it?'

'I haven't thought about it,' Hailey said flatly.

'Then perhaps you should.'

'You could, Caroline. I *couldn't*.'

'You're bloody right I could, and I did when I caught the second one at it. Then I made *sure* he knew I was screwing someone, too.'

'And it finished your marriage.'

'It was finished anyway.'

'Well, mine isn't.'

'I hope you're right.'

Hailey sighed. 'I still feel so bloody angry with him,' she admitted.

'And why shouldn't you? Don't feel guilty about it. Rob's the one who should feel guilty – not you. I still say you should have left him.'

'It's not that easy. I have to think about Becky.'

'Then it looks like my other idea is favourite: have an affair yourself. What is it they say: "Don't get mad, get even"?' She raised an eyebrow.

Hailey ran a hand through her hair and sighed.

'As a matter of fact,' she said, 'I was thinking of going back to work.'

'What kind of work?' Caroline wanted to know.

'My old job. Jim Marsh rang me a couple of days ago and asked me if I'd go back part-time. We've kept in touch since I left them. I just thought it would give me less time to sit around wondering about what Rob's been up to.'

'So, do it,' Caroline urged. 'You loved that job.'

'I told him I'd think about it.'

'Hailey, you owe it to yourself. Call him and say you'll do it.'

'You know what it was like: the hours were irregular. I might not always be here when Becky needs me, and . . .'

Caroline cut her short. 'Stop putting obstacles in the way,' she said. 'I'll pick Becky up from school if you can't manage it. Do it, Hailey. Go back and work for him.'

'I haven't talked about it with Rob yet.'

'You know what *he's* going to say anyway. He'll try to put you off. He never liked you doing that job in the first place, did he?'

Hailey shook her head.

'Well, sod him,' Caroline said, touching her friend's arm. 'Do what *you* want to do. That's your trouble, you don't think about *yourself* enough.'

Hailey shrugged.

'Perhaps you're right,' she conceded.

'I know I am. Besides, if you go away on business somewhere, you might meet some good-looking bloke in one of these posh hotels Marsh books you into and, if you do, who knows what might happen.'

'Caroline, stop trying to push me into an affair, will you?' Hailey smiled.

'What's good for the goose,' Caroline said quietly.

The doorbell rang.

Hailey hesitated a moment, her arms full of shopping items.

'I'll put these away,' said Caroline. 'You answer that.'

Hailey wandered through the hall, thoughts tumbling around inside her head.

Leave Rob?

She glanced at the coat-rack and saw one of his jackets hanging there. As she reached the door, she touched the sleeve of the jacket lightly.

Yes, go back to work for Jim Marsh. To hell with what Rob thinks.

She opened the front door.

Adam Walker stood smiling at her.

23

For interminable seconds, Hailey merely stared at Walker, as if she couldn't remember who he was.

He remained on the front doorstep, still wearing that infectious grin.

Finally the spell was broken.

'Adam,' she said, smiling too, 'I wasn't expecting you.'

'I'm sorry if I've disturbed you,' he said. 'I was passing by and I hoped you wouldn't mind me calling in.' He chuckled. 'God, that sounds like the worst cliché in the world, doesn't it?'

She nodded blankly.

Just like some stupid schoolgirl. Get a grip.

'Where's your car?' she asked eventually.

'I parked it round the corner. Look, if it's inconvenient, I can go. I just wanted to see if you were in.'

She stepped aside and ushered him in.

'No, please come in,' Hailey said. 'You caught me by surprise, that's all.'

He accepted her invitation.

'It's a beautiful house,' he said, looking around inside the hall.

'Thanks. Come through.' She motioned for him to follow her into the kitchen. 'Aren't you working today?'

'I've got to go into London later today. I was just on my way to the station to check on train times, then I realized how close I was to your house.'

Caroline Hacket turned to look at the newcomer.

Walker smiled at her.

'Caroline, this is Adam Walker,' said Hailey. 'The man I was telling you about. The one who found Becky.' As she introduced them, she could see approval in Caroline's eyes.

They shook hands and Walker continued smiling at her friend.

'Would you like a coffee?' Hailey asked.

'I'm disturbing you,' said Walker, motioning towards the shopping spread out on the worktops and the kitchen table.

'No, you're not,' Hailey reassured him.

'Any excuse for a break,' Caroline echoed, her gaze lingering on the newcomer that little bit too long.

He was wearing the same black jeans and leather jacket he'd sported for his lunch with Hailey the previous day. When she moved past him, she could smell its musky aroma again.

'Are you local, Mr Walker?' Caroline wanted to know.

'I live locally, if that's what you mean,' he told her.

'Adam's an artist,' Hailey said.

'What do you paint?' Caroline enquired.

'Whatever pays the most money.' Walker grinned again.

'I've always wanted my portrait painted,' Caroline said. 'In the nude.'

Hailey raised an eyebrow in her direction.

'I could give you an estimate,' Walker chuckled.

All of them laughed.

Hailey put a cup of coffee down before him, then handed another to Caroline and sat down herself.

'One sugar, isn't it?' she said to Walker.

He nodded. 'How's Becky?' he wanted to know.

'She's fine.'

'And your husband?'

'He gets back from Manchester tonight. It's a pity you couldn't have met him. I'm sure *he'd* like to thank you for what you did for us.'

'I told you, I didn't do anything.'

'You rescued my daughter.'

Walker looked over at Caroline, who was still running appraising eyes over him.

'Are you married, Caroline?' he enquired.

'I *was*, twice,' she told him.

'But not now?' he continued.

Caroline shook her head. 'What about you?'

'I never met the right woman,' he said, glancing at Hailey briefly.

'I never met the right *man*, but it didn't stop me getting married twice.' Caroline laughed. 'Marriage is a lottery anyway, isn't it? Sometimes Mr Right turns out to be Mr Wrong.' She looked at Hailey, then sipped her coffee.

'Do you live nearby?' Walker asked her.

'Round the corner,' Caroline told him.

'We've been friends for years,' Hailey said, 'God help us. We used to go to dance classes together, didn't we?'

Caroline nodded.

'What kind of dancing?' Walker asked.

'Ballet,' Caroline informed him. 'I studied for five years after I left school.'

'Why did you stop? You could have been a famous ballerina by now.'

'I developed back problems. The doctor told me if I didn't give up dancing I'd be in a wheelchair by the time I was twenty-five.'

'And you did ballet, too, Hailey?' Walker persisted.

'Only as a form of exercise,' she told him. 'We used to have a class at one of the local community centres. It was just a kind of less violent aerobics.' She laughed.

'Do *you* work out, Adam?' Caroline asked.

'No, why do you ask?'

'You're in good shape. I wondered if you did weights or something like that.'

'I hate gyms. Sweaty blokes standing in front of mirrors staring at themselves and comparing the size of their biceps.'

'Sounds like heaven to me,' Caroline offered, sipping her coffee.

'Most of them are probably gay anyway,' Hailey said. 'Or too obsessed with their own bodies to care about anyone else.'

'Well, they say all the best ones are either gay or married, don't they?' Caroline said.

'And what do they say about good-looking women?' Walker's gaze strayed to Hailey.

'They're bitches,' Caroline told him. 'All good-looking women are total bitches.' She smiled.

'Not all of them,' Walker said.

He took another sip of his coffee.

'I should leave you ladies alone,' he said. 'I shouldn't have disturbed you – but, like I said, I was passing and . . .'

'You're not disturbing us. Besides, Caroline was just going,' Hailey interjected.

'Was I?' Caroline said, smiling. 'Oh, yes, that's right, I was.' She got to her feet.

'Nice to have met you, Caroline.' Walker rose.

He shook her hand, and she felt the strength in his grip.

'I'll see you out,' said Hailey to her friend.

Caroline gathered up her own bags of shopping and headed for the front door. On the doorstep she smiled at Hailey.

'I can see why I'm in the way,' she said. 'He's gorgeous. Call me later and tell me what happens.'

'Nothing's going to happen,' Hailey told her.

'It would if *I* was alone in there with him.'

'Well, you're not,' Hailey chuckled.

'Are you going to tell Rob about him?'

'There's nothing to tell, except he was the one who found Becky.'

'*And* he's gorgeous, *and* you fancy him? And don't try to deny it. I've seen how you look at him.'

''Bye, Caroline,' Hailey said, smiling.

Caroline leant close to her ear, her voice a whisper.

'Tell me if he's good with his tongue,' she murmured.

Hailey slapped her on the arm.

'I'll call you later,' she laughed.

'Lucky bitch,' Caroline said, heading towards the path.

Hailey closed the front door.

She stood there for a moment, trying to control her breathing, aware too that her heart was thudding that little bit more urgently against her ribs. Then she headed back into the kitchen.

24

SHE'D BEEN GONE when he'd woken up.

Rob Gibson had rolled over in bed and reached out towards where he'd expected her to be, but had found only a rumpled sheet.

He had no idea what time Sandy Bennett had left the hotel. At first he'd wondered if she *had* left. He'd wondered if he would arrive at the trade fair to find her waiting for him there. But, no, that was not to be.

He'd smelled her scent on the sheets when he woke, rolling across to where she had lain.

There had been no warmth there, so she'd obviously been gone for some time. He'd must have been sleeping more soundly than he thought, for her to dress and pack her meagre belongings and to slip unheard from his hotel room.

Going where?

Back to his company offices?

Would he arrive there tomorrow to find her sitting at her desk as usual?

Rob had rolled onto his back and stared up at the ceiling.

He had thought back to the previous night: the passion.

Could you really feel such passion with someone you didn't love?

He was now sure you could. He knew that was possible, because he didn't love Sandy.

That was one of the rules. You didn't fall in love with your mistress, did you?

Did you?

He was now standing on the BG Trucks stand in the G-Mex centre, surrounded by other trade stands, enveloped by the noise of so many voices. And yet he felt isolated. Faces passed by and glanced at him; some even stopped and spoke to him, and he answered with practised, robotic words and actions. It was as if he was functioning in some kind of limbo – outside himself. Rob felt as if he was standing to one side, looking back at his own body. A kind of astrally projected selling, he mused.

His mind was elsewhere.

With Sandy?

He inhaled deeply.

Or with Hailey and Becky?

What would Hailey do if she ever found out what had happened last night?

He took a sip from the styrofoam cup close by, wincing when he discovered his coffee was cold.

That was it, he told himself: it was over now. The previous night had been a one-off. 'For old times' sake,' Sandy herself had said.

She understood it was over between them, too.

Didn't she?

He glanced at his watch and wondered how much longer this fucking trade show was going to last.

How much longer before he could go home.

Home to what? To more questions from Hailey?

What had he done here? Who had he spoken to? Some of her questions would be innocent. And then the *other* questions would begin.

Had he phoned anybody?

Had he contacted anybody?

Anybody. Jesus Christ, couldn't she just say 'Sandy'?

But, no, that was part of *her* rules, wasn't it?

You never mentioned the other woman by name. She was always a bitch, a slag, a whore.

He could feel the beginnings of a headache gnawing at him.

25

As HAILEY WALKED back into the kitchen, she found Walker standing looking at some photographs that hung on the wall near the cooker.

Photos of Becky.

'She was a beautiful baby,' he commented, without turning.

Hailey smiled and joined him, eyeing each of the four framed colour ten-by-eights in turn.

'Those were taken at three months, six months, nine months and one year,' she explained.

'Who do people say she resembles?' Walker wanted to know.

'My mum and dad reckon she looked like Rob when she was a baby, but she's grown more like me as she's got older.'

He nodded, his eyes still fixed on the photos.

'Yes, she has. She's beautiful,' he said quietly.

'Would you like another coffee?' Hailey asked. 'Perhaps you can drink *this* one in peace. Caroline does tend to go on a bit.'

'She seemed friendly enough.' He smiled, eyes still scanning the kitchen walls.

He noticed a couple of roughly drawn crayon sketches, which he guessed had been done by Becky. On another wall hung a calendar featuring different views of New Zealand. Opposite it, next to the phone, a small piece of paper cut from a newspaper had been Blu-tacked to the wall. It featured Sky TV's live-televised match schedule.

There were a couple of small framed prints, of the Vatican and the Bridge of Sighs, and another of the Duomo in Florence. Beneath it a framed menu from Lindy's Restuarant in Times Square.

'You've travelled a lot,' said Walker, studying this array of memorabilia.

'That's stuff Rob and I brought back from Italy and New York,' she told him.

'What about your trips abroad with Jim Marsh? Didn't you bring back anything from those?'

She put the cup in front of him, and sat down opposite.

'Just odds and ends,' she said. 'Usually presents for Becky. I never got too much chance to go shopping, you know. It *was* hard work.'

He nodded and sipped his coffee.

'What does your friend Caroline do for a living?' he wanted to know.

'Believe it or not, she's a writer.' Hailey chuckled. 'I know you might find that hard to believe.'

Walker looked suddenly interested.

'What does she write?' he asked enthusiastically.

'She's done a couple of non-fiction books about crime. One of them about serial killers. I don't think either of them sold *that* well, but she doesn't need money from her writing anyway. It's more of a hobby for her.'

'Why doesn't she need money?'

'Both her ex-husbands paid her large divorce settlements, and she invested the money wisely.'

'Does she still write now?' he persisted.

Hailey nodded. 'I think she's working on something at the moment.'

'Another crime book?'

'I'm not sure. She doesn't talk about it much.' Hailey grinned. 'I'm sure if you ask her, she'll let you have copies of what she's written.'

'She sounds like a talented woman. I admire talent in anyone.

If they've got it, they should use it. Talent keeps boredom at bay.'
He smiled.

'I don't think Caroline's ever had a boring day in her life,'
Hailey said wistfully.

'And what about you, Hailey?'

'I haven't got *time* to be bored. Not with a house, a child and
a husband to look after.'

She was aware of him gazing at her. She met his stare and held
it.

'I'm sorry if I interrupted anything, I should have called first
and asked if it was OK to come round,' he said apologetically. 'But
I didn't think you'd mind.'

'I don't,' she said softly.

They sat in silence for what seemed like an eternity, drinking
their coffee, gazing at one another. But it wasn't an uncomfortable
silence, Hailey realized. There was no need for them to speak. No
desperate attempts were necessary to fill the gulf between their
snippets of conversation.

It feels right, doesn't it?

She watched as he finished his coffee.

This stranger.

*You've met this guy only twice, and you're now sitting drinking
coffee with him in your own kitchen.*

'You certainly have got a beautiful house,' he said finally. 'It
must have involved a lot of work.'

She nodded.

'A lot of ambition too,' he added. 'This place is like a sign that
you're both successful, isn't it?'

'It's not meant to be. We liked the house, so we bought it.
Quite simple really.' She smiled, but her smile wasn't returned.

'But people will look at this house and know that someone
successful lives here – someone with money,' he insisted.

'It's our home, Adam, not a status symbol.'

'When I'm famous I'm going to have a house so big you'll need
golf carts to get from room to room.' He laughed.

'And servants?'

'Probably. A couple of maids, a cook, a butler. Whatever famous people have.'

They both laughed.

'Call me if you need a PA,' she joked.

'I will,' he told her, reaching across the table.

Even without thinking, she touched his outstretched fingers with her own.

The contact felt as if someone had pumped a small electrical charge through her.

'I'd better go,' he said quietly.

'You don't have to rush off, Adam,' she assured him.

'I was intending to visit my father,' he told her. 'I ought to go now.'

She nodded. 'Is he very bad?'

'He probably won't even recognize me,' Walker said philosophically. 'But at least I'll be there for him, for an hour or two.'

'It *must* be hard for you.'

'Sometimes he remembers things. He'll talk about things that happened years ago. Other times he just stares at the wall – or at me. He asked one of the nurses to throw me out once. It's a horrible disease.'

'What about the rest of your family?' she wanted to know. 'Do they visit too?'

'I don't know,' he said quickly. 'We've never been a close family. We don't keep in touch.'

'Not even with your sister, the one whose little boy was killed?'

'Like I said, we're not that close.'

Hailey nodded, deciding not to press her point.

'I once said to my father that it was ironic – with him having been a vicar all his life. He'd served God, and then God had done *that* to him: taken his mind. Amusing in a perverse kind of way, isn't it? God must have one hell of a sense of humour.'

Walker got to his feet.

She walked with him to the front door.

'Thanks for the coffe,' he said. 'Sorry again for barging in.'

'I'm glad you did.' She touched his hand and held it for fleeting seconds.

'Give my regards to your husband,' he told her.

She nodded.

'He won't mind that I came by, will he?' asked Walker.

'He'll be sorry he missed you.'

She moved to open the door, in the process leaning close to him, close to his face.

Hailey could smell him distinctly, that musky scent from his leather jacket.

She swallowed hard.

Again her heart was thudding that little bit faster.

'Tell Becky I called,' said Walker, as he stepped out into the porch.

'I hope things go all right with your father,' she said.

He nodded and turned to walk away.

'See you again,' she said.

I hope.

He waved.

She watched until he had disappeared around the corner.

26

THE WIND WHIPPED around the Scorpio, occasionally shifting it slightly to one side.

Adam Walker sat behind the steering wheel, looking out at the building before him, his eyes fixed hypnotically on the red-brick edifice that faced him.

Bayfield House Nursing Home was a modern building in about four acres of its own grounds. It housed around twenty-five residents, between the ages of sixty and ninety, some disabled in mind or body, others merely losing the battle with advancing years.

There was a good ratio of staff to residents, and they did their best to make day-to-day life enjoyable for their charges. There was a doctor on the premises twenty-four hours a day.

Walker swung himself out of his car, and headed up the short path towards the double doors that led into the main reception.

He pulled up the collar of his jacket, then muttered something to himself, spun round and headed back to the Scorpio.

He reached onto the back seat and grabbed the cellophane-wrapped bunch of flowers. He'd bought them at a garage on the way.

Every time he visited here, he brought flowers.

That was what you were supposed to do, wasn't it?

Adam trudged back up the path and pressed the security buzzer next to the front door. The closed-circuit TV camera peered down at him as he looked up into its single eye.

A moment later there came a whirring sound, and the doors opened to allow him access.

The main reception area was empty.

There was a large, low table surrounded by leather-upholstered chairs in the centre. Corridors led off from the reception area like spokes from a wheel hub.

Walker made his way slowly along the central corridor, glancing into open rooms along the way. They, too, all seemed to be empty.

For one bizarre moment it appeared that the entire nursing home had been evacuated. As if its residents had merely disappeared. He wondered if he might come across a steaming cup of tea left unattended. This place was like an earth-bound *Marie Celeste*.

Then he heard voices coming from the day-room up ahead.

Through a pair of glass double-doors he could see several of the elderly residents seated in high-backed chairs in front of a television. As he walked in, he also noticed two nurses in attendance.

First one, then the other smiled at him, and he reciprocated, crossing over to the younger of the two.

She was wearing a light blue uniform, her long hair tied in a ponytail pulled back so severely from her hairline that it looked as if someone was trying to tug her scalp off.

The small badge pinned to her left lapel announced that her name was ANNA COLEMAN.

'How are you, Anna?' He grinned.

'Are those for me?' She nodded towards the flowers.

'If they were for you, this bunch would be twice as big,' Walker told her.

'You smoothie,' interrupted the other nurse. 'She loves all that stuff.'

'Haven't you got some work to do, Nurse Stinson?' replied Anna with mock irritation. Her cheeks had coloured slightly.

'Yes I have, Nurse Coleman.' The other woman smiled.

Two or three of the residents gazed blankly at Walker. The others seemed more intent on the TV screen, although Walker wasn't sure they even understood what they were watching.

'I'm looking for my father,' he said.

'He's in his room.' Anna's smile faded.

Walker nodded, turned, and headed back down the corridor, back into the reception area and off to the right.

There were more bedrooms in that direction. He knew that at the far end of the corridor there was even a small chapel.

Beyond it, outside, was a beautifully kept garden, even an orchard where apple trees blossomed in spring. The setting was idyllic.

Strange therefore, he thought, that he hated this place so much.

He passed two rooms with their doors wide open.

In the first a man in his seventies lay on the bed, reading a newspaper.

In the second another man sat staring out of his window, tapping out a Morse-like tattoo on the sill with one arthritis-twisted forefinger.

The door of the third room along was firmly closed.

Walker paused outside, holding the bunch of flowers before him like some aromatic, cellophaned cosh.

He swallowed hard, then – without knocking – walked in.

The man sitting up in the bed, propped there like a puppet with its strings cut, turned to look at him. But the eyes were blank, no recognition registered there.

The patient was in his early seventies, white hair combed back from a heavily lined forehead, wisps of hair also curling from each nostril and ear.

Closing the door behind him, Walker stood at the end of the bed.

'Hello, Dad,' he began flatly.

27

If there was any recognition in the eyes of Philip Walker it didn't show.

He watched silently as his son moved around to the side of the bed and brandished the flowers at him.

'I brought you these,' said Adam.

On the bedside table there was a vase filled with dead flowers, its water beginning to smell rancid.

Adam took out the dead blooms and dumped them in the waste-bin beneath the sink, then he swilled out the vase and set about replacing the old flowers with the new.

The room was about fifteen feet square: carpeted and tastefully decorated, but otherwise fairly spartan. There were a couple of pictures on the wall. Copies of El Greco's *The Agony in the Garden* and Antonio Allegri da Correggio's *The Mystic Marriage of St Catherine* hung on either side of a large crucifix.

Reminders?

Adam put down the replenished vase, aware that his father was peering up at him. He was frowning slightly, as if trying to remember who this newcomer was, and what he wanted here.

Adam sat down beside the bed and looked at him.

'How are you feeling?' he asked.

No answer. Only blank eyes staring back.

'When you weren't in the day-room, I thought there was something wrong.'

Philip Walker was plucking gently at the flesh on the back of one liverspot-dappled hand.

'Has the doctor been in today?' Adam asked.

'Doctor?'

His father spoke the word whilst looking directly at Adam.

'Doctor,' he repeated.

Adam shook his head.

'No,' he said softly, '*I'm* not a doctor. Do you know who I *am*?'

Silence again.

Still plucking at the flesh.

'Do you fancy going for a walk?' asked Adam. 'The fresh air might do you good. Better than being stuck in here all day.'

He looked again into those blank eyes, then across at the wheelchair in the corner.

His father turned to look at the flowers.

'"Man cometh up and is cut down like a flower",' he said slowly, as if considering each word before he spoke it.

It was Adam's turn to stare silently at the old man.

'At how many funerals did you say those words?' he said finally. 'How many did you see off? How many good men and women did you bury?'

The old man was plucking at the back of his hand again.

'How many children?' Adam persisted.

'"Suffer the children to come unto me",' his father intoned.

'So, is there still something in there?' Adam said, tapping his own temple. 'Still a light in the forest?'

'"I am the light",' said his father.

Outside, the wind seemed to be growing stronger. It swirled around the building angrily.

Inside Philip Walker's room there was only silence.

His son sat motionless for long moments, then leant forward and flipped open the bottom section of the bedside cabinet.

The smooth white band of stiff material was where it always lay.

The dog-collar.

He smiled ruefully to himself and held it up before him.

'It's like a badge, isn't it?' he said, without looking at his father. 'A badge for a club that you never leave.'

The old man continued pulling at his hand.

'You'll *never* leave it, will you?' said Adam. 'You'll *never* tear up your membership card.'

He continued to gently stroke the white dog-collar.

'Do you think He still cares?' Adam asked flatly, turning his eyes skyward briefly. 'Do you think He cares about *any* of the things you did?'

Fingers plucking at mottled flesh.

'He would have seen everything, wouldn't He – over the years?' Adam continued. 'All the good and the bad. I wonder what He thinks about you now.'

They sat in silence, only the ticking of the clock interrupting their solitude.

When Adam finally got up to leave, the hour hand of the clock had shifted more than once.

'I'll see you again soon,' he said, one hand on the door handle.

His father stared blankly at him.

'When those flowers are dead,' Adam murmured.

And he was gone.

28

Hailey heard the key in the front door and sat up.

The magazine she'd been reading slipped from her lap as she got to her feet. She padded across to the sitting-room door.

It opened a moment or two before she could reach it.

Rob stood and smiled at her.

She took a step towards him and they embraced.

'I thought you might have been here earlier,' she said, kissing him lightly on the lips.

'Traffic was bad on the M6,' he told her. 'I spoke to Frank on the way back and he said there'd been some problems at work, so I nipped in there before I came home. Otherwise I'd have been earlier.'

'Well, work has to come first, doesn't it?' she said, trying to control the irritation in her voice.

Rob exhaled but said nothing.

'Becky in bed?' he wanted to know.

'She's looking forward to seeing you in the morning. As I didn't know what time you were getting in, I didn't want her sitting up until all hours.'

'You've made your point, Hailey,' he said, slumping into an armchair.

'I'm just *telling* you, Rob. I'm not looking for a fight.'

He ran appraising eyes over her. Freshly washed hair, baggy sweater, tight black leggings tucked into a pair of floppy white socks. She looked great, but he noticed there were dark smudges beneath her eyes.

'You look tired,' he told her.

'I haven't been sleeping too well,' she confessed.

'Worried about me?' He smiled.

She nodded, and sat down beside him on the arm of the chair. He snaked an arm around her slender waist.

'So, how did the show go?' she asked.

'It went well. It was a worthwhile trip.'

And I got to fuck Sandy again.

'Did you see anyone you know there?'

'Like who?'

Take it easy. Don't be too defensive.

'Other reps. You've been to quite a few of these shows now, so I just wondered if you knew anybody else there.'

'You usually do see the same faces. I can't always remember their names, though. That's one good thing about everyone wearing a name badge. You just read their badge, call them by their name, and they all think you're a long-lost mate.'

'Just part of the bullshit, eh?'

'You know me, babe: king of the bullshit.'

'And everyone falls for it, don't they?'

'Everyone except you.'

'Did you fuck anyone while you were there?'

'Hailey, please . . .'

'Did you?' she insisted.

'I told you before I was going on my own, and I'm sure you checked up on me, didn't you?'

'I only asked you a simple question, Rob. You could have met someone in the hotel bar or something. I know what you're like.'

'I didn't fuck anyone,' he lied. 'Jesus, I've been back home for five minutes and you've started already.'

Take it easy.

'Listen, Rob. I've been thinking while you were away, and I've decided to go back to work for Jim Marsh.'

He opened his mouth to say something.

'Just part-time,' she assured him. 'I start tomorrow.'

'So that's it. You've decided. We don't discuss things any more?'

'I've been talking about doing it for ages now – you know that. It would only be for three or four hours a day, when he needs me.'

'And what about Becky – how does *she* fit into your plans?'

'Caroline said she'll pick her up and drop her off at school, if it comes to that.'

'I'm glad to hear you've got it all sorted out. It's a good job I *did* go away for a couple of days, isn't it? I mean, you might not have been able to arrange all this with me here in the way.'

'What *is* the big deal?'

'You could at least have had the decency to tell me before you made up your mind you were going back to work.'

'Sorry, Rob, did I betray your trust? Is that what this is? Because if it is, you're the last one to start handing out lectures about honesty, aren't you?'

'Fuck it. Go back to work, I don't care.'

'I'm trying to help,' she snarled. 'Why can't you see that? You never used to object to the money I brought in working for Jim before. I know you didn't like me being away from home, but you never complained about the money, did you?'

'I told you, if you want to do it, then do it.'

'I intend to, Rob. We'll all benefit: especially Becky. That's what *you* usually say, isn't it – if *you* have to work late or work seven days a week? It's for Becky's sake in the long run, isn't it?'

'I suppose Caroline thinks it's a great idea, doesn't she?' he rasped.

'What the hell's Caroline got to do with this?'

'She gets to look after Becky even more. I bet she was over the fucking moon.'

'I don't know what you're talking about.'

'She treats Becky as if she were *her* child.'

'At least she cares about her. I'd have thought you'd be pleased about that.'

'She *uses* her because she can't have kids of her own.'

'That's not *her* fault, Rob.'

'Three abortions before she was nineteen, *that's* why she can't have kids of her own. If she hadn't been such a fucking slag when she was younger, she wouldn't be paying for it now, would she?'

'You bastard,' said Hailey quietly, her eyes boring into Rob. He could see the anger there. 'Perhaps you should have stayed in Manchester. At least until you were back in a better frame of mind.'

He nodded. 'Perhaps you're right,' he snapped. 'I wish I had.'

Hailey was about to say something else when she heard the doorbell.

29

FOR INTERMINABLE SECONDS, neither of them moved, although both had heard the two-tone chime.

They continued to glare at one another until it sounded again.

'Who the hell is that?' said Rob wearily.

'I can't see through walls,' Hailey hissed. 'But I'll go and see before they wake Becky.'

She headed for the hall, running a hand through her hair.

Her mind was spinning. The argument with Rob. Wondering who was at the door. She looked at her watch and saw that it was 8.15 p.m. Who would be calling now?

She slipped the bolt at the top of the door, but left the security chain attached.

The hinges squealed as she opened it.

'Twice in one day,' said Adam Walker, smiling at her.

She smiled thinly, almost asked him sharply what he wanted.

'I was driving back this way,' he said, answering her unspoken question, 'and I saw your husband's car outside. You said that he might want to speak to me, so I thought I'd call in.'

Oh, not now. Please!

She hesitated for a second, her fingers on the chain.

'If it's not convenient . . .' he said quickly. 'I know it's a bit late. I nearly didn't call. I was worried about waking Becky. She *is* in bed, isn't she?'

Hailey nodded and slid the chain free, opening the front door to allow him access.

'Come in, please,' she said. 'I'm sorry. You took me by surprise, that's all.' She managed to smile again, ushering him towards the sitting-room door.

Rob was still slumped in the armchair when she walked in, urging Walker to join them.

He hesitated, but she put one hand tenderly on his shoulder: a gesture for him to follow.

'Rob, I'd like you to meet Adam Walker,' Hailey said.

She watched as her husband stared in bewilderment at the newcomer – then at her.

'He's the one who found Becky when she got lost in the shopping centre,' Hailey continued.

Rob stood up and extended his right hand, which Walker shook warmly.

'It's good to meet you,' Rob said.

'You, too,' Walker replied.

Rob felt the strength in his handshake.

He had always felt you could tell a lot about a man by his handshake. If he encountered a feeble grip, that usually tainted his opinion of the man. It was surely a sign of weakness. Not so with Walker: there was power in that grip.

'We've got a lot to thank you for, Mr Walker,' Rob said.

'Adam,' the other man insisted.

Rob nodded. 'It's a good job you were around that day,' he said. 'Christ knows what would have happened to Becky otherwise.' He shot an almost accusatory glance at Hailey, who was not slow to notice the underlying vehemence of it.

'Would you like a drink?' Hailey asked, smiling at Walker.

'No, I'm fine. I won't disturb you any longer,' he said. Then, looking at Rob: 'Hailey asked me to call in, so I did. But I'm sure you've got other things to do.'

'Hailey forgot to tell me you might call in,' Rob said, his eyes narrowing slightly. 'I much appreciate what you did for Becky. Thank you.'

'Anyone else would have done the same,' Walker insisted.

'Not everyone,' Rob interjected.

There was an awkward silence.

'Are you sure you won't have a drink?' Hailey said, becoming aware of the wordless interlude.

'No, honestly,' Walker said. 'I'll get off now.'

Walker, too, was anxious to get away from this oppressive atmosphere. He looked briefly at Hailey, who forced a smile.

'I'll see you out,' she said.

As Walker stepped out into the hall, Hailey glared over at Rob, then she followed the other man to the front door, opening it for him.

'I'm sorry if I caused any trouble,' Walker said quietly. 'I should have realized this was too late for social calls.'

'*You* didn't cause any trouble, Adam,' she answered softly. 'How was your father?

He shrugged.

'The same as ever,' he told her. 'Like I said, you get used to it after a while.'

She nodded.

'You get used to anything after long enough, Hailey,' he said cryptically. 'Don't you?'

He turned and headed down the path.

'I'll see you,' he added gently. 'Take care.'

'Adam?' she said, taking a step out into the porch.

He turned.

'Call me again,' she asked, touching his hand lightly before she backed away.

He nodded.

Hailey stepped back into the house.

30

By the time Hailey wandered into the living room again, Rob had changed into a pair of jeans and a denim shirt.

She carefully carried two mugs of tea, and set his down on the table beside him.

There was already a glass there, and she could smell the whiskey it contained.

'I needed it – before you ask,' he said.

She sat down at the opposite end of the sofa from him, legs tucked up beneath her.

Rob took a sip of the spirit, wincing slightly as it burned its way to his stomach.

'Adam,' he said, without inflection.

She looked at him.

'Adam Walker.' His eyes were still fixed on the TV screen.

'I said I wanted him to meet you,' Hailey told him. 'I *said* you'd like to thank him.'

'Oh, I *did* want to thank him. He seems like a nice enough bloke. Is he? You probably know more about him than I do.'

'He rang me later to see how Becky was.'

No need to mention their lunch.

Rob nodded. 'You invited a complete stranger to our house,' he muttered, still without looking at her.

'I invited the man who *saved* our daughter to meet you.' Her voice was heavy with scorn. 'After all, it was me who fucked up,

140

wasn't it? I let her get lost, didn't I, Rob? I mean, you're never going to let me forget *that*, are you?'

He sipped at his drink.

'He's a good-looking bloke, isn't he?'

'Are you asking me or telling me?' Hailey wanted to know.

'A nice bloke.'

'What are you going on about, Rob?'

'I'm just saying he's a nice bloke. What's so wrong with that?'

'Yes, he's a nice bloke. Yes, he's good-looking. What do you want to hear? How about, "Yes, I'd suck his cock if he asked me"?'

'There's no need to get stupid about it, Hailey.'

'Don't patronize me, you bastard. I *know* you.'

They locked stares.

'I'm going to bed,' said Rob. 'Perhaps *you* should, too. You'll need to feel fresh for the morning, won't you? I'm sure Jim Marsh wouldn't want you fucking up on your first day back.'

Rob got to his feet.

He drained what was left in his glass and left it empty on the coffee table.

'It's great to be home,' he said, with a humourless grin.

'You're pathetic at times, Rob.'

He closed the sitting-room door behind him. Hailey heard his footsteps on the stairs.

She felt the first tears welling up in her eyes.

Tears of anger? Of pain? Of loss?

It felt as if there was a huge empty hole inside her.

In her very soul.

She continued to stare blankly at the television.

*

When she first heard the phone, Hailey had no idea how long it had been ringing.

She forced open her eyes, emerging from a troubled sleep to register its electronic shrillness.

Rob flapped out a hand and grabbed the receiver, pulling it to his ear, his eyes still closed.

'Hello,' he croaked.

Hailey saw that the glowing red digits on the radio alarm showed 12.49 a.m.

'Hello?' Rob said again, clearing his throat.

She rolled over and looked at him – at the phone.

'Either say something, or get off the fucking line,' he snapped into the mouthpiece.

After a moment or two he slammed the receiver down.

'Who was it?' she wanted to know.

'Some dickhead with the wrong number,' he told her.

'Are you sure?'

He exhaled deeply. 'Go to sleep, Hailey,' Rob murmured.

'Didn't she speak? Perhaps she was frightened I'd overhear. Never mind, you'll see her again tomorrow, won't you?'

'There was no one there,' he said angrily. 'If it happens again, *you* pick it up. It might be your friend Adam.'

They lay with their backs to each other.

It was a long time before either slept.

OAK LANE, MANNINGHAM PARK, BRADFORD

She stood banging on the roof of the car and shouting.

He spotted her as he drove closer, and it took him a moment or two to realize that the car was empty.

What was the stupid bitch playing at?

She was screaming obscenities at the empty vehicle, reeling from it every now and then, and he could see that she was obviously drunk.

Probably done the rounds tonight. The Perseverance, the Carlisle, and now, he guessed, she was heading towards the International.

Drunk, pathetic, plying her filthy trade for anyone desperate enough to pay her.

He slowed down as he drew closer, and she noticed his car.

In fact she started to walk across towards it.

She was dressed in jeans, a short leather jacket and a blue shirt. Most of the buttons were undone.

He shook his head. They were all the same.

She bent down and smiled drunkenly at him through the passenger side-window, then reached for the door handle.

He made no attempt to stop her. In fact he smiled as she slipped into the seat beside him.

He looked at her for a moment, listening to her drunken babble. To the same sort of thing that they all said: to him and to every other man who paid them for the use of their bodies.

This one was different, somehow.

She was in her mid-twenties but the ravages of working the

streets didn't seem to have affected her the same way it did so many of the others.

This one was even quite pretty – in a cheap kind of way. Her skin was still fresh and taut, her long dark hair lustrous.

He could smell the booze on her breath as she directed him to her flat.

He parked the car and allowed her to climb out, watching as she headed towards the ground-floor bedsit.

As she pushed the key into the lock, still with her back to him, he slid his hand beneath the driver's seat and pulled out the clawhammer.

He hid it inside his coat, and then followed her inside the flat.

She was prattling on about a drink, but he paid little attention. He hung up his coat, ensuring that the hammer was still concealed inside. Within easy reach.

Arms folded before him, he looked around the tiny bedsit.

The walls were a little discoloured by cigarette smoke and by the central heating. The bedspread could have done with a good wash, but apart from that it was a passable dwelling.

For someone like *her*.

She sat on the edge of the bed with her back to him and began pulling off her shoes.

He pulled the hammer from his coat and struck.

The shuddering impact seemed to shock her into silence.

Sometimes they screamed, but not this one. She merely tried to rise – even when he struck her again.

The third blow sent her sprawling back across the bed.

The fourth caused her to roll off onto the floor.

He bent down and slid his hands beneath her armpits, lifting her back onto the bed.

Moving quickly, he pulled open her shirt, exposing her breasts. He tugged her jeans down past her hips too, and stood for precious seconds gazing at her.

He shook his head slightly, thinking how cheap she looked.

How many other men had seen her like this?

Blood was already pouring form her head wounds, soaking into the bedspread underneath.

He then hit her again. And again. Occasionally he would flip the hammer, using the claw to gouge into her flesh, watching the welts rise where he raked her body with its twin prongs.

He wasn't sure if she was dead when he finally stuck the knife into her stomach. He was more transfixed by the fact that her blood looked so red. So vivid. With the others, before her, it had appeared black in the darkness. But now he almost marvelled at its brightness.

He pulled the bedsheets over her, watching the blood soak through the cotton. He could hear gurgling sounds coming from underneath them as she gargled with her own blood.

She was obviously still alive but would be in no state to tell anyone what had happened.

Death would follow fairly quickly. It was what she deserved.

Filthy whore.

He walked out, closing the door carefully behind him.

He would throw the hammer from his car on the way home, having cleaned it carefully of fingerprints.

You could never be too careful.

23 April 1977

The women I killed were filth-bastard prostitutes who were littering the streets. I was just cleaning up the place a bit.
Peter Sutcliffe, 'The Yorkshire Ripper'

OK, now you're on your own.
Your self-righteousness has grown . . .
The Ruts

31

HAILEY COULDN'T DECIDE exactly how she felt as she parked the Astra.

Was the fluttering in her stomach caused by exhilaration or nerves?

She sat for long moments looking up at the main entrance of SuperSounds, wondering how much the place had changed since she had last entered those carefully polished doors. The two brass handles were each cast in the shape of a letter S. Beyond them she could see the reception area.

The factory itself wasn't that large, considering the amount of merchandise it produced, but its site still covered over half an acre.

The offices immediately before her were where the clerical work was done. Ordering, despatching, designing – that kind of thing. The manufacturing warehouses extended to her left. Large grey brick and glass edifices that housed over eighty workers.

She could see one of the delivery lorries pulling out onto the main road as she glanced in her rear-view mirror. It carried the same distinctive black livery and gold S's that appeared everywhere in and around the building itself. Or, in fact, on anything to do with James Marsh's business. Even the guitars made here at the factory bore that same symbol, etched in gold on each machine head.

It was a huge operation – worldwide – and it had all begun from this same site. Once only a warehouse, and with three other men apart from Marsh himself. He would design the guitars, even help in their manufacture. But, as time went on, the business expanded, growing larger and more successful until it became the global concern it was now.

As she stepped out of the Astra, Hailey could see Marsh's black Jag parked in its usual spot.

She headed for the main doors, the wind ruffling her hair.

As she passed through into the reception area, her heels rattled noisily on the marbled floor.

The young receptionist looked up and smiled welcomingly.

'My name's Hailey Gibson,' she said. 'I'm here to see James Marsh.'

As the receptionist checked her appointment book, Hailey ran a hand through her hair again, glancing around.

Behind the reception desk there were a number of gold and platinum discs. All were dedicated to James Marsh, from a list of bands that read like a *Who's Who* of the rock-and-pop world.

AC/DC.

Ozzy Osbourne.

Eric Clapton.

Iron Maiden.

Queensrÿche.

The Rolling Stones.

U2.

And many more.

There were more discs on the left-hand wall. Above them were a number of guitars: from the earliest designs produced here by the Marsh factory, right up to the most advanced and up-to-date models.

To her right were two lifts.

She heard a whirring noise, and a bell sounded as the lift descended to a halt.

'Mr Marsh said you could go straight up,' the receptionist said. 'You'll find him on the fifth floor.'

'She knows where I am.'

The voice had come from out of the lift, and Hailey recognized it immediately.

James Marsh stepped from the lift and strode across the reception area to embrace Hailey. The receptionist looked on in silent bemusement.

'I saw you pull up,' Marsh told Hailey.

'Checking to see that I wasn't late?' She smiled.

'As if,' he said, holding up his hands. 'Come on, I'll show you your office.' He beckoned her towards the lift.

The receptionist still looked on, smiling.

'It's OK, Julie,' Marsh said. 'She'll be safe with me.'

All three of them laughed.

32

'THEY'RE BEAUTIFUL, JIM. Thank you.'

Hailey gestured towards the huge bouquet of red carnations that lay on her desk. She smiled broadly.

'Just a little welcome-back present,' Marsh told her.

He was in his fiftieth year but looked much younger, the only clue to his advancing years being the profusion of crow's feet at his eye corners. His hair was flecked with grey but still lustrous, swept back from his forehead.

The office they now stood in was huge. It contained an enormous desk, a leather sofa, a glass coffee table, and two other high-backed leather chairs. There were even more flowers in vases set on either side of the large picture window that overlooked the car park fronting the building.

Hailey walked back and forth, gazing out of the window, while Marsh took a seat behind her desk.

'It's good to have you back, Hailey,' he said finally. 'I know it won't be *just* like it used to be, with you being part-time now, but I hope it'll do for you.'

'It's good to *be* back, Jim. Thanks for keeping my old office for me.'

'I knew you'd be back eventually. You were made for this job.'

She smiled and leant on the window sill, pulling down her skirt slightly.

'Things haven't changed much around here,' he told her. 'A lick of paint, a few new faces. That's about it.'

'You never did like change, did you, Jim?'

'Mr Predictable, that's me. Anyway, I'm not the one who's changed – it's you. What's it like being a mum?'

'Tiring.' She smiled.

'How are your family?'

'Fine.' She kept the fixed smile in place.

'Rob didn't mind you coming back to work for me?'

'Not at all,' she lied.

Very convincing.

'I'm delighted you agreed to come back,' he told her. 'I've tried other girls here, but they just haven't got it.'

'Got what?'

'What you've got?'

'And what's that?'

'It's indefinable,' he chuckled, getting to his feet. 'I had one girl here a while ago. Lovely girl, long blonde hair, good-looking, legs up to her armpits. You get the picture?'

'Decorative.' Hailey smiled.

'I even paid for a boob job for her. Five bloody grand.'

'Jim, for God's sake,' she laughed.

'She *looked* great, but she didn't have it up here.' He tapped his temple.

'You sexist pig,' chuckled Hailey.

'No, don't get me wrong. I don't mean she was thick. Like I say, she *looked* great. Wherever we went together, she turned heads. I took her to Rome, New York, you name it. But she couldn't do the job. Not like you used to do it.'

'Did she become another notch on the Marsh bedpost?'

'What's that got to do with it?' he wanted to know.

'Oh, come on, Jim. You don't usually employ your PAs for their typing skills.'

'You're still the only one who's had it all, Hailey. Looks, brains, and the same sort of work ethic as me. You get the job done.'

'Jim, you can stop the bullshit now. I'm back, OK?' She sat down behind her desk after he stood up and moved to the other side of the room. 'Just don't forget: it's only part-time. No more trips away. No more working until midnight.'

He held up his hands. 'I hear you.'

'So, what's first on the agenda?'

'Well, I thought I'd give you a few hours to settle in, get the feel of the place again. You might have become a bit rusty.'

She raised an eyebrow.

Marsh smiled. 'All right,' he said, 'here's the deal. Have you heard of a band called Waterhole? They've just released an album called *Playing with Andy Warhol*, whatever the hell that means. Advance sales are huge.'

'I'd have to have been living in a cave on the moon *not* to have heard of them.'

'Right. Well, as you know, in less than a month it's the twenty-fifth anniversary of the founding of SuperSounds, and I've managed to negotiate a deal with Waterhole to play a gig locally in celebration. They use only our gear.' He sat down in one of the high-backed chairs, after pulling it closer to her desk. 'That's high-profile. The advance ticket sales are over ten thousand already, and they'll be double that by the time the gig takes place. All the proceeds go to charity.'

'So where do *I* come into all this?' Hailey wanted to know.

'They're a big band, Hailey. About the biggest there is at the moment. The only problem is they're arseholes. I know they haven't exactly got the monopoly on that in the music business, but these guys have raised being pricks into an art form.'

'Yes, I've read all about them. Didn't one of them get arrested last week?'

'For decking a journalist at some showbiz party. The guy was just taking pictures and the guitarist got the hump and broke his nose.' Marsh shrugged. 'I think that dozy slag he's going out with objected to the intrusion.' He shook his head.

'They're in Canada at the moment, aren't they?'

'They fly back tomorrow. They've been in trouble out there, too: mouthing off about the Royals and shit like that. Very original.

They want to be the new wild men of rock, but they're only *playing* at it. Sticking two fingers up at cameramen and spitting at your own fans doesn't make you the new Sex Pistols. Try biting the heads off a few bats, driving cars into swimming pools, or lobbing TVs out of hotel windows – that's more like it.' He grinned.

'So what do *I* do with them?' she wanted to know.

'You liaise with their press office and their record company, make sure this gig goes off without any hitches. With all the proceeds going to charity, I've managed to get some local big nobs involved too. The local MP is going to attend. And we've got a big party lined up too, after the gig. Yours truly gets to present the cheque to the heads of the chosen charities. I need you to work closely with *them*, too.'

She nodded.

'So, let me get started,' she said. 'By the way, Jim, what about getting one of the guitarists from Waterhole to donate a signed guitar after the gig, for auction? You could raffle it at this party you're having. I'm sure those local dignitaries would be only too happy to fork out for it. Especially as the money *is* going to charity. It'll make whoever buys it look good too, won't it?'

'And you wonder why I wanted you back?' Marsh grinned.

He turned and headed towards the door.

'All the info you need is on the computer,' he added. 'Any problems, give me a shout.' He paused at the entrance. 'Thanks again, Hailey.'

'Thank me when it's all over,' she said, smiling.

He closed the door, leaving her alone in the office.

33

THE PUBLIC BAR of the Tawny Owl was relatively empty for a
lunchtime. The smell of liquor mingled with the odours of food;
the sound of a dozen conversations competed with music from the
jukebox.

Rob Gibson sat back in his seat, glancing around, tapping one
finger on the table as he listened to the music.

'. . . I'm all out of faith, this is how I feel . . .'

He saw Frank Burnside paying for the drinks, then make his
way carefully back through the light crowd of customers towards
their table.

'. . . I'm cold and I am shamed, lying naked on the floor . . .'

Burnside set down the two glasses of Jameson's, and seated
himself opposite his partner.

'. . . Illusion never changed, into something real . . .'

'Maggie would go mad if she could see me drinking.' Burnside
smiled.

'Oh, come on, Frank,' Rob protested. 'If you can't have a drink
to celebrate becoming a father, when can you?'

'I suppose you're right.'

'Of course I'm right. Get it down you. And congratulations.
When's it due again?'

'November. I didn't want to say anything until we were sure
this time – after Maggie lost the last one. And neither of us is
getting any younger.'

'Cheers, Dad,' chuckled Rob, raising his glass in salute.

The two men drank.

'I remember when Hailey got pregnant,' Rob mused. 'I felt like a kid with a new toy. I don't think I've ever been so happy. She moaned because I wouldn't touch her, but I was scared of hurting the baby. And when Becky was born . . .' He allowed the sentence to trail off. 'She was born by Caesarean. I was the first one to hold her. I couldn't believe it. Hailey and I just looked at each other and burst into tears. When I was ringing people afterwards, I kept crying too. I think it's relief as much as anything. You know that they're all right, they're healthy. It's like the wait's been worth it.'

'How *are* things between the two of you now?' Burnside wanted to know. 'If you don't mind me asking?'

'It's still difficult,' said Rob. 'It's been worse since I got back from Manchester. She started work again today, too.'

'Well, that's good, isn't it?'

The look on Rob's face told Burnside that it wasn't.

'She claims it's only part-time, but I know what she's like. She loved that job. If Marsh asks her to put in a few extra hours, she'll do it.'

'What's the problem?'

'I don't want her working too many hours. I don't want her with *him* any more than she needs to be.' He sipped his Jameson's.

'Why?'

'He fancies her – I'm not stupid. When they used to go away together on business, I reckon he had a crack at her. He might even have fucked her.'

'Come on, Rob, don't you trust her? Hailey wouldn't do anything like that.'

'How do *you* know, Frank?'

Burnside looked at him evenly, then took a sip of his own drink.

'She might feel that she wants to get back at me now, especially after what happened with Sandy. If Marsh comes on to her again, she might just go for it. Just to get back at me.'

'How old's the guy? I thought he was in his fifties.'

'So what?'

'Give Hailey a bit of credit, Rob. If she really wanted to get back at you, I'm sure she could find some other way.'

'Yeah, maybe. But then she doesn't know what happened while I was in Manchester, does she?'

'Meaning?'

'Sandy came up.'

'For Christ's sake, Rob. I thought that was over.'

'It *is*. I didn't fucking plan it. She turned up at the hotel. She spent the night.'

'You fucked her?'

'She put it on a plate, Frank.'

'I don't understand you . . .'

'Don't come over all sanctimonious on me. It doesn't suit you,' Rob snarled.

'As long as she's around, it'll never be over, will it?'

Rob drained what was left in his glass.

'Are you in love with her?' Burnside continued.

'How many times do I have to tell you? *No!* I told you before, this *never* had anything to do with love.'

Burnside, too, finished his drink. 'I'm going back to work,' he said.

'What's wrong, Frank? Are you disgusted? Do I offend your sensibilities? Your morals?'

'I told you, I just don't know what's going on inside your head.'

'Well, that makes two of us.'

Rob got to his feet and headed for the bar.

'I'll see you in a while,' he said. 'I need another drink.'

Burnside opened his mouth to say something, then realized it would be pointless.

When Rob turned around again he saw his partner disappearing out of the door.

He held the Jameson's in his hand for long moments, then downed it in two huge swallows.

34

HAILEY WAS BEGINNING to wonder if she'd lost her touch.

Either that or it was going to take her longer to ease back into this job than she'd originally thought.

Or maybe it was just the people she was dealing with.

Yes, that was it. It was the people she was dealing with.

She looked at the computer screen before her, then at the phone. Only seconds before she had been speaking to one of the girls

(*well, be fair, she didn't sound much older than about twenty*)

in Waterhole's press office. *Her* name had been Catrina

(*with a 'C', she'd stressed, not a 'K'*)

and she'd informed Hailey that she really needed to speak to someone called Trudi

(*without the 'e'*)

who was out of the office for the time being. So, Hailey thanked Catrina with a 'C', and asked her to get Trudi, *without* an 'e', to call her as soon as she came back into the office.

The screen showed the names, addresses and phone numbers of everyone relevant, ranging from Waterhole and their record company, press office and management office, to the local MP and *his* offices, both at Westminster and locally. There were also the names of numerous other local dignitaries that Marsh wanted present at the after-gig party.

Also listed were the promoters, limo firms for transporting VIPs, hotels, helicopter transport firms . . .

It was never-ending.

Hailey smiled. She had missed this job more than she realized.

The organization involved, the hectically ringing phone – it was like a circus where all the acts were insane and the trainers were on drugs. You never knew what was going to happen, from one minute to the next. And she loved it. She felt energized. For the first time in months, she felt as if she was in control. Despite the organized chaos before her, she revelled in the situation.

She decided to call the local office of Nicholas Barber, the MP Marsh had persuaded to attend. She wanted to know what time he would be arriving, and there had also been a fax from his secretary requesting further details of the gig itself – more particularly, how many backstage passes Barber was entitled to. His twin daughters, the fax informed her, were huge fans of Waterhole, so Mr Barber would appreciate it if his daughters could meet the band.

'You and twenty thousand others,' murmured Hailey.

She was about to pick up the phone, when it rang.

At last: Trudi without the 'e'?

'Hello,' she began. 'SuperSounds. Hailey Gibson speaking.'

'How's it going?'

She recognized the voice instantly.

'Adam?'

'Sorry to disturb you,' said Walker.

She sat back in her chair.

'I know you must be busy,' he said. 'I just wanted to know how your first day back at work was going.'

Why couldn't Rob have done that?

'It's great,' she told him. 'As if I've never been away. The music business is still as crazy as always.'

'The whole world's crazy, isn't it?' Walker chuckled.

'Are *you* working today?' she asked him.

'Always working, Hailey. If I don't work, I don't eat. It's a great motivator.'

'How did you get my number?'

'I looked up the number for SuperSounds, then just called their switchboard. The receptionist put me through straight away.'

'Listen, Adam, I'm glad you rang. I wanted to say sorry for last night – when you called round.'

'Sorry for what?'

'Oh, come on, you don't have to be so tactful. You must have noticed the atmosphere.'

'Just a bit.' He laughed.

'Rob can be so bloody rude sometimes. I do apologize for his attitude. And he and I'd just had a few cross words. So you sort of walked into the middle of it.'

Why tell him about their argument? Looking for his sympathy?

'Forget it,' he said. 'No harm done.'

'Well, I'm sorry anyway.'

'Prove it,' he said flatly.

'How?'

'Have lunch with me tomorrow. And this time *I'm* paying. What do you say?'

She smiled.

'I'd love to. Thank you.'

Ask him about that phone call late last night. Ask him if it was him who phoned.

'What time, and where?' she wanted to know.

Surely it wasn't him who called? Why should he?

He gave her the name of a pub about five miles out from the city centre. She wrote it down on a piece of paper.

She knew it: the Happy Brig.

'How does one o'clock suit you?' he asked.

'It suits me fine. See you there tomorrow.'

'I hope the rest of your day goes well,' he said. 'Take care.'

Such a nice thought.

She put down the receiver.

One o'clock tomorrow.

Hailey folded the piece of paper and slid it into her purse.

35

THE AFTERNOON HAD dragged interminably, thought Rob. It seemed as if each minute had become stretched and elongated – to ensure that time moved excruciatingly slowly.

He had glanced at his watch and up at his wall clock more times than he could ever remember doing before.

He'd walked back to work after Burnside had left him in the pub, ostensibly to clear his head, but also to avoid reaching the office too quickly.

When he entered, Burnside had glanced at him from behind his desk but merely shook his head before turning back to his work.

For the rest of the afternoon the two men hadn't spoken.

Rob looked at his watch yet again, and saw that it was almost five o'clock. He was going to leave early: get out of this place, get home.

He'd seen Sandy only twice that day. When she first came in, and when he left for lunch with Burnside.

Both times she'd smiled at him.

There had been something behind that smile that he hadn't liked: a kind of smugness that irritated him. He had tried not to look at her too closely.

Why not? Like what you see a little too much?

Once or twice he'd heard her voice outside his office, but otherwise, he'd managed to avoid her.

This couldn't go on, he tried to persuade himself more forcefully.

What couldn't go on? These feelings you have for her?

And yet he had managed to convince himself he *had* no feelings for the woman. Never had. Never would.

His musings were interrupted by a knock on his office door.

Sandy Bennett walked in before he had time to call out.

'This fax just came through,' she told him. 'I thought you might like to see it.'

'Show it to Frank, I'm getting ready to go home,' he told her.

She was wearing a dark brown jacket and trousers, and Rob couldn't help but notice how tightly the trousers clung to her legs and buttocks.

Sandy laid the fax on his desk.

'It's about those vans you were going to buy,' she continued. 'They've agreed to meet your price.'

'I can read it myself,' he muttered.

'What's wrong, Rob? Are you in *that* much of a hurry to get home? Worried that Hailey might check up on you?'

He didn't like the disdain in her voice.

'Leave the fax,' he said flatly.

'Do you want me to send a reply?' she asked.

'No. I want you to get out of my fucking office.'

'Charming. You didn't throw me out of your hotel room so quickly, did you?'

'Get out,' he snapped, reaching for his jacket.

'You were pleased to see me – don't deny it. Don't tell me you didn't have a good time. I know *I* did.'

'Is that why you sneaked out in the morning before I woke up?'

'Perhaps you should be grateful I did.'

'What the fuck is *that* supposed to mean?'

'Well, if I'd still been there the next morning, you might never have got out of the room at all.' She smiled. 'We'd probably still be there now.'

'I doubt it.'

He pulled on his jacket and pushed past her to the door.

'See you tomorrow, Rob.' She smiled. 'Is there anything in

particular you'd like me to wear? I know you like that skirt with the split.'

He took a step towards her, his face dark.

'Don't push it, Sandy,' he rasped angrily.

He turned and walked out, slamming the door behind him. Leaving her inside.

'See you tomorrow,' she murmured, her smile narrow.

36

So many books. So many titles. So many authors.

But not the one he sought.

Adam Walker wandered slowly up and down the racks of shelves in the library, eyes flicking over each of the titles.

He had already looked for an alphabetical listing, but found nothing.

He had the right name: Caroline Hacket. But there was no sign of anything written under that name.

Perhaps she'd used a pseudonym, he wondered.

No, surely Hailey would have mentioned that.

Besides, why would Caroline Hacket want to hide her identity behind a fake name? Why would *anyone* seek anonymity when they could have notoriety instead?

Hailey had mentioned that neither of Caroline's books had been big sellers, Walker remembered. That probably explained why he'd been unable to find either in any of the city's bookshops.

Hence this trip to the library.

He continued to walk slowly between the high shelves, occasionally passing other borrowers as he moved.

The library was fairly deserted, apart from two pensioners sitting reading newspapers, and a woman returning books at the counter.

Walker tried the Thriller section. Nothing.

He looked under True Crime. Nothing.

It made no sense. Her books *should* be here.

He glanced again at titles in the True Crime section.

Beyond Belief

The Shrine of Jeffrey Dahmer

10 Rillington Place

Helter Skelter

He pulled the last volume down and flipped it open.

Photos of Charles Manson.

Of Sharon Tate.

One famous for being an actress, the other famous for ordering her death.

Perhaps *more* famous, for that reason.

He looked at another of the books.

At the photos of Myra Hindley and Ian Brady.

Famous.

More people knew *their* names than knew the names of their young victims.

The book itself smelled old, as did the next one he took down and flipped through.

There was a picture of John Reginald Halliday Christie.

He had murdered nine women.

Gassed them. Raped them. Strangled them. Then hidden their bodies in the walls and garden of his house.

Famous.

Walker shook his head.

More titles.

Serial Killers

Hunting Humans

Deviant

Who Killed Hanratty?

A woman in her sixties ambled past him, glancing first at him, then at the books he was perusing.

She gave him a brief, distasteful look and hurried on towards the Romance section.

Walker smiled to himself, then headed for the information desk.

The young woman who sat behind it was sipping tea from a mug that bore the legend: I'M IN TOUCH WITH MY INNER BITCH.

She looked up and smiled as Walker approached.

'I need some help,' he said, grinning.

She nodded inquiringly.

'I'm looking for some books,' he told her.

'You're probably in the right place then.' She ran appraising eyes over him, and smiled.

He smiled again, that infectious smile.

'I suppose I asked for that,' he said.

'Which books?' she prompted.

'Well, I don't actually know their titles,' he said, almost apologetically. 'Just the author. Her name is Caroline Hacket. Someone told me they're crime non-fiction.'

'Hacket,' the young woman murmured as she punched in the surname, looking at her computer.

Walker stood studying her as she watched the screen. She was aware of his gaze.

'This will only take a minute,' she said. 'It's very thorough. It gives you date of publication, ISBN, publisher – everything really.'

'Don't worry too much about it.'

Her cheeks flushed slightly as she looked up at him, then back at the screen.

'Hacket, Caroline,' she said triumphantly. 'Two titles. Do you want me to order them for you?'

'Yes, please. What are they called?'

'Well, you were right, they *are* crime books. One's called *Murderous Minds* and the other is *Fame and Foul Play*.'

Walker smiled.

37

Hailey sipped at her mineral water as she glanced around the dining room of the Happy Brig.

It was what purists scathingly called a plastic pub, complete with reproduction horse-brasses on the artificially aged walls, and a huge fireplace stacked high with logs that would never feel flame.

She and Rob had visited the place two or three times, and always enjoyed the food here.

Today was no different. All that had changed was her companion.

She looked across the table at Adam Walker, who was finishing his steak, pushing the final piece into his mouth.

Hailey had been a little late arriving. Trudi from Waterhole's press office had finally called her back, and their conversation had taken longer than expected.

She'd managed to persuade Trudi to set up a meeting between her and the band in a few days' time, so that Hailey could speak to them in person about the forthcoming gig.

Trudi had seemed almost reluctant: fiercely protective of the band, adamant that only the lead singer and the drummer were available on the day Hailey requested.

Hailey had finally relented, weary of Trudi's hip ravings and Americanisms. If she'd used the word 'cool' once, she'd used it a dozen times.

'You must be excited at the thought of meeting them,' Walker said.

'I don't know if "excited" is the word,' Hailey told him.

'They're famous – big stars.'

'Jim says they're arseholes. And, from what I've seen of them on TV, I think he might be right.'

'You shouldn't say that about them, Hailey. No matter what they're like, they've made it, haven't they? People *know* them, look up to them.'

'I suppose you're right.'

'I'd love to meet them, just to shake their hands. To tell them I admire what they've done.' He smiled. 'You never know, if they saw some of my artwork, they might like it enough to use it on an album cover.'

'I could show something to them, if you like. See what they think.'

'I couldn't ask you to do that.'

'You're not asking. I'm offering.'

'I wouldn't take advantage of you like that, Hailey.'

'I wouldn't have suggested it if I thought you were. Please, Adam, let me take some of your work along to them. You don't know *what* might happen then.'

'They'd probably just laugh at it.'

'Well, you won't know until you let me show it to them, will you? Please. I'd *like* to do that for you.'

'Don't do anything out of pity, Hailey.'

She glared at him, irritation in her eyes.

'Do you actually like their music?'

'Not really, but I still respect what they've achieved. I admire anyone who succeeds, anyone who makes a mark. It doesn't matter *how* they make that mark.'

'Is fame that important to you, Adam? I mean, would you want it at any cost?'

'What do you mean?'

'Well, these pop stars, film stars and people like that, they don't have any privacy. Everything they do is put in the papers. They can't even walk down the street without someone sticking a camera in their faces. Would you want *that*?'

'It goes with the territory, doesn't it? That's exactly what annoys me with some of these stars. They want the money and the fame, but they aren't prepared to put up with what goes with it. *I* would be, in their position.'

'Perhaps you chose the wrong profession to become famous,' she mused. 'I mean, artists aren't exactly up there with actors and musicians, are they?'

'Picasso? Dali? What are they?' he wanted to know. '*They* were famous, weren't they?'

'You know what I mean.'

'David Bailey? Herb Ritts? Photography's a visual art, but they're famous too, aren't they? Christ, even dress designers are famous these days. Calvin Klein. Armani. Versace.'

'And look what happened to *him*.'

'It's a risk you take when you become famous, Hailey. And I'*d* be prepared to take it.'

'You'd risk your life for fame?'

He nodded slowly, sipping at his drink.

'Even murderers are famous,' he said slowly.

She looked at him and shook her head gently.

Walker smiled. 'It's true,' he said. 'I bet your friend Caroline knows all about it.'

Hailey laughed.

'I went to the library today and tried to find her books.'

'I'm sure she'd be flattered if she knew,' Hailey chuckled.

'You shouldn't take the piss. She's made her mark too, hasn't she? Those books she wrote mean that her name will live for ever. People will know she was here long after she's dead. And that's what it's all about. What's that saying, "Life's a bitch and then you die"? It's true.'

Hailey regarded him over the rim of her glass.

Walker held up his hands. 'All right, I'll shut up. I'm starting to sound like a nutter, aren't I?' he said.

She shook her head. 'You sound passionate, Adam,' she told him. 'There's nothing wrong with that.'

'You know about passion, don't you? You're passionate about your job. You must be or you wouldn't have gone back to it.'

She nodded.

'Are you still enjoying it?' he enquired.

'It's good to be back.'

'Is Rob pleased you're back?'

'Not really. I told you before, he was never too keen. But, then again, I didn't exactly expect him to throw a party when I went back to work.'

She sipped at her drink again, finally putting the glass down and running the tip of one index finger around the rim.

'What's wrong, Hailey?' Walker wanted to know.

'How long have you got?' she said bitterly.

'If you want to talk about it . . .' He allowed the sentence to trail off.

'OK,' she said quietly.

When he looked into her eyes, he saw they were glazed with tears.

Walker leant forward and touched her hand softly.

'Shall I start with Rob's affair?' she murmured.

38

She had no idea how long she'd been talking. It felt like hours.

Every now and then Hailey would stop and take a sip of her drink but, other than that, she felt as if she'd been spewing out words for ever.

Walker merely sat gazing at her, nodding occasionally, sometimes shaking his head.

But always listening intently. Sometimes touching her hand as it rested on the table.

The only thing that seemed to be missing was 'Bless Me, Father, for I have sinned'.

It felt like a confession.

'And that's it,' she said finally. 'Now you know.'

Walker didn't speak.

'Are you going to tell me I should have left him?' Hailey wanted to know. 'Caroline thinks I should.'

'Who else knows about it?'

'Just you. It's not the sort of thing you shout from the rooftops, is it? I don't know who *Rob's* told.'

He shook his head almost imperceptibly.

Happy now? You've told a complete stranger one of your most intimate secrets.

Hailey reached for her glass and realized it was empty. She sipped at the melted ice in the bottom.

'And he still works with the girl he had this affair with?' Walker said finally.

'Yes, he sees her every day.'

'Why didn't he sack her?'

'He claims it isn't as easy as that.'

'I'm sorry, Hailey,' Walker said quietly.

'So am I, Adam.'

'Do you still love him?'

'Of course I do. When it first happened, I hated him for what he'd done. Not *him* – but what he'd *done*.'

'Has it affected Becky?'

'It's difficult to say. We've kept it from her. At least we think we have. No real slanging matches in front of her – that kind of thing. But she's not stupid. She doesn't know *exactly* what's going on, but she knows everything's not like it used to be between me and Rob.'

'I wish I could say something that would help.'

She reached across and touched his hand.

'You *have* been a help,' she told him, tracing a pattern on the back of his hand with her index finger.

You want him, don't you? And you want him to know it.

'I only met you a few days ago and I feel like I've known you all my life, if you'll excuse the cliché.' She forced a smile.

Beneath the table her foot brushed against his calf, but she didn't move it away.

'Those paintings you mentioned: the ones you want me to show to Waterhole. When can I see them?'

'Whenever you like. They're in my studio at home.'

She squeezed his hand.

'Take me there now,' she said flatly.

Confrontation

DAVID LAYTON FELT the sweat running down the side of his face. A combination of the heat inside the large kitchen and also of his current exertions.

The boxes each held twenty-four tins of baked beans, and by anybody's reckoning that was fucking heavy. He'd been humping them for most of the morning, from the back of the lorry in the prison yard into the kitchen, then beyond to the storeroom.

Beans, tinned spaghetti, Smash, tinned fruit . . .

Boxes and boxes of tins, all of them heavy.

He'd been allowed a fag break only once since he had started, and that felt like hours ago.

The man helping him, a small thin-faced individual whose name he didn't know, seemed to be having even more trouble than Layton. He was pale and looked undernourished, and hadn't said much during the time they'd been working together. Hadn't said much during the entire time he'd been working in the kitchen. He looked frightened, nervous.

Layton had come to the conclusion this must be his first time inside.

Shit-scared, forever looking over his shoulder. Silent. Whatever he'd been dubbed up for couldn't have amounted to much, or he wouldn't have got kitchen detail. Layton thought maybe burglary, or receiving — some bullshit charge that had got him probably six months. He looked the sort who cried himself to sleep every night.

But what did he care. He was out in a couple of days. This pasty-faced little cunt could rot as far as he was concerned.

171

He set down the latest box of beans and headed back to the lorry outside.

The driver was sitting in his cab, talking with a warder. Another uniformed man stood at the rear of the lorry, watching the two prisoners as they unloaded the goods.

Layton recognized him: a screw called Collinwood.

Big-built, scrub-headed cunt who used to be a security guard for a firm of stockbrokers in the City, before he started locking other men up for a living.

He snapped orders at them, telling them to move quicker.

Layton cursed under his breath as he lifted another box and headed back inside with it.

He felt the bottom of the box beginning to give. Realized he was going to drop it.

'Shit,' he snarled, trying to slide his hands beneath the torn cardboard.

It was no use.

The tins burst through the bottom of the box and landed with a loud clang on the kitchen floor.

'What the fuck are you doing?'

The voice that boomed through the kitchen was Scots: a Glaswegian bellow that caused the other men working in the room to look round.

'Pick them up, you dozy cunt,' roared the voice.

Layton looked up to see James Gorton advancing towards him.

'Get them picked up, you fucking prick,' Gorton snarled, standing over Layton as he struggled to gather up the scattered tins.

The uniformed officer in the kitchen stood back, allowing Gorton to handle this situation. The Scot had been in charge of the kitchen for the past seven months. His temper was legendary amongst the other inmates. He was doing a nine stretch for assault, Layton had heard. He'd blinded some bloke with a piece of broken glass, during an argument about money. But he knew the system inside out and he'd conned his way into the kitchen job by convincing the Governor he'd once worked in a restaurant.

That much was almost true. He'd worked the door at a club in

Birmingham and, according to the prison grapevine, smashed a man's hand to pulp with a meat-tenderizing hammer. So he knew how to handle at least one kitchen utensil. It was one more than most of the other men who worked in there.

Layton continued to gather up the fallen tins, carrying them through to the stockroom as best he could.

Gorton followed him through, slamming the door behind him.

'You get out of here soon, don't you, son?' the Scot growled menacingly.

Layton nodded.

'Good,' Gorton said. 'Because I don't want you fucking up my kitchen again, you understand?'

'I understand,' Layton told him.

'I think you should say sorry.'

Gorton took a step towards him.

Layton didn't speak.

'I didn't hear you,' Gorton persisted.

Silence.

'I said, you should say sorry. So, say it, you little cunt.'

Gorton was standing so close now he was breathing his rancid breath into Layton's face.

'Sorry,' Layton said flatly.

'That's better,' Gorton told him.

'Sorry, you sheep-shagging Scotch cunt.'

Gorton's face darkened. He brought his knee up into Layton's groin so hard, he felt it connect with the pelvic bone.

Layton dropped to his knees, or at least he would have done had Gorton not grabbed him by the lapels, lifted him up and held him like a rag doll.

He stared into Layton's watering eyes for a second, then drove his head forward, slamming his forehead into Layton's face.

The headbutt caught him on the left eyebrow.

'Pick those fucking tins up.' Gorton released his grip, allowing Layton to fall to the floor, opened the stockroom door and walked away.

Layton slumped against some large bags of salt, unsure which pain was worse, the one in his groin or the one in his head.

He sucked in a couple of deep breaths and pulled himself upright.

'Fucking bastard,' he groaned under his breath.

He steadied himself for a second, then limped slowly back out into the kitchen.

Gorton smiled as he saw him, then turned his attention back to the large pots of soup that were bubbling on the range nearest to him.

As he drew nearer, Layton noticed that the handle of one was sticking outwards.

Gorton was no more than a foot away.

The movement was so fast no one, including Gorton, saw it.

Layton brought his hand down with great force onto the outstretched saucepan handle, causing the entire thing to flip up.

He couldn't have planned the trajectory better if he'd worked it out with a slide-rule and protractor.

An immense geyser of boiling soup shot into the air, most of it hitting Gorton straight in the chest and face.

As Layton went down, pretending he'd slipped, he heard the Scot scream in agony as the searing fluid struck him.

Where it touched his skin, the flesh immediately turned red.

Layton was aware of footsteps rushing towards them. Collinwood was there.

Other hands were hauling him to his feet.

Figures were gathered around Gorton, who was now rolling about on the kitchen floor shrieking, his suffering intolerable.

'I slipped,' Layton said. Then those same hands that had picked him up pushed him aside.

He heard one of the screws shout for a doctor.

Layton backed away, looking down at Gorton, who was still screaming. Blisters were already forming on his seared flesh. Layton thought how excruciating the pain must be.

He smiled faintly.

39

HAILEY ADJUSTED THE heating control inside the Astra for the second time, seeking cooler air.

She felt warm. Uncomfortably warm.

The weather was mild but no more. No extremes of temperature to cause this occasionally unpleasant feeling.

She kept her eyes on the Scorpio ahead, aware that Walker was glancing over his shoulder at her every now and then. Ensuring that she didn't lose him on the narrow, winding roads, that led from the Happy Brig.

More than once, when they stopped at traffic lights, she found herself, almost unconsciously, checking her appearance in her rear-view mirror.

Want to look your best for him?

Her hands felt sweaty on the wheel.

Like first-date nerves?

She glanced at the dashboard clock: 2.32 p.m.

Plenty of time.

She didn't have to collect Becky from Caroline Hacket's house until five if necessary.

Plenty of time.

For what?

She switched on the cassette, wondering how much longer the journey to Walker's house would take. The music filled the car, but she hardly seemed to hear it. Her mind was elsewhere, her gaze firmly fixed on the Scorpio as it moved along.

Hailey began to see more houses appearing now and she realized they were drawing closer to the outskirts of the city.

Closer to his house.

The house where you want to go.

A part of her said that this was insane. The sensible, married mother, with a husband and a career, told her it was insane.

But the woman who had been cheated on – who felt attracted to this good-looking, kind and considerate man – told her otherwise.

Two voices. Conflicting.

She would look at his work, she would take some of it away with her. She would try to help him.

Simple.

You want him. You want him inside you. There's moisture between your legs already.

She shifted slightly in her seat.

Do you wish Rob could see you now? Would you like him to know what you intend to do with this man?

The Scorpio turned left and she followed.

If he offered her coffee, she would accept. She would look carefully at his work, offer opinions if he sought them.

Hold him tightly to you. Let him feel how much you want him. Show him.

Her head was spinning.

If only you could see me now, Rob. I'm paying you back. As I make love to this man, I'm taking revenge.

She swallowed hard. Caroline would be proud of her, she mused.

She knows you want him. She said so. Said she could see it in your eyes. If she slid a finger between your legs, she would also feel how much you wanted him.

Hailey saw the Scorpio slowing down, turning into the driveway of a large, 1930s-style house.

She swung the Astra in behind, and switched off her engine as she saw Walker clamber out.

The house stood on a wide street, both flanked and faced by buildings of similar appearance. It sported a fairly big front garden; not particularly well kept, she noted. The paintwork of the house itself looked as if it could do with freshening up.

As she slid from behind her steering wheel, she saw Walker heading towards the front door.

Her legs felt a little shaky.

A sudden breeze ruffled her hair as she followed him towards the door, which was now open.

He gestured for her to enter.

Go on. It's what you've been waiting for.

She stepped into the hall.

He closed the door behind them.

40

THE HALLWAY SMELLED of air-freshener and furniture polish, as if it had been freshly cleaned that morning.

Hailey stood motionless for a moment, glancing around.

There was a staircase directly ahead of her. To her left, slightly ajar, was the door to the sitting room. To her right, another room. The door was tightly closed.

'Would you like a coffee?' said Walker, smiling.

Hailey nodded. She followed him through into the kitchen.

'Sorry about the mess,' he said as they entered a room to the rear of the house. 'It seems almost obligatory for blokes who live on their own to have untidy houses, doesn't it?'

'I've seen worse.' She smiled at him.

Apart from a couple of unwashed bowls in the sink, the kitchen was actually very neat.

He took some mugs from one of the wall cupboards, and flicked on the electric kettle.

'My own place can get pretty chaotic,' she assured him, watching as he spooned coffee into the mugs.

'Well, that's understandable with you having a little child,' he said.

'Yes,' she murmured.

Becky? Are you betraying her too?

Hailey crossed to the kitchen window and looked out onto the back garden. It stretched for a good seventy feet towards a high privet hedge that enclosed the lawn on three sides, effectively screening it from the neighbours on both sides.

The grass needed cutting.

'Do you see much of your neighbours?' she wanted to know.

He shook his head. 'We nod at each other in the street.' Walker smiled. 'That's about it.'

He filled the two mugs with hot water and set them on the kitchen table. They sat down opposite each other.

'It's a big house for one person,' she commented.

'I like my own company.'

'That's just as well.'

'It wasn't much different when my father lived here. I didn't see that much of him.' He sipped his coffee. 'We didn't have much to talk about.'

Hailey sensed that she should change the subject.

Walker was gazing past her, as if staring at something behind her that she couldn't see.

'What about your brother and sister?' she asked. '*They* were here, weren't they?'

He looked blank for a second.

'Oh, right,' he murmured. 'It was still like being alone, though. We all kept ourselves to ourselves. They both moved out when they were eighteen: went to university. We don't keep in touch. We're not very close.'

'Have you spoken to your mother since she left?'

He shook his head. 'She could be dead for all I know,' he muttered. 'I'm not sure what I'd say to her after all these years. I suppose I might ask her *why* she left – if she knew how much pain she was causing.'

'It must have been hard for you, Adam.'

He shrugged. 'I wouldn't be the only one it's happened to, would I? I mean, marriages split up every day, don't they?'

He looked straight into her eyes.

Hailey found it difficult to hold his gaze.

Yes. They break up every day. Over things like infidelity.

She sipped her coffee.

'I used to wonder how my father felt when he discovered my mother had left him for another man,' Walker said. 'I'm not even sure it bothered him that much. With him being a vicar, he probably thought it was the Will of God or some shit like that.' There was disdain in his voice. 'How did *you* feel when Rob cheated on you?'

'Angry, hurt, and puzzled. I know it might sound big-headed, but I'd always thought I was quite good-looking – good figure and all that. I didn't understand what *she* could give him that *I* couldn't. Perhaps she was better in bed than I was.'

'Aren't mistresses supposed to do things in bed that wives *won't* do?' Walker smiled. 'That's the usual excuse, isn't it?'

'Rob never missed out on anything,' she said defiantly.

That's it. Tell him your sexual details too.

'Even after I had Becky, we still had a good sex life,' she continued. 'He didn't have to look anywhere else for blow-jobs or any of his little fantasies.' She lowered her gaze. 'I'm sorry, Adam.'

'Are you *still* angry with him?'

She nodded. 'I wanted to hurt him the way he hurt me.' She smiled wanly. 'Caroline said that *I* should have an affair.'

She looked deeply into Walker's eyes. The silence between them seemed to stretch into an eternity.

She reached out and touched the back of his hand gently.

Go on. Do it. Do it now.

'And what do *you* think about that?' he wanted to know.

She could feel her heart thudding more insistently against her ribs, her breathing becoming a little more ragged. There was both heat and moisture between her legs as she squeezed her thighs together and shifted on the chair.

'I think if you're going to do that, you have to be careful who you do it *with*,' she breathed. 'It's a dangerous game to play.'

And do you want to play it?

She was still tracing her index finger gently across the back of his hand, aware that the digit was shaking slightly.

He put his hand over hers and squeezed gently, closing his own fingers around hers.

Hailey could feel her nipples pressing insistently against her bra. Her whole body felt as if it was ablaze. Her cheeks were flushed.

Walker, too, fidgeted slightly on his chair, his gaze never leaving hers.

'Is that what it would be?' he said softly. 'A game?'

He felt her foot rubbing slowly against his calf.

As Hailey crossed her legs she felt a steadily growing warmth envelope her. It was as if her blood had been replaced by liquid fire. She sat back slowly, allowing her hand to slip from his, aware of the almost palpable atmosphere in the room.

She ran a hand through her hair and swallowed hard.

'Show me this artwork you were talking about,' she said finally.

Walker smiled again.

41

THE ROOM ALSO lay towards the rear of the house. Perhaps twenty feet square, it was in complete darkness. Any light that might have encroached was kept out by a pair of thick velvet curtains.

As Walker flicked on the lights, and the two fluorescent tubes in the ceiling sputtered into life, Hailey could smell paint. She could also see that the walls on two sides were covered by illustrations of various kinds, and in assorted styles and mediums.

Paintings, sketches, pencil drawings, even watercolours.

There were a number of empty canvases to her right and, at one end of the room, several others of varying sizes, covered by sheets. There was a desk with a single high-backed chair, the desk surface littered with all the paraphernalia of an artist. Tubes of oil paint, brushes, pencils.

She took a step inside the room and Walker closed the door behind her.

'Well, this is it,' he said. 'It used to be a dining room but it's my studio now.' He smiled thinly. 'That sounds so grand, doesn't it?'

He walked to the other end of the room and pulled open the velvet curtains, allowing some natural light to flood in.

Hailey looked around, mesmerized by the array of pictures, amazed at their diversity and also at the skill that had gone into creating them.

'Tell me about them,' she said quietly, moving towards one painting on the wall. It showed a pair of red, cat-like eyes leering towards the viewer, framing a clenched fist that held a long knife.

'That one was a book cover,' Walker said. 'I forget the name of the book. The one beside it was for a record company.'

It showed a slender, naked woman reclining in the arms of a powerfully muscled creature bearing the head of a goat and looking down at her. She was smiling towards the viewer, the tip of her tongue touching her upper lip.

'I called that "Animal Passion",' said Walker, smiling.

Hailey then noticed that the goat-headed body sported a large erect penis.

'Did they actually use it?' she wanted to know, nodding towards the massive erection.

Walker shook his head.

Next was a pencil drawing, about ten by eight, of two beautiful women, both naked, facing each other. The one on the left had her hand on the other's breast; the one on the right had pushed one index finger between the labia of the other.

'What about this one?' Hailey asked.

'That was for *me*,' Walker chuckled.

'Did someone model for it?'

'I should be so lucky.'

'Was it done from memory?'

'One of the girls was a friend.'

Hailey ran her own index finger over the sketch, then moved to the next one.

This was a painting of a small baby being held aloft by its ankle, dangling over the gaping, tooth-filled mouth of a tiger.

'*Feeding Time*,' said Walker, standing close beside her. 'Another one for a record company.'

'Which band used it?'

'They didn't tell me. Just said what the album was called, and left it up to me.'

There was another nude: another woman. One arm stretched above her head, nipples painted to appear erect. The eyes were closed as if she was in ecstasy, the legs open. Her other hand rested between them, fingers stirring the carefully painted pubic hair.

'Another one from memory?' Hailey asked, her voice catching as she stared at the picture.

It was so detailed, so accurate, it might have been a photo.

Walker nodded.

She was aware of how close he was standing. She could practically feel his breath on her neck, but she made no attempt to move.

You don't want to move, do you?

Her eyes remained on the painted breasts. Hailey's own nipples were stiffened points now.

You want his hands on you, don't you?

There was another large painting towards the end of the room.

This was a crucifixion. Christ was naked, his face upturned to heaven, but the eyes were closed not in agony but in pleasure. He was smiling, despite the nails driven through his wrists and feet, the blood dripping from the wounds.

It took Hailey a second to realize that the Christ figure bore the face of Adam Walker.

Instead of angels, naked women and huge rabid dogs sat around the cross. In places, the dogs were mounting the women, the white foam of their madness dribbling from their open jaws like ejaculate. There were mounds of excrement, both human and canine, around the foot of the cross. One of the women, a statuesque blonde, gripped the penis of Christ and was licking the swollen glans with her tongue. But the tongue itself was that of a snake.

'That was for my father,' said Walker flatly. She caught a hint of hostility in his tone.

'What did he say when he saw it?' she wanted to know.

'He's never seen it. I'll show him one day, before he dies.'

'It's very powerful,' she told him.

'They say the best art comes from rage, don't they?'

He was staring at the painting. Hailey was staring at *him*.

The knot of muscles at the side of his jaw was pulsing angrily.

'Perhaps I should thank him for giving me that,' snapped Walker. 'It was all he *did* give me, apart from the scars.'

She looked puzzled.

'You can't see them of course,' he continued bitterly. 'Mental scars are invisible, but they mark you more deeply than any fucking knife ever could.'

'What happened?'

'Does it really matter?'

'If you don't want to talk about it—'

He cut her short.

'No, I'll talk about it,' he said. 'What would you like to know? The beatings? Would you like to know the first time he put me in hospital? I think I was only nine. A hairline fracture of the left tibia. Strange how you remember things like that, isn't it? He learnt some caution after that. He used a belt instead. Its marks usually faded after a couple of days. And all the time he was hitting me, he'd be telling me how useless I was – how I'd disappointed him. How I'd never amount to anything. If I did badly at school, he hit me. If I was late in, he hit me. He used to claim that if I was a failure before *him*, then I was a failure before God. That carried on until I was seventeen.'

His eyes were blazing furiously.

'I'm sorry, Adam.' Hailey wanted to touch him, to comfort him.

'Most priests get their calling when they're young,' Walker said evenly. 'In their teens or early twenties. Not *him*, no. He got his call when he was thirty-eight, when it was time to clear his conscience. When it was time for redemption. Why would God want a cunt like that?'

'Did he beat your sister and your brother?' Hailey asked quietly, almost reverentially.

'I don't know. We never spoke about it. He always warned us not to speak about it.'

'I didn't mean to pry. I really am sorry.'

He smiled. 'Perhaps the old bastard helped me in some ways. Like I said, the best art comes from rage. He *gave* me that rage.'

Walker was looking around at some of the other paintings that adorned the room.

'You learn to deal with it in time,' he said quietly. 'You learn to deal with *anything* eventually. If you get beaten enough times, it gets to the stage where it becomes routine. You think that's the way it is – that everyone lives like that.'

'And you still visit him now? Despite what he did?'

'He's still my father,' replied Walker flatly.

Hailey reached out and touched his hand gently.

He smiled at her and gestured around him.

Yet more paintings. More products of a great talent, thought Hailey, astonished by the diversity and power in some of them.

'I don't know how Waterhole's record company would react to some of these,' she said, studying a painting of a small boy holding a gun, forcing the barrel into the mouth of a besuited bald man who was kneeling before the child as if in prayer.

'They'll probably reject them,' Walker said, 'just like everyone else has.'

Hailey turned to look at him.

He nodded. 'No one has ever bought a single one of my paintings. No publisher, no record company, no one. I'm a fraud, Hailey.'

42

For long seconds she stood in silence, looking first at the picture-covered walls and then at Walker.

'You told me earlier you'd done work for both record companies and publishers,' she said.

'I have. I've submitted work, but they've always rejected it,' he admitted.

'But, Adam, this stuff is brilliant. I know some of it's a bit controversial, but it's great.'

'I wish everyone else agreed with you.' He lowered his gaze. 'I should have come clean. I shouldn't have lied, but I didn't want you to think I was a failure. I'm sorry.'

'Don't be. You're not a failure when you can produce work like this.' She turned and made an expansive gesture with her hand, designed to encompass the contents of the room.

'I'm a failure until someone *pays* me for my work.'

'But if you haven't sold any paintings, how do you survive? How do you manage to live here and supprt yourself?'

'There's no mortgage on the house, and I've got money in the bank. When my grandmother died, she left me some money. It's been in a trust fund since I was a child. It keeps me going if I'm careful: the interest is enough to pay for my expenses every month. I just paint every day. I love it. I still submit things to publishers and record companies, and the rejections still keep coming back. But, you never know, one day I might crack it. Perhaps with *your* help.'

She nodded.

He moved towards one of the sheet-covered canvases, took hold of one corner of the material and gently pulled it free.

'I did this for you,' he said quietly.

Hailey stepped forward, eyes widening.

'Adam, it's beautiful,' she whispered.

The painting was of Becky.

Hailey reached out to touch the image. It was perfect. As if her daughter had sat for hours while Walker painstakingly fashioned this portrait.

'From memory,' Hailey murmured, still awestruck by the painting.

'It's what she was wearing the day she got lost,' he reminded her. 'The day I found her.'

Hailey nodded, her eyes drawn particularly to the bright red coat. It was virtually luminous in its brilliance.

'I hope you don't mind,' he said, almost apologetically. 'I wanted you to have it.'

'Thank you,' she murmured, turning towards him.

He smiled. 'At least *someone* likes my work. I hope Becky likes it too.'

'She'll love it,' Hailey told him, reaching out to gently brush his cheek with her hand.

As she did so, she stepped forward.

He leant towards her and their lips brushed.

She closed her eyes as they kissed more passionately. Hailey pushed her tongue past the hard white edges of his teeth and stirred the warmth within.

He responded with surprising tenderness, drawing her closer to him, into his arms, kissing her deeply.

When they finally parted, she was breathing heavily, gazing up into his eyes.

'I want you,' she breathed and kissed him again.

She felt his erection pressing against her as they clung to each other, and with one hand she squeezed it through the material of his trousers.

Walker groaned as he felt her urgent movements and he allowed one hand to glide up inside her skirt, brushing the smooth flesh of her thighs, his fingertips trailing over her skin with featherlight delicacy.

Hailey parted her legs slightly, allowing him better access.

Wanting him to touch her in that most intimate place.

When his fingers caressed the damp cotton of her panties she gasped aloud, feeling the pressure slowly and gloriously build.

Walker's touch was expert, teasing. Allowing her excitement to build to even greater heights.

She allowed her head to loll back, allowed him to flick his tongue into the hollow of her throat, and then across to her earlobe.

He pushed her back towards his worktop, closing strong hands around her waist. Lifting her until she was sitting on the edge of it.

She lay back, stretching one leg out before her.

He slipped off her shoe, his gentle fingers stroking her foot, gliding between her toes. Then he dipped his head and took her little toe into his mouth. He sucked it gently for a moment, then moved to the next one, and the next, his tongue now probing where his fingers had been.

Hailey arched her back as she felt that slippery tumescence gliding up the inside of her ankle – then her calf. He paused at her knee, kissing the soft flesh at the rear, and she gasped aloud as he pushed up her skirt and continued to lick his way up her slender leg.

She felt his warm breath between her legs, even through the flimsy, sodden material of her panties.

He kissed her there, tasting her through the cotton.

Hailey lifted her bottom slightly, gripping the edge of the desk with both hands, pushing her pubis towards his eager mouth. Allowing him to slide her panties down her thighs.

Her skirt was up around her waist now.

She opened her eyes as she felt his tongue glide into the slippery wetness of her sex.

The pleasure was exquisite and growing by the second.

When the tip of his tongue slid across the stiff nub of her clitoris, she felt the first unmistakable feelings of warmth spread through her lower body.

She gripped the worktop even more tightly, her breathing now almost uncontrollable.

Hailey pushed herself against his tongue and mouth, her back arching once more as the sensations became stronger.

She turned her head to one side.

The portrait of Becky stared accusingly at her.

What are you doing?

Hailey could feel his tongue working more urgently, playing in and around her swollen vaginal lips and clitoris, as anxious to bring her to a climax as she was to reach one.

No, you can't do this.

She felt two of his fingers outlining her labia, smearing her moisture through the downy hair of her pubis.

Stop it now. Stop him!

She stared across at the portrait of Becky, and those painted eyes fixed her in a piercing gaze.

No more. This isn't just betraying Rob. It's betraying Becky.

The waves of pleasure were building. Her climax was seconds away.

No.

She said it aloud.

'No,' she gasped.

For a second, Walker continued with his expert ministrations.

'No,' she insisted.

This time she pulled away from him, squirming across the worktop, her face flushed, and flecked with the perspiration of pleasure.

Walker stared at her.

At the expression on her face that had turned from one of pure pleasure to one of

(*shock?*)

distaste.

'What's wrong, Hailey?' he asked, genuinely concerned.

'I can't do this,' she breathed, pulling up her panties, pulling down her skirt.

He opened his mouth to say something.

'This isn't right,' she said, stepping into her discarded shoe. 'I can't.'

Walker was also breathing heavily, his own excitement evident.

'I'm sorry,' she told him, and she was already heading for the door.

'Take the painting,' he called helplessly, motioning towards Becky's portrait.

He heard the front door slam.

Heard the sound of her car engine bursting into life.

Walker bowed his head and exhaled deeply.

Almost painfully.

43

She wasn't even sure where she was when she at last stopped the car.

Hailey had been driving as if she was in a trance, grateful that the roads had been so quiet.

Now, finally, she pulled the Astra over and switched off the engine, her breath still coming in deep, racking gasps.

For what seemed like an eternity she sat behind the wheel, gazing aimlessly out of the windscreen at the trees that rose tall on both sides of the road. A light breeze whipped along the road, stirring fallen leaves – occasionally scooping them up into miniature whirlwinds that died as quickly as they had risen.

When Hailey shifted in her seat, she could feel the wetness between her legs – the desire still strong.

She looked into the rear-view mirror.

The face of Adam Walker looked back at her.

She blinked hard and looked again, but the image was gone.

She was looking at her own flushed features.

Hailey fumbled in her handbag for a cigarette and lit up, the Superking quivering between her fingers.

She closed her eyes and allowed her head to slump back against the headrest.

She thought about Walker.

About his tongue sliding so expertly between her legs.

Her eyes jerked open, as if to banish that image.

To force such feelings from her body.

You wanted him.

She sucked hard on the cigarette, took another couple of drags, then clambered out of the car.

The wind ruffled her already unkempt hair and she pulled her jacket tightly around her as she walked, unsteadily, along the path at the roadside.

There was a wooden bench about twenty yards further along, and she made for that, finally seating herself. She sucked in deep lungfuls of air, glancing up and down the road as if expecting to see Walker's Ford Scorpio approaching.

What did you think you were doing back there?

She massaged her forehead with her fingertips.

You wanted him, and then you turned your back on him. Why?

Hailey knew that what she had intended was wrong.

But it felt so good, didn't it?

Becky?

Becky wasn't there. She would never have known. You led him on. You're *to blame.*

Such thoughts whirled around madly inside her head.

You had your chance. You wanted revenge against Rob. You wasted that chance.

Becky?

Hailey still felt the excitement she'd felt as Walker had held her. As he'd lifted her onto the worktop. As he'd explored her most intimate desire.

She got to her feet and walked back to the car, the passion still burning between her thighs.

Barely thinking, she slid her right hand down the front of her panties. Her other hand gripping the steering wheel.

The sensations built quickly as she used the tip of her index finger to stroke her inflamed clitoris.

Her orgasm hit her with a speed and intensity that surprised her. She gripped the wheel, her knuckles whitening, her breath loud and guttural inside the car.

For long seconds she writhed in ecstasy, squeezing her thighs together to increase the sensations. Her body shook violently three or four times, then she lay back in her seat, her eyes half open.

A car drove past, but she paid it little attention.

When she pulled her fingers free they were glistening.

She glanced at the dashboard clock and knew she had to leave now.

Hailey started up the engine.

*

Adam Walker leant on the desk, head down.

He'd remained in that position ever since Hailey left the house. It seemed to take a supreme effort of will from him to straighten up and look around the room.

He could smell her: the delicate scent of her perfume; the musky aroma of her desire. He could still taste her in his mouth.

Walker let out a long breath and shook his head.

He couldn't understand what he'd done that was so wrong. What awful act had he perpetrated to make her rush out of the room so quickly?

Walker wandered round behind the desk and slumped down in the high-backed chair, gazing slowly around the room. The eyes from all his paintings stared back at him blankly. There was no sympathy in those blind orbs, no understanding in those expressions.

He wanted to hold her in his arms again. To ask her *what* he had done wrong. To enquire how he could put it right.

Perhaps he shouldn't have told her what happened between himself and his father.

The abuse he had suffered.

Some things were best left unsaid, weren't they?

He shouldn't have burdened her with that kind of knowledge. It was bad enough having to live with the memories, without sharing them with others.

And yet she had said she wanted to know.

She had said she wanted *him*.

She wanted him to hold her, didn't she? She had *told* him she did.

A great feeling of sadness enveloped him like a shroud.

He looked across at the portrait of Becky.

He had painted her smiling.

Walker wished that Becky could see the painting. It had been done for *her*.

It was only right that she should see the painting.

If only Hailey had taken it with her.

If only . . .

Outside in the hall, the phone began to ring.

44

Hailey was staring at the VDU screen when she heard a knock on the door.

Without looking up, she called for the visitor to enter.

James Marsh peered around the door, then walked in.

'I won't be a minute, Jim,' she said, scribbling down a phone number from the vast array before her.

'Take your time,' Marsh said, wandering further into the office.

He walked around slowly, finally crossing to her desk and reaching for a small framed photo of Becky that he picked up, smiling at her image.

Hailey finally turned to look at him.

'She's got her mum's looks,' said Marsh, replacing the photo.

'Thanks.' Hailey smiled.

'I just nipped in to check that this meeting with Waterhole is going ahead.'

'I rang the hotel this morning and checked. I'm due there at one.'

'They're staying at the Crest, aren't they?'

'Two of them: Craig and Matt.' She grinned. 'The others are doing interviews in London. Their PR girl said they were very busy. We're lucky to have *two* of them.'

Marsh snorted indignantly. 'Jumped-up little shits,' he said irritably.

'Their manager's with them, too. *And* their girlfriends. *And* a couple of people from their record company.'

Marsh shook his head.

'What's their manager like?' Hailey wanted to know.

'Ray Taylor? He's like *most* managers. As long as he gets his twenty per cent, he's happy. He's been in this bloody game for years. I knew him when he was a record plugger. He's got plenty of rabbit, but he's bearable – you know the type.'

She nodded.

'What's Rob said so far about you coming back to work for me?'

'He doesn't mind,' she lied. 'He knows how much I like this job. Besides, he's got his own business to keep him occupied.'

'Did you tell him you were meeting Waterhole?'

She nodded. 'He wasn't very impressed.' She smiled.

'I'm not surprised.'

'My little girl was excited about it. She asked me to get their autographs.'

'You'd better check if they can *write* first,' Marsh chuckled.

'Is there anything specific you want me to go over with them, Jim?'

'Just make sure they know the deal. That the gig's for charity. That there's a big party afterwards. That they're expected to meet a few local big nobs. That sort of thing.'

'Shall I mention the auction for the signed guitar?'

'Did you get that sorted then?'

'I got them to agree to it. They're bringing a mobile unit with them too, to record their set. The record company have agreed to press a limited edition of twenty thousand CDs. Half the proceeds will go to charity.'

'And Ray Taylor agreed to that?' Marsh said, grinning.

'With a little persuading,' she told him.

Marsh laughed loudly. 'Jesus, that must have hurt him.'

'Jim, I'd better get going.' Hailey glanced at her watch.

He nodded and headed for the door.

'Let me know how it goes,' he said. Then he was gone.

Hailey waited for him to disappear, then picked up her handbag.

She was fumbling for her car keys when there was another knock on the office door.

'Come in,' she called.

The flowers seemed to appear like a huge multicoloured cloud, the cellophane sheath crackling in the hands of the young woman who carried them.

'These just arrived for you,' said Emma Grogan.

Hailey looked surprised, and took the immense bouquet from her secretary.

'I wish I had someone to send *me* flowers like that,' said Emma, staring at the array of blooms longingly. She stood a moment longer, then left.

Hailey pulled a card from the small envelope stapled to the clear wrapping and glanced at it.

> *Dear Hailey*
> *Sorry about yesterday.*
> *Adam*

She held the card in her fingers for long seconds, then slid it back into the envelope.

Sorry.

She glanced down at the flowers.

Sorry.

'So am I,' she murmured.

Hailey picked up the bouquet and dropped it into the waste-bin.

45

ADAM WALKER HAD seen the same words before. Many times.

And one in particular.

Rejection.

It appeared in nearly all the letters he had received from publishers or record companies over the years.

He had assumed that the idea of rejection, the very *act* and process of being rejected, would somehow lose its sting. Surely if he suffered rejection often enough, it would become easier to live with.

He had found that wasn't the case.

It still hurt.

Perhaps that was a good thing. Perhaps when rejection ceased to bother him, then that was finally the time to give up. But that idea never entered his thinking.

Yet it hurt. Every time it happened, it hurt. And it angered him. To think that someone could dismiss his work so easily was annoying.

He looked at the letter again, re-read it.

The record company thanked him for sending samples of his work (he always sent transparencies), but they didn't use freelance artists for their album sleeves. Hence this latest rejection.

Rejection.

He crossed to a small filing cabinet in his study and slid open one of the drawers.

From inside he withdrew a black clip-file and flipped it open.

There were over forty rejection letters and slips inside it already.

He knew, since he had placed each one there carefully.

Walker found the hole-punch, snapped open the file and added the latest letter to the batch, then he shut the file and slid it back.

Out of sight, out of mind?

If only it was that easy.

He looked around at his canvases, his work.

What now?

Walker knew what he must do.

He found a fresh canvas and prepared himself.

Never give up.

As he moved about the study, he glanced occasionally at the portrait of Becky.

The sight of the child made him think of Hailey.

He'd rung her office three times that morning. The first time, she hadn't arrived yet. No return call had been forthcoming, despite his urgent request to her secretary.

Perhaps she'd forgotten to tell Hailey.

Yes, that was it. The secretary hadn't told her he'd rung. Otherwise she'd have called him back, wouldn't she?

He'd rung twice since then.

Hailey was out at lunch, he was told. Again he'd asked if she could call him on her return. He hoped the secretary would give her the message *this* time.

He wanted to make sure she got his flowers. Wanted to be certain that she *knew* he was sorry for what had happened the day before.

If he could just *speak* to her.

He would stay in and work, wait for her call.

He had to leave the house later, though. If she called and he wasn't there, he could catch her tomorrow or the next day.

She would understand if he wasn't at home.

He wouldn't be out very long.

But there was something he had to do.

46

THE BAR OF the Crest Hotel was relatively empty when Hailey walked in.

However, she got the impression that, even if it hadn't been, she would still have had little trouble finding the person she sought.

The young woman was in her mid-twenties: tall, statuesque even. She was wearing a black dress that ended several inches above her knee. A slit in the material revealed what little thigh was unexposed already. She was tottering around on a pair of platform boots that laced up as far as her knees. These platforms, plus her normal height, convinced Hailey that the woman was fully six feet tall. Her hair was so brilliantly platinum blonde it was practically luminous.

She wore purple eyeshadow and, as she strode towards Hailey and extended one sinewy hand, the black fingernails she sported seemed to glint menacingly.

'Trudi,' said the girl.

'Without the "e",' Hailey said, smiling, shaking the proffered hand, feeling how thin it was.

This young woman, Hailey felt, was likely to be on intimate terms with an eating disorder. Had been, would be, or was currently.

'You must be Hailey,' Trudi said, looking down at her. 'Would you like a drink?'

She spoke quickly, distractedly, one hand constantly brushing through her hair.

Hailey accepted a Bacardi and Coke.

Trudi ordered a margarita and sipped at it like a sparrow drinking at a bird-bath.

'Where are the band?' Hailey wanted to know.

'They're up in their rooms. They're very busy doing interviews with the local press. One of my colleagues is up there with them.'

Hailey nodded slowly.

'It's quite an event for a place like this to have them here doing interviews. A big thrill for the local journos,' Trudi announced. 'I mean it's not exactly London, is it?'

'That's why so many people like it,' Hailey told her. 'How long have you been in this business?'

'I went in straight from college. Messed about, really. Didn't know *what* I wanted to do. I originally studied drama, but the music business is more me. The vibe is awesome.'

Again Hailey nodded. 'Isn't it just?' she said, barely managing to suppress a grin.

'What about *you?*' Trudi asked. 'Have you been in the business long?'

'Long enough.'

'And you work for Jim Marsh?'

'Part-time now. I've got a little girl.'

Trudi shrugged.

'I couldn't have kids,' she said, almost dismissively. 'They tie you down too much, don't they? All that shitting and puking all the time. Not very cool, is it?'

'There's a bit more to it than that,' Hailey informed her.

'A friend of mine had a baby a few months ago. God, she put on *so* much weight. She still hasn't got her figure back.'

Hailey was aware of Trudi running appraising eyes over her.

Perhaps you could do with having one then, you elongated stick insect.

Hailey laid her handbag on the bar as she sipped her drink.

'I don't recognize the make,' said Trudi, peering at the bag as if it was some kind of precious stone.

'You wouldn't. I got it locally,' Hailey told her.

'I bought a Versace bag last week. It's *so* cool. It cost me half a week's wages, but it was worth it. I got it down the King's Road.' She sipped her margarita. 'How do you manage, being so far out of London?'

'We're only thirty miles away. Twenty minutes on a train.'

'But you have to be at the hub of things in my business. You know, on top of it all. And I *couldn't* live anywhere but London. I'd feel too cut off. You must go mad sometimes.'

'This whole city is mad actually,' Hailey replied earnestly. 'We have the highest incidence of insanity per head of population anywhere in the country. Especially women. Apparently it's the lack of designer shops that does it.'

Trudi looked on with concern. 'Really?' she murmured, gazing at Hailey as if mesmerized.

'Still, they've got running water in most of the houses here now, and they think that in a couple of years we might even have television.'

Trudi's look of concern turned to one of bemusement.

Hailey saw a flicker of irritation on those gaunt features.

'We can go up now,' Trudi said brusquely.

'I can't wait,' Hailey told her.

She watched as the tall PR girl slid off the bar stool and wandered away in the direction of the lifts.

Hailey picked up her handbag and followed.

They rode the lift in silence, standing on either side of the mirrored car until it bumped to a halt on the third floor.

'Do you enjoy working for the band?' Hailey said conversationally.

'It's mega,' Trudi said. 'They're so cool, so funny. Especially Craig. He writes all the lyrics, you know. His wife's really nice, too. She used to be an actress.'

Hailey nodded.

'If you wait here a minute I'll check they're ready,' Trudi told her.

She disappeared inside one of the rooms, leaving Hailey alone in the corridor.

She shook her head, smiling.

No, the record business never changes, does it?

She inspected her reflection in the large mirror opposite, satisfied with what she saw.

The door opened and Trudi stuck her head out.

'You can come in now,' she said, almost reverentially. 'They're ready for you.'

23 CRANLEY GARDENS, MUSWELL HILL, NORTH LONDON

He brought the Dyno-Rod van to a halt and checked his clipboard to ensure he had the right address.

Yes, this was it. Number 23.

It looked a little run-down compared to some of the properties in the same street, and the address he'd been called to was actually converted into flats. It had been one of the residents who'd called, complaining that she'd been unable to flush her toilet. This problem had been going on since the previous Saturday – almost a week now.

No wonder she wasn't happy.

Michael Cattran wrote down the current time on his work-sheet, then hauled himself out of the van, moving round to the rear of the vehicle to collect his tools.

The sky was darkening with the onset of evening. Great banks of dark cloud gathering in the sky promised rain.

Best get this job finished with and get home. It was his last call of the day and he wasn't sorry.

He made his way up the path to the front door, rang the bell and waited for someone to answer.

When a woman appeared at the door, he saw the look of relief on her face.

It had been she who had called him, and Cattran listened while she rambled on about blocked drains and inconvenience, adding his own sympathetic comments every now and then.

She showed him round to the side of the house and stood there.

Cattran hated it when customers stood and watched him work,

peering down at him while he toiled away. He warned her that he would have to inspect the blockage first, and that could take some time.

She offered to make him a cup of tea and he accepted readily, happy when she retreated back inside number 23 and closed the front door.

He looked down at the manhole cover then reached into his toolbox for the metal implement he would use to prise it open.

The cover was rusted slightly around the rim, and he was forced to use more strength than he'd anticipated, but finally, with a loud clang, it came free and he lifted it away from the manhole.

The stench that erupted was vile beyond belief. A putrid, virulent odour that clogged his nostrils and sent him reeling backwards, clutching his stomach. It was all he could do to prevent himself vomiting.

For a moment or two he stood away from the yawning hole, sucking in several lungfuls of clean air, as if to flush away the noxious smell that filled his nostrils. Finally he returned to the manhole, bracing himself for a fresh dose of the nauseating stench it contained.

A rusted ladder led down into the cistern itself, and Cattran realized that this was indeed a major blockage. He would have to take a closer look to determine how bad.

He took a torch from his toolbox, jammed it into his belt, and began his descent, the stench growing even more intense as he drew closer to the bottom.

Cattran was beginning to wonder if he would make it. Was he going to faint before he reached the foot of the ladder? But he persevered, and finally made it into the conduit itself.

It was about three feet round, and he pulled the torch from his belt and shone it in both directions.

When he saw what was blocking the drain it took an almost superhuman effort to stop him vomiting.

Lumps, chunks, scraps of rotting meat clogged the drain.

The entire conduit was packed with the decaying white matter, much of which had already begun to putrefy. At first it looked like chicken flesh, but when he touched it he realized it had a different consistency: softer. There was something familiar about this seething mass of carrion. Something appallingly familiar.

The stench. The feel of it.

The realization hit him like a thunderbolt.

This rancid flesh wasn't chicken.

It was human.

8 February 1983

I wished I could stop but I could not.
I had no other thrill or happiness.
Denis Nilsen

I've crashed to the bottom of the barrel,
I've got feelings that could kill . . .
Harlow

47

IT SOUNDED LIKE an explosion.

As Rob Gibson heard the first rumble of thunder, he turned in his chair and looked out at the slate-grey sky.

Rain was already pelting down on the Velux windows of his office. Beating out a machine-gun tattoo on the glass.

He stood up and looked out, seeing the first phosphorescent shaft of lighting tear across the heavens. It looked like a luminescent vein against the mottled grey flesh of the sky.

Rob thought about Becky. She was terrified of thunderstorms. Had been since she was a baby.

He remembered, on more than one occasion during the last five years, how he and Hailey had woken to find she had climbed into bed between them. Or was crying for them in her own room.

Rob himself had gone in to comfort her the last time. Cuddled her and held her close. Told her that the storm was nothing to worry about.

The thunder, he'd told her, was just the clouds bumping together. Then he'd taught her the trick his father had taught him. The one where you counted between the flash of lightning and the rumble of thunder, so you could tell how far away the storm really was.

He'd stayed with her for an hour or more that night, counting the seconds between each flash and rumble. Counting the miles as the storm moved away. Then he'd sat in silence beside her bed until she fell asleep.

The thought of it brought a smile to his lips.

Hailey would be thinking about her too, he guessed.

Wherever the hell she was. Whatever she was doing.

The rain hammered even harder on the roof and windows, as if trying to break through them.

Hailey?

He wondered precisely what she was doing, how her meeting was going.

Taking an interest in her job? Watch it, you're slipping.

He watched the sky, washed out by so much rain. The clouds that only promised more.

Rob glanced at his watch. He'd be home in another three hours. He'd see them both.

His wife and his daughter.

He smiled again.

The office door opened and he turned slowly to see who it was.

Sandy Bennett looked at him and smiled.

He didn't return the smile.

'Am I missing something?' she asked.

'I was just watching the rain,' he told her.

'The storm's getting worse. I think we're in the best place. Although I could think of one better.'

She pushed the office door shut and moved across to his desk.

'Like where?' he wanted to know.

'Bed. We'd be nice and cosy tucked up in bed together.'

'What do you want, Sandy? I'm busy.'

'I typed up that stuff you wanted, and there's a couple of faxes.' She handed him the sheets of paper, touching his hand as she did so.

'Is that it?' he said, glancing at the fax communications.

'I wondered if you might want to nip round for a drink tonight. You could always call Hailey and tell her you'd got a meeting or something.'

He regarded her impassively.

'Yeah, I *could*,' said Rob quietly, 'if I wanted to. The thing is, I don't *want* to.'

'Rob, I know how you feel. I know you didn't want to stop what was going on between us. If Hailey hadn't found out, we'd still be together.'

'We were never *together*, Sandy,' he reminded her. 'The sooner you get a grip on that, the better.'

'Don't tell me it isn't a problem for you, too,' she hissed. 'Because I don't believe you. You see me here every day, and you still want me.'

'You're right about one thing: it *is* a problem. And it's about time I did something about it. You're sacked. I want you out of my firm as well as my life. I'll have your P45 sent on with any wages we owe you.'

'You can't do that.'

'I'm doing it. Don't come in tomorrow, Sandy. I mean it. I'm doing what I should have done when all this first happened. Hailey was right.'

'I thought it *would* be her fucking idea. Is she scared she's going to lose you? Scared she can't compete?'

'I tell you what: don't wait until tomorrow. Get your stuff and go now.'

Sandy held his gaze for a moment, then spun round and left his office, slamming the door behind her.

Rob stood up, watching, as she crossed to her desk, picking up her handbag, pulling on her jacket. He saw Frank Burnside peering out, also watching the activity.

Then Sandy was gone.

Burnside had already left his office. Rob met him at the door.

'What the hell is going on?' Burnside wanted to know.

'Come in, Frank,' Rob said quietly. 'I'll explain.'

Outside, there was another loud rumble of thunder.

Redemption

ALL HE HAD in the world, he carried with him in a Puma sportsbag. Some socks. A clean pair of jeans. A couple of shirts. A broken Walkman. T-shirts. A Zippo lighter.

There were a few other things in the bag that David Layton carried towards the main gate of HM Prison Wandsworth, but nothing of any worth.

He walked between two warders: the tall screw, Collinwood, and another man he hadn't seen before.

None of the trio spoke. Not even when Collinwood selected a large key from the many on his chain and slotted it into the lock of a smaller door set in the larger gates.

He pushed open the door and motioned with his head for Layton to step out – when he gladly did.

He looked up at the sky, feeling the rain on his face. Glad to feel it.

It felt like freedom.

It was freedom.

'Anyone meeting you?' Collinwood asked, surveying the empty street beyond.

Layton shook his head.

'There isn't anyone,' he said, looking around.

'What will you do?'

'What do you care? I'm not your responsibility any more, Mr Collinwood.'

He stared directly at the uniformed man.

'That's the first time in eighteen fucking months I haven't had to call you "sir",' he snarled. 'And it feels good.'

'You'll be back. Your kind always are.'

'We'll see. Don't wait up for me.'

'The nearest train station is—'

Layton cut him short.

'I know where it is,' he interrupted.

'See you soon, Layton,' the uniformed man intoned.

'Mr Layton,' he said, grinning.

The door closed behind him and, for long moments, he stood motionless in the rain. Staring back at the locked gate. The gate that kept him out now.

'Fuck you, Collinwood,' he rasped under his breath.

He swept his wet hair back, and began walking. He had about twenty-five quid on him.

It would be enough to get him where he wanted to go.

48

HAILEY'S FIRST THOUGHT: 'Jim was right.'

As she entered the hotel room occupied by two members of Waterhole, she smiled at them, surprised when they both stood up ... then turned their backs to her, bent over and broke wind in unison.

They both laughed hysterically and flopped back down on the sofa.

Trudi was laughing also. A high-pitched caterwaul of a laugh that echoed through the spacious room.

Hailey recognised the two men immediately.

Craig Levine and Matt Dennison. Vocalist and drummer respectively. Early twenties, unshaven, long shirts undone and flowing loose outside their grubby jeans. Levine was wearing a pair of Caterpillar boots, which he had resting on the coffee table in front of the sofa. Hailey noticed chewing gum stuck between the treads of the sole.

Dennison was wearing a pair of yellow wrap-around Ray-Bans, despite the fact that every light in the room was on.

Sitting next to him was a girl Hailey thought could be no older than twenty. She was blonde, dressed in a pair of jeans that looked as if they'd been sprayed on, and a tightly fastened black jacket that pushed her ample breasts together to form a cleavage you could lose a Filofax in.

She was stroking Dennison's hair, occasionally flicking at

strands of it with one index finger. Every time she did so, she giggled.

There was a large ghetto-blaster propped on top of the television in the corner of the room. Hailey recognized the sound of Waterhole's latest album coming from it.

'This is Hailey Gibson,' Trudi said, waving a hand in Hailey's direction.

'I suppose you know who *we* are?' said Levine, grinning. 'Most people do.'

The room was filled with raucous laughter again.

'Jumped-up little shits.'

From the bedroom of the suite another man appeared.

Mid-thirties, a little overweight. The Armani suit he wore fitted a little too snugly, Hailey thought, as she shook his hand.

'Ray Taylor,' the man said. 'Manager.'

'You're supposed to curtsy now,' Levine said.

More raucous laughter.

Hailey sat down opposite the two band members, trying to prevent her gaze from straying too often to the blonde, who was still stroking Dennison's hair.

'Leave it out, Sophie,' said the drummer finally, looking round at the girl, who pouted for a moment then wandered off towards the bedroom.

'I'm going to help Jenny try on those clothes she bought,' said Sophie before disappearing from view.

'Women,' said Dennison, shrugging his shoulders and grinning.

Hailey was aware of his gaze travelling up and down her slender legs. He had barely looked at her face since she entered the room.

I'd eat you alive, you little bastard.

'You're from Jim Marsh, aren't you?' said Taylor, pouring himself a drink from the mini-bar.

Hailey nodded.

'Worked for him long?' Taylor persisted.

Hailey told him.

'Would you like a drink?' he asked.

214

'Yeah, *we're* going to have one, aren't we, Matt?' said Levine, also grinning.

Trudi hurried to the mini-bar to fetch what they wanted.

'I know you're busy, so I won't keep you,' Hailey said.

And the quicker I can get out of here the better.

'I just came to check some details about the gig, and the party afterwards.'

Are *you* coming?' Levine wanted to know.

'No, it's just the way she's sitting,' Dennison offered.

More laughter. Hailey smiled politely.

Christ, it was an effort.

'I'll be there, yes,' she said.

'I've seen the guest list,' said Taylor. 'Why the local politicians?'

'It's a charity gig, isn't it? It's good publicity for them. It makes them look hip and they're doing something for a good cause. The local papers will be running the pictures for weeks.'

Taylor smiled.

'So we've got to have our photos taken with a load of old cunts, just for charity?' Dennison sneered.

'It won't take long,' Hailey reassured the drummer. 'And Jim wants some photos of the band taken inside his factory, too. But that can be done the following day.'

Taylor nodded and sipped at his gin and tonic.

'I hope he realizes how lucky he is getting us to do this gig,' the manager said. 'I can't remember the last time I let the boys do something for nothing. It's against my principles.' He smiled crookedly.

'Well, it'll be good publicity for the band, too,' Hailey reminded him.

'The last thing this lot need is more publicity,' Taylor told her.

'Making headlines for helping people is better than making headlines for trashing hotel rooms and punching photographers,' mused Hailey.

'I don't *like* fucking photographers,' Levine interjected.

Trudi laughed, but found she was the only one. Her cheeks coloured and she looked down, fumbling for a cigarette in her handbag.

'Well, as long as you promise not to hit any of them before, during or after *this* gig,' said Hailey, looking directly at Levine.

'I'll do my best,' he said scornfully. 'The last one was trying to get pictures of Jenny's tits. He wasn't showing her any respect. That's why I smacked him.'

'He was a creep.'

Hailey looked across towards the bedroom as she heard this new voice.

Jennifer Kenton emerged wearing a black trouser suit. She ran a hand through her shoulder-length blonde hair and crossed to the sofa. She leant forward and touched Levine's face.

Hailey recognized her immediately. She'd been in half a dozen failed feature films during her career. She still made films now, but most of her work was for television. She too was wearing Ray-Bans.

'I don't like creeps hanging around me,' she continued. 'You'd better make sure the photographers that cover this gig and the party afterwards behave themselves.'

Hailey nodded. 'Don't worry about it.' She smiled.

'*You'd* better worry about it, otherwise I'll have your job,' Jennifer Kenton told her haughtily.

'That's it, babe, you tell her,' Levine chuckled.

Hailey glared at the former actress for a second.

Bitch.

Jennifer Kenton sat down on the arm of the sofa, and Levine snaked his arm around her waist.

'Get me a tequila sunrise, Trudi,' the former actress said. 'You'll probably have to call room service for it.'

Trudi rushed to comply.

'We've nearly finished, babe,' said Levine, looking up at his wife.

'Thank God for that,' Jennifer Kenton muttered wearily. 'I'm fed up with this hotel. It's like a prison. The only trouble is if I go out I'll probably get so many people asking me for bloody autographs.'

In your dreams.

Hailey glanced at her watch. 'Well, I'm just about finished,' she said. 'I'll let you all get on.'

'Thank fuck for that,' said Dennison, getting to his feet and hurrying across the room. 'I reckon Sophie's waiting for me in there.' He pointed to the bedroom and flicked out his tongue.

Hailey also rose.

She shook hands with Ray Taylor.

'See you at the gig,' she said, smiling.

Jennifer Kenton looked her up and down disdainfully.

'Don't forget what I said about those photographers,' she said.

'It's all right, Jenny,' Trudi interjected. '*I'll* make sure it's cool.' She ushered Hailey towards the door.

'I told you they were cool, didn't I?' said the PR girl as she and Hailey emerged into the corridor. 'I love working with them. And I said Craig was so funny, didn't I?'

'I could tell he reads a lot of Oscar Wilde,' Hailey told her.

Trudi looked blank.

Hailey headed towards the lift.

'I'll be in touch,' she called without looking back. 'It's been mega.'

All she heard was the sound of the door closing.

49

THERE WERE ALREADY a number of cars parked outside the school as Caroline Hacket arrived.

She selected a position about twenty yards from the main exit and swung her red Saab into it.

The rain, she was delighted to see, had eased to little more than drizzle. The storm had passed and the sky, though still bruised with cloud, seemed to have released the worst of the deluge.

Caroline sat for a moment behind the wheel, checking her reflection once or twice in the rear-view mirror.

There was a car parked a few yards away from her, its windows badly steamed. The passenger side-window was open a few inches, and she could see a harassed-looking young woman in her mid-twenties trying to pacify a child of two or three who was strapped in the car-seat. The child was crying, struggling to get out, and the woman had gone from cajoling and reasoning to shouting and threatening.

Caroline looked away. That was one thing she *didn't* miss about kids.

And yet, people said it was different if they were your own.

She would never know.

Caroline continued to gaze through the windscreen, trying not to dwell too much on that subject. Aware that unwanted thoughts and memories arose with this kind of self-analysis.

The abortions.

The string of lovers

*(no, lovers wasn't the word, was it? Love had never been involved.
It had been sex, pure and simple)*

she'd had during her teens and early twenties.

The operation.

She still remembered that day when a doctor had told her she'd
be unable to ever have children. How the news had not hit her like
the thunderbolt she'd expected. Instead the realization of it had
festered and grown within her, slowly. Like some kind of cancer.

It was this inability to have children that had caused her
second marriage to break up. That *and* her husband's affair, of
course. For a short time she had blamed herself. If she had been
able to give him the child he wanted so badly, then perhaps he
wouldn't have gone to another woman.

But any feelings of guilt she had harboured left swiftly.

She was left with the pain instead.

Caroline looked across towards the car closest to her and saw
that the small child in the front seat had stopped crying. His
mother was kissing him on the cheek and the child was laughing.

The realization that *she* would never know that joy struck her
as hard as it had ever done.

She brushed a single tear from the corner of her eye, inspecting
her reflection once again in the rear-view mirror. She didn't want
Becky to see that she'd been crying.

It was while she was retouching her mascara that she noticed
another car parked about thirty yards behind her.

Or, more to the point, its driver.

It only took her a second to realize it was Adam Walker.

She had never seen the Scorpio he drove before. She had only
ever seen *him* on that one occasion, but she knew instantly who it
was.

He was leaning against the side of the Ford, gazing towards the
school, hands dug deep into the pockets of his leather jacket.

He looked distracted, his eyes scanning the cars already
stationed outside the school, and also those constantly pulling up
and parking.

Caroline turned in her seat to get a better look at him.

After a moment or two he slid back behind the wheel, but didn't drive off.

He merely sat.

Waiting.

Caroline glanced at her reflection once again, then swung herself out of the Saab.

50

THE TAPPING ON the window startled him.

Adam Walker looked round as he heard the sound, at first unsure where it was coming from.

Then he saw Caroline Hacket standing beside his Scorpio, smiling in at him.

Walker wound down the window.

'You were miles away,' she said to him. 'You didn't even see me coming.'

'How did you know I was here?' he wanted to know.

'I'm parked just along there.' She indicated her own vehicle. 'Are you waiting for somebody?'

He nodded slowly.

'Get in,' he said, reaching across and unlocking the passenger door. 'I think it's going to rain again.'

Caroline accepted his invitation.

'How are you, Adam?' she said as she scrambled in beside him.

'I'm fine. I didn't expect to see *you* here.'

'You were waiting for Hailey, weren't you?'

He looked surprised.

'It's OK.' She grinned. 'I'm very discreet.'

'What's Hailey said to you, then?'

'Nothing. She doesn't *have* to. We've been friends for long enough.'

He nodded slowly.

'You're out of luck today though,' Caroline informed him. 'She asked *me* to pick Becky up. Hailey's still at work.'

'What would you say if I told you it was *you* I was looking for?'

'I'd say you were a liar.'

He reached into the glove compartment of his car and pulled out a battered paperback.

Caroline laughed as he showed her the cover.

'Where did you get that?' she wanted to know, inspecting the book.

She flipped it open and glanced at the author photo inside the back cover, shaking her head. Still smiling.

It showed her sitting on what looked like a bar stool, with legs crossed. She looked very efficient, in a black two-piece and court shoes. There was no smile though. That was her enigmatic face, she mused.

'I got it from the local library. They ordered them both for me. I've already finished *Murderous Minds*.'

'And?'

'Very interesting.'

'Just interesting? Not devastating, or ground-breaking, or incredibly powerful? Just interesting?'

'I didn't mean it to sound like an insult. It was very good. I enjoyed it. Why didn't you say you were a writer the first time we met?'

'It's not the sort of thing you just drop into a conversation, is it? And besides, I'm hardly Catherine Cookson, am I?'

'*I'm* impressed,' he said, smiling.

She handed the book back to him.

'Why the fascination with murderers?' he enquired.

'I've always been interested, ever since I was a kid. All the gory details – but not *just* that. It's *why* people kill that fascinates me. What drives someone to take another life?' She shrugged.

'Hailey told me you were working on a new book at the moment. What's it about?'

'It's like a dictionary of murderers.'

'I'd like to read it when it's published.'

'I'll let you have a copy. At least then I'll know *someone's* read it.'

'How long have you been writing?'

'Over ten years. I was a journalist on a local paper before that. That's how I met my first husband. He owned the paper.'

'I admire anyone who can write – or can do anything creative.'

'*You* know what it's like. You paint, don't you?'

Walker nodded.

'What else did she tell you?'

He looked perplexed.

'About me?' Caroline continued.

'Just that writing was your hobby,' Walker said. 'She wasn't talking behind your back, if that's what you're worried about.'

'I *wasn't* worried about that. I'm just curious about *you* and Hailey.'

'There's nothing going on between us.'

'Adam, I saw the way you looked at each other. And I know Hailey. Her marriage has been on the rocks for the last six months. Rob's been acting like a complete bastard. If you and her have got a thing going, then good luck to you. Both of you. I certainly wouldn't blame Hailey, and *I'm* not going to drop you in it.'

She glanced at the dashboard clock.

'I'd better go,' she told him. 'Becky will be coming out any time now.' She paused and touched his arm. 'If there is something going on between you and Hailey, then that's *your* business. If there *isn't*, then give me a call.' She laughed and closed the door.

He watched as she walked back to her car, then beyond towards the school gates.

Only when he saw Becky emerge from the school, among the hordes of other children, did he drive off.

And from the heaving skies the rain began to fall again.

51

'HE SAID HE was waiting for *you*,' Caroline Hacket said as they sat in her kitchen.

She watched Hailey sip her coffee, then look towards the door, which was half open. In the sitting room beyond, Becky was watching TV. Hailey crossed to the door and pushed it shut.

'Did he say why?' Hailey wanted to know.

'He didn't have to,' Caroline told her. 'Listen, I told Adam and I'm telling you, Hailey, whatever's going on between you two is *your* business.'

'Did *he* say we were having an affair?'

'He said there was nothing going on.'

'But you didn't believe him?'

'I just thought that *you'd* tell me if you were sleeping with him.'

'I'm *not*,' Hailey insisted.

Caroline eyed her friend impassively.

'Oh, Christ,' Hailey groaned. 'Listen, Caroline, what I'm telling you is the truth. I had lunch with him a couple of days ago. We ended up going back to his house . . .' She allowed the sentence to trail off.

'And nothing happened?' Caroline said quickly.

'I'd suggested showing some of his work to Waterhole, to see if they were interested in using it on their album covers, that kind of thing,' Hailey murmured. 'Things got out of hand. I was mad with Rob. I wanted to get back at him because of his affair with that slut.'

'So you *did* have sex with Adam?'

'I wanted to, but I couldn't. I *told* him I wanted him. We started – but I couldn't go through with it.' She explained more fully, slowly. She told Caroline *everything*. Like some kind of confession. As if it was difficult to speak the words.

Truth hurts, doesn't it?

'You led him on,' Caroline said flatly.

'No,' Hailey snapped angrily. 'It wasn't like that.'

Wasn't it?

'Hailey, you let the guy go down on you. I think he could be forgiven for thinking you wanted to be a little more than just friends.'

The two women regarded each other silently for a moment.

'Why did you want him to stop?' Caroline said finally.

Hailey shrugged.

'Maybe I wasn't as mad at Rob as I thought I was,' she muttered.

'So where does that leave Adam?'

'Who cares? I'm just grateful nothing happened. I shouldn't even have had lunch with him. I suppose I got carried away. I wanted to show him how grateful I was for him finding Becky. It got out of hand.'

'You can't blame *him*, Hailey.'

'I didn't *ask* him to send me flowers – or ring me at work.'

'You bitch,' Caroline said, smiling. 'You led him on and now you just want to drop him.'

'I thought *you* would have understood,' Hailey retorted, snatching up her coat.

'No, I don't.'

'Look, if I sent out the wrong signals, then I'm sorry, but it's too late now.'

'Don't you think you should be telling Adam this, not me?'

Hailey pulled on her coat.

'I don't want to speak to him again, Caroline. It's as simple as that.'

'You mean, as long as you can't see him, you can't be tempted.'

Hailey headed for the sitting room.

Caroline heard her calling to Becky.

'Just because Rob was stupid doesn't mean *I* have to be too,' Hailey announced.

'At least have the decency to return his calls, Hailey. Put the poor sod out of his misery. He only wants to speak to you. Where's the harm in that?'

Hailey didn't answer.

'Thanks for picking Becky up,' she said brusquely, ushering her daughter towards the front door.

''Bye, Auntie Caroline,' Becky called as she left the house, wandering towards the waiting Astra.

'See you soon, darling,' Caroline called after her. Then, to Hailey: 'Speak to him. You owe him that, at least.'

Hailey hesitated a moment, then headed towards the car.

Caroline stood at the door as the Astra pulled away.

52

THE EVENING HAD passed in relative silence since Rob had taken Becky up to bed.

He and Hailey had barely exchanged ten words. Both of them seemed enveloped by a feeling of weariness. As if each was carrying some crushing weight on their very soul. They sat staring blankly at the television, watching a film both of them had seen before, but which neither seemed willing to switch off.

They had exchanged the usual small talk over the dinner table. Anxious to perpetuate in front of Becky the façade that all was still well between them.

As the credits began to roll, Hailey stretched out her legs before her and glanced across at Rob, who was slumped in the chair, almost asleep.

He stirred, aware of her gaze.

'It wasn't much good the *first* time, was it?' he said, nodding towards the screen.

Hailey smiled and shook her head.

'Do you fancy a coffee?' she wanted to know.

'If you're making one.'

She got to her feet and headed for the sitting-room door.

Rob caught her hand and held it.

'Hailey?'

He looked up at her.

'I sacked Sandy today,' he said flatly.

Hailey held his gaze.

'She's finished at BG Trucks,' he continued. 'You were right. I should have done that at the beginning.'

'Why now?' she asked, kneeling beside his chair, still holding his hand.

'I *wanted* to do it. I didn't want her around any more.'

'What did she say?'

'Does it matter? She's gone. That's the most important thing. I thought you'd be pleased.'

'I am. I just wish you'd done it earlier.'

He nodded. 'So do I.'

She thought how calm his voice was: no confrontational edge to it. He just seemed so tired.

'Why did you sack her *now* if you wouldn't do it when your affair ended?' she enquired.

'She kept on saying she thought there was still a chance for us. She still wanted me.'

The way you wanted Adam Walker?

'Do you still want *her?*'

'I never did. I would never have left you and Becky for her. You know that.'

'What was it, Rob? Didn't you want the temptation around any more?'

'You've got what you wanted, Hailey. Can't you just leave it at that?'

'*I* wanted her to go, Rob. But are you sure *you* did?'

'Very sure.'

'What did Frank say about it?'

'Not much. He understood why she had to go.'

She reached out and touched his cheek. 'Promise me you'll never see her again,' she whispered.

'Hailey . . .'

'Promise me.'

He looked directly at her. 'I'll never see her again,' he murmured.

She got to her feet and kissed him gently on the top of the head.

'I'll make the coffee,' she said quietly.

He heard the sitting-room door close behind her.

Feel better for that? Conscience not pricking quite so badly now?

Rob prepared for the weight to lift from his shoulders.

It didn't.

53

Fucking bastard.

Lousy, gutless, fucking bastard, thought Sandy Bennett.

She wondered what he was doing now. Sitting playing happy families with his wife and kid, no doubt.

And there was nothing she could do about it.

She exhaled deeply and padded through the small flat to the kitchen, where she found a can of Diet Coke. She'd been toying with idea of getting drunk: downing enough vodka to blot out his memory, at least on a temporary basis.

Instead she'd taken a bath, sitting in the warm, soapy water for what seemed like hours. Thinking about her life – about Rob Gibson.

Bastard.

What was she meant to do now? She didn't care about losing her job. She knew she'd find another without too much trouble. No, it wasn't that which preyed on her thoughts. It was the way he had discarded her.

She managed a smile as she wondered if his child had a rabbit. Perhaps she should boil it . . . throw acid over his car.

If it was good enough for Glenn Close, then . . .

She laughed out loud. Actually laughed.

No. She wouldn't do that. Nothing like it. She wouldn't cut her wrists, then call him. She wouldn't attack him. She wouldn't pretend she was pregnant.

Nothing like that.

She did, however, feel that it might be worth pursuing a claim for unfair dismissal. She made a mental note to visit the Citizens' Advice Bureau the following morning. First there, and then the temping agency which had found her the job at BG Trucks in the first place.

The mortgage on her flat wasn't exorbitant, and she was confident enough of her own ability to secure a new job before a problem with finances even arose.

She wandered back into the living room, switched off the TV and reached for the remote that controlled the small CD system.

She skipped through tracks, avoiding any that were slow and moody.

Sandy wasn't in the mood for crying. It was anger she felt, not desperation.

She adjusted the volume on the CD and reached for the discarded copy of *Elle* that lay on the floor beside the sofa. Sipping her Diet Coke straight from the can, she found her page.

At first she didn't hear the knock on the door.

She looked up and shook her head gently, then continued reading.

Again the knock, more insistent this time.

She frowned and glanced across at the clock on the video: 22.17 p.m.

Sandy sighed.

She hoped it wasn't that miserable old bastard from the flat below to complain about the music. Christ, it was barely audible.

She got to her feet and headed for the front door.

Rob?

A smile flashed across her face. Had he changed his mind?

Had he come to tell her that there *was* a future for them? That she could have her job back? That he'd been too hasty?

She ran a hand through her hair as she reached for the chain and slipped it into place, before gently easing the door open.

Her smile faded rapidly.

'My God,' she whispered, gazing at her visitor. She removed

the chain, opening the door, ushering the newcomer inside. 'Well, you'd better come in,' she insisted. 'You can't stand *there* all night. What the hell are you doing here?'

'That's a nice way to greet your brother,' said David Layton.

54

THE FLOWERS HAD arrived around two that afternoon. A huge bouquet of mixed blooms.

Hailey hadn't even needed to look at the card.

He'd phoned four times that day, on each occasion leaving a message with Hailey's secretary.

Would she please ring him back?

Please?

Hailey got to her feet and wandered across to the window, gazing out.

The sky threatened rain. Large banks of grey cloud were gathering menacingly.

'Speak to him. You owe him that, at least.'

He'd get the message, surely. A day or two more and the calls would stop.

Wouldn't they?

She tried to push thoughts of Adam Walker out of her mind. There were more important things to concern her.

She looked across at the bouquet.

She'd give them to Emma. Let her secretary take them home.

'At least have the decency to return his calls.'

Hailey tried to concentrate on work. Just as she'd been trying to do since arriving at the office.

She'd spoken to someone from Nicholas Barber's office. It seemed the local MP was looking forward to the charity bash in honour of SuperSounds' anniversary. The organization for it was coming along well: everything seemed to be falling into place with relative ease. Hailey was glad that she clearly hadn't lost her touch.

Not your touch – just your nerve perhaps?

What harm could it do to speak to Walker? The next time he rang, just take the call. Tell him that things had got out of control and ask him not to call again. What could be simpler?

She wondered what Rob would say if he ever found out about her liaison with Walker.

About the kissing . . . the sex?

No, it didn't count. It hadn't been sex. Not full sex. That made it OK, didn't it?

She ran a hand through her hair.

What was it if it wasn't sex? His tongue between your legs. His expert touch bringing you so close to that supreme pleasure.

Hailey turned away from the window, crossed to her desk and snatched up her jacket.

It was time to go. Time to pick up Becky. Time to get home to wait for her husband.

The phone rang.

For interminable seconds she started at it, the breath frozen in her throat.

If it's Walker, then speak to him.

Still it rang. Hailey gazed at it as if it were some kind of venomous reptile.

She reached for the receiver, noticing that her hand was quivering slightly.

This is bloody ridiculous.

'Hello,' she said, her voice a little stern.

'Mrs Gibson, I've got Trudi on the line, from Waterhole's press office,' Emma Grogan told her.

Hailey relaxed.

'Tell her I'll call her tomorrow, Emma,' Hailey said and put down the receiver.

Thank God. Now get out of the office before he does call.

She breezed through the outer office, waving a goodbye to

Emma, who was still on the line to Trudi. The secretary smiled and returned her wave. Then she cupped her hand over the mouthpiece.

'Do you want me to put those flowers in water for you?' she said, hooking a thumb in the direction of the office.

'*You* take them home if you want to,' Hailey told her.

Emma's face lit up. 'Thanks,' she said happily, and returned to her conversation with Trudi.

Hailey was already on her way to the lift.

55

SHE NEVER NOTICED him.

Only heard his voice at the last minute. Just as he reached out towards her.

Hailey spun round, startled as she heard Adam Walker close by.

'Hailey,' he said quietly.

She turned to face him.

He managed a smile. It looked almost apologetic.

'I *had* to see you,' he said. 'I wanted to speak to you.'

She didn't answer, merely stood there, the keys to the Astra still in her hand.

'Did you get my flowers?' he asked.

She nodded.

Silence.

Awkward, unwieldy silence.

They were like two strangers. Two people who had just met and were struggling for words.

Hailey knew she couldn't ignore him *this* time. Not face to face.

'I've tried calling you,' he said. 'I left messages with your secretary. I just assumed she hadn't passed them to you.'

'I've been busy,' she told him.

'I know that. I know you're busy. I just wanted to make sure you got the flowers. I couldn't call you at home. I wouldn't want your husband to get the wrong idea.' He shrugged.

Another silence.

They both began to speak simultaneously.

'Go on,' he said, smiling.

'Adam, I don't know what to say to you,' she muttered, every word a struggle.

'Look . . . what happened at my house the other day. I'm sorry, I—'

She cut him short.

'Yes, *I'm* sorry too. I think things got out of hand.' She was fiddling nervously with her car keys. 'I should never have got myself into that situation.'

He nodded.

'We all make mistakes,' he said, the understanding tone in his voice not helping her.

'I think it would be best if you didn't ring me again,' Hailey said flatly.

He looked bemused.

'And no more flowers, eh?' she continued.

'But I just wanted to say sorry. To check how you were,' he protested. 'I didn't want to embarrass you.'

'I think you got the wrong message at your place.'

'Meaning what?'

'What happened, or nearly happened, between us, it shouldn't have done.'

'You said you wanted it.'

'You picked up the wrong signals.'

'Do you blame me? You asked me to take you back to my house. *I* didn't suggest it.'

'Let's just leave it, Adam,' she snapped, turning towards her car and sliding the key into the door.

'Hailey, I'm sorry if I've done anything wrong.'

'Don't call me again, please.'

'Why are you being so hostile? *You* were the one who started it.'

'No, I didn't.'

'You invited *me* for lunch. You were the one who asked to go back to my house. You led *me* on.'

'I asked you to have lunch with me in the first place to say thanks for finding Becky. That was all. The rest of it should never have happened.'

'Nothing *did* happen,' he reminded her.

'Look, Adam, if I didn't do the job I did, you wouldn't want to know me anyway.'

'What are you talking about?'

'You couldn't make it as an artist, so you thought I could give you some help. You asked me to show some of your work to Waterhole.'

'You volunteered to do that. I never asked you.'

'You didn't want *me*,' she said scathingly. 'You wanted what I could *give* you.'

'That's not true and you know it.'

'Do I? I don't know *you*, Adam. How do I know you didn't have some ulterior motive for wanting to get close to me?'

'I can't believe you're saying this. I found your little girl, and I brought her back to you. I didn't know what *you* did for a living that day. I didn't *care*. It didn't matter then, and it doesn't matter now. That day I saw a little girl who was lost and frightened and in danger, and I helped her. I didn't expect a *reward* for finding her and bringing her back to you. I just did what any decent person would have done.'

'And I thanked you for it.'

'I appreciate that. You bought me lunch. You didn't have to – it was very kind. I thought we were becoming friends. And that's all.'

'So you're trying to tell me you never wanted anything else? You didn't want to sleep with me?'

'Hailey, you're a very attractive woman. I'd have to be stupid *not* to want to sleep with you. But that wasn't why I wanted to get to know you.'

'You knew I was married.'

'And you were the one who told *me* you were unhappy. You told me your husband had had an affair. You told me all the details of your life, and all I did was listen.'

'I've got to go,' she said sharply, pulling open the driver's door.

'At least take this,' he said, and she could see that he was holding something fairly large and square in his hand.

It was the portrait of Becky.

'I can't,' she said flatly.

'Please, Hailey. Take it for Becky. I did it for her.'

She slid behind the wheel and started the engine.

'Don't call me again, Adam,' she snapped.

'The painting,' he insisted.

'You keep it.'

'What have I done that was so wrong?' he wanted to know.

He grasped the door, as if to open it.

She glared at him and he withdrew his hand quickly.

'I'm sorry,' he said quietly. 'But please take this.' Again he pushed the painting towards her.

She shook her head.

He smiled thinly. 'OK, then,' he said quietly. 'Say hello to Becky for me, will you?'

No answer.

'Hailey. I promise I'll still remember you, even when I'm famous,' he offered, his smile fading. He swallowed hard.

'Goodbye, Adam,' she said, looking at him briefly.

He opened his mouth to respond, but then realized it was pointless. He took a step back as she guided the car away from him.

'I'm sorry,' he murmured as it moved further away.

Hailey glanced in her rear-view mirror, and saw him trudging back towards his own car.

Happy now?

She swallowed hard and pressed her foot down on the accelerator, anxious to be away from this scene of confrontation.

A little hard on him, weren't you?

She switched on the radio and turned the volume up as far as it would go.

The first drops of rain began to spatter the windscreen.

56

'FUCKING THING,' SNARLED Russell Poole, banging the fruit machine.

He stood glaring at it, while fumbling in his denim jacket pocket for some more small change. He fed in more coins and watched as the three reels spun once more.

Again nothing.

'Fucking fix,' he rasped and turned away in anger.

The Black Squirrel was busy. Both bars were full of noisy drinkers. It was one of the most popular pubs in the city centre despite its reputation. There were five or six other pubs, each with a somewhat calmer atmosphere, but Poole had always looked on this one as his local. All his mates drank here. He'd met his last two girlfriends here (fucked one of them in the Gents to be exact). The recollection brought a grin to his ravaged features.

He was twenty-seven: slightly built and with long, lank hair. His hands and most of his neck were covered in pink, puckered skin that a doctor had once told him was eczema. A scar ran from the corner of his left top lip to just above the nostril, giving him the appearance of constantly sneering.

Poole pushed his way through the mass of drinkers to the bar, downed a pint of Carlsberg, then made his way to the toilets to ease his already over-filled bladder.

The stench hit him as soon as he walked into the Gents.

'Fuck sake,' he hissed.

The other man inside glanced round from the urinal where he stood, ran appraising eyes over Poole, then continued urinating.

The doors of the three cubicles were open and Poole chose the first one.

'Dirty fucking bastard,' he grunted, looking at the filthy, excreta-filled pan. 'Don't people know how to flush toilets?'

He moved to the next cubicle.

Clean.

He smiled and bolted the door.

Poole urinated gushingly, then zipped up and sat on the cracked seat.

He slid the small plastic bag from his inside pocket and regarded it on the palm of his hand, grinning down at it.

He pulled the small bag open carefully and dipped the tip of his index finger into the powder.

The cocaine tasted cold on his tongue.

It was the only drug he dealt in that he actually used.

He never touched crack or smack, and E was for stupid fucking teenagers. Another one had died at the weekend. Taken a tab at some fucking club and died bleeding from every orifice. One less clubber, he mused, grinning. One less arsehole.

Stupid cunt – had it coming.

But he still sold them. He sold anything and everything if people wanted it. But the only stuff he'd touch himself was Charlie.

The odd joint, naturally, but otherwise he was very particular about what he shoved into his body.

Some silly fucker had asked him for acid the other week.

He'd got it, naturally. Poole prided himself on being able to deliver, no matter what the request.

Even the nitrous oxide had been easier to obtain than he'd thought. He had a contact at the local hospital.

Piece of piss.

He tipped a little of the coke onto the palm of his hand and regarded it almost lovingly.

Poole snorted the tiny pile: some of it into each nostril.

Fucking ace.

He re-sealed the bag and slipped it back into his inside pocket.

It was good shit. He only used the good stuff himself. The stuff he *sold* was chopped with washing powder, Vim and any other fucking thing. But what did *he* care. The punters paid the same price, no matter what the quality.

He flushed the toilet again and brushed his nostrils with the back of one hand.

The Gents was empty when he emerged from the cubicle.

At least he thought it was.

He never saw the hand that grabbed him around the throat.

57

Poole felt a moment of panic as he was pushed back against the cubicle door.

'Still using that shit?' a voice rasped close to his ear.

Poole found himself gazing into a face he knew.

The grip on his throat eased.

David Layton was grinning at him crookedly.

'Good job I wasn't the Old Bill,' Layton said.

'What the fuck are you doing?' Poole demanded, massaging his throat with one hand and looking at Layton warily.

'I saw you come in here. I thought I'd surprise you.'

'Well, you fucking did *that* all right. When did you get out?'

'A couple of days ago.'

Poole walked across to the row of basins on the other side of the room and washed his hands, glancing at Layton's reflection in the cracked mirror.

Layton was puffing on a cigarette.

'You don't seem very pleased to see me, Russ,' he mused. 'Something bothering you?'

'Like what?'

'Like some money you owe me.'

Poole shrugged and wiped his hands on the grubby roller-towel nearby.

'Just before I went down,' Layton reminded him, 'I helped you shift some gear. You owe me for that. Two hundred sheets.'

'I haven't got that sort of money on me, Dave.'

'Then get it,' Layton snapped. 'I need some cash.'

'You could sign on,' Poole offered, attempting a smile.

Layton regarded him contemptuously in silence.

'What are you going to do now you're out?' Poole enquired.

Layton shrugged. 'I haven't got anything lined up yet. But I'm sure something'll come along.'

'Where you staying?'

'With my sister, until I can find a place of my own.'

'She was always a cracking bit of cunt, your sister. She—'

Layton had stepped towards Poole and grabbed him by the front of his jacket, shoving him back against the sink.

'She's what?' he snarled.

'A good-looking girl,' Poole corrected himself, seeing the fury in Layton's eyes.

Layton released his grip.

'Sorry,' Poole said, swallowing hard.

'Yeah, you're right. She is a good-looking girl. Way out of your fucking league, so don't even think about it.'

'She still married?'

'No. The geezer was a twat anyway.' He flicked his cigarette butt onto the floor, where it hissed in a puddle of spilled water.

'So, are you back for good, then?' Poole wanted to know.

'I told you, I'm looking around. Testing the water, you could say.' He grinned.

'What was it like inside?'

'Same as it always is. *You've* done bird. You know the s.p.'

'I was in a remand home, not proper nick.'

'Yeah, that's right. You always *were* small-time, though, weren't you, Russ?'

'So what *do* you want from me, Dave?'

'You mean apart from my two hundred quid?'

'I'll get it for you, right?'

'I *know* you will. In the meantime you can buy me a drink. There's some business I want to talk to you about.'

58

ADAM WALKER OFTEN asked himself why he still bothered to visit his father.

It wasn't guilt that brought him regularly to the nursing home. Not his *own* guilt.

And it wasn't love.

Was it?

Why did he come here to see this shell of a man? This wrinkled effigy who looked as if all the life had been sucked from him. What did he hope to gain by it?

Adam sat opposite his father, gazing at the old man, watching as he pulled at the flesh on the back of his hand. Sometimes his lips would move, as if he was about to say something, but no words would spill forth. There would be no sound.

Just the silence.

Sometimes the old man would look at Adam. Very occasionally there would be a flicker in those glazed eyes. Adam then wondered if a miracle was about to happen: if the dementia that was slowly consuming his father's brain was about to be wiped away. Was Philip Walker about to regain his powers of thought? Would he look at his son and suddenly remember who he was?

And what he'd done to him?

Adam wondered what he might say to his father if such a miracle were ever to happen.

But it wouldn't, would it? There were no miracles left. Not for

Philip Walker anyway. His God had not so much abandoned him as simply lost interest – or so it seemed to Adam.

He had changed the water in the vase. Thrown away the dead flowers from last time, and replaced them with the new blooms he'd brought along. He'd tidied up the room – even sat for a few moments combing the thinning strands of his father's hair.

All in total silence.

Outside the room, a bird sat singing happily on one of the lower branches of a tree, its song filling the room. When it finally took off, the silence returned, thick and oppressive.

'I've got to go,' said Adam, getting to his feet.

He took a step towards his father.

The old man was still sitting up in bed, gazing blankly across the room. His expression didn't change.

Adam moved towards the door, took one last look at his father, then stepped out into the corridor.

He exhaled deeply and leant against the door, as if trying to recover his strength. Strength that felt as if it had been sucked from him during his time inside that room.

As he turned to make his way towards the reception area, he saw one of the nurses approaching him.

Adam smiled at her, but she returned the smile weakly.

'Have you got a minute?' she asked.

'What's wrong?' he wanted to know.

'Dr Simmons wants to speak to you. It's about your father.'

*

'So, why isn't he in hospital?'

Adam Walker sat forward in his chair and looked across the desk at Dr Raymond Simmons.

He was a tall, sinewy man in his late forties, with sad eyes and waxy skin.

The suit he wore was immaculately pressed and had, Walker thought, been dry-cleaned recently. Simmons took off his glasses and massaged the bridge of his nose between his thumb and forefinger.

'Mr Walker, the state your father is in, we can do as much for him here as any hospital could,' the doctor said quietly. 'There's no need to move him unless his condition worsens.'

'And is it likely to?'

'I'm afraid it's only a matter of time.'

'Renal failure,' Walker mused. 'What will happen to him?'

'His kidneys will simply stop working. Dialysis can prolong their function but . . .' He allowed the sentence to trail off.

'He's going to die,' Walker offered.

Simmons nodded. 'I'm very sorry.'

'Don't be,' Walker said flatly.

Simmons looked surprised, and met the younger man's gaze.

'It's probably a blessing in disguise,' Walker explained. 'I mean, he isn't going to get any better, is he?'

He got to his feet.

'His mind's gone,' he continued, heading towards the door. 'Now his body is decaying too. There's nothing left for him.'

'We'll do all we can, Mr Walker,' Simmons reassured him.

'I'm sure you will. How long's he got?'

'It's difficult to say. A month? Perhaps longer with the right treatment, and provided there are no more complications.'

'You know he used to be a vicar, don't you?' Walker said quietly.

Simmons nodded, looking a little perplexed.

'A man of God,' Walker continued, smiling. 'I wonder where his God is now? Sitting up there laughing at him?' He reached for the door handle. 'Thank you, Doctor.' And he was gone.

Walker headed back to his car and slid behind the wheel of the Scorpio, sitting there for a moment.

So his father was dying.

At last it was happening.

'A month? Perhaps longer.'

Walker gazed through the windscreen at Bayfield House Nursing Home.

He wondered how many more times he would have reason to return here.

'A month? Perhaps longer.'

And then what?

He'd expected to feel something akin to exultation upon hearing the news that this man who had made his life such a misery was going to die. But, no, all he felt was a kind of emptiness. And he wondered why.

Just as he wondered why a single tear rolled down his cheek.

He wiped it away almost angrily.

Don't cry for him. *He doesn't deserve your tears.*

Walker started the engine, swung the car round and guided it back down the long, tree-lined drive.

Bayfield House disappeared behind him.

59

HAILEY CLOSED HER eyes as the excited babbling around her began to grow in volume.

There was a moment of near silence. Then the screams began.

And she joined that chorus of shrieks.

She gripped the safety bar with both hands as the rollercoaster hurtled down the precipitous slope. It sped down with such incredible speed it seemed certain it must crash. But, instead, it merely shot up the next incline, its momentum carrying it onwards.

As the brightly coloured carriages began to climb, Hailey continued to cling tightly to the rail.

She, Rob and Becky sat side by side in the lead car. All three were clutching the bar. All three were yelling at the tops of their voices.

Becky was laughing, too, amused by her mother's apparent terror and also at the sheer exhilaration she felt. Rob looked across at Hailey as they prepared to speed down the next slope. He grinned broadly, reaching out quickly to touch her face before the rollercoaster went hurtling towards the bottom again.

Hailey kissed his outstretched hand, then looked down at Becky, opened her mouth and screamed again as they were catapulted earthwards.

The rumble of the wheels on the track was loud in her ears and she could feel the car vibrating beneath her as it took each curve.

Becky was loving it – just as she had loved all the other rides before it. As she'd loved the funhouse and the dodgems. She'd earlier watched Rob at the rifle range, shooting down the small metal targets. Cheering, like her mother, as each one fell. Then she'd watched him hurling small beanbags at a pyramid of tin cans. She had shouted in delighted triumph as the pyramid was shattered, hugged him when he presented her with the large fluffy panda he'd won. It sat between them now, blank eyes watching every twist and turn of the rollercoaster.

Hailey felt the wind surge through her hair, pull at her face, and, when she screamed, it rushed into her open mouth.

The feeling of exhilaration was infectious.

It had been Rob's idea to visit the funfair, which was in town for four days. He had mentioned it that lunchtime, and his suggestion had taken Hailey by surprise.

They had arrived here about four, oblivious to the threatening clouds above, all three of them determined nothing would spoil their evening out. And now, three hours later, with the whole fairground illuminated by the multicoloured lights and flashing neon of the stalls and rides, they were still enraptured by it all. As the rollercoaster reached the top of another incline, Hailey looked out over the sprawling mass of brilliant lights below. They burned in the darkness like fallen, multi-hued stars.

Up and down, the rollercoaster careened madly for another few minutes, then came to a halt. Laughing passengers spilled from the cars, to be replaced by others eager to taste the thrill.

'That was great,' said Becky, reaching up to hold Hailey's hand. 'You were scared, weren't you, Mum?'

'Petrified,' Hailey admitted, laughing.

'We'd better get home soon,' Rob said, as they walked along.

'Oh, Dad,' Becky complained.

'Dad's right,' Hailey told her. 'We have been here for a long time, haven't we?'

Becky nodded reluctantly.

'One more ride?' she said imploringly.

'We've been on all the rides there are,' Hailey insisted.

'We haven't been in *there*,' said Rob, pointing ahead of him.

The hall of mirrors bore a huge clown's face that leered down at them as if daring them to enter.

Hailey looked at the large wooden face, and thought how menacing it appeared. Not the usual benevolent visage of a clown, but something darker. The mouth looked more like a sneer than a smile.

Rob saw her slow her pace and he reached for her hand.

'What's wrong?' He smiled.

'Nothing,' she told him, squeezing his hand. 'Nothing at all.' She leant across and kissed his cheek.

'Come on,' said Becky, pulling them both towards the entrance. She ran ahead, beckoning to her parents, who sauntered along behind.

'I got lost in one of these when I was a kid,' Hailey said quietly. 'I was in there for ages before they got me out. I was terrified.'

'Well, hold my hand,' Rob told her. '*I'll* make sure you don't get lost.'

They looked at each other for brief seconds, then Becky's excited cries sent them running towards the cashier.

Rob paid the entrance fee and they walked in.

Immediately, Becky began to laugh as she was confronted by a bank of distorting mirrors that elongated and squashed her image alternately.

Hailey and Rob also stood gazing at their own warped reflections.

Oh, how appropriate.

Both of us twisted. Bent out of shape.

A little like how some marriages get.

All three of them posed before each mirror in turn, Becky's musical laughter filling the musty, wooden-floored hall. Then they moved on.

The labyrinth of mirrors seemed impenetrably confusing.

On all four sides, Hailey saw her reflection staring back at her.

Guilt on every side? Is Rob feeling the same thing?

She glanced across at him, or at his reflection, she wasn't sure which.

He seemed more intent on gazing after Becky, who was picking her way carefully through the maze ahead of them.

Hailey felt a wave a panic rising inside her.

Memories?

She looked into one mirror and saw herself as a child again. Standing alone, sobbing – lost.

When she blinked, the image vanished.

In another she saw Rob and Sandy Bennett, both naked, coupled together. Sweat pouring from their undulating bodies, pleasure etched across their faces.

Again the image disappeared when she blinked.

The image of Adam Walker loomed at her from another of the mirrors.

He was looking at her angrily. There was pain in his expression.

She looked away, but the image was still there.

Hailey felt her heart thud rapidly against her ribs.

She reached out to touch his image.

'Come on,' said Rob, touching her bottom with one hand.

Hailey spun round, her face pale.

'Are you OK?' Rob wanted to know.

She looked back at the mirror.

The vision of Walker was gone.

Hailey nodded. She leant forward and kissed her husband.

'I love you,' she whispered.

Rob looked suprised.

'I know,' he murmured. 'Even though I don't deserve it.'

'Come on.'

Becky's excited shout came from just ahead of them. 'I've found the way out,' she called.

They hurried to catch up with her.

60

'Shit,' grunted Rob as the gears of the Astra crunched.

'Do you mind,' Hailey said, slapping him gently on the thigh. 'This is *my* car you're wrecking.'

'Bloody Astras.' He grinned.

'Well, it's more reliable than yours, or we'd be in yours now instead, wouldn't we?' she said smugly. 'When are you getting it fixed?'

'It goes in for a service tomorrow. Christ knows how much that'll cost. I think the exhaust is fucked.'

'Watch your language,' Hailey said quietly, inclining her head towards the back seat.

'She's asleep,' Rob said, glancing in the rear-view mirror. 'She has been since we left the fair.'

He could see Becky safely strapped into the rear seat, the panda he had won for her still clutched in her arms. She was breathing slowly and evenly.

'I'm glad we went,' Hailey said. 'It was a good idea. Becky loved it.'

'So I do have my uses, then?'

'Sometimes.'

As he swung the Astra into the drive, Rob glanced at the dashboard clock: 7.38 p.m.

He brought the Astra to a halt next to his own Audi, peering briefly across at the other vehicle.

'Jesus Christ,' he snarled.

Hailey turned to look at him, at his angry expression.

Rob switched off the engine and swung himself out of the car.

'Rob, what is it?' she asked.

'Come and look,' he told her, standing back from the Audi to examine it.

Hailey slipped out of the passenger side and wandered around to join him.

'Oh, no,' she murmured, looking down.

Both offside tyres had been slashed.

No, that was an understatement. They had been shredded.

Huge lumps of rubber had been cut from them. The now exposed inner tubes, looking like pieces of protruding intestine, had been gouged and ripped with incredible savagery.

The Audi was listing to one side, its chassis sloping down at an angle, the car's frame resting on the offside axles.

Rob walked around the vehicle to look for more damage.

The other two tyres were untouched. He could see no harm to the bodywork itself.

In the back seat of the Astra, Becky began to stir.

'You get her inside,' Rob said wearily, 'I'll sort this out.' He walked back round and looked down at the slashed tyres, shaking his head.

Hailey lifted Becky from the rear seat of the Astra and carried her towards the front door.

The little girl stirred and opened her eyes.

Hailey put her down as she fumbled for her front door key.

Becky stood motionless, the panda still held firmly in her grip.

'Soon be in bed, darling,' said Hailey, pushing the key into the lock.

It was as she did she first noticed the smell.

Foul, noxious – and horribly familiar.

It clogged her nostrils as she eased the front door open, the sound of the alarm soon filling her ears.

Hailey thought she was going to vomit.

She put out a hand to hold Becky back, not wanting her to step into the hallway.

The vile smell was even stronger now, and Hailey saw why.

She put one hand to her face, covering her nose and mouth.

The dog excrement had been loosely wrapped in clingfilm, then pushed through the letterbox. The several reeking parcels had burst open to spill their fetid load all over the carpet. There were half a dozen of the rancid packages lying all around.

Hailey stared at them with disgust, the stench filling her nostrils.

She felt her stomach contract.

The alarm continued to ring.

*

'Fucking kids,' snarled Rob, gazing at the ceiling.

Beside him, Hailey rolled over in bed and moved closer to him.

'I'd like to get my hand on the little bastards who did it,' Rob continued.

'Why would kids do something like that?' she wanted to know.

'They probably thought it was funny. Ha-bloody-ha. Those tyres are going to cost me seventy quid apiece. Still, I suppose it could have been worse. At least they didn't break into the car.'

Hailey nodded slowly.

'Kids,' she murmured distractedly.

She hoped he was right.

61

CAROLINE HACKET GAZED at the screen of the word processor, then down at her fingers as they rested on the keyboard.

She reread the words on the screen, then leaned back in her chair, stretching.

There were several books spread out on the desk around her.

Pieces of paper, too, with notes scribbled in biro and pencil.

She worked in one of the spare bedrooms, as she always had done. The room looked out onto her back garden, but her desk was arranged so that she had her back to the view. Some days she found it difficult enough to work anyway, without the distraction of something to look at.

It had been easier in the office when she'd been a journalist. She had always found the seething chaos around her there more conducive to work than the silence and loneliness of this small bedroom. Strange, she thought, how easy it had been to shut herself away mentally in the middle of a newspaper office, surrounded by others of like mind. Easier than this. Easier than the silence she had now.

It was a peculiar paradox. But, she reasoned, not the only one in her life.

She got up from the WP and headed for the stairs. She couldn't think straight anyway. Perhaps a coffee would help. Some caffeine might kickstart her creative juices. She smiled to herself as she reached the bottom of the stairs.

In the kitchen she flicked on the small music centre that was perched on top of the fridge. The CD began to fill the room with the strains of Celine Dion.

During a break between tracks she heard the doorbell.

Caroline hesitated. She wondered for a second if she should ignore it. Her concentration was wavering enough already, without further interruption.

In the end she decided to see who was calling.

In the kitchen the kettle began to boil.

She pulled open the front door.

Adam Walker smiled at her.

She returned the smile.

'I hope I'm not disturbing you,' he said.

'Not at all. I was having a lousy day anyway. Come in.'

He hesitated.

'The kettle's just boiled,' she told him. 'Can I tempt you to a coffee. I was making one anyway.'

'Thanks.'

He followed her through into the kitchen.

'It's a nice house,' he told her, seating himself on one of the high stools beside the breakfast bar.

She smiled again and pushed a coffee mug towards him.

'Sugar there,' she informed him, nodding towards a bowl close by.

There was a brief silence, finally broken by Caroline.

'If it's any consolation, Adam, I think Hailey was wrong.'

He looked puzzled.

'What are you talking about?' he wanted to know.

'She told me what happened. Said you'd been phoning her. I know she hasn't returned your calls. So, if it's any consolation, I think she's wrong. I told her she should at least speak to you.'

'What else did she tell you?'

Caroline shrugged. 'What happened between you at your house,' she explained.

Walker sipped his coffee, his gaze never leaving her.

'I didn't force her into anything,' he said. 'I don't care what she said to you.'

'Look, I'm on *your* side.'

She sat down beside her.

'Then help me,' Walker said.

'How?'

'Get her to speak to me.'

'She won't listen to me, Adam.'

'You're her best friend, aren't you?'

She gazed at him for a moment, then looked away almost guiltily.

'What do you want from her?' Caroline asked.

'I just want her to listen. All I wanted to do was apologize for what happened. I didn't intend all that to happen. I thought it was what Hailey wanted. She was the one who was always going on about what a bad marriage she had. I wanted to be her friend. I never wanted to start an affair with her.'

'Not even if she was willing?'

He smiled. 'Well, maybe.'

They both laughed.

'I just don't know why she's become so hostile,' he said finally. He then told Caroline about their meeting in the car park of SuperSounds.

She listened intently.

'Well, *I* wouldn't have turned you down,' she said, smiling.

'I don't need your pity, Caroline,' he replied flatly.

'I'm not giving it.' She looked directly into his eyes.

'I shouldn't have come here,' he sighed. 'This isn't your problem. I just thought that if you spoke to her, told her how I felt, then she might call me back. That's all I want her to do. It sounds pathetic, doesn't it?'

'And if she *does* call you back, what do you think she's going to say? "Everything's all right, Adam. Sorry I wouldn't speak to you. Tell you what, let's go ahead and *have* that affair." Is *that* what you want her to say?'

He didn't speak.

'Let it go, Adam,' Caroline said quietly. 'I don't normally give advice, and if you told me to mind my own business I wouldn't blame you, but for *your* sake forget about Hailey.'

'It's not that easy.'

'Oh, come on, you'd only known her for a couple of weeks. It's not like you were life-long friends, is it?'

Walker looked at her, his eyes narrowing slightly, and Caroline saw something behind those eyes.

Something like rage.

It vanished as rapidly as it had appeared.

A smile again creased his features.

'You're right,' he said finally, slipping from the stool. 'But when you see her again, tell her I said hello and tell her I understand.' He put down the mug. 'Thanks for the coffee.'

'Adam, wait. I was just about to have some lunch. Nothing fancy: something out of the microwave. If you'd like to join me . . .' She allowed the sentence to trail off.

'Thanks,' he said, still smiling. 'But I've taken up enough of your time. Besides, I'm stopping you working, aren't I?'

'Any excuse is welcome.' She grinned.

'How's the new book coming along?'

'You don't want to know.'

'No, you're wrong. I *do* want to know. I really respect what you do. And, by the way, I finished your other book. I thought they were both excellent.'

'Thanks very much. Why don't you tell me how brilliant I am over lunch?' She pointed towards the microwave.

They laughed and Walker sat down again.

62

Hailey glanced at the dashboard clock as she drove, guiding the Astra with one hand, holding the mobile phone with the other.

She finished her conversation with Nicholas Barber, confirming their meeting for the following day. The local MP seemed a little less pretentious and self-important than some she had encountered, but nevertheless Hailey wasn't relishing the meeting. Still, she reasoned, it couldn't be any worse than her encounter with Waterhole.

They were to meet for lunch the following day to discuss final details of the charity concert that Barber was to attend.

He said his secretary would be on hand to take notes. Hailey assured him this would be unnecessary, but, despite her protestations, he insisted. She thanked him for his time and switched off the mobile, swinging the Astra around a corner.

Up ahead she could see her home.

There was over an hour before she had to pick Becky up. The little girl was playing a game of rounders after school. Hailey decided she had time to shower and change before she set out.

She was pleased with the way preparations for the charity gig were progressing. Jim Marsh too was delighted with her work.

Even Rob had been asking her about it. His interest seemed genuine, too, she mused.

They had gone through too much during the past year for

everything to return to normal soon, but they were making more progress, she felt. They had agreed to suspend their Relate counselling sessions for a time.

Just see how things go.

Hailey smiled to herself.

And there'd been no further calls from Adam Walker.

No calls. No flowers.

No contact.

Just as well.

She had been stupid. She knew that. But at least things hadn't got out of hand.

Not quite.

She shuddered when she thought how easily the pair of them could have become involved.

How easily *she* could have become involved with this man whom she hardly knew, but felt she understood so well. And who understood her.

Better to have ended it when she did.

She brought the car to a halt outside the house and sat behind the wheel for a moment, glancing up at the sky – at the dark clouds gathering.

With a sigh she slid from behind the wheel, picked up her briefcase and headed for the front door, fumbling in her jacket pocket for her keys.

Rob had called her at work that afternoon to say that he'd be coming home late. Something about having to meet a customer for a drink. He and Frank Burnside were going along to meet the man together.

When she had asked him what time he'd be back, it had taken a supreme effort not to ask him if it was really Burnside whom he was going with. If it was really a customer he was meeting.

The spectre of Sandy Bennett still remained, like the dying vestiges of a bad dream.

In the end she hadn't asked. He promised her he'd be home around seven, and she'd believed him.

Perhaps she'd ring the pub later.

Just in case.

Hailey selected the front door key from the others on her chain and pushed it into the lock, then stepped into the hall.

Silence.

She frowned.

Why wasn't the alarm going off?

She crossed to the key-pad and opened its plastic flap.

She had set it when she left that morning – she was sure she had.

Perhaps there was some kind of fault.

She'd check it now and call the maintenance firm if necessary.

She pressed the reset keys.

Nothing.

She glanced up.

The sensor that normally flickered red in the top right-hand corner of the ceiling was dead.

The alarm wasn't working.

She wandered into the kitchen to retrieve the alarm-system maintenance firm's business card from the noticeboard.

As she stepped into the room she felt a draught. It was coming from the window over the sink.

Hailey swallowed hard as she moved closer.

The window was slightly ajar.

And in that split second she knew why. Just as she knew why the alarm wasn't working. The realization set her heart hammering.

Whoever had broken into their house had disabled the alarm first.

63

FOR INTERMINABLE SECONDS, Hailey stood motionless in the centre of the kitchen.

The silence seemed to crowd in on her until the only thing she could hear was the rushing of blood in her ears.

She swallowed hard and looked around.

There didn't appear to be anything missing. And if someone had broken into the house, they had been very careful. Even the crockery on the draining board close to the open window didn't seem to have been disturbed.

Hailey moved back into the hall.

She glanced across at the phone.

Call the police. Do it now!

Instead she passed through into the sitting room, the breath now catching in her throat.

What if the intruder was still inside the house?

Intruder?

Even the *word* frightened her.

There was so much to steal.

TV. Video. Stereo.

She pushed open the sitting-room door.

It was as neat and tidy as it had been when she'd left earlier in the day.

The television still occupied its usual position in one corner of the room. The VCR was still beneath it. Untouched.

Hailey took a couple of steps inside the room, glancing round to make an inventory of their other possessions.

Nothing was missing.

Except . . .

There was something, but she couldn't quite work what it was.

Something was missing, but . . .

She noticed some mud on the carpet close to the sofa.

Brought in on the shoes of the intruder?

She looked around the room again.

Call the police. For Christ's sake, call the police!

Someone had definitely been inside the room, and yet it remained undisturbed.

She spun round, passed through the hall and began climbing the stairs, cursing every creaky one.

Slowly she made her way towards the landing, ears alert for the slightest sound from above.

If the intruder was still inside the house . . .

Above her, a floorboard groaned protestingly.

Didn't it?

She froze, straining her ears.

Outside, the wind was gathering ferocity as it swept around the house.

Perhaps it hadn't been a floorboard she'd heard. It must be some trick of that violent wind.

Of her mind?

Hailey waited a moment longer, then began to climb the last few steps to the landing.

When she reached it, she stopped again. She glanced at the four firmly closed doors that confronted her.

More mud on the carpet close to one of the guest rooms.

She remained motionless.

Hailey was having trouble controlling her own breathing now.

Which room first?

She crossed to the guest room which had mud trodden into the carpet outside it.

She waited a moment, then pushed the door open.

It swung back on its hinges and she peered in.

Everything in its place. Untouched.

Nothing stolen.

She quickly checked the second guest room.

Also nothing missing.

Hailey moved towards the master bedroom she and Rob slept in, moving as quietly as she could across the groaning floorboards of the landing.

She pushed the door gently and stepped inside.

More mud inside this room, trodden into the thick-pile carpet.

Hailey tried to swallow, but her throat was dry.

Then she saw the heads.

64

One on each pillow.

Hailey moved further round the room, eyes riveted on the double bed.

She put her hand on the wall, as if to support herself, as she approached the bed.

The heads had been propped up carefully so that, as Hailey advanced towards them, their sightless eyes held her in an unblinking gaze.

One with flowing black hair; the other with long blonde hair.

Had she been able to think straight, she may well have realized which of Becky's dolls they had been taken from. As it was, all she could do was stare down at them.

For fleeting seconds she wondered if this was some kind of bizarre joke perpetrated by Becky herself, but the thought disappeared almost instantly.

This was no joke.

There was real malice in this act.

Becky would never have . . .

Becky?

Hailey turned and ran into her daughter's room.

Like the other rooms in the house, it appeared relatively undisturbed. Apart from the toys.

Three of her dolls heads had been removed. Pulled free. Two

of them were now in Hailey's own bed. The third, she saw immediately, lay on the pillow of her daughter's bed.

Three tiny plastic bodies lay together on the floor close by.

Hailey picked one up and it made a mechanical crying sound.

She dropped the doll and sat down on the edge of Becky's bed.

Now what?

She sat trembling for what seemed like a long time, her heart hammering inside her chest.

Now *will you call the police?*

Hailey sat a moment longer, then wandered back into her own bedroom. She retrieved the two dolls' heads and returned to Becky's room, where she carefully restored the small mannequins to their correct appearance by replacing the heads of each. The blank eyes gazed at her as if they were wondering what she was doing. When all three were repaired, Hailey replaced the dolls in their usual position.

Everything in its place.

The fear she had felt before had been replaced by a kind of foreboding as she moved around the house in a trance-like state.

She had already made up her mind she wouldn't tell Rob what she'd found today.

She would tell him that the burglar alarm needed fixing. That was all.

And there was certainly no need for the police.

Hailey changed into jeans and a T-shirt, stepped into ankle boots, and made her way back downstairs.

The dried mud on the landing and in the bedroom would brush off later.

No need for Rob to know.

Nothing had been taken. Nothing had been damaged.

Whoever had broken in had done it not for gain, but merely to prove a point. And that point had been admirably illustrated. The intruder had got in easily once. A second time would be a formality.

Hailey checked her watch.

Another forty minutes before she had to collect Becky from school.

She had time.

There was something she must do.

65

'WHAT WAS ADAM Walker doing *here*?'

Hailey Gibson looked at Caroline Hacket with a curious mixture of anger and bemusement.

'It's a free country, Hailey,' Caroline told her.

'But what did he want?' Hailey demanded.

Caroline sighed.

'He came to talk,' she said quietly. 'Mostly about *you*, if it makes you feel any better. You hurt him, Hailey.'

'Well, I'm so sorry about that.'

'You should be.'

'What bullshit has he been giving you, Caroline?'

'You led him on. *I* told you that. He just wanted to know why you wouldn't talk to him.'

'I *did* talk to him. I told him to keep away from me.'

'Perhaps it was the *way* you did it he didn't like.'

'So you're on *his* side now?'

'Don't be so bloody ridiculous. It isn't a matter of sides.'

'It sounds as if it is. Why did he come here in the first place?'

'I told you. He needed someone to talk to.'

'So you obliged? Very thoughtful. I suppose the fact that you fancy him has got nothing to do with it?'

'He came here. We talked. About you. About my books. He stayed for lunch. That was it. And to be perfectly honest, Hailey, it's none of your business whom I have lunch with. Just because you don't want to speak to him any more doesn't mean *I* have to ignore him.'

'What time did he leave?'

'About half-past two. Why?'

Hailey exhaled deeply.

'I think he might have broken into the house this afternoon,' she said finally.

'*What?*' Caroline asked, a slight smile on her lips. 'Why the hell would he want to do that?'

'Revenge.'

'And what did he take?'

'Nothing. But he was in our bedroom *and* in Becky's.'

'Was any damage done?'

Hailey shook her head.

'You can't accuse Adam of something like that,' said Caroline. 'Not without proof. What sort of man do you think he is?'

'He was angry with me for not speaking to him.'

'I don't blame him, but that was no reason for him to break into your house.'

'I think it gave him *every* reason.'

'Then why didn't he steal something – ransack the place?'

'He wanted to show me he could get into the house any time he wanted to.'

'And what do you think he's going to do if he *does* break in again? Murder you all in your beds?'

'You don't know *what* he might do.'

'Be careful, Hailey. Your paranoia's showing.'

'Don't patronize me, Caroline,' Hailey snapped. 'I know what I saw.'

'What *did* you see? Just let me refresh your memory. You say Adam Walker broke into your house, but he took nothing and he damaged nothing, right? Where is your proof that it was him?'

'Who else would do something like that?'

'Have you told Rob yet?'

'I'm going to sort this out myself. I'm going round there tomorrow to speak to Adam and tell him to stop what he's doing.'

'You've got no proof he's doing *anything*,' Caroline reminded her.

'Why are you defending him?'

'Because you're making him a scapegoat for your own guilt.'

'What guilt?' rasped Hailey. 'Nothing happened between us.'

Caroline regarded her impassively.

'Did you fuck him while he was here?' Hailey wanted to know.

'What difference does it make if I did or not? *You* don't care about him. *Do* you?'

Hailey looked away from her.

'Do you?' Caroline persisted.

'I don't want him in my life,' Hailey said flatly.

'Good. Then leave him alone.'

'He's the one pestering *me*. Sending flowers, phoning all the bloody time, trying to speak to me. I didn't ask him for that. I don't know why *you* have to get involved with him.'

'I like him.'

'I *know* that.'

'It's *my* life, Hailey. If you can't cope with it, I'm sorry.'

The two women gazed at each other for a moment longer, then Hailey reached for her car keys.

'I'd better go,' she said brusquely.

'Yes,' Caroline added quietly. 'I think that might be best.'

She heard the front door slam as her friend left, followed moments later by the sound of the Astra's engine.

Caroline waited a moment, then crossed to the phone.

66

'AM I BORING you, Miss Gibson?'

Hailey looked directly at Nicholas Barber and saw a look of mild irritation on his face.

'I'm sorry, what did you say?' she asked, forcing a smile and shifting uncomfortably in her chair. She swallowed hard, aware that the MP's gaze had settled on her unwaveringly.

At other tables in the restaurant, people chatted amiably, and the babble of their conversation mingled with the chinking of cutlery on crockery. The odd loud laugh punctuated the background hubbub.

Come on, get a grip.

'Your attention seemed to be wandering,' said Barber. 'I realize that's something of an occupational hazard in *my* position. People don't exactly tend to hang on my every word.'

She met the MP's stare and ran a hand through her hair.

Barber pushed a spoonful of crème brulée into his mouth.

He was a narrow-shouldered individual with pinched features and enough grey hair to suggest that he lied about his age. Hailey had figured him for mid-fifties, but he insisted he was yet to reach the half-century. But then again, she reasoned, he was a politician. Why should he be truthful about his age when he spent his life lying about everything else?

'I *was* listening,' Hailey assured him. 'There's so much to think about, though. The organization behind this gig is incredible.'

'Well, fortunately, that's *your* problem not mine, Miss Gibson.'

'Mrs Gibson,' she corrected him.

It was Barber's turn to look bemused.

'So, how many guest passes will you want for the gig, Mr Barber?' Hailey said finally.

'I think half a dozen should cover it.'

'Well, we are trying to limit them to two per person, it being a charity event.'

Barber shook his head. 'And how many are the pop group themselves getting?' he wanted to know.

'I'm not sure yet. That side of it is being handled by their record company. And it is *their* gig after all.'

'I was under the impression this was Jim Marsh's event.'

'There wouldn't *be* an event without Waterhole,' Hailey reminded him.

Barber sat back in his seat, dabbing at the corners of his mouth with his napkin.

'I've known Jim Marsh for years,' he said. 'I knew him when he didn't have a pot to piss in.'

Hailey tried to hide her surprise at the MP's words.

'I was a local councillor and he was running a business with just two people working for him,' Barber said. 'Things have changed for both of us, Mrs Gibson. He's a multi-millionaire employing eighty people in this town alone. He's created jobs, and that's good for the community. I've done my bit, too. I've been MP for this borough for the last fifteen years. I've served it well. It's flourished, and I like to think that people like myself and Jim Marsh can claim some responsibility for its vibrancy.'

Pompous bastard.

Hailey sipped her cappuccino.

'I'm sure everyone who lives here is grateful to you, Mr Barber,' she said, barely able to hide her sarcasm.

All she wanted to do was get away from the rambling sod. She had other things on her mind.

Lunch had taken an eternity, or so it seemed. More than once she'd chanced a surreptitious glance at her watch.

'Yes, this concert will be good for the town,' Barber decided. 'It'll bring more money in. My family are looking forward to it, so I wouldn't want to disappoint them.' He smiled and leant forward. 'Do *you* have family?'

She told him about Rob and Becky.

'And they'll be attending the concert, will they?' Barber wanted to know.

'Yes.'

'And the party afterwards?'

Hailey nodded.

'How many guests will be at the party?' Barber enquired.

'Fifty or sixty. We're running competitions in a number of music magazines too, so there'll be four winners there to meet the band.'

'A pop group *and* a Member of Parliament,' Barber said smugly. 'It should be a night to remember for them.'

'I'm sure it will be,' Hailey said in her most convincingly reverential tone.

They won't even know who you are.

'So, you'll see that I have all the passes I need?' Barber persisted.

Hailey nodded resignedly.

Anything. Just let me out of here.

It was Barber's turn to check his watch.

'Well, I've just got time for a brandy,' he smiled. 'This is going on your expense account, I trust?'

Hailey ordered him his drink and herself another coffee.

The restaurant was beginning to empty. There were only three or four tables still occupied. Elsewhere, the staff were busy clearing up, some of them glancing over in the direction of Hailey and Barber.

'Here's to a successful concert,' said the MP, raising his glass.

Hailey smiled dutifully. Again she looked fleetingly at her watch.

There were things she had to do.

One in particular.

67

Hailey parked the Astra about a hundred yards from Adam Walker's house and sat behind the wheel motionless.

The street was relatively empty of vehicles and, if Walker was home, she didn't want him to see her. Not just yet.

During the drive she had gone over in her mind what she would say to him. Rehearsed her part of the conversation until she knew it by heart. Decided what she was going to say to him, and how. She wasn't going to lose her temper. She wasn't going to raise her voice. She just wanted to speak to him.

If you'd spoken to him in the beginning, then none of this would have happened.

She sucked in a deep breath, held it, then exhaled slowly.

Her heart was thudding insistently in her chest.

Afraid to face him?

She swung herself out of the car and locked it, checking her reflection in the window before she set off towards his house.

Be firm, not rude. Just firm.

Her heels clicked on the pavement as she walked. The only sound, it seemed, in the stillness of the thoroughfare.

There were two or three birds singing in the trees that lined the street, but apart from that she seemed to be alone.

Hailey paused at the entrance to the short driveway that led to Walker's house, gazing at the dwelling for long moments before finally heading towards the front door.

Keep calm.

Walker's Scorpio wasn't in the drive.

It could be in the garage, she reasoned.

He was probably in.

Watching you from one of the windows. Waiting for you.

She reached the front door, hesitated a minute, then rang the doorbell.

Her heart was beating even faster now.

Why are you concerned? He's the one in the wrong. He's the one who should be apologizing for what he's done. The dog shit through the letterbox, the slashed tyres on Rob's car, the break-in. He should be grateful you didn't call the police.

Hailey took a step back and looked up at the first-floor windows.

No sign of movement behind the curtains.

Perhaps he *wasn't* home.

And if he's not? How many times do you come back?

She rang the bell again.

Still no answer.

Hailey crossed to the bay window, cupped her hands around her eyes and peered through the glass.

She could see very little.

The path led on to a wooden gate at one side. This obviously led to the back of the house.

She saw a latch on the gate and lifted it, pushing against the weathered wood.

The gate didn't budge.

Hailey muttered under her breath and pushed harder.

The gate swung open and she almost overbalanced.

A narrow path continued down the side of the house, flanked on the left by some out-of-control privet hedge that also acted as a barrier between Walker's house and the dwelling next door.

Hailey moved slowly along the path, pieces of untrimmed privet scratching at her clothes and face. She emerged into the back garden.

For a moment she stood still, remembering the last time she had been here at Walker's house.

Remembering it because you enjoyed it?

She crossed to the back door and knocked.

No answer.

Hailey peered through various windows, but saw nothing. If Walker *was* inside, then he had no desire to speak to her.

Because he had something to hide? Because he was ashamed?

She returned to the back door and twisted the handle.

Locked.

In frustration, she banged again, harder this time. Only silence.

Hailey murmured something angrily and headed back up the path to the side of the house.

The gate had swung shut.

She wrenched it open.

The figure before her seemed to appear from nowhere.

68

Hailey barely managed to suppress a scream.

She took a step back, colliding with the gate.

The woman standing there looked in her late fifties: pudgy-faced and dressed in a blue cardigan and brown slacks. She seemed as surprised as Hailey by this sudden confrontation, and she too stepped back.

'Sorry,' Hailey said breathlessly. 'You scared me.'

The woman eyed her appraisingly for a moment, then managed a smile.

'I didn't mean to,' she said and Hailey heard a slight Northern lilt in her accent. 'Only I saw you arrive and I was coming over to tell you that Mr Walker's out. I wasn't being nosy, you understand, but we've had a few burglaries in the area, so we all keep an eye out. We've got this neighbourhood-watch thing – very good idea. I thought I remembered seeing *you* here with Adam once before. That's why I came over. I didn't want to leave you hanging around. I don't think Adam would be too happy if he came back and found his girlfriend standing out on the doorstep, would he?'

'No,' said Hailey softly. 'He probably wouldn't.'

His girlfriend? What the hell had he been saying?

'I suppose you were trying to surprise him,' the woman said.

Hailey nodded.

'We live next door,' the woman added, motioning towards the house on the left.

She paused a moment longer, then turned to leave.

'How well do you know, Mr Walker – Adam?' Hailey said, as if anxious that the woman should remain.

'Well, he keeps himself to himself mostly. People do around here, don't they? My husband's always laughing at me for saying that. You know, that Northerners are more friendly than Southerners.' She grinned. 'We've lived here for more than forty years. We've seen lots of people come and go. We moved down here in 1949 – no, I tell a lie, 1950.'

'Do you know Adam's family?' said Hailey, interrupting her musings.

'Well, like I said, everyone minds their own business around here, but we used to speak to his father quite regularly. A very nice man. It's a terrible shame he's ill.'

'What about his mother?'

The neighbour looked away from Hailey and crossed her arms.

'I don't agree with what she did,' said the woman indignantly. 'Running around with another man. And the worst thing is, she made no attempt to hide it. I mean, you don't do things like that when you're married, do you?'

No, you don't, do you?

Hailey shook her head slowly.

'And married to a vicar as well,' the woman continued. 'It's a disgrace. I felt for Adam, poor little chap. I think he was only six or seven at the time. It's always the kiddies who suffer when marriages break up, isn't it?'

Hailey nodded almost imperceptibly.

'Mind you, his father did a good job of bringing him up alone. It's not easy for a man on his own, is it? Especially not a man in *his* position. But he can be proud of what he's done. Adam is a lovely lad, but then you don't need *me* to tell you.'

She laughed warmly.

'Did you see much of the brother and sister before they left home?'

The woman looked vague. 'Whose?' she asked.

'Adam's. He's got a brother and a sister, he told me.'

'Well, if he has he's done a good job of keeping that quiet.' The woman smiled.

'The sister apparently had a small child, a boy. Adam said the boy was killed in an accident about a year ago. You *must* have seen them about.'

'I think you've got your wires crossed somewhere, love. Adam never had a brother or a sister. He's an only child.'

69

SHE COULDN'T SLEEP.

Despite the fact that Hailey could barely keep her eyes open, the merciful oblivion of sleep still eluded her.

She sat up, exhaling deeply. Thoughts whirled around inside her head like some kind of emotional twister.

Walker was an only child.

Hailey ran a hand through her hair.

There had been no terrible hit-and-run accident involving his nephew, because he didn't have one.

What the hell was going on!

'You OK?'

She looked across to see that Rob was lying on his side looking at her.

'Yeah,' she lied, 'I'm fine.'

He raised one eyebrow.

'All right,' Hailey confessed, 'I'm not.'

'Do you want to talk about it? Is it *me?*'

She almost laughed.

'For the first time in ages, no,' she said, and now Rob smiled too.

He reached across and held her hand.

Tell him the truth.

She swallowed hard.

But what is the truth?

'It's work,' she told him, lying back on her pillow and gazing straight ahead. 'As the gig gets closer, everyone's more tense. The organization is a bloody nightmare. Trying to make sure everyone's got what they want. Making sure no one's toes are stepped on. Dealing with so many fucking egos.'

'It's what you wanted.'

'I know, and I don't regret going back, but things are starting to get a bit frayed around the edges at the moment, that's all. The gig's in two weeks. I just wish it was all over.'

'And?'

She looked at him. 'And what?' she wanted to know.

'What *else* is bothering you?'

'Nothing. Really, Rob. I'd tell you if there was.'

Liar.

'Are you sure it's not me?' he enquired. 'More of *those* thoughts about what happened with me and Sandy?'

'I think about it from time to time. I'd be a liar if I said I didn't. And it's going to be a long time before I ever completely forgive you, Rob. But this time it *isn't* you that's bothering me.'

'Thanks for that vote of confidence,' he said, swinging himself out of bed.

She watched as he padded towards the bathroom, pausing by one of the windows, peering out.

'What is it?' she asked, seeing him cup his hands around his eyes, squinting into the gloom.

'I'm not sure,' he murmured.

Hailey also got out of bed, joining him at the window.

He snaked an arm around her waist.

'I thought I saw something move,' he whispered. 'Down in the garden. Over by the bushes.'

At the bottom of their garden, a thick growth of wild blackberry and gorse bushes separated their property from the one adjacent. In the blackness of the night it was almost impossible to pick out shapes.

'Probably a cat,' Hailey said, hoping she was right.

'Yeah, probably,' Rob echoed.

He turned to kiss her on the cheek, then they both squinted through the gloom once more, watching for any signs of movement. At that moment, the security alarm went off.

70

HAILEY'S BREATH FROZE in her lungs as the deafening explosion of sound ripped through the night.

'Shit,' hissed Rob, his voice barely audible above the shrill two-tone alarm.

He ran to his side of the bed and pulled on a pair of jogging bottoms, then he slid his hand beneath the bed and pulled out the baseball bat he kept there.

Protection?

Hailey pulled on a long T-shirt, her hands shaking as she draped it over her head.

'Mum.'

She heard Becky cry out from her room, and Hailey hurried off to be with her daughter.

Rob was already advancing across the landing, the bat held in one hand.

'Rob, don't go down there,' Hailey called to him as he paused at the top of the stairs.

'Just call the police,' he shouted back, and she realized that these words were as much for the benefit of whoever else might be inside their house as for her. Somewhere in the back of her mind she remembered reading something in a magazine advising that if you suspected burglars had broken in, you make as much noise as possible. Frighten them off.

Frighten them off? That was a fucking laugh.

Hailey's heart was hammering madly against her ribs as she

entered Becky's room to find the little girl sitting up in bed, arms outstretched. Hailey swept her up and held her tightly.

'It's all right, babe,' she said, wishing she believed that.

Becky clung tightly to her mother, the sound of the alarm still screaming in her ears.

'Rob, be careful,' Hailey called, watching as her husband still peered over the balustrade, trying to see into the gloom of the hallway below.

If he heard her, he didn't acknowledge her. She watched as he descended the stairs quickly.

'What's happening, Mum?' Becky blurted.

Hailey held her more tightly. 'It's all right,' she said again. 'The alarm's gone wrong. Dad's going to fix it.'

She heard Rob reach the bottom of the stairs.

He looked at each of the closed doors facing him in turn, then reached for the alarm control-pad, jabbed in the numbers and silenced it.

The silence seemed worse than the constant ringing.

He could hear his own blood rushing in his ears.

Rob looked at the panel and noticed that one of the blood-red zone-lights was flashing.

Zone Four.

Wherever the fuck *that* was.

Each of the rooms bore a different zone number, but he couldn't remember which was which.

Zone Four?

Kitchen? Sitting room? Dining room? Study?

He would have to check them all.

He moved to the sitting-room door first, rested his hand on the handle, then shoved it open, simultaneously slapping at the light switches.

The room was instantly illuminated.

Rob stepped inside. He hefted the bat before him.

If you're in here, you fucker, I'll beat your lousy fucking brains out.

The room was empty. Nothing looked disturbed.

He headed across the hall towards the study.

Again he pushed the door open. Again he snapped on the lights.

Again there was nothing.

Dining room or kitchen next?

If it was the kitchen, then the intruder would have had time either to escape the same way he'd entered, or to have armed himself with any number of implements.

Knife? Carving fork? Cleaver?

Rob held the bat with both hands as he approached the door, pausing a moment, trying to slow his breathing as much as anything.

He threw open the door and hit the light switch.

The fluorescents in the ceiling sputtered into life, for fleeting seconds their cold stroboscopic glare faltering.

Rob gripped the bat tightly and advanced into the room.

Empty, too.

That only left the dining room.

'All right, you cunt,' he said at the top of his voice, one hand on the door.

He shoved it open.

Slapped the lights on.

Nothing.

Rob swallowed hard and lowered the bat, then he wandered slowly back across the hall, past the open doors of rooms now bathed in light.

From upstairs he heard Hailey call his name.

'It's clear,' he told her, wiping perspiration from his brow with a trembling hand. He was no hero – he would be the first to admit it.

'The alarm must be faulty,' Hailey heard him say.

Like it was the other day?

'Who was Dad shouting at?' Becky wanted to know.

'Just the alarm,' Hailey said, smiling. 'You know how he gets sometimes. It's OK now.'

She herself closed her eyes tightly as she heard doors downstairs being shut.

'Did you check the downstairs bathroom?' Hailey called.

She heard him open a door.

Then she heard his grunt of pain.

'Rob,' Hailey shouted.

Silence.

'Rob!' she yelled again, her eyes bulging wildly.

She got to her feet and moved towards the landing.

'Mum.'

Becky was climbing out of bed, following her.

'No, stay there, babe,' Hailey said, her mouth dry, her voice cracking.

'Rob,' she shouted again, moving towards the doorway of Becky's room.

She heard another groan of pain. Louder this time.

Then she heard footsteps on the stairs.

Uncontrollable panic seized Hailey, and for brief seconds she considered slamming Becky's door and trying to haul the chest of drawers across to block the path of any intruder.

She daren't even think about what had been done to Rob down there.

What had . . .?

Rob appeared halfway up the stairs, his face creased with pain, his eyes narrowed.

'Stubbed my bloody toe on the bathroom door,' he said.

Hailey wanted to laugh with relief. Wanted to shriek hysterically that it didn't matter. So what if he'd stubbed his toe? At least he was all right. Their house hadn't been broken into.

'The alarm must be playing up,' Rob said. 'Or a spider crawled across one of the sensors, or something. That would set it off.

They're pretty sensitive those things.' He was still holding the baseball bat. 'I've reset it anyway.'

'Can we go back to sleep now, Mum?' Becky wanted to know.

'Yes,' Hailey said, stroking her daughter's hair. 'Yes, we can.'

71

She replaced the mobile phone and sat staring at it for a moment.

Hailey rubbed her eyes. She'd felt tired all day. A combination of precious little sleep the night before and a steadily growing feeling of something akin to depression.

Time for a wallow in self-pity?

She felt as if she carried the weight of the world on her shoulders – a weight that was growing by the day. Hailey hadn't felt this down since she'd first discovered Rob's affair.

Rob's affair?

Pressures of work?

Fear?

Was that the newest burden she carried?

Did fear feel like a crushing weight on your mind and soul?

She had received no phone calls from Adam Walker for more than a week now. But the knowledge that he was responsible for slashing the tyres of Rob's car, for the dog excrement . . .

The knowledge that he'd broken into their house.

It was an assumption, nothing more. There was no proof that was Walker.

She started the car.

The trip to his house the previous day had done little to allay her

(*fear. It seemed to be the most apt description*)

concerns about the man.

Why had he lied to her about his family?

If the sister and brother were inventions, then how much more of what he'd told her was fantasy?

The abuse?

Thoughts whirled around inside her head as she drove.

It should take less than fifteen minutes to reach Becky's school. She had phoned Caroline Hacket earlier in the day and told her she'd do the run herself.

Caroline?

As long as *she* was involved with Walker, it kept him in the picture.

Kept him around.

Hailey exhaled wearily.

And now Rob's phone call . . .

There were problems at work that he had to sort out immediately. One of their biggest customers hadn't received a delivery he needed, blah, blah, blah.

He wouldn't be home until late tonight.

When he'd told her this, for fleeting seconds she'd almost asked if that was the *real* reason he would be late.

A totally unwanted image of Rob with Sandy Bennett slipped into her mind, and she pushed it aside with difficulty.

But she *hadn't* asked him that. She would keep her fears to herself this time.

So many things to think about.

She switched on a cassette, hoping the music would divert her attention from the thoughts and worries that closed around her so tightly.

When she finally pulled up outside the school, there were already several cars parked there. Some of the women she recognized, and she waved greetings to a number of them. Hailey slid out from behind the steering wheel, leant against the Astra and lit a cigarette, drawing deeply on it.

She heard the school bell sound, and looked across to the main entrance, awaiting the tide of excited children that would stream forth at any moment.

She took a couple more drags on the Silk Cut and then ground it out beneath her foot.

The Ford Scorpio cruised slowly past the main gates.

Hailey was sure she recognized this car, and she took a couple of steps forward.

She *did* recognize it.

She could see Adam Walker quite clearly behind the wheel.

The Scorpio headed for the end of the road and disappeared around a corner.

Hailey watched it go.

A moment later it returned.

Moving at that same deliberately slow speed. And now she could see that Walker was looking over towards the school.

What the hell was he doing here?

She hurried to the roadside, watching as the Scorpio vanished once again, this time into a side street.

Hailey crossed to the school gates, eyes fixed on the turning in the road that had swallowed up the Scorpio.

She heard voices around her as the first of the children began to flood out. But her attention was still fixed on the end of the road.

The Scorpio was heading back the way it had come.

Walker gazing over at the school.

He looked straight into her face, his expression blank.

But *this* time he speeded up.

He must have seen her. So why didn't he stop?

'Adam,' she called after the car, oblivious to the bemused stares she was getting from the other mothers waiting to pick up their kids.

The Scorpio was gone.

72

Rob Gibson flicked the windscreen wipers of the Audi on to double speed.

It did little to help.

The hammering rain was striking the car with such ferocity that visibility was almost non-existent. The combination of driving rain and badly lit roads had forced Rob to slow his speed.

He glanced at the dashboard clock and saw that it was already approaching 10 p.m.

Most of the work problems had been sorted out. Deliveries that had been promised but not arrived had been rescheduled. Customers had been pacified where possible. Frank Burnside had left an hour earlier, on Rob's prompting. Rob was beginning to wish that he too had begun the journey home when his partner did. At least then he might have avoided this downpour.

A brilliant white flash of lightning lit the sky. It illuminated the heavens for fleeting seconds, then blackness returned again, like a wet cloak.

Inside the car, the rain sounded like a hundred angry woodpeckers slamming against the bodywork. Rob reached forward and wiped condensation from the windscreen, cursing when he almost lost control of the wheel as the car passed through some water lying on the road. It sprayed up on either side of the Audi like a miniature tidal wave.

Thunderclaps like cannon fire filled the sodden air, and Rob was sure he felt the Audi vibrate as one particularly savage rumble swept across the sky – followed immediately by a blinding explosion of lightning.

He slowed to forty, then thirty, the wipers still swiping frenziedly back and forth across the windscreen, but still making little impression on the downpour.

A car passed him going in the other direction, its driver also moving slowly as he negotiated the elements.

Rob reached for the mobile phone, anxious to tell Hailey that the weather would delay him even further.

He dialled, careful to keep one eye on the road.

There was a high-pitched beep and the legend NO SIGNAL appeared on the handset.

Rob muttered something under his breath, realizing that the storm had destroyed the reception.

He replaced the phone and gripped the wheel with both hands again.

The other car came out of nowhere.

All Rob saw was the sudden glare of its headlights in his rearview mirror.

It was as if it had appeared out of the umbra, and now it was sitting on his tail, no more than ten or twelve feet behind him.

He wondered briefly which of the small side roads the car had emerged from. There were a number of narrow thoroughfares leading off this main artery into the town, but most were little more than dirt tracks. Wherever this particular vehicle had come from, its driver seemed determined to stay as close to Rob as possible.

He pumped his brakes once or twice, hoping that his flaring tail-lights would cause the other driver to pull back.

They didn't.

Rob pressed his foot down with a little more force on the accelerator, not wanting to go too fast in the downpour, but anxious to deter the vehicle following.

It too speeded up.

Rob shook his head.

The lights that filled his rear-view mirror were dazzling. So bright he was forced to narrow his eyes as he attempted to get a proper look at the make of car that was behind him. It was impossible to tell.

In the driving rain and the darkness, it was difficult to see further than ten yards, and the blazing headlights behind gave him no chance at all of identifying the other vehicle.

He tried a different tactic. Rob allowed his speed to drop to twenty-five.

He was hoping that the driver behind him would tire of this snail's pace and overtake him.

But the vehicle behind also slowed down.

Rob winced as he looked into the rear-view mirror again, and now he had to lean forward to prevent himself being dazzled by the beams. The bloody idiot was driving with headlights full on.

The two cars rounded a corner, still no more than three yards apart.

Rob raised a hand to wave the car past.

'Go on, then,' he muttered irritably.

The car behind slammed into him.

73

The impact jolted him forward in his seat.

For long seconds Rob thought that the other car had skidded on the wet surface. Maybe the driver had panicked, hit the brakes hard and been unable to stop.

Perhaps that would teach the silly bastard not to get so close in future.

Rob accelerated away.

The other car followed.

Seconds later, Rob felt another shuddering impact. Even more powerful than the first.

'Fucking idiot,' roared Rob, looking again at the rear-view mirror, but still seeing only glaring headlights.

The rain continued to pelt down. Above him the heavens were illuminated by another searing white flash, and soon thunder rumbled loudly.

The car behind rammed him again.

'What the fuck are you doing?' Rob shouted angrily.

He stepped on the accelerator, sending a curtain of spray up behind him.

The other car followed, swung out into the road and kept pace about three yards behind, but slightly to his right.

Rob looked in the wing mirror, and saw that the vehicle was now driving down the centre of the road.

It suddenly swerved across and slammed again into the Audi,

the clash so great it was all Rob could do to keep his own car under control.

There was another impact almost immediately and, this time, he felt the Audi skidding. He was careering towards the sodden grass and mud that flanked the road.

For terrifying seconds he thought he was going to lose control – hit the small ramp of earth and crash into the trees beyond. But he guided the car back onto the road, great geysers of mud spewing up from under churning tyres.

The darkness was lit momentarily by the cold white glow of lightning, and in that instant Rob saw the other car drawing up alongside him.

He glanced to his right, trying to see the driver, gesticulating madly at this fucking moron who seemed so intent on running him off the road.

But the rain and darkness hid the occupant and, despite its proximity, still also masked the make of vehicle.

They were coming to a corner.

The pursuing car veered sharply to the left, and caught the Audi broadside.

Both cars swerved on the waterlogged surface. Rob gripped the steering wheel furiously and twisted it.

'Come on then, you prick,' he bellowed, sending the Audi back across the road towards the other vehicle.

As they collided, the other car swung away slightly but, before Rob could enjoy his victory, it had crashed back into him so hard he felt something prod against his leg.

Looking down, he realized that his door had been dented so badly that part of the interior frame had come loose.

What the fuck was this bastard playing at?

Rob accelerated again, the needle on his speedometer touching sixty.

He knew this was too fast for safety in such treacherous conditions, but his only thought now was to escape this madman – whoever the fuck he was.

Another jarring collision.

The other car was level with him again, bumping into him almost continuously, nudging him towards the muddy verge.

Rob's anger was mixed with fear now.

He had no idea what this bastard was doing, why he was doing it – and, more worryingly, how far he would persist in taking this dangerous game.

The Audi was battered yet again, and Rob could see now that the other car was moving ahead of him.

Trying to cut him off?

Rob hit his brakes, allowing the other driver to get in front of him. Then he accelerated. Out, and across into the other lane, so that Rob was on the outside now.

He was driving on the wrong side of a darkened road.

Perhaps if he could push the offending vehicle off the tarmac . . .

Just nudge it onto the verge.

Disable it long enough to escape from it . . . then he would phone the police and . . .

The entire car interior was filled with such blinding light that Rob actually raised a hand to shield his eyes.

The lightning now lit up the heavens with a savage explosion of whiteness.

But it was not lightning, Rob realized.

It was the headlights of a lorry.

And it was heading straight for him.

74

ALL HE HEARD was an incredible cacophony of sound.

The blaring of the lorry's horn.

The squealing of tyres on wet tarmac.

The ever-present rumbling of the thunder.

It fused together to create one unholy eruption of noise that filled his head and drummed in his ears.

'*No!*' shouted Rob and wrenched the wheel to one side, desperate to get out of the lorry's path.

But the other driver saw his predicament and slammed back into him, keeping him pinned in the right-hand lane. Keeping him in the path of the oncoming lorry.

Ploughing through the rain, the juggernaut hurtled down the road, sending up geysers of spray all around it. Its driver was gesturing wildly with one hand, trying to wave Rob out of his path.

Rob stared at the lorry. There were less than fifty yards between them.

He tried to draw back, to slip behind the other car, to get back across onto the correct side of the road.

But the other car dropped back too, shunting him again into the path of the oncoming juggernaut.

Forty yards now.

Rob wrenched the steering wheel to one side, and slammed again into his aggressor, but the car held firm and its driver sent it careening back into the Audi.

Thirty yards . . .

There was no way past.

Still stuck in the way of the speeding juggernaut, Rob glanced down at his speedo.

Forty miles an hour.

That was too fast. He would never avoid the lorry.

Twenty yards . . .

The distance between them was closing too fast. But the other car wouldn't allow him to pull over. Wouldn't allow him to get out of the way.

Fifteen yards . . .

One chance?

Rob drove his foot down hard on the accelerator, and the Audi roared straight towards the lorry, as if intent on ramming the massive vehicle.

The needle now touched fifty-five.

And, all the time, the juggernaut came nearer.

Ten yards . . .

Rob pressed down harder.

Sixty-five.

The lights almost blinded him.

He could now hear the roar of the lorry's engine.

Seventy miles an hour.

The Audi sped past the car on the left, still screaming its way towards the lorry.

Five yards.

He spun the wheel suddenly.

There was barely enough space for the Audi to slip through. As he worked the wheel madly, Rob felt a tremendous crash shake the entire vehicle. He realized that the lorry had clipped his offside rear wing.

But he was through!

Again the Audi skidded on the wet road. He desperately fought to regain control, turning into the skid, and aware that there was now a thick hedge running alongside the road.

Aware that he was spinning straight towards it.

The pursuing car rammed him with incredible force.

As the Audi left the road, Rob gripped the steering wheel with one hand. The other he raised to protect his face.

As if fired from a catapult, the Audi hurtled off the tarmac and exploded through the hedge, carving its way effortlessly through the bracken and overgrown hawthorn.

Rob grunted as he felt a thud, his sternum connected hard with the steering column, and his seat-belt jerked him back, fresh pain shooting across his shoulders.

But the car had stopped.

'Shit,' he hissed, unbuckling his seat-belt.

He sat behind the wheel, heart hammering against his ribs, his breath coming in gasps.

Apart from his shoulders and his chest, there was no pain.

Even the Audi's engine was still running.

He thought about switching it off, then turned in his seat to look back towards the road – through the gaping rent that the Audi had carved in the hedge.

The road seemed deserted.

The lorry was gone; so was the other car.

The only light came from flashes of lightning.

Rob stuck the Audi in reverse and manoeuvred back onto the roadside, but he remained inside the car, looking anxiously up and down the thoroughfare. As if expecting the mystery car to return at any minute.

The road remained empty.

Rob leant forward, resting his head on the wheel, his eyes closed tightly.

'Jesus,' he whispered breathlessly.

He had to get home.

Had to tell Hailey about the fucking maniac who'd tried to kill him.

Had to phone the police. Tell them someone had tried to murder him.

He tried his mobile once. NO SIGNAL.

Rob stuck the Audi in DRIVE and pulled away, gripping the wheel so tightly his knuckles turned white.

The storm continued to rage.

75

HAILEY THOUGHT HOW pale he looked.

Rob sat right on the edge of the chair, a tumbler of brandy cradled in his hands. Hair, plastered by the rain, sticking to his forehead.

Every now and then he would take a sip of the Courvoisier, gazing down into its depths as if seeking answers there.

Hailey perched on the arm of the chair beside him, gently massaging his shoulders.

He had blundered into the house less than fifteen minutes ago, eyes bulging, face set in hard lines. She had been thoroughly frightened by his appearance, especially when he brushed past her into the sitting room without speaking. His clothes were soaked with rain and perspiration. His skin was cold and waxy.

When he had finally managed to force out words, they were ones like 'police' and 'murder' and 'maniac'. What he was saying made no sense. His sentences were garbled, like a message breaking up over radio waves.

Outside, the storm continued to rock the night, and not for the first time Hailey glanced upwards. The thunder had already woken Becky once that night, and it had taken a while to get her back to sleep. But at the moment Hailey's main concern was for her husband, who just sat gazing blankly ahead. It was as if he was seeing something *beyond* the walls of the house. Something that she could not see herself.

'He tried to kill me,' Rob said finally, still staring ahead.

'Who?' Hailey wanted to know.

'The fucking nutter who tried to run me off the road.' He swallowed more brandy.

'Did you get a look at him?' she asked.

Rob shook his head.

'What about the make of his car?' Hailey enquired.

'It was too dark, what with the rain and everything...' He allowed the sentence to trail off.

'Why would someone want to kill you, Rob?'

'How the fuck would I know?' he snapped, downing what was left in his glass and getting to his feet, swaying unsteadily.

Hailey took the glass from him and refilled it before handing it back to him.

'All I know is that's what happened,' Rob said, slumping back down in his seat. 'Some fucking maniac came out of nowhere and tried to run me off the road.'

'It could have been a drunk driver you annoyed. Or some delinquent kids in a stolen car.'

'Could have been.' He ran a hand through his hair. 'Jesus, Hailey, you should have seen it happen. I thought I was going to die.'

She put both arms around his neck and pulled him closer to her.

'I've got to call the police,' he said, moving away slightly.

'What's the point?'

'Are you serious? There's some fucking lunatic out there on the road, pissed or drugged up, or both. He might decide to have a go at someone else, and *they* might not be as lucky as me.'

'But, Rob, what can you tell them? You didn't see the driver, so you can't give them a description. You didn't even see the *car*.'

He swallowed more brandy and got to his feet.

'I've got to tell them,' he insisted.

Hailey stood too, blocking his way to the phone.

'No,' she said flatly.

'What the hell is wrong with you?' he demanded.

'Don't call the police.'

His brow furrowed. 'Why not?' he wanted to know. 'What am I supposed to do?'

'I can handle it, Rob.'

'*You* can handle it?'

'I know who tried to kill you – *and* why.'

76

'His name is Adam Walker,' Hailey said quietly.

Rob didn't speak, merely looked at her aghast.

'You remember, when Becky got lost over in the shopping centre that afternoon, I told you a man had found her and brought her back. It's him.'

'You're not making any sense, Hailey. He saves my daughter, then tries to kill *me*? Why?'

'It's because of me. What happened tonight *and* what happened with your car. The slashed tyres, the dog shit pushed through the door: that was Walker too.'

Why not mention the break-in while you're at it?

Rob waved a hand in the air.

'What has he got against *you*?' he wanted to know.

She lowered her gaze.

'Hailey,' Rob persisted. He took a step towards her.

'He kept ringing me at work,' she said, a note of anger in her voice. 'I wouldn't return his calls. I didn't want it to go on.'

He glared at her.

'You were fucking him, weren't you?' he said sharply.

'No,' she protested. 'It didn't get that far.'

'How far *did* it get?'

'We had lunch a couple of times. I wanted to thank him for what he did for Becky. He got the wrong idea. He kept pestering me. *He* wanted an affair. Not *me*.'

'You fucking bitch,' Rob said quietly. 'You fucking two-faced

307

bitch. You were giving me a hard time about what happened with Sandy, and all the time you were getting shafted by this cunt.'

'Don't start lecturing me about affairs, Rob. You're not in a position to do that.'

'At least Sandy didn't try to *kill* you,' he shouted.

'Rob, please. You'll wake Becky. I don't want her to hear this.'

'No, I bet you don't. That would take some explaining, wouldn't it? "Sorry to wake you, darling, but Dad's a bit upset because the man who's been fucking Mum has just tried to kill him."' He took another step towards her, and for a second she thought he was going to strike her. 'I hope it was worth it. I hope he was good.'

'It wasn't *like* that,' she snarled.

'Well, what *was* it like,' he roared. 'Tell me.'

She saw tears in his eyes.

'Wasn't his fucking dick big enough?' Rob continued venomously. 'Didn't he make you come? Is that why you finished it, or did you think that spreading your legs a few times was payment enough for him finding our daughter?'

He raised his hand and she stepped back involuntarily.

She saw the fury in his expression.

And the pain.

'Now you know how *I* felt,' she said, tears suddenly coursing down her cheeks. 'Rob, I didn't mean any of this to happen. I didn't know what he was going to do. I was so mad at you because of what happened with that slag you worked with. But I didn't have an affair with Adam Walker. I swear to you. Something happened, or nearly happened, but I stopped him. I didn't have sex with him.'

'And you expect me to believe that?' he rasped.

The knot of muscles at the side of his jaw pulsed furiously.

'That cunt came here, didn't he?' he growled. 'He came to this house. I shook hands with him. I thanked him. And all the time he was fucking *you*. He was laughing at me. So were you, you fucking bitch.' He pushed her to one side and wrenched open the sitting-room door, pounding up the stairs.

Hailey followed.

'Rob, please,' she called after him.

'Keep away from me,' he told her threateningly.

'All right, call the police if you want to. Tell them who it was. Tell them what Walker's been doing,' she blurted.

'No. You know him so fucking well, *you* sort it out.'

She saw him pull an overnight bag from one of the wardrobes. Watched as he hauled open drawers and cupboards, and stuffed clothes inside.

'What are you doing?' she wanted to know.

'Getting away from you,' he snarled.

'Rob, please. Think what you're doing.'

'What *I'm* doing?' he spat. 'We spent time in those fucking Relate sessions trying to save a marriage that looks as if it wasn't worth saving. *I* was supposed to be the bad guy. *I* was the one who was breaking up the happy home, wasn't I? Until Mr Adam fucking Walker came along. If you'd kept your eye on Becky that day, *none* of this would ever have happened. Because then he wouldn't have had to find her, and you wouldn't have had to spread your fucking legs to thank him.'

He snatched up the bag and barged past her.

When they emerged on the landing, Becky was standing in the doorway of her room. She was clutching a small teddy bear and crying softly.

'Dad,' she said, her voice cracking.

He crossed to her and kissed her.

'I'm going away for a while, sweetheart,' he said softly. 'Your mum will explain.'

He looked round and shot Hailey a scathing glance, then he made his way down the stairs.

'Rob,' Hailey called after him.

He slammed the front door behind him.

'Why were you and Dad shouting?' Becky wanted to know.

Hailey swept her up into her arms and held her tightly, both of them weeping.

'Where's Dad going?' the little girl sobbed. 'When is he coming back?'

Hailey wished she knew.

77

HAILEY LOOKED ACROSS at the glowing red digits on the radio alarm: 2.03 a.m.

Outside the storm had abated. The thunder and lightning replaced by rain spattering insistently on the windows.

In the bed beside her, Becky slept fitfully, tossing and turning in her sleep, occasionally moaning aloud. Some bad dream, Hailey assumed.

Like seeing her parents shouting at each other?

There had been lots of tears that night: from Becky and from herself. She had lied

(*what the hell else was she supposed to do?*)

about why Rob had left the house. Saying that he had been called away on business, and wasn't sure when he'd be back.

The lie had worked for the time being.

It's a pity not all lies work as effectively, isn't it?

Becky had asked about the raised voices. Hailey had found it more difficult to explain *that*. Even now, she wondered if her daughter believed her. Only natural. She didn't know what the hell to believe herself.

How many times had she looked across at the phone?

Who should she ring first? The police?

Tell them about Walker.

Frank Burnside?

Find out if Rob was staying there.

She swung herself out of bed and crossed to the window,

peering out through the curtain of rain into the deserted street beyond.

Walker?

That was who she *should* be ringing.

The irony was not lost on her, but it didn't force a smile. She didn't know what would ever make her smile again after the events of the last few days. How long had she tried to avoid him? And now she needed to speak to him – *wanted* to.

Perhaps she should call Caroline Hacket. He might even be with her.

Then she looked back at the clock and remembered the ungodly hour. Any calls would have to wait until morning.

Wouldn't they?

Hailey crossed to the bed and pulled the duvet up around Becky's shoulders, then she bent down and kissed her little daughter on the cheek. Satisfied that she was well settled, Hailey edged out of the room and made her way downstairs.

She stood beside the phone in the hall for a moment, then picked up the receiver. Her index finger was shaking as she pressed the digits.

It was ringing.

She swallowed hard. Waiting.

Still it rang.

Put it down.

Two more rings and she'd try again tomorrow, when . . .

The phone was picked up.

'Hello,' said a voice thick with sleep.

'Adam,' she said quietly. 'It's me, Hailey Gibson.'

She transferred the phone to the other ear.

'We need to talk,' she said.

Silence.

'Adam, are you still there?' she persisted.

'Talk about what?' he said sleepily. 'I thought it was all over between us.' He coughed. 'Besides, have you seen the time?'

'Meet me on Friday,' she said. 'Please.'

'Why not tomorrow?' he wanted to know.

'I'm too busy. Can you meet me, or not?'

Another silence.

'Where?' he asked.

'The Happy Brig.'

'Just like old times,' he said, but the laugh that followed was grating and hollow. 'I'll be there.'

'Adam . . .'

He hung up.

78

THE ROOM WAS small.

Rob had stayed in Travelodges before, so he knew what to expect: the basics. Bed, bathroom, TV, tea- and coffee-making facilities: that was about it.

He'd unpacked his meagre supply of clothes, and now he lay on the single bed gazing at the ceiling.

What a fucking night!

Almost killed by a nutter in a car, then discovering that his wife had been unfaithful with the man who had tried to kill him.

He rubbed both hands across his face and let out a deep sigh. Thoughts were still spinning around inside his head.

And, worse still, an idea was beginning to form that he could barely stand to entertain. What if Hailey had *known* that Walker planned to kill him?

He sat up slowly, the very thought almost unbearable.

What *had* gone on between Walker and his wife?

Had his own affair with Sandy Bennett driven her to such lengths, such frenzies of rage? How far would she go to gain revenge on him? He knew he had hurt her, and hurt her badly.

But surely not this . . .?

She couldn't want him dead.

Could she?

Rob swung himself off the bed and padded into the bathroom, slapping on the light.

The fluorescent light above the mirror sputtered into life and

314

he studied his tortured reflection. His red-rimmed eyes, his pale skin.

He shook his head. His reflection imitated his movement.

The face he was gazing at was that of a man totally at the end of his tether. Shattered, drained, as if every emotion has been torn from him.

She had betrayed him with another man. Lied to him.

(*As he had done to her*)

But surely she would not have plotted to kill him? To rob their daughter of a father?

He refused to believe it, and yet there was something gnawing away at the back of his mind. Some cancerous thought that refused to leave him: a feeling of such terrible malignance that it ate into his subconscious.

He wouldn't believe it.

He *couldn't*.

Tears began to flow from his puffy eyes and he gripped the sink tightly, watching that tortured visage before him.

'Why?' he whispered.

He pushed his head forward, connecting with the mirror, pressing his flesh against the cold glass for a moment.

Then he drew back and repeated the action. Harder this time.

The impact left a small white mark on his flesh.

He held onto the sink so hard it seemed he might pull it off the wall.

For the third time he drove his head against the mirror – so hard this time that he felt momentarily dizzy. Still the tears ran down his cheeks.

'Why?' he said again as he did so. And the word was accompanied by an angry crack.

The mirror had splintered. The glass was split cleanly from top to bottom.

Rob studied his distorted reflection in it.

Saw the blood running down his face from the gash just below his hairline.

He watched as droplets of crimson fell into the sink and flowered.

Rob felt little pain from the wound. In fact he looked at it with something akin to bemusement, watching the red trickle coursing down his face as surely as the tears that still flowed from his eyes.

The real pain was inside him.

Inside his heart.

Inside his soul.

And it was excruciating.

79

HAILEY WAITED FOR the ringing phone to be picked up, the receiver of her own jammed between her shoulder and ear as she typed. The words flickered on the screen before her, but she hardly saw them.

She'd managed barely three hours' sleep the previous night, and it felt as if someone had attached lead weights to her eyelids.

The phone continued to ring.

She sat back from her keyboard, stifling a yawn.

Perhaps later she'd ring Becky's school and make sure *she* was OK. The child hadn't wanted to go to school that morning, and there'd been more tears.

After last night, life looked like being one endless catalogue of tears again, she mused.

Still the phone was ringing.

The answerphone wasn't switched on, so the person she sought was home. They just weren't answering.

She was on the point of setting the receiver down.

'Hello,' said the voice.

'Caroline, it's Hailey. Sorry to interrupt you if you were working.'

There was a moment's awkward silence.

'I wasn't sure if you and I were still talking,' Caroline Hacket said.

'I need to ask you something.'

'Go on.'

'Did you see Adam Walker last night?'

Hailey heard the weary intake of breath. 'Just tell me, please,' she persisted.

'I *could* tell you to mind your own business.'

There was an edge to Caroline's voice that Hailey hadn't expected.

'Please yourself,' Hailey said defensively.

'I could, but I won't,' Caroline insisted. 'I saw him for lunch, OK? Why? What's the problem now?'

'I think he tried to kill Rob last night.' She explained briefly.

'Don't be so bloody ridiculous,' Caroline said finally. 'It seems as if you're trying to blame Adam for *everything* lately. You wanted him out of your life – and he's gone. Why don't you drop it?'

'I told Rob what happened between Adam and me. Rob walked out and I don't know where he's gone.'

There was another silence.

'Caroline . . .?'

'I heard you. You can't blame Adam for *that*.'

Hailey swallowed hard. 'Are you seeing him tonight?' she wanted to know.

'Look, I've got to go,' Caroline told her sharply. 'I'll speak to you later.'

She hung up.

Hailey slammed the receiver down and sat forward in her chair. Her office door opened and she looked up.

Jim Marsh walked in, smiling.

The smile faded as he saw the expression on Hailey's face.

'Are you all right?'

'Fine,' she lied. 'I just didn't get much sleep last night. I've got those details on the gig and the party afterwards that you wanted.'

Marsh sat down opposite her. 'Are you *sure* everything's all right?' he asked.

My husband was nearly killed last night, then he walked out on me. My closest friend is seeing the man who tried to kill him. My daughter is almost suicidal, and I'm close to a nervous breakdown. Everything is fan-fucking-tastic!

'I told you, Jim, I'm just tired.' She handed him a couple of pieces of paper. 'The guest list for the gig, the travel arrangements, and the details of the party afterwards. I think everything's covered.'

Marsh scanned the documents, nodding approvingly every now and then.

'It looks fine,' he said, smiling. 'Are Rob and Becky looking forward to it?'

She felt the tears building.

'Can't wait,' she said, her voice cracking slightly. She coughed. 'Jim, would you mind if I left a bit earlier today? There's a few things I've got to do.'

He nodded. 'I thought you trusted me,' he said quietly.

She looked puzzled.

'How long have we known each other?' Marsh continued. 'Eight years?'

'Jim, what are you getting at?'

'I just thought that you'd let me help if I could. I know there's something wrong. If there's anything I can do . . .?'

She managed a smile.

'I wish there was,' Hailey told him. 'But *I'm* the only one who can sort this out. Don't worry, it won't affect my work.'

'For Christ's sake,' he said irritably. 'Sod the work. You'd never let me down. I'd like to do something to help *you* for a change.'

Marsh got to his feet. 'If you change your mind, you know where I am.'

'Thanks, Jim, but, like I said, this is *my* problem. *I've* got to deal with it.'

'Good luck.'

'I think I'm going to need it.'

80

Rob Gibson raised a hand to attract the barman's attention. He picked at the bowl of peanuts before him while he waited for his glass to be refilled with Johnnie Walker. Once it had been, he sipped at the fiery liquid, feeling it burn its way to his stomach.

The pub was fairly quiet. Other than two or three youths gathered around a fruit machine in one corner, and another group of men about his own age playing pool just behind him, there wasn't much activity inside the building.

Rob had been there for about an hour. He'd driven there straight from work.

Frank Burnside had tried to persuade him to leave the office earlier, but Rob had insisted he had work to complete, and allowed his partner to leave him alone in the solitude of BG Trucks.

There was work to do: there always was. And he was certainly in no rush to get back to the Travelodge. Hence the stop-off at the pub.

It was like many such places in and around the city centre, new, characterless and totally lacking in charm, but Rob hadn't come in to enjoy the ambience. He sipped more of his whisky and looked around the bar disinterestedly.

There was a couple in their early twenties huddled in one corner over their drinks. Laughing and smiling, occasionally kissing. Rob watched them for a moment, until he became aware that the young man had noticed his intrusive stare and was meeting it almost challengingly.

Rob smiled, raised his glass in salute, and turned on his stool.

More peanuts. Another drink.

He was sure that he'd had too much already. He wasn't drunk – nowhere near it – but it didn't take too much to tip a breath-alyser, did it? Just as well he wasn't too far from the Travelodge. The last thing he needed at the moment was some over-zealous copper pulling him over for drink-driving.

What he'd needed *last* night was a fucking copper. One of the good old boys in blue to arrest the arsehole who'd been trying to kill him.

The arsehole who was shagging his wife.

Rob lowered his head, unwelcome thoughts spinning around in his mind.

Thoughts of infidelity.

Visions of Hailey on her back with her legs wrapped around some other bastard's back.

Visions of her mouth on some other guy's cock.

Doesn't feel too good, does it? Boot on the other foot and all that shit. How do you like it? Can you imagine what Hailey felt like whenever she thought about you and Sandy?

Sandy?

For insane seconds after he'd first left his own house the night before, he'd contemplated driving over to her flat.

Revenge?

Revenge for revenge? Remember who started this little merry-go-round of infidelity going. Take a bow, Rob Gibson.

He downed what was left in his glass and looked at the empty tumbler.

One more?

Rob ran a hand through his hair and looked up, catching sight of his reflection in the mirror behind the bar.

He ordered a mineral water instead, to wash down the last few peanuts that he scraped from the bowl.

The clock at one end of the bar told him it was after ten.

Becky would be in bed by now, asleep with any luck.

He finished half the water and got to his feet, fumbling in his jacket pocket for his car keys. He passed the young couple on the way out. They were still kissing.

Rob sucked in several deep breaths as he stepped into the pub car park. He shivered a little, surprised at how chilly it had become.

The gravel crunched beneath his feet as he walked across to the waiting Audi.

It was parked beneath a large oak tree, and he noticed there were several dollops of bird shit on the roof.

That was meant to be good luck, wasn't it?

On any other occasion, he probably would have smiled.

The car park was dimly lit, illuminated only by two sodium lights near the exit onto the main road.

Rob squinted in the gloom, trying to make out the door lock.

The tree towering above him and the bushes that grew so thickly around this side of the car park helped to blot out any natural light, and he was forced to bend forward to find the lock.

He heard the rustle of leaves, and was about to straighten up.

More crunching of gravel close behind him.

He realized in that split second that he wasn't alone.

And then the first blow landed.

81

Rob felt a crashing impact on the back of his head.

The blow was so hard it slammed his head forward, smashing it against the side window of the Audi.

He fell to his knees, the gravel digging into his skin, adding to the pain he already felt. But at least this added pain kept him conscious.

A foot connected hard with his ribs – once, twice.

The breath was torn from him, and he felt a crack as one of his ribs snapped from the force of the kick.

He tried to roll over, tried to clamber to his feet in an effort to protect himself from this sudden assault.

If he could just get up . . .

Something struck him in the face.

He wasn't sure whether it was a fist or the same object that had clouted him around the back of the head.

Whatever it was, it split his bottom lip and he tasted blood.

Rob shot out a hand to block the next kick aimed at him, and he succeeded in deflecting the worst of the impact, but he shouted out in pain as his little finger was crushed.

With his other hand he clawed at the door handle, trying to pull himself upright, desperate to at least defend himself against this frenzied onslaught.

Another blow caught him in the mouth and shattered a tooth, but he grabbed at the hand that struck him and managed to ensnare the wrist in a vice-like grip. He pulled his assailant towards him, driving his own forehead towards the onrushing face of his attacker.

Rob felt the impact, but heard a satisfying groan from his assailant as he was headbutted.

He had little time to savour his triumph.

Another powerful blow caught him across the bridge of the nose, pulverizing the bone. Blood burst from it, and Rob fell to his knees once again.

He took another kick to the stomach. Then several to the small of the back.

He curled into a foetal position, hands covering his head in an attempt to prevent further damage.

But his attacker seemed to become more incensed by this, and started stamping on his head, on his protecting hands.

Rob was convinced he was going to die.

He was battling to remain conscious while kicks rained in from all directions, mainly aimed at his head now.

Where the fuck was everyone? Why hadn't someone from inside the pub come to help him?

Blood was pouring down his face, and he felt agonizing pain from his broken finger and rib.

Still the blows rained down, and Rob was beginning to wonder if this madman was ever going to run out of energy.

This madman . . . ?

One thought flickered briefly into his head.

Was this the same person who had tried to kill him the previous night?

Was . . . ?

The assailant was now stamping on his arm, trying to knock it away from his face.

A kick cracked part of Rob's bottom jaw. Two teeth spilled onto the gravel as he opened his mouth in pain. The blood that poured from his burst lips and lacerated face looked pitch-black in the gloom.

Rob was losing consciousness.

A particularly powerful kick sent him onto his back.

Like an upturned turtle.

He couldn't protect himself any longer.

More kicks to his sides and stomach.

He couldn't focus properly any more. Blood in his eyes. Pain.
Fear.

A thunderous kick to his head.

Someone was using his skull like a football.

Something else broke. Another bone shattered.

Rob's eyes rolled upwards in the sockets.

Darkness . . .

82

S<small>HE WAS DREAMING</small>: that was the only explanation.

Hailey rolled over in bed, trying to force her eyes open. Expecting the residue of her dream to vanish with the intrusion of waking.

She heard the sound again.

The doorbell?

She looked across at the radio alarm: 11.56 p.m.

Hailey was gripped by a feeling of unease.

Who the hell would be ringing her doorbell at this time of night?

Somebody playing a joke?

She was grateful she'd put the security alarm on. She glanced across at the phone beside the bed, thought how easily she could reach it if she needed to.

The doorbell sounded again.

Whoever was down there wasn't giving up easily. She began to wonder how long they'd already been there.

She swung herself out of bed and pulled on a T-shirt, then she crossed to the window and looked out.

Either the person standing at the door had no transport or their car was parked out of sight.

Walker?

Why would he have come to the house tonight? She was meeting him tomorrow.

A smile flickered across her lips.

What if it was Rob? He'd tried his key and not been able to

get in because of the bolts. Even now he could be standing there waiting for her to let him in. He'd had time to think, and he wanted to talk. That *had* to be it.

Surely?

She hurried towards the stairs, pausing briefly to look in on Becky, who was sleeping undisturbed by the persistent ringing.

Hailey hurried down the stairs, crossing to the key-pad and jabbing in the four-digit cancel code. For long seconds she stood in the darkness of the hall looking towards the front door.

She could see shadows outside.

Two figures.

It wasn't Rob.

Did you really think it would be?

Not Walker either, unless he had someone with him.

Perhaps he'd brought Caroline with him. Perhaps they had needed to tell her of their undying love for each other.

She exhaled deeply.

The doorbell sounded again.

Hailey took a step towards the front door, pausing to squint through the spyhole.

She'd been right: there were two figures standing in the porch.

The breath froze in her lungs. Her heart thudded alarmingly against her ribs.

Please God . . .

With shaking hands she slipped the bolts free, then scurried into the kitchen and fetched her front door keys. She left the chain on as she opened the door, feeling a blast of cold night air sweep into the house. It raised goose pimples on her flesh.

'Mrs Hailey Gibson?' said the first of the policemen.

She nodded. 'What's wrong?' she murmured, barely able to force the words out.

'It's your husband,' the uniformed man told her.

'Oh, no,' she said, her voice cracking.

'If you get dressed, we'll run you to the hospital.'

'An accident?' she said.

'We'll give you the details on the way,' the other policeman said, smiling understandingly.

She wondered how many previous times he'd performed a similar task – or worse.

'Is he badly hurt?' Hailey wanted to know.

'Yes, he is,' said the second man.

She slipped the chain free and let the two men in, turning and bolting up the stairs.

Tears were already forming in her eyes.

You've got to be strong for Becky's sake.

She stood in the doorway of her daughter's room, looking at the little sleeping form.

Hailey waited a moment, then hurried into her own bedroom.

She dialled the number quickly.

Caroline Hacket was still up, still working.

'I'm really sorry, Caroline,' Hailey said. 'I've got to go to the hospital. I need someone to watch Becky for me. I won't be long. It's Rob. I think he's in a bad way.'

Caroline said she'd be there in five minutes.

'Thanks,' said Hailey, wiping her eyes with the back of one hand. She hung up.

She pulled on jeans, socks, stepped into trainers, then ran a hand through her hair and headed for the stairs, pausing once more at the door to Becky's room.

The little girl was still sleeping soundly.

No need to wake her.

Not yet.

Hailey made her way downstairs to the waiting policemen.

83

THE DRIVE TO the hospital seemed to take an eternity.

All the way there, Hailey sat gazing blankly out of the side window of the police car.

There were questions she wanted to ask, but she couldn't seem to force the words out. And, as they drew nearer to the huge building, she felt as if her vocal cords had seized up.

The car pulled up outside the entrance to Accident and Emergency, and the younger of the two policemen led Hailey through the reception area into the hospital itself.

An ambulance had just arrived, its blue lights turning silently. Hailey briefly glimpsed someone being lifted onto a gurney from the back of the vehicle. She saw blood, heard a moan of pain, then it was gone.

She followed the policeman along a series of corridors; they passed nurses and porters on the way. But Hailey's overwhelming impression was one of silence. At such a late hour most patients were sleeping: some soundly, some with the aid of painkillers. In this monolithic structure, people were in pain. Some were dying. Some were already dead.

She forced the thoughts to the back of her mind, or at least she tried to. And, all the time she trudged along with the policeman, that antiseptic smell she hated so much clogged her nostrils. To Hailey hospitals smelled of pain and suffering.

They passed a cleaner using a buffing machine to polish the floor of one of the corridors. He looked up briefly as Hailey passed, no doubt wondering who this sad-looking woman was here to see. Then he returned to his work.

Hailey and the policeman rode the lift to the third floor and he stepped out ahead of her.

There was a small nurses' station to her left, lit only by a dull night-light. There didn't seem to be anyone on duty.

The policeman crossed to the desk and looked behind it, towards a small inner office.

A tall, thin-faced nurse in a blue overall emerged and smiled efficiently at him.

'Robert Gibson?' he said.

'Room 311,' the nurse told him, returning to her duties, as Hailey and the policeman made their way towards the room she had designated.

There was a single plastic chair outside it, and perched on that chair, a copy of the previous day's *Mirror* in his hand, was a man in a brown suit and a pair of unpolished shoes. He stood up when he saw Hailey and managed a smile.

'Mrs Gibson?' he said.

She nodded.

'My name is Detective Constable Matthew Tate,' he told her. 'I've been assigned to your husband's case.'

'Please let me see him,' Hailey asked.

'Look, I'll warn you now,' Tate said almost apologetically, 'he's taken a bad beating. The facial damage is severe but . . .'

'Please, just let me see him,' she said irritably, and barged past the plain-clothes man.

During the drive to the hospital she had tried to prepare herself for every possible eventuality. Imagined what he might look like. How bad his cuts and bruises would be.

'Oh my God,' she whispered softly, and the tears began to flow immediately.

Nothing could have prepared her for what she now saw.

Rob lay propped up on three pillows.

'Oh my God,' Hailey repeated, moving closer to the bed.

There were drips running into both arms. His right hand was heavily bandaged. So too was his scalp and most of the left side of his face. What remained exposed was a collage of purple, red and black flesh. Bruises and gashes seemed to overlap, and his whole face looked as if it had been inflated, so great was the swelling. Both eyes were almost closed. The skin around them was blackened with bruises, and one eyelid, she noticed, was slightly torn. Two stitches had been inserted into it.

His lips were cracked and split and his head lolled to one side, despite the neck brace he wore.

His upper body was uncovered, and that too showed a patchwork of cuts and bruises. Every single inch of flesh seemed to have been damaged in some way: his shoulders, his arms. His stomach and sides were tightly strapped.

Hailey crossed to the bed, only now noticing that there was a nurse in the room. She'd been so mesmerized by the appalling sight of her husband as soon as she'd entered, she hadn't even seen another figure in the small room.

'Rob,' Hailey whimpered.

'He's heavily sedated,' the nurse told her quietly.

Hailey stared again at the terrible injuries. She wiped tears away.

'He's stable now,' the nurse insisted. 'He's going to be OK.'

'How bad are the injuries?'

'He's got a broken finger, two broken ribs. He's lost a couple of teeth. There's a hairline fracture of the jaw and some very bad cuts and bruises. We did a scan when he was brought in. There's no damage to his brain, despite the head injuries. No severe internal damage either.'

'Can he hear us?'

'Probably, but he can't speak. His jaw is wired at the moment.'

'I thought you said it was only a hairline fracture.'

'It's just a precaution. He'll be chattering away again in a few days, you'll see.'

The nurse paused by the door. 'I'll leave you for a few minutes.' She smiled.

Hailey sat on the edge of the bed and looked down at her husband.

'Oh, Rob,' she said, her voice cracking. She wiped her tears away. 'Who did this to you?'

His eyes flickered open slightly – at least as far as the puffy swollen flesh around them would allow.

'Can you hear me?' she persisted.

He tried to speak, but the effort caused great pain. He winced instead.

She gripped his unbandaged hand.

'Tol' police,' he croaked.

She leaned forward, anxious to hear his garbled words.

'Did you see who did it?' Hailey wanted to know.

'Didn't know them,' he continued, pain creasing his battered features.

She gripped his hand more tightly.

'Rob,' she said urgently.

He closed his eyes.

84

'NOTHING WAS TAKEN,' said DC Tate. 'Not even your husband's wallet. So the motive obviously wasn't robbery.'

Tate and Hailey sat in a small anteroom on the ground floor of the hospital.

The young DC sipped at his machine coffee, grimaced, and watched as Hailey ran her fingertip around the rim of her own plastic cup. She seemed uninterested in its contents.

'The attack could have been random,' the policeman continued. 'Some bloody idiot from the pub – drunk? There doesn't seem to be any *real* motive for it. Or if there was, we haven't found it yet. I'm afraid your husband just seems to have been in the wrong place at the wrong time. I'm sorry.'

'He couldn't identify who attacked him, then?' Hailey asked, gazing past Tate towards a sign that proclaimed: AIDS – BE SAFE, WEAR A CONDOM.

'Do you know of any enemies your husband might have had?' the DC wanted to know.

It couldn't have been Adam Walker, could it?

Hailey shook her head.

Perhaps the same person who tried to run him off the road the other night?

She looked directly at Tate. Perhaps now was the time to mention that?

'Your husband couldn't think of anyone either,' Tate said. 'Mind you, in *his* state I'm not surprised. I'll have a word with him in a couple of days, when he's feeling better. Perhaps I could call around to your house?'

Hailey nodded.

Why? Rob won't be there, anyway.

'Yes, that'd be fine,' she told him.

Had it really been a random attack? Would someone almost kill a complete stranger just for the hell of it? Would Walker do that?

'I understand your husband was staying at the local Travelodge when this attack happened,' said Tate. 'We found their key-card in his jacket.'

So that was where he'd gone.

Hailey nodded. 'He'd been away on business,' she lied.

Tate looked at her quizzically. 'Who else knew he was there?' he wanted to know.

'I don't know. Why does it matter?'

'Well, your husband's a businessman, isn't he? Runs his own company? Men like that sometimes make enemies.'

'He's got a haulage company,' Hailey sighed. 'It's hardly the Mafia, is it?' She stretched her arms, hearing the joints pop. She had the beginnings of a headache. The product of tiredness and tears, she reasoned.

She sipped at her tea, wincing when she found it cold.

'Can I see my husband again now?' she said, almost pleadingly.

'It's not up to me, Mrs Gibson,' Tate told her. 'But if the hospital don't object . . .' The sentence trailed off.

She got to her feet and turned towards the door.

'I can leave a car here to get you home,' the DC told her.

'I'll call a cab. Thanks, anyway.'

He smiled. 'I'll be in touch,' he told her.

And he was gone.

Hailey made her way back towards the lifts, and rode the next car to the third floor.

*

She had no idea how long she'd been sitting there at his bedside.

Every now and then he would groan softly in his pained sleep, sometimes open his swollen eyes as best he could. Once he looked straight at her.

Hailey sat by the bed holding his unbandaged hand, her own head lolling forward onto the sheet.

'Hailey?'

She heard the voice through a veil of sleep.

Hailey jerked her head up and stared at Rob. There was a jug of water on the bedside table and she poured him some, holding it to his ravaged lips, watching as he managed to take a couple of sips.

The effort seemed monumental and it caused him pain.

'Oh, Jesus,' he murmured finally.

'I'm so sorry, Rob,' she said, tears welling up.

He squeezed her hand. 'I saw his face,' he said, each word forced out with effort.

'Who was it?'

'Don't know.' He winced.

She began to stroke his hand slowly.

'Just rest,' she urged him.

'Don't know who it was,' Rob continued. 'But it wasn't Walker.'

85

HAILEY SAT IN the car park of the Happy Brig, puffing on a cigarette.

She wasn't sure how many she'd smoked since she'd arrived, but her throat was feeling raw. However many it was, she had a feeling it was *too* many.

He was late. Perhaps he was doing it on purpose.

Paying you back?

More than once she had wondered if Walker would show at all.

Why should he? After everything that had happened between them, who could blame him if he failed to appear?

Feeling sorry for him now?

She tried to push the butt into the ashtray, but it was already full. She tossed it out of the side window instead.

Again she checked the dashboard clock: 1.16 p.m.

How much longer?

Even when he arrived, if he ever did, she wasn't sure exactly what she was going to say to him.

'*I know you didn't beat my husband almost to death, but did you push dog shit through our letterbox, slash the tyres on Rob's car, and then try to kill him by running him off the road?*'

Simple.

She was reaching for another cigarette when she saw his Ford Scorpio swing into the car park.

Hailey watched as he parked about three vehicles away from

her and clambered out. She, too, slid from behind the steering wheel and walked towards him.

'Sorry I'm late,' Walker said.

'I thought you weren't coming,' she told him.

'I wouldn't have missed it for anything,' said Walker, and she heard the slight hint of sarcasm in his voice. 'I couldn't imagine why you wanted to speak to me. After all, you've gone to such great lengths to avoid me.'

'Don't make this harder than it already is, Adam.'

He shook his head. 'You're amazing, Hailey.' He smiled humourlessly. 'Why is it so hard for you? I'm the one who's been treated like an idiot. All I wanted to do was talk to you, and when I tried you didn't want to know. And, all the time, all I wanted to do was apologize to you. What's so bad about that?'

She exhaled deeply.

There was a long silence, finally broken by Walker.

'So what do we do now?' he wanted to know. 'Stand here and talk about the weather? You were the one who called me at two o'clock in the morning. So I assumed it must be important.'

'Things have been happening,' she said vaguely.

'What kind of things?'

She told him about the slashed tyres, the dog shit, the incident with Rob and the maniac in the other car.

'And last night Rob was beaten up,' Hailey told him finally.

'You think I'm responsible, don't you?' It sounded more like a statement than a question.

'At first I did. I—'

'How could you?' he interrupted angrily. 'Why would I want to do anything like that? Why would I want to hurt you or your family?'

'It started not long after you and I . . .' She hesitated, as if reluctant to finish the sentence. 'After I asked you to stop calling me.'

'And you thought it was some kind of sick fucking revenge?' he rasped. 'What do you take me for, Hailey?'

'I didn't know what to think, Adam.'

'You think I'd do that just because you wouldn't speak to me? Give me *some* fucking credit, will you? I think you're flattering yourself a little, too, don't you?'

'Meaning what?' It was Hailey's turn to be angry.

'I think a lot of you, but not *that* much,' he snapped. 'I don't want revenge. I just wanted to be friends.'

She nodded slowly.

'Rob knows what happened between us,' she told him. 'Or at least he *thinks* he does. He thinks we were having an affair. He's walked out on me.'

'Didn't you tell him the truth?'

'I tried. I told him everything, but I can understand the way he feels.'

'After what he put *you* through? Don't you think he's being a little hypocritical?'

'So what was I supposed to do? Call you and get you to come round to our house and explain that we didn't ever have an affair? That it wasn't really anything for him to get worked up about, because we didn't have sex? Not *real* sex, as we didn't go all the way. Do you think he'd have accepted that?'

Walker looked at her in silence. He could see how tired and wan she looked.

'Who *did* attack Rob?' he said finally.

'No one knows,' she told him. 'Rob didn't recognize them. And the police don't have any idea.'

'How is he?'

She shrugged. 'I saw him this morning,' Hailey said. 'He's feeling much better. The doctors say he can come home in a couple of days. He's worried about how Becky will react. He still looks pretty bad, even though the worst of the bruising and swelling has started to go. He really doesn't look very pretty.' She swallowed hard.

'How's Becky?' Walker wanted to know.

'She's fine, I think. We've managed to keep most of this from her. Well, until Rob got beaten up.'

'Have you got any idea who would want to do this to him?'

Hailey shook her head. 'I wish I had. And I wish I knew where the bastards lived, because I'd like to do to them what they've done to us.'

'What do the police say?'

'They try their best, but they haven't even got any suspects. What's that expression: "We're all pissing in the wind"?' She smiled bitterly.

'If there's anything *I* can do, let me know. *Anything.*'

She met his gaze and held it. 'I'm sorry for thinking you might have been behind this, Adam. But I didn't know *what* to think.'

'It's all right,' he said softly.

He reached out and touched her cheek.

Hailey pressed her own fingertips to his hand, then stepped back.

'I'd better go,' she said, her voice low.

He watched as she climbed into the Astra.

In her rear-view mirror she could see him still standing out in the car park, watching as she pulled away.

She touched her cheek where he'd put his fingertips.

It was as if she could still feel his warmth on her flesh.

·

86

'HE HURT YOU, so I hurt *him*.'

David Layton sat back on the sofa, gazing at the television set. He took a swig from the can of Special Brew he held.

Sandy Bennett looked at him, her face expressionless.

'I thought you would have thanked me,' Layton continued.

'What exactly did you do?' she wanted to know.

'I taught him not to fuck around with my sister,' Layton said.

Sandy switched the TV off.

'I was watching that,' Layton proclaimed with mock indignation.

'I want to know what you did,' she repeated.

'What's your fucking problem? This bastard Gibson had been messing you around. You said that yourself. He sacked you. You loved him, Sandy, and he took advantage of you. *You* told me that.'

He drained what was left in the can and crushed it in his fist.

'What am I supposed to do?' he continued. 'Sit around like a cunt while somebody makes my sister look like an idiot?' He shook his head. 'No way. He got what was coming to him. He's lucky he didn't get it worse.'

'How long has this been going on?' she demanded.

He shrugged. 'A couple of weeks, on and off.'

'And what exactly did you *do*?'

'I frightened him a bit, that's all. Played a couple of little tricks on him.' Layton smiled crookedly. 'I wasn't going to sit back and see you used, Sandy. I know you: you would have let him get away with it. He fucks around with you, gets fed up, and goes running back to his wife and kid. Now he knows he can't get away with it.'

Sandy ran a hand through her hair and glared at her brother.

'How badly is he hurt?' she wanted to know.

'Does it matter?'

'Yes, it matters,' she rasped.

'We put him in hospital.'

'*We?*'

'Russell Poole helped me. He owed me a favour, and he seems to enjoy things like that.' Again that twisted smile.

'I don't believe this,' Sandy said quietly. 'You could have killed him.'

'He's lucky we didn't. Like I said, it'll teach him not to fuck around with you again.'

'Am I supposed to thank you for this, Dave?' she snapped.

He looked blankly at her.

'I told you that it was over between Rob and me – that he'd sacked me.'

'You said you loved him.'

'Perhaps I did. But I didn't ask you to start some sort of bloody vendetta against him. I didn't ask you to put him in hospital. Jesus Christ, if the police find out it's you, you'll be back inside again.'

'Let *me* worry about that. Besides, they *won't* find out, will they? The only two people who know what's happened are Russell and you. And Russell's not going to open his mouth.' He looked accusingly at her. 'The only one who can grass me up now is you. But why would you want to do that? I did you a favour. What are brothers for, eh?' He chuckled.

'I never wanted this,' she said quietly.

'Well, you got it. Perhaps you should be thanking me.' Layton got to his feet and took a step towards her. 'And I'll tell you something else: if he ever comes near you again, I *will* kill him. Him, his wife *and* his fucking kid.'

87

HAILEY SQUEEZED ROB'S hand and looked into his face.

The worst of the swelling had receded. There was still puffiness around his eyes, but now he was able to open them both with relative ease, although blackened by bruises too. Several blood vessels in the right eye had been ruptured during the attack, and a crimson mark stood out vividly against the surrounding white.

The intravenous drips had also been removed. On the whole the doctors had expressed delight, and also surprise, at the speed of Rob's recovery. However, he was all too conscious of the cuts and bruises that still crisscrossed his face and upper body.

There were several bunches of flowers in the room, including a small bouquet of lilies that bore the note: HOPE YOU ARE FEELING BETTER, DAD, LOVE BECKY.

There was also one from Jim Marsh: a large bunch of white carnations.

A smaller arrangement of mixed blooms had arrived from Frank Burnside. There were Get Well Soon cards too.

Hailey hadn't told too many people what had happened to her husband, but those she had informed seemed to have responded with some gesture of concern.

Hailey herself kissed his hand, noticing the bruises on his knuckles and wrist.

'The doctors said you must be pretty strong to recover so quickly,' she said.

'I don't *feel* very strong,' said Rob, shifting position slightly, wincing in pain. 'These bloody ribs are killing me.'

'It's going to take time, Rob. You were hurt badly.'

'Tell me about it,' he said sardonically.

There was an awkward silence broken by Hailey.

'You *are* coming home when they release you, aren't you?' she wanted to know.

He tried to take a deep breath, but the pain from his broken ribs prevented even that simple action.

'Rob?' she persisted.

'I suppose I was unlucky,' he said. 'Storming out and leaving you was supposed to create more of an impact. Now I'm going to need your help just to get in and out of a fucking chair.'

'Would you really have left us?' she wanted to know. 'Permanently, I mean?'

'I needed time to think things through. I still do – but I suppose what you said was right. I wasn't in any position to preach to you about having affairs, was I?'

She opened her mouth to say something. She was going to remind him that what had gone on between her and Walker *wasn't* an affair. In the end she said nothing.

'I suppose we're even now,' said Rob sadly.

'That isn't how it was supposed to be.'

'No, but that's the way it *is*.'

Hailey glanced at her watch. 'I'd better go,' she said, getting to her feet. 'Becky will be worried.'

'Give her my love.'

'You can give it to her yourself when you come home.'

'If I don't frighten her too much.' He touched a hand to his battered face.

Hailey leaned forward and kissed him on the forehead and lips.

'I love you, Rob,' she whispered.

'I know,' he said, squeezing her hand.

She picked up her handbag and headed for the door. As she reached it, she looked back at him and smiled.

He returned the smile.

Then she was gone.

88

He was sleeping when Sandy Bennett entered the room.

She moved slowly towards the bed, her eyes narrowing as she saw again the mass of abrasions and bruises that covered his face and body.

Clutching a small bunch of flowers in one hand, Sandy stood at the end of the bed, watching the gentle rise and fall of Rob's chest.

She had bought the blooms from a small shop in the foyer, just after she'd entered the hospital almost three hours ago.

There was a florist, a coffee shop and a small gift shop on the ground floor, where she'd sat patiently since her arrival, watching the visitors come and go. So many people.

Some had arrived with packages, with flowers. Some with balloons, some with toys.

She had wondered where they were all heading – what kind of illnesses the patients they were visiting suffered from.

That passed the time.

She had seen Hailey arrive around 7.30, watching her as she strode towards the row of lifts.

Sandy had been sure to remain well hidden amongst the other visitors and patients who populated this busy area of the hospital. She had positioned herself at a table behind a concrete pillar, able from there to see both the lifts and the main entrance to the hospital, but hidden from view should Hailey glance in that direction.

At one point a man in his mid-forties, dressed only in a dressing-gown and pyjama bottoms, had joined her at her table and sat there drinking his tea. He'd told her all about his prostate operation, and she listened politely, her attention hardly wavering from the lifts across the way.

The man had finally left her in peace to continue her vigil, drinking more of the strong coffee that the café sold. Continuing her game of guessing who each visitor had come to see. New-born children? Relatives with terminal illnesses? Mothers with arthritis? Fathers with kidney trouble?

She'd seen Hailey leave about fifteen minutes ago, but Sandy had waited deliberately before she'd headed briskly towards the lifts. When she'd first entered the hospital she'd checked with the receptionist which floor and room he was in. She now rode the lift to the third floor.

She was forced to lie to the ward sister at the nurses' station, telling her she was Rob's sister. She said she'd come a long way to see him, and that was why she was so late. But she'd promised not to stay long. Visiting hours were almost over.

The sister had relented and allowed her into his room.

Sandy moved nearer to him.

'I'm sorry,' she whispered close to his ear.

He didn't stir.

Sandy laid the small bunch of flowers on the bedside cabinet.

The small card bore the words: FROM SANDY.

She stepped back, gazing at him once more, before turning and heading for the door. She didn't look back.

As she closed the door behind her, a draught swirled across the room.

The card on the flowers fell to the floor. It floated down like an autumn leaf, and lay unseen beneath the bed.

*

Sandy never realized she was being followed.

The same eyes that saw her clamber into the Nova also watched the car from behind as she drove home.

In the gloom, she wasn't even aware that there was another car within fifty yards of her during the whole drive home. Similarly unaware that those same eyes watched her parking outside the flats where she lived.

Watched the light go on in her kitchen window.

She had no reason to think that anyone was interested in her movements.

Or those of her brother.

The same eyes that had watched her saw David Layton return to her flat just before 11.00 that same night. Saw Russell Poole wave him off as he headed into the small block.

The watcher waited another ten minutes, then left.

89

'YOU DIDN'T HAVE to do this, Jim,' said Hailey, smiling.

She looked across at James Marsh, who was sipping his Southern Comfort.

'I know I didn't *have* to,' he told her. 'I *wanted* to – just to say thanks and all that old crap.'

'Thanks for what?'

'Coming back to work for me. Organizing this anniversary gig and the party so efficiently.'

'You're paying me well to do it, Jim, remember?'

'Christ, that's a point,' he chuckled. 'Perhaps I should let *you* buy the lunch instead.'

He signalled to the waiter to bring him another drink. The restaurant of the Pavilion Hotel was fairly quiet. The main rush of diners had long since departed, back to their offices or wherever else they plied their various trades. Marsh had no such need to hurry.

The Pavilion was an old building – early 1920s he guessed – but it had undergone such major refitting and refurbishment during the past five years that it looked as if it belonged with the new structures that made up the rest of the small town that had sprung up around it. The only thing that hadn't changed much was the restaurant itself. It was a massive conservatory-like building framed on three sides by huge glass panels that allowed diners to look out over an orchard and an ornate garden.

Sumptuously decorated with original furniture and carpets, it also boasted an enormous chandelier suspended from the centre of the glass roof. To Hailey, it looked as if thousands of crystalline tears had been fused together to create this magnificent adornment.

Marsh had hired the entire hotel for the night of the gig. Members of Waterhole would stay here, too. The party itself would be held in the room in which they now sat. Huge oak tables, each seating up to twenty, would be attended by waiters and waitresses bringing food prepared by three master chefs.

The list of guests had swelled from sixty to over one hundred. Record company people, local dignitaries, media, friends and family.

Family . . .

Marsh ran his finger slowly around the rim of his glass.

'What's the matter, Jim?' Hailey wanted to know, noticing his pensive expression.

'I was just thinking about my kids,' he told her.

'Aren't any of them coming to the party?'

'I doubt it,' he said bitterly, draining what was left in his glass. 'They don't approve of their dad's plans.'

'Are you still going to announce your wedding at the party?'

He nodded. 'Do you think there'll be lots of disapproving looks? Much silent tutting amongst the morally righteous?'

'Who cares if there is? Who you marry is *your* business,' said Hailey defensively.

'Even if that someone is half my age?'

'It's your life, Jim.'

'One of my sons called Paula a gold-digger. I don't think he likes the idea of having a stepmother who's only a year older than himself.'

'It doesn't matter what *they* think, as long as *you're* happy. You love Paula and *she* loves you. She wouldn't be marrying you otherwise.'

'Oh, I don't know. A personal fortune of thirty million does make a man that *little* bit more attractive, doesn't it?' He smiled.

Hailey also managed to grin.

'Anyway, what about *your* family?' Marsh asked. 'How's Rob?'

'He's due home tomorrow. I'm picking him up from the hospital.'

'And the police still haven't got any idea who attacked him?'

Hailey shook her head.

'I wish *I* had,' she said quietly. 'I'd kill them.'

He regarded her silently across the table. Saw the anger in her expression.

'He'll be well enough to come to the gig and the party afterwards, won't he?' Marsh asked.

Hailey nodded. 'I think Becky would drag him along, even if I didn't,' she said, grinning. 'She can't wait to see Waterhole in the flesh.'

'Even though they *are* a bunch of arseholes. I was right, wasn't I? People like Lennon, Hendrix and Janis Joplin would be spinning in their graves if they could see those dickheads now. Tell me I'm wrong.'

'I can't,' she admitted.

'At the risk of sounding like an old fart,' Marsh said, 'this world really has turned to shit, hasn't it? It makes you long for the good old days.' He chuckled. 'Do you know what we had in the good old days? Malnutrition, rickets, TB and poverty.'

They both laughed.

'You've come a long way, Jim,' Hailey said. 'We *all* have.'

'Let's drink to that,' he echoed.

They both raised their glasses.

'To rickets,' he said.

Again they laughed.

90

'Please let us call an ambulance.'

Dr Raymond Simmons stood beside the bed, looking down at Adam Walker, watching for any flicker of emotion on the younger man's face.

Adam sat in a chair beside his father's bed, staring at the old man lying on his back, eyes closed.

Every now and then his lips would flutter silently, as if he was trying to speak. But no sound would emerge.

'Mr Walker—' Simmons began.

'I heard you, Doctor,' Adam said flatly, without taking his eyes off his father.

'The longer we delay, the less chance there is for your father. Please let us call.'

'You once told me that you could cope with his condition *here* as well as any hospital could.'

'I meant his ongoing condition,' Simmons protested, 'his kidney problems. This is entirely different. This is a medical emergency.'

Adam heard the urgency in the doctor's voice, but it made little impression on him.

'You called me an hour ago,' he said, his tone measured. 'I told you then that I wanted no ambulance. That I didn't want my father taken to a hospital.'

'He's my responsibility while he's here at Bayfield House.'

'He's *my* father,' rasped Adam, finally turning to look at the doctor.

'Then let us help him,' Simmons said. 'Let the hospital help him.'

Adam continued to gaze down at his stricken father.

'A stroke you said?' he murmured.

'It looks like it,' the doctor answered. 'And that means speed is important. The quicker he can be taken to hospital, the better his chances of survival.'

Adam chuckled sardonically. 'Survival,' he muttered. 'What has he got to look forward to, Doctor? If the hospital manage to keep him alive, he's looking at weeks – months, if he's lucky – on a life-support machine. That's about it, isn't it?'

Simmons nodded slowly.

'Not really much in the way of survival, is it?' Adam said, shifting slightly in his seat. His hands were resting on his lap, the fingers entwined. Slowly he pulled them apart, and pressed one to his father's temple. 'He's dead in there now. He has been for years. Alzheimer's, renal failure – he's better off dead.'

'I can't just stand here and watch a man die, Mr Walker,' Simmons protested.

'Then get out,' Adam said flatly, looking up at the doctor once more. 'No one's asking you to stay.'

Simmons was momentarily taken aback by his tone. He looked into the other man's eyes and saw nothing.

No emotion. Nothing . . .

Just a cool detachment that raised the hairs on the back of the doctor's neck.

'I'll stay with him,' said Adam quietly, returning his attention to his father. 'This is what he would have wanted. He never wanted to die in a hospital. He always said that.'

Simmons hesitated.

'Please go, Doctor,' Adam insisted.

He heard the door close as Simmons left.

The only sound now seemed to be the ticking of the clock.

'You're going to die,' he said softly to the wizened form in the bed before him.

Philip Walker made a low gurgling sound in his throat.

'And I'm going to watch you,' Adam said, leaning closer.

For fleeting seconds his father's eyes opened, and Adam found himself gazing into those watery orbs. He saw something there, didn't he?

Was it a final moment of clarity?

Was it pain?

Or fear?

His father reached out a hand, gnarled fingers scratching across the sheet towards Adam, who sat motionless.

Still he gazed into his father's open eyes.

'You're going to your God,' Adam whispered. 'You should be pleased – or perhaps not. How are you going to explain to Him some of the things you did to me?'

His father's eyes closed again, but his hand continued to flex as if seeking contact with his son.

Adam looked down at the hand.

'Don't touch me,' he said scathingly. 'You're never going to touch me again.'

Again the eyes opened. Wider this time.

'Just die,' Adam said, his words barely audible.

In the silence of the room the clock continued its somnolent ticking.

Each second a fragment of life.

Adam sat back in the chair and looked on.

91

AT FIRST SHE'D been terrified.

Becky had looked up at her father's face and recoiled from the sight that greeted her. The patchwork of cuts and bruises: some still vivid purple, others yellowed and black at the edges.

But, within a matter of minutes, she had run to him and embraced him.

Hailey had carried his holdall as they'd walked to the car, happy to see that Becky had chosen to hold his hand.

On the way home she and Rob had chatted in the car, while Hailey drove in virtual silence. Now, as they pulled into their driveway, Hailey hurried around to help Rob out.

'I can manage,' he said sharply, pulling himself out of the car, but wincing as he felt the pain from his still-healing ribs. He paused a moment, sucking in lungfuls of air, as if the effort of clambering out of the Astra was too great. He straightened up, then made his way slowly towards the front door, Becky close by.

Once inside, Becky hurried off to play in her room. Rob wandered into the sitting room and slumped in an armchair.

'Do you want a coffee, or something stronger?' Hailey asked.

He sat in silence for long moments, gazing around the room as if he'd never seen it before.

'Coffee, please,' he told her. 'Whisky doesn't mix too well with the painkillers they gave me.'

'Do you want anything to eat?'

He shook his head.

'Can I get you the paper?' Hailey persisted.

'Stop treating me like a fucking invalid, Hailey,' he snapped. 'I'm not a cripple.'

'I'm just trying to help,' she protested.

'Then let me do things on my own. *You* might not always be around.'

She pushed the sitting-room door shut. 'Meaning what?' she demanded.

'You might not be here if there's something I want,' he repeated. 'I've got to learn how to manage. Besides, it's only two cracked ribs I've got, not a broken spine.'

'The doctors said you had to take it easy for a week or so,' she reminded him.

'I can't afford to take it easy for a week or so,' he told her. 'I'm going in to work as soon as I can.'

'Rob, for Christ's sake!'

'What do you *want* me to do? Sit around here in an empty house every day feeling sorry for myself? Thinking about how lucky I am to be alive? Thinking about the bastard who did this to me? Thinking about *other* things, too?'

She knew what he meant.

'I'm not going to *keep* telling you, Rob,' Hailey said wearily. 'Nothing happened between Walker and me.'

In fact, Adam had asked if there was anything he could do to help.

Rob didn't answer.

She crossed to his chair and sat on the arm.

'What have I got to do to convince you?' she wanted to know.

He could only shake his head.

'What about that coffee?' he asked finally.

She reached out a hand and gently touched one of the yellowish bruises on his left cheek.

'If I knew who'd done this to you,' she said softly, 'I'd kill them.'

Rob met her gaze. 'Am I supposed to say thanks?'

'Don't make it any more difficult than it has to be, Rob.' Hailey got to her feet.

'If it's any consolation, I now know what *you* felt like – when you found out about me and Sandy.'

'No, Rob,' she told him, one hand on the door, 'it *isn't* any consolation.'

92

SANDY BENNETT TURNED the key in the lock, then twisted the handle once or twice to check it was secure. Satisfied, she made her way towards the lift and jabbed the CALL button.

She rode it to the ground floor, then strode out into the cool night air.

She paused for fleeting seconds, looking up at the darkening sky, searching the heavens for signs that it was going to rain or turn colder. She wondered about returning for a heavier jacket, but finally decided she'd be fine in what she wore already.

The black trouser suit was made of wool; it should be absolutely fine.

She selected her car keys from her pocket and wandered over towards the Nova. It was, she realized, the first time she'd been out socially since she was sacked from her job at BG Trucks. A friend of hers she'd known since college had called and asked her out for a drink. Sandy had hesitated, then finally decided that she couldn't spend the rest of her life living like a hermit, so had accepted the invitation.

She was looking forward to it now. It would give her a chance to forget about Rob.

The bastard!

She was angry with herself for even thinking about him. Where would he be now? At home playing happy families with his wife and kid?

Forget about him.

She opened the driver's door and slid behind the wheel.

Her brother was out for the night, and she didn't even dare to imagine what *he* might be up to.

Sandy was wondering how much longer she could let him stay with her. How long before he became a burden? She knew all the clichés about family and blood being thicker than water, but all the same he couldn't stay with her indefinitely, could he?

She twisted the key in the ignition.

Nothing.

No spark. No sound.

She tried again, glancing at the dashboard.

Flat battery?

'Shit,' she murmured. Typical! Her first night out for Christ knows how long, and the car's playing up.

She turned the ignition key again.

Still the car didn't react. Not even the splutter of an engine *trying* to start.

Sandy banged the wheel irritably, and swung herself out.

She had two choices now: either ring the RAC and stand around waiting, or call a taxi and deal with the car tomorrow.

Sandy looked at her watch. She wasn't due to meet her friend until 8.30.

Taxi or RAC?

She slammed the door and headed back towards her flat, where she dialled a cab.

He'd be there in five minutes, he told her. Still slightly irritated, she made her way back outside again.

The Nova stood there defiantly.

Try it once more. If it works, you can always cancel the cab.

She crossed to the car and slid behind the steering wheel again.

Sandy pushed the key into the ignition and turned it.

This time the Nova started immediately.

'Yes!' said Sandy, fists clenched in triumph.

It was then that she noticed the condensation on the windscreen.

It was on the *inside*.

As if someone had been breathing on the glass.

Someone inside?

Someone . . .

She heard a grunt behind her, then came a terrifyingly powerful impact just below her left ear.

Sandy felt agonizing pain, but she couldn't scream.

Not even when she realized that the knife had been rammed into the angle between her jawbone and skull, so powerfully it practically shattered the lower mandible. Blood erupted from the wound and spattered noisily against the side window.

She felt her head flopping backwards. Felt a strong hand grabbing her hair, slamming her back against the headrest.

Then she felt the freezing blade against her throat. Felt the grazing as its serrations rasped against her flesh.

Then the knife was drawn across her throat with incredible force.

The gash it opened spread from one ear to the other, her riven throat yawning like the gills of a fish. Blood exploded from the massive wound, arteries and veins spewing their crimson load onto the windscreen.

She felt consciousness slipping from her.

By the time the knife was driven into her face for the third time, she was already close to death. Slumped in her seat, the life draining from her.

Even when the tip of the blade sliced one of her eyeballs in two, and sent vitreous fluid spilling down her chest to mingle with the thick viscosity of her blood, she didn't move.

And she knew nothing of the ten wounds that followed.

93

THE RAIN BEAT out a steady tattoo on Adam Walker's umbrella but he barely noticed it.

He stood gazing at the grave, every now and then drawing in a deep breath.

The smell of wet earth and grass was strong in his nostrils. Piled high on either side of the deep hole, the clods of dirt were turning to brownish-yellow mud under the downpour.

Raindrops battered the cellophane-wrapped flowers around the grave, the crackling sound mingling with the beating of rain against his black umbrella, and he glanced up at the sky, wondering when the dark clouds would pass. Great solid banks of them hovered there. All they offered was the promise of more rain – more misery.

All the mourners had left.

He'd been surprised at how many people had turned up to see his father laid to rest. Some staff – even some patients – from Bayfield House. Even a few of the old man's ex-parishioners. Other people he didn't recognize.

He'd accepted their condolences and their apologetic handshakes, then thanked them for coming. Expressed his gratitude for their floral tributes.

All these tasks he'd performed like some kind of automaton. And most of the time he'd looked right through them, in the direction of the grave itself. As if afraid that his father wasn't actually dead. Perhaps the old man was going to clamber up from that six-foot-deep hole and announce his own resurrection. Just as he'd spent his time as a vicar preaching about the resurrection of Christ.

Perhaps, Adam told himself, that was why he had stayed so close to the grave for so long. Maybe he had to be sure that his father was gone for good. He wondered if that realization would only come when the hole was filled in with earth. When the headstone finally stood there. When the floral tributes had died and rotted away.

The vicar performing the short ceremony had babbled on about his father going to a better place, then he'd shaken hands with Walker and told him not to worry about his father any more. That he was at peace now.

Walker had nodded slowly.

A peace the old man didn't deserve.

He had looked into the eyes of the vicar, then at his dog-collar, and he had felt anger. Whether it had showed or not, he neither knew nor cared.

And what words would the headstone bear?

'Beloved Father. Sadly missed.'

'At Peace.'

'Rot In Hell'

Walker gripped the umbrella more tightly, and prepared to turn away from the grave at last.

'Adam.'

He heard the voice and recognized it immediately.

Hailey Gibson made her way slowly across the wet grass towards him.

Walker smiled.

'What are you doing here?' he wanted to know.

'I heard about your father's death,' she explained. 'Caroline told me. She said the funeral was today.'

'It's good of you to come – but why *did* you? You didn't *know* him.'

She caught the slight edge to his voice.

'I came to see *you*,' Hailey said quietly, her voice almost lost beneath the falling rain. 'To see how you were coping. Whatever's happened between us, I still wanted to say I'm sorry about your father.'

His expression softened a little.

'I appreciate it,' he told her. 'Especially considering, a week or two ago, you wouldn't even *speak* to me.'

Hailey opened her mouth to say something but then decided against it.

Walker turned back to face the grave.

'I always thought I'd feel differently when it happened,' he said. 'I thought I'd throw a party when I found out he was dead.' He smiled wanly.

'He was still your father,' Hailey reminded him, 'no matter what happened between you.'

'You mean even though he brutally abused me when I was a child, I should still shed a tear for him? I don't think I've got any tears left, Hailey. Not for *him*. I cried them all when I was younger. Usually after he'd just left me alone in my room, when he'd finished punishing me. After he'd told me it was God's Will. And I believed him *then*. Stupid, wasn't I?'

Hailey shook her head. Thought about reaching out to touch his arm. To offer some words of comfort.

She realized there were none that were adequate.

Above them, the wind set the lower branches of the trees rustling. The rain continued to fall.

Hailey regarded him silently for a moment, then turned away.

'Thanks for coming,' he said softly. 'I mean it. I'll see you around.' She nodded.

'Do you need a lift back?' she wanted to know.

'I'll walk. Perhaps it'll clear my head. Thanks, anyway.'

Hailey was a few feet away from him when he spoke again.

'I *am* sorry he's dead,' Walker said. 'Do you know why? Because *I* had to sit and watch it happen. And what really bothers me is that he died too soon, too quickly. He didn't have *enough* pain. I wish he'd died in agony. I wish *I'd* killed him.'

94

DAVID LAYTON SWALLOWED what was left in his glass and banged it down on the bar top.

'Your round,' he said, belching loudly, and prodding Russell Poole.

Poole was fiddling around with a small calculator, and muttered something under his breath as the figures suddenly disappeared. He ordered two more pints and readjusted his position on his bar stool.

The Black Squirrel was busy. The jukebox was thundering out the latest sounds and the never-ending electronic buzz of numerous fruit machines mingled with several loud conversations to form one discordant cacophony.

Layton surveyed the other drinkers dispassionately, glancing at their faces – taking a little more interest in the young women who occasionally entered. One in particular, a blonde in a black mini-dress who had come in with two friends, had already smiled coyly at him. If she was more than eighteen, he'd be surprised. Perhaps not even that: the make-up was too heavy, and she tottered on her high heels like a tightrope walker. Still, she looked good, and eighteen months inside had made him less discerning. He smiled back at her.

The youth who approached Russell Poole did so nervously.

Layton saw him coming: easing his way through the crush near the bar, his gaze never leaving Poole.

Late teens, thought Layton.

The lad's face was pitted, and his hair was so slick with gel it looked as if someone had dipped his head in a vat of grease.

He stood looking at Poole, then reached out and touched his shoulder.

Poole spun round to face the youth.

'Someone told me to talk to you,' said the younger man, swallowing hard. 'They said you could get stuff.'

Poole hawked and swallowed. 'Fuck off,' he snapped, turning his back.

'I've got money,' protested the youth, and shoved a balled-up twenty onto the bar in front of Poole.

'What the fuck are you doing?' Poole rasped, looking first at the money, then at the youth.

'Do you know this cunt?' Layton wanted to know.

Poole shook his head.

'I need some stuff,' the youth repeated.

'And I told you to fuck off,' Poole said.

'What kind of stuff?' Layton enquired.

'Well, you know . . .' The youth smiled.

'No, I don't. You tell me,' Layton demanded.

'Whizz,' the youth told him, the smile fading. He was picking nervously at a whitehead on his cheek.

'Listen, spotty,' Layton said quietly. 'Who told you to come over here and interrupt our conversation?'

'Spotty' looked bemused.

'What's the stuff for?' Poole asked.

'A party,' the youth explained.

'And you think that my friend can get it for you?' Layton insisted.

'Spotty' nodded.

'Come back tomorrow night, same time,' Poole told him. 'It'll cost you fifty.'

'Fuck', said the youth dejectedly.

'You don't like the price, then fuck off,' Poole said.

'We've got overheads.' Layton grinned. He picked up the twenty and stuffed it into his jeans.

'That's mine,' the youth protested.

'Call it a finder's fee,' Layton chuckled. 'Now fuck off, spotty.'

The youth hesitated, picked at the whitehead a few more times, then disappeared into the crowd.

'Fucking kids,' said Poole.

Layton drained what was left in his glass and got to his feet.

'I'm off,' he said. 'I'll give you a call tomorrow.'

'Where are you going?'

'I might hang around outside and wait for that little blonde,' Layton chuckled.

'She's only about fifteen.'

'Who cares? Old enough to bleed, old enough to breed.'

He ruffled Poole's hair, and pushed his way through the crowd towards the exit.

The blonde smiled at him again as he left.

As he stepped outside, he pulled up the collar of his jacket. The wind had grown cold and he headed down the street towards the bottom of the hill, past closed or empty shops, most of which sported security grilles over their windows. Several of the streetlights were broken. The road was dark, and few vehicles used this thoroughfare at night.

Except the one that now sped towards Layton, accelerating as it saw him step into the road.

The driver had sat patiently outside the pub for the last hour – and now the wait was over.

The approaching car was driving without headlights.

All Layton heard was the roar of the engine, as it bore down on him.

Even if he'd seen it, his chances of avoiding the speeding vehicle would have been slim.

It hit him, doing sixty.

The impact sent him hurtling into the air, where he seemed to be suspended for precious seconds before crashing back down and bouncing off the car's roof.

As he hit the ground, he heard the screech of tyres.

The car was turning round.

Coming back towards him.

Agonizing pain ran the full length of his left leg, and up most of his back.

Movement was difficult.

His head was spinning, but even in his battered state he realized that, if he didn't get out of the road, the car was going to run over him.

He looked up, saw the vehicle speeding towards him.

It skidded to a halt a couple of feet away, engine still running.

Layton could feel the heat from the radiator grille, the car was so close. He smelled petrol and rubber.

Heard the sound of a door opening.

Tasted blood in his mouth, felt it running down his face.

The pain in his leg seemed to intensify.

He saw that the driver was carrying something.

Something heavy.

There was a thunderous impact across the top of his head.

Darkness.

95

HE WAS BLIND.

For terrifying seconds, David Layton was convinced he had gone blind.

His heart hammered against his ribs and he tried to cry out, but then he realized that the darkness was caused not by blindness, but by the strip of material fastened so tightly around his eyes.

The same material that had been used to bind his wrists and ankles?

Indeed, even if he had wanted to scream, he couldn't.

His mouth was sealed shut by several strips of masking tape wound right around the back of his head. It stuck to his hair and pulled at his scalp when he tried to move.

The pain from his injured leg was almost unbearable, and he realized that it must be broken. Somewhere around the thigh, he guessed.

Had the blindfold been removed, he would have noticed the gleaming point of bone protruding through his ripped jeans, its end bloody and leaking dark red marrow.

He had no idea where he was, or how long he'd been unconscious.

More to the point, he had no idea who had run him down, then bundled him into the car, and spent so long carefully blindfolding, binding and gagging him.

Pain and fear filled his mind in equal measures.

He tried to shout through the masking-tape gag. Tried to tell whoever had run him down that there had been some kind of mistake.

That he had money he could give them.

That he needed medical treatment for the shattering pain in his broken leg.

He was sitting on grass: that much he did know. He could feel its damp blades beneath his hands. Could smell wet earth in his nostrils.

Wherever he was, it was deadly quiet.

No passing cars. No dogs barking. No voices.

He guessed he was in the countryside somewhere. He didn't know how long he'd been travelling in the car. Didn't know how long his captor had been driving.

He didn't even know what time it was.

From the silence, though, he guessed it was still night.

He heard movement close to him.

Tried to gauge where it was coming from. His left? His right?

Jesus, if only he could see. If only he could get free. Get his hands on the bastard who had done this.

Anger now began to enter his mind, but it disappeared rapidly.

The fear returned.

He heard more movement. Realized that his captor was standing only feet away.

The pain in his leg had not diminished and each movement brought fresh waves of agony.

For frenzied moments he struggled to free his hands, then gave up and slumped back exhausted.

His captor had moved closer now. Layton felt a hand against his thigh. Against the protruding bone that stuck out through his torn skin and ripped jeans.

It was that same hand that gripped the marrow-weeping bone and pulled.

Pain unlike anything he had ever experienced before enveloped his entire body.

Inside the gag he shrieked in unimaginable agony, felt consciousness slipping away from him, but a series of sharp slaps to his face kept him hanging on. Denied him the oblivion of a blackout.

Blows began to rain down all over his legs.

Blows that combined effortless expertise with tremendous power. Blows with the same heavy object that had first struck his head. Blows that shattered more bone.

The tibia splintered with a harsh crack.

The patella of the right knee took three whacks before it finally broke.

The left one went after just one thunderous strike.

This time he could not retain consciousness and he welcomed the darkness, but it would not come. More sharp blows to his face. Water splashed onto his cheeks and something freezing cold against his neck that he realized instantly was a blade.

Tears were coursing down his cheeks. Pain? Fear?

His entire lower body felt as if it was ablaze.

Then he felt another blow, this time to his shoulder.

The left clavicle broke easily.

So did the right.

The knife was pressed against his cheek again.

Drawn quickly across it to open the flesh to the bone.

When he felt hands pulling at his shirt, ripping it open, he prayed to a God he didn't believe in to help him.

When those same hands tore open his trousers and tugged them down slightly, he began to sob uncontrollably.

When the tip of the blade was forced into the eye of his shrivelled penis he prayed for death.

It was a long time coming.

96

As HAILEY WALKED into the sitting room, Rob said nothing. He merely tapped his watch and shook his head.

'All right,' she said, kicking off her shoes, 'I'm sorry. I know it's late. I *did* phone, if you remember.'

'Yeah, two fucking hours ago,' he snapped. 'It's after eleven, Hailey.'

'I know what time it is, Rob, and I said I'm sorry. If I could have been here any quicker I would have been.'

'When you went back to work for Jim Marsh, you said it would be part-time. You didn't say anything about being out until all hours of the fucking night.'

'Don't exaggerate. It couldn't be helped – you know that. I didn't want this any more than you.'

'That's *two* nights this week you've been out so late. What about Becky?'

'You're her father. It doesn't do you any harm to look after her once in a while. How many nights have *you* been out late? Or how many nights didn't you come home at *all*?'

'Don't start that shit again.'

'Then how many times do I have to say I'm sorry? This gig is important to Jim. It's important to *me*. *I've* done most of the work organizing it. So I want to make sure it runs smoothly.'

'I thought everything was meant to be sorted.'

'There were a couple of last-minute hitches: they had to be cleared up. It all happens in two days, you know.'

'I know. Becky keeps reminding me.'

'She's looking forward to it, Rob – that's why. *She* understands that I have to work on it. Why can't you?'

'I'll be pleased when the whole fucking thing is over. Perhaps we can get back to normal.'

'What the hell is *normal* around here any more? Our relationship?'

She slumped down in the chair opposite him.

'After what we've been through, Rob, I'm not sure I'd know normal again if I fell over it,' she said wearily.

He regarded her silently.

'How do you feel?' she asked finally.

'I took a couple of painkillers earlier, so I'm OK. I was more concerned about you, and where you were.'

She was aware of his gaze trailing over her.

'You're wearing a different blouse,' he said. 'That's not the one you had on when you left this afternoon.'

'I spilt some coffee on the other one.'

'Whose coffee?'

'You think I've been with Walker, don't you?' she said irritably.

'I didn't say that.'

'You didn't *have* to. Christ, Rob, when are you going to believe me? Nothing happened between us and, like I've said to you before, *you're* in no position to start lecturing me about adultery, are you? I mean, you wrote the fucking book.'

She got to her feet.

'I'm going to bed,' Hailey told him. 'Are you coming?'

'In a bit,' he said, gazing at the television.

'We can't go on like this, Rob,' she said, pausing at the door.

He didn't look round.

'No,' Rob replied. 'We can't.'

She stood there a moment longer, then gently closed the door – leaving him alone in the room.

97

SHE HADN'T SLEPT well the night before.

Hailey yawned, and studied her reflection in the mirror – noting that the image staring back at her had dark rings beneath the eyes.

Dressed in just bra and panties, she carefully put on her make-up, occasionally glancing across at the bed.

She had no idea what time Rob had come up the previous night. One o'clock? Later? He'd slipped into bed beside her, and soon she had heard his low breathing.

She'd thought about rolling across to lie nearer to him but, when he turned onto his side and showed her his back, she'd decided against it.

He'd left the house about half an hour ago. Despite her protestations, he'd announced that he would first take Becky to school, then later that morning he was going back to work. He needed, he'd told her, to get out of the house.

Hailey finished doing her make-up and crossed to the wardrobe, where she selected a grey two-piece and black shoes.

She was buttoning the jacket when she heard the front door open. Heard footsteps climbing the stairs.

'Was she OK?' Hailey asked as Rob walked into the bedroom.

He nodded. 'Fine,' he announced, running appraising eyes over her. 'Like you said last night, perhaps it's about time I started doing more for my own daughter.'

'That *wasn't* what I said.'

'It's what you meant. I didn't realize I was so useless as a father. Perhaps you should have told me before.'

'Now you're being ridiculous. Stop being such a bloody martyr, Rob. You twist everything I say to suit *you*.'

He regarded her silently.

'I'll pick Becky up,' Hailey said, brushing fluff from her skirt.

'If you're not too busy?' he chided.

Hailey exhaled. 'Don't start, Rob,' she said. 'Not now.'

'I was just making sure. I didn't know if you might be out until late again. I didn't know what Jim Marsh might have in store for you today.'

She heard the disdain in his voice.

'What time are *you* getting home?' she wanted to know.

He shrugged.

'You shouldn't really be going in to work yet, Rob,' Hailey told him. 'The doctor said you had to rest, and I'm sure Frank can manage without you. Even *you're* not indispensable, you know.' She smiled, but he didn't return it, merely looked at her indifferently.

She was about to say something else when she heard the doorbell.

'*I'll* go,' Hailey said, making her way down the stairs.

They creaked protestingly as she hurried down to the hall, running a hand through her hair before she opened the door.

There was something familiar about the man who stood there. Dressed in a dark brown suit and shoes that looked as if they hadn't tasted polish for a while, he smiled thinly at her.

'Mrs Gibson?' he asked.

'Yes,' said Hailey.

'You don't remember me, do you?' said the newcomer. 'I'm not surprised. The last time we met you had a lot on your mind.' He fumbled inside his jacket for a slim leather wallet that he flipped open. 'Detective Constable Tate.'

Hailey smiled.

'Yes, I remember,' she told him, her smile fading slightly. 'You were at the hospital the night my husband was attacked.'

He nodded.

'What can I do for you?' Hailey wanted to know.

'It's your husband I'd like to speak to. Would that be possible?'

'Is there something wrong?'

'Yes, there is.'

98

'I'm GLAD TO see you're feeling better now, Mr Gibson,' said Tate as he shifted position on the sofa.

'Thanks,' Rob murmured.

Both he and Hailey were looking at the policeman intently. They saw his brow furrow, and he sat forward slightly.

'I know you're both wondering what I want, so I'll try to get this over with as quickly as possible,' Tate told them.

He looked directly at Rob. 'Mr Gibson, you knew a young lady called Sandra Bennett, didn't you?' Tate made it sound more like a statement than a question.

Hailey glared at Rob.

'She worked for me until recently,' he said flatly.

Tate glanced at Hailey, saw the venom in her expression.

'We know that,' said the DC. 'But you were personally involved with her too, weren't you?'

Rob swallowed hard.

'I'm sorry. I know this is difficult,' Tate continued.

'How do *you* know my husband had an affair with her?' Hailey demanded.

'We found some correspondence from your husband at her flat,' Tate informed her. 'A number of letters. There were some gift tags too, with your writing on them, Mr Gibson.' He looked at Hailey. 'You knew this affair was going on, Mrs Gibson?'

'I found out in the end,' said Hailey sharply.

Tate nodded, suddenly feeling very intrusive.

'I didn't know it was against the law to have an affair,' said Rob, attempting a smile. 'You're not here to arrest me, are you?'

Hailey shot him a furious glance.

'When was the last time you spoke to Sandra Bennett?' Tate wanted to know.

'When I sacked her,' Rob informed him. 'Why?'

'She was murdered three days ago.'

'Oh God,' Rob murmured, colour draining from his cheeks.

'I would have come here sooner, but there were other developments, and we weren't sure of a positive identification at first.'

Rob ran a hand through his hair.

'Who killed her?' he said slowly.

Hailey looked at him angrily.

Still such concern? Even now she's dead?

'I wish I could tell you, Mr Gibson.' Tate looked across at Hailey. 'Did *you* ever meet her, Mrs Gibson?'

Hailey shook her head.

'How was she killed?' Rob asked quietly.

'She was stabbed,' Tate informed him.

'There's been nothing in the papers,' Rob muttered.

'A murder doesn't merit many column inches in the nationals these days. It's become too commonplace, I'm afraid. We haven't released too many details to the media anyway.'

'What's this murder got to do with my husband?' enquired Hailey. 'Or did you just assume he'd be interested because he'd been fucking her?'

Tate regarded her evenly. He had heard the vehemence in her voice.

'During your, er . . . relationship, did you ever meet her brother, Mr Gibson?' the DC continued.

'I didn't even know she *had* a brother,' Rob explained. 'She never mentioned him.'

'I'm not surprised. He was a small-time villain. Spent most of his life in and out of prison. Not the kind of sibling you'd want to talk about. It's just that we have reason to believe it was Sandra Bennett's brother who attacked *you* last week.'

Rob looked puzzled.

'Forensics came up with hair and fibre samples that linked him to you. We think it might have been some kind of revenge for what you did to his sister.'

'I didn't do anything to his sister,' Rob protested.

'You sacked her from her job. You ended your affair with her. It's possible that her brother, in some kind of twisted way, thought he was protecting her by attacking you. It's unlikely she knew anything about it. However, it also gives *you* motive.'

'For what?' Rob asked.

'For killing him. He was murdered last night.'

'And you think *I* did it?'

'No, Mr Gibson, I don't. Just as I don't think, for one minute, that you killed Sandra Bennett. But I'll ask you anyway where you were last night.'

'Here, with my daughter,' said Rob.

'Thank you,' he said. 'I won't take up any more of your time.'

'Do you think the same person killed them both?' Hailey wanted to know.

'It's more than likely. I can't say any more.' Again the policeman smiled.

'I'll see you out.' Hailey followed him towards the door.

Tate paused on the doorstep.

'I'm sorry I had to drag up your husband's involvement with Sandra Bennett,' he told her apologetically.

'Don't worry about it,' Hailey replied, forcing a smile. 'I know you're only doing your job.'

'Thank you for your time,' said Tate, and set off back to his waiting car.

She closed the door behind him and leant against it for a moment.

Her smile grew broader.

99

'I THOUGHT YOU were going to burst into tears when he told you,' said Hailey acidly.

Rob merely shook his head. 'I can't believe it,' he said quietly.

'What? That she's dead? Or that it hurt you so much to hear it? You still care about her, don't you?'

'Jesus Christ, Hailey, she was fucking stabbed to death,' Rob snarled angrily. 'How am I supposed to react? It was a shock hearing it. Whoever it was, I would have felt the same.'

'But the fact that you knew her so intimately just made it worse,' Hailey said, her voice heavy with scorn. 'And she'd even kept some of your letters – how touching. And gift tags? What kind of presents did you buy her, Rob? How much money did you waste on that fucking slag?'

'You're glad she's dead, aren't you?'

'I won't shed any tears over her.'

Rob shook his head. 'I don't expect you to.'

'She had it coming,' Hailey said flatly.

'You're a cold bitch sometimes.'

'Perhaps it was someone else whose marriage she'd ruined. She seemed to make a habit of that. Who else had she fucked other than you, Rob? How many other married men had she used?'

'Give it a fucking rest, will you?'

'Why? Is the memory painful?'

'It was over between us, Hailey – you know that. How would you feel if some copper walked in here and told you that your friend Adam Walker had been murdered?'

'There was nothing between us.'

'I've only got your word for that.'

They regarded each other angrily for long moments.

'I'd have thought *you'd* have been pleased, too,' Hailey exclaimed. 'I mean, if she thought that much of you, why did she get her brother to beat you up and nearly kill you?'

'You heard what Tate said. He didn't think she knew anything about that business.'

'He didn't *think* she knew.'

'Perhaps he was the one who tried to run me off the road that night.'

'And the one who pushed dog shit through the letterbox? And slashed your tyres? And broke into the house?'

Rob shot her an angry glance.

'What are you talking about? What break-in?' he demanded.

She told him about the dolls.

'Why the fuck didn't you tell me about that?' he rasped. 'Why didn't you tell the police?'

Go on, tell him the truth. At the time you thought it was Walker. You were protecting him, weren't you?

'It doesn't matter now,' Hailey said. '*He's* gone too. They're both out of our lives. That's all *I* wanted.'

'Well, you got your wish, didn't you? I hope you're happy.'

'You don't know what he might have done next, Rob. What if he'd attacked Becky? Or me?'

Rob exhaled wearily. 'Well, we won't know now, will we?'

He glanced at his watch.

'You'd better go,' he said. 'You're going to be late. You don't want that, do you?'

She put a hand on his shoulder.

'What happened to her, and to her brother,' she said quietly, 'it's for the best. You'll see.'

'Are we sending flowers to the funeral?' he said flatly.

Hailey smiled humourlessly.

'That isn't funny, Rob,' she told him.

She left him sitting alone.

100

IN THE MORTUARY the smell was always the same.

The pungent odour of chemicals, mingled with the more caustic aroma of antiseptic.

And the heavy, cloying stench of death.

It was a smell that DC Tate had come to know well, but one that he'd never got used to. Never would get used to either, he told himself.

He closed the door behind him and walked slowly into the large, high-ceilinged room. It was painted a uniformly dull green: the same colour as the smocks of those who worked within. There were two or three smocks also hanging on pegs of the far wall.

Four mortuary slabs.

Tables, the staff liked to call them, but to Tate they were slabs, pure and simple. Stainless steel with a gutter and a number of strategically placed holes, for drainage.

Beyond them were the lockers where bodies were stored for various reasons.

Some corpses were awaiting examination. Some were waiting to be removed – perhaps for burial. Others would remain there for months. Unclaimed. Unwanted.

It was a storehouse for sightless eyes.

There was a small office just beyond, its door firmly closed. It bore a sign saying PRIVATE.

A small trolley stood beside one of the slabs, a linen cloth hiding the gleaming instruments it carried.

Tate wondered if another body was about to be brought in. No one had mentioned it to him.

He crossed to the closest slab and leant against it, feeling how cold the metal was beneath his palms. The temperature was kept at a constant fifty degrees, which chilled the metal even more.

It chilled his blood too.

He crossed to the lockers and ran his gaze over them.

The contents of numbers four and five concerned him.

They concerned him greatly.

He reached out to touch the handle of number five.

'We can't keep you away, can we?'

The voice startled him and he spun round, his heart thudding a little quicker in his chest.

Bernard Swain, the chief pathologist, was in his thirty-ninth year, four years older than Tate. A tall, wiry man with thinning hair swept back severely from his forehead, he sported a goatee beard which, despite his belief that it made him look trendy, actually looked to Tate as if someone had glued a dead mouse to his chin.

'They're still in there, Matt, if that's what you're worried about,' Swain said to him, nodding towards the lockers. 'Brother and sister.'

Swain passed through into the office and slid open a drawer in his desk, rummaging around for some papers he wanted.

'Someone really didn't like *that* family, did they?' the pathologist observed. 'Layton would have been better off staying inside.'

'You're sure the same person killed them both?' asked Tate.

'You read my report.'

'Yes, I did.'

'Then what's the problem? The same knife was used in both murders.'

'A blade approximately twelve inches long, serrated on one edge.'

'Exactly. The angle of the cuts was the same in both cases. So was their nature. There were approximately fifteen stab wounds to the upper part of Sandra Bennett. Another six to the vagina, probably inflicted *after* she was dead.'

'Thank Christ for that,' Tate breathed.

'Twenty-two stab wounds to the body of David Layton, including four to the genitals. One of which, as you know, split his penis from top to bottom. He wasn't so lucky: he was still alive when that was done. In addition, there were fractures to eight major bones, all inflicted with a heavy object made of metal. Probably an iron bar.'

'The killer would have been covered in blood,' mused Tate.

Swain nodded.

'And yet we found no fingerprints or fibres at either scene,' Tate muttered. 'No clues, no motive, no suspects.' He exhaled wearily. 'What about the other business? You didn't make any mention of it in your report.'

'My job's to examine the bodies they bring in here, Matt, not speculate on cases.'

'But you must be curious. Why *did* he take their heads?'

101

CAROLINE HACKET SAT back from the table, and patted her stomach appreciatively.

'That was a beautiful meal, Adam,' she said. 'Thank you.'

'My pleasure,' said Walker, raising his wine glass. 'It's surprising how easy it gets when you're cooking for yourself every day.'

'Tell me about it. I'm just grateful for microwaves and frozen meals,' Caroline chuckled.

She eyed him over the kitchen table, watching as he sipped at his wine.

'Perhaps next time you'll let me cook *you* a meal,' she said.

He nodded almost imperceptibly.

'There *is* going to be a next time, isn't there?' she persisted.

Walker met her gaze. 'Of course,' he told her.

'You don't sound too sure.'

He finished what was left in his glass and pushed it away empty.

'It's a nice house,' Caroline said, aware that his mind was elsewhere. 'It must get lonely here, though.'

'Do *you* get lonely?'

'Sometimes.'

'I've been on my own for so long now, I prefer it that way. Did Hailey tell you about this house?'

Caroline looked puzzled.

'She mentioned it briefly, but . . .' She allowed the sentence to trail off.

'You know what happened here, don't you? You said that Hailey had told you.'

'Yes, she did, and I know she's treated you badly since. *She* knows that she was wrong.'

Caroline got to her feet and walked around the table towards him. She stood behind him, gently massaging his shoulders with her slender fingers.

'Does her husband know?' Walker asked.

'Why don't you forget about Hailey?' Caroline said, a slight note of irritation in her voice.

Walker stood up suddenly, turning to face her.

'Why?' he said. 'So I can concentrate on you?'

He pulled her face towards him and pressed his lips against hers, feeling them part, feeling her tongue anxiously seeking his.

He slid one hand between her legs, brushing the inside of her left thigh, allowing his fingers to climb higher until they touched the soft cotton of her panties.

Caroline pushed herself against him, surprised by the ferocity of his kiss.

When they finally parted, she was panting.

He kept his hand between her legs, fingers stroking softly, expertly.

'Is this what you want?' he said, looking into her eyes.

She nodded.

He slid two fingers beneath the gusset of her panties, stirred the moisture there, then lifted those same two digits to her mouth and touched them gently against her lips.

'Taste yourself,' he said softly, watching as she licked his outstretched fingers, her tongue flicking over his wet digits. Caroline closed her eyes, her breathing now ragged.

He held her face between his palms and kissed her lightly on the lips.

'You should go,' he whispered.

Her eyes jerked open. Walker was smiling.

'*Now?*' she said, almost incredulously. She opened her mouth to say something else, but he put a finger to her lips to silence her.

'Now,' he repeated.

She stepped back from him slightly, trying to control her breathing.

'I can stay if you want me to,' she told him.

'Another time,' he smiled.

She ran a hand through her hair.

'You really are a puzzle, Adam,' she told him, touching his cheek.

'It's not the right time,' he explained. 'I've got things on my mind. Besides, we'll have plenty of other nights together.'

'I'm sorry,' she told him. 'I should have realized. With what happened to your father and . . .'

'It's not *your* fault,' he told her.

She managed a smile.

'So, you're throwing me out, are you?' Caroline joked.

'Yes, I am.'

He walked her through to the hall, helped her on with her coat, then pulled her to him again. Once more she was surprised at the passion of his kiss.

'You're a bastard,' she told him, grinning.

He looked at her indignantly.

'For sending me home like this,' she continued.

'I'll pick you up at seven tomorrow,' he said.

'The gig doesn't start until nine. Let me cook *you* a meal tomorrow, before we go.'

He kissed her lightly on the lips. 'We'll go in my car,' he said.

'No, let me drive. I—'

He cut her short. 'My car,' he insisted.

She nodded.

He watched as she turned and headed back to the waiting Saab.

Watched her slide behind the steering wheel and start the engine.

Watched her drive off.

He closed the front door and made his way back through the hall, but he bypassed the kitchen and made straight for his study.

The smell of paint was welcoming and he shut the door behind him.

His latest canvas was positioned in one corner of the room. It was already close to completion. Walker looked at it for long moments, taking in every detail, his face expressionless.

It was huge: fully fifteen feet across, and half that again in width.

But this was for no eyes but his.

Not yet.

It was almost complete.

Almost ready.

He studied it again and smiled.

102

HAILEY WALKED SLOWLY between the tables set out in the ballroom of the Pavilion Hotel. Every now and then she would pause to check the names on the place-card settings against those she carried on her own seating-plan. Satisfied that each was in its correct place, she then moved on.

Around her, staff dressed in white jackets and black trousers swarmed like monochrome bees inside a crystal hive. Hailey had been there for an hour already. She had run through the lists of hors d'oeuvres and canapés to be served. And what time they were to be served. She had checked that all the champagne was well chilled, that the smoked salmon was in perfect condition. And a hundred other jobs.

The ballroom looked magnificent. There was no other word for it.

She stood at the top of the small flight of stairs that led down onto the highly polished parquet floor, and afforded herself a smile.

This party was to honour James Marsh and his factory, but its whole organization was *her* doing. She had arranged the party, the backstage passes, the limos, the accommodation, the guest list . . .

Everything.

The centrepiece of the buffet was to be an enormous ice sculpture in the shape of a guitar. It would be brought into the dining room minutes before Marsh himself arrived, and then unveiled.

Hailey checked her watch. She had more than an hour to get home and change before she, Rob and Becky were due to leave for the Waterhole gig.

But everything had to run like clockwork.

She decided on one final inspection.

*

The explosive sound of drumstick upon cymbal brought a shout of approval from the waiting crowd.

The roadie who had struck the instrument smiled and looked out at the sea of faces before him.

He performed a couple of drum rolls, each of which met with a similar roar of approval, then contented himself with striking each of the floor toms and mounted toms once or twice – according to the instructions he was receiving through his headset.

Guitar technicians were performing similar tasks around him. Levels were being checked, and one man in black jeans and a T-shirt bearing the legend FUCK DANCING, LET'S FUCK spoke into each of the microphones set up on the stage.

The instructions came from the mixing desk. It was positioned high on a purpose-built gantry about a hundred yards from the stage itself, facing the platform that was flanked on either side by huge video screens.

'Twenty thousand people,' said James Marsh, looking out at the crowd from the wings.

'Yeah,' Ray Taylor mused. 'Don't remind me. When I think of the gate receipts we're missing out on.'

Marsh grinned. 'It's for charity, you bastard. Look on it as a good deed.'

'I'd rather look on it as more money in the bank,' Taylor said.

Marsh took a couple of steps out onto the stage, peering first at the crowd, then across towards another purpose-built structure to the right. This was the VIP viewing platform. Designed to take over one hundred people, it was a covered construction filled with temporary seating that gave a clear view of the stage over the heads of the heaving crowd on the ground.

'Let's just hope it doesn't rain,' Marsh mused, looking up at the darkening sky.

'That's what outdoor gigs are all about, Jim, you know that. If the punters aren't up to their knees in shit by the third song, they're not happy. When can you remember it being dry at Reading or Donington? But no one gives a toss. They're happy enough.' He made an expansive gesture with his hand, designed to encompass the entire crowd.

'And you're sure this is going to work? This spectacular bloody entry?' Marsh sounded concerned.

'They did it in Paris,' Taylor assured him, 'they did it in Rome, and it worked a treat. Half an hour before Waterhole are due on stage, the chopper starts buzzing the crowd. They all know the band are inside it. Then, it hovers. The rope ladders are dropped, and they climb down straight onto the stage. Straight into the first song. It looks fucking great, and the crowd love it.'

Marsh nodded. 'I trust you,' he said quietly.

'You wait and see,' Taylor told him. 'You won't forget tonight in a hurry, I promise you.'

*

The cemetery was closing.

As Adam Walker swung himself out of the Scorpio, he saw that one of the main gates was already shut.

He hurried towards the entrance, noticing half a dozen people still inside the vast necropolis.

There was still time.

He walked purposefully along the wide tarmac thoroughfare that cut through the middle of the cemetery, then turned off on a gravel path that led to the newer plots on one side.

Many of the graves he passed were badly neglected, but he reasoned they were so old that many of those buried within would have been since joined by those who had previously tended their resting places.

He passed a middle-aged man on the narrow path, and saw he was carrying some dead flowers wrapped in paper. The man glanced at Walker and met his gaze.

Walker saw the sadness in his eyes and assumed he too had been visiting a grave.

A wife?

A sister or brother?

Possibly a child?

Who had he lost?

The man tossed the dead flowers into a nearby dustbin and wandered off, head down.

Walker could see his father's grave just ahead. Flowers, wrapped in their cellophane, still lay on the plot, but most of them had begun to rot.

As he stood beside the grave, the stench of their putrefaction was strong in his nostrils.

'They're decaying,' he said, looking down at the dark earth, 'just like you. Lying there rotting ... But, then, you were rotten even when you were alive, weren't you? Deep inside you were rotten. Filth! Well, at least I'll never have to see you again. And I hope that, wherever you're watching me from, you can hear this.' He smiled crookedly. 'As if you'd be watching *me*.'

He dug his hands into his pockets.

'Man of God,' he grunted. 'Do you think God would want *you*? What kind of God would have let you get away with doing what you did to me?'

Walker stood staring down at the grave.

'Enjoy Judgement Day,' he whispered.

*

The car was spinning out of control.

Rob Gibson could see that it was going to crash. Beside him, Becky opened her mouth to scream.

There was a bright red flash.

'I won,' shouted Becky.

Rob gazed at the TV screen and watched the remains of his own car going up in smoke.

'I win again, Dad,' Becky said, holding up the Playstation joypad triumphantly. 'Shall we have another go?'

'On a different game,' Rob insisted, tickling her.

He grinned as his daughter dissolved into fits of giggles.

'I might have a better chance of winning without that racket in the background too,' Rob observed, looking towards the CD player. 'I can't concentrate with that noise going on.'

'That's not noise, Dad,' said Becky, searching through her other games. 'It's Waterhole. They're great.'

'Do all your friends listen to them as well?'

'Some of them are going to the concert tonight. Billy and Megan asked me if I could get them autographs.'

'I don't know if we'll get to meet them, sweetheart.'

'Mum said we could.'

Rob nodded. 'Then I'm sure we will.' He smiled.

He watched as Becky selected another game, held it up and then pushed it into the Playstation.

'This one's tennis, Dad. You might have a better chance with this one,' she told him.

'Thanks. Haven't you got any football games?' he wanted to know.

'No,' she told him. 'You never bought me any.'

Rob laughed. 'Tennis it is then.'

They began playing.

'Dad,' Becky said, staring at the screen. 'You still love Mum, don't you?'

Rob looked at her, but saw that she was concentrating on the game.

'Of course I do, babe,' he said softly. 'Why do you ask?'

'I've heard you and Mum shouting at each other, and people who don't love each other shout at each other, don't they? Megan said *her* mum and dad used to shout at each other a lot, and then her dad moved away.'

'I love your mum,' Rob told her. 'People sometimes disagree about things, so they shout. It doesn't mean they don't love each other.'

Becky looked at him and smiled.

'That's good,' she said. 'Look, I've just won the first game.'

She laughed out loud.

In the background, Waterhole continued to thunder from the stereo.

*

Caroline Hacket spun the taps, then tipped some bubblebath into the churning water, stirring it around with one hand.

The delightful aroma of lemon began to rise from the steaming water.

She was wearing just a bathrobe as she padded back through the bedroom and into her office.

She'd been working most of the day. The book was nearly finished, and she'd always found she wrote quicker when she was nearing the end. The thought of a publisher's cheque due on delivery of the manuscript always seemed to aid creativity, she mused, listening to the water running into the bath.

She had another hour before Walker arrived to pick her up.

A nice soak would ease away the aches.

Caroline looked at the screen, reread what she'd written.

One more paragraph should do it.

She decided to finish it while the bath was filling up.

THE GUN METAL felt cold against his hands.

The weapon was heavy as he hefted it in his fist, admiring the sleek lines of the pistol.

The Steyr Model GB.

Nearly six inches long and weighing over twenty-nine ounces, the entire gun was constructed of steel, even the grip plates.

He checked the eighteen-round magazine, thumbing several more of the hollow-tip rounds into the slim steel frame. Then he worked the slide and laid the pistol inside the case, alongside the four spare clips.

The Scorpion machine-pistol, the CZ68, was only slightly larger, but infinitely more lethal. Capable of spewing out over eight hundred 9mm rounds a minute. It had been chambered to take the same kind of slugs as the Steyr.

Like the rounds he'd loaded into the pistol, the bullets he'd fed into the six spare magazines of the Scorpion were also hollow-tipped.

When fired, they would be travelling in excess of one thousand feet a second, but when they struck their target they would explode.

The Scorpion also had a folding shoulder stock and a silencer, but he doubted if he would need either.

The Heckler and Koch MP5SD3 featured a telescoping butt, should he require it. But, again, he didn't expect the need to arise. Both of the machine-pistols could be held in one fist, if necessary. The MP5's thirty-round magazines were capable of firing six hundred and fifty shots a minute.

It was a beautiful gun and he couldn't resist running his hands over the frame before he slid it into the case with the other two weapons.

The Sig-Sauer P225 was, like the other weapons, a 9mm. Eight-round magazine. Capable of putting a hole in a brick wall from close range.

He studied the pistol a moment longer, then laid it alongside the others.

Before he sealed the small carrying case, he looked almost lovingly at the awesome array of firepower before him. Then, smiling, he fastened the two combination locks of the case.

The time had come.

103

HAILEY COULDN'T HELP but think how lacking in genuine VIPs the VIP stand was.

There were lots of music-industry people, friends of James Marsh, business associates, local dignitaries – but precious little to satisfy the hordes of celebrity-spotters who had gathered close to the rear of the stand, hoping to catch a glimpse of someone even remotely recognizable.

As another limo drew up and disgorged its faceless passengers, Hailey saw one watching girl shake her head in irritation.

The area behind the makeshift stand had been roped off, its perimeter patrolled by enormous men in yellow jackets with SHOWSEC stencilled on them. Hailey had watched the desultory dribble of nobodies entering the VIP stand, and thought that the security men might be better employed elsewhere. It didn't seem likely that the arrival of two more local councillors was going to test their crowd-handling abilities.

Hailey smiled dutifully as she showed the two councillors to their seats in the makeshift stand, hearing the older of the two men complaining about the sound from the stage.

One of the support bands was in the middle of its set, and was meeting with nothing short of indifference from the waiting crowd. Still, Hailey reasoned, indifference was better than the hail of urine-filled plastic bottles that had accompanied the departure of the first support band. The lead singer had dashed back and forth across the stage looking for hands to slap, but had received only an apple core on the back of his head for his trouble.

The joys of being in a support slot, thought Hailey.

She gazed across the stand itself, which was already three-quarters full.

Rob and Becky were sitting in the front row, Becky mesmerized by the sight of the huge crowd and by the spectacle before her.

Rob spotted Hailey and waved. Then he pointed at Becky and held up one thumb.

Hailey waved back.

She saw several more cars approaching, and went over to meet them.

Nicholas Barber stepped out of the first. The MP nodded a greeting and sniffed the air.

'The smell of the great unwashed,' he sneered, and looked around at some of the main crowd.

'Good of you to come, Mr Barber,' Hailey said, trying to disguise the irritation she felt.

She showed him quickly to his seat, and returned to greet the next two cars.

At last the watching celebrity-spotters raised a few cheers. Jenny Kenton climbed out of the first car, closely followed by three other young women.

All wives and girlfriends of the band, Hailey assumed. One of them, the bass-player's girlfriend, had just been given a job on an early-morning TV show and she was revelling in her new-found fame.

Hailey thought how easy it was for these women: famous, rich partners and a jet-set lifestyle. They were famous themselves for nothing else other than the fact they were sleeping with celebrities. It was either amusing or nauseating, depending on your view.

'It's a bit tacky, isn't it?' said Jenny Kenton as she climbed the stairs to the platform.

'Well, it's not the Hollywood Bowl, but then Waterhole aren't the Beatles, are they?' Hailey said, smiling. 'As much as they'd like to think they are.'

Jenny Kenton glared furiously at her.

'You're the one who does the publicity for Marsh, aren't you?' she sneered. 'His personal assistant?'

'Nice to see I made an impression,' Hailey told her.

Jenny Kenton pushed past her towards the seat Hailey indicated.

'Bitch,' Hailey whispered under her breath.

The other women followed and seated themselves.

Hailey heard a great roar and looked up to see that the support band were now leaving the stage.

She checked her watch. Another forty minutes and the helicopter carrying Waterhole would begin its first swoop over the crowd.

The guest cars continued to arrive.

104

IT WAS BECKY who spotted them.

She turned in her seat to look around at the array of faces in the VIP stand. They registered expressions ranging from boredom to indifference, bemusement to excitement.

The little girl pulled at Hailey's arm and pointed excitedly.

'There's Auntie Caroline,' she said, 'and Adam's with her.'

Rob looked round and saw them both, but his attention was drawn to Walker, who was still gazing towards the stage.

'What the fuck is *he* doing here?' Rob rasped, leaning close to Hailey's ear. 'Did *you* invite him?'

'Don't be ridiculous,' Hailey said, not looking round. 'I gave Caroline two invitations. I didn't instruct her on who she could or couldn't bring with her.'

'So, he's screwing *her* now, is he?' Rob hissed. 'I wonder how she compares to you. I wonder if he's been taking notes on you both.'

Hailey glared at him. 'Not here, Rob, please,' she said through clenched teeth.

Becky was still looking round excitedly. She waved in Walker's direction but he didn't see her.

'Did you *know* she was bringing him?' Rob persisted.

'I just told you: I gave her two guest passes. That was it.'

'So he'll be at the party with her, too?'

'Yes.'

'Well, I'm sure you'll want to speak to him. You might want to talk about old times.'

'I didn't ask Caroline to bring him. It was none of my business who she invited. She could have turned up with Lord Lucan for all I care. It's nothing to do with me.'

'Not any more.'

'Rob, drop it, please.'

He looked at her, held her imploring gaze. Then he glanced at Becky, who was now aware of their mutterings and had turned to face them.

Rob forced a smile. 'Are you OK, babe?' he said, ruffling her hair.

Becky laughed.

'Are you enjoying yourself?' Hailey added.

The little girl nodded. She was looking out over the crowd, who had spontaneously begun chanting the name of Waterhole.

Another section began singing their latest hit, and Becky joined in.

Hailey looked across at Jenny Kenton, who had just lit up a cigarette and was puffing at it. She adjusted her dark glasses and glanced in Hailey's direction.

'Isn't that the one who's married to the singer?' Rob asked.

'Yes. Objectionable bitch,' said Hailey.

'She used to act, didn't she?'

'She still does,' Hailey said acidly. 'She's giving a command performance now.'

There was a mechanical roar above them. It began as a low drone, then grew steadily louder.

Immediately several spotlights near the front of the stage burst into life, sending their powerful beams cutting through the night sky.

The crowd stopped singing and chanting, and began cheering loudly.

More lights flashed on around the stage: strobes that bathed all those watching in a cold, white glow.

Becky grabbed Hailey's hand in excitement.

The helicopter swooped over the crowd like a massive, power-driven bird of prey.

It sped down, then hurtled upwards in a wide arc, trailing an illuminated message from its tail section.

The sign bore one word: WATERHOLE.

There were lights on the helicopter's skids too: brilliant red lights that flickered and flashed and left crimson imprints on the retinas of those who watched. They looked like splashes of blood across the sky. And, all the time, the lights from the ground shone up into the blackness, sometimes glinting on the shiny hull of the swooping, circling helicopter.

The roaring of the crowd grew louder – so loud it drowned out even the noise of the chopper's rotor blades and engine.

More lights came on around the stage, and across the top of it – in blinding white, one letter at a time – the name of the band lit up. It shone like a beacon in the night. Then the huge illuminated logo began to flash rhythmically. Pulsing vividly.

Some of the crowd began to clap in time to the moving lights, as if directed by their phosphorescent glow. Others pointed up at the swooping helicopter, or punched the air expectantly. The noise was deafening.

Becky was on her feet, also clapping. Enraptured by the awesome spectacle.

Hailey looked across at James Marsh, who smiled back at her.

Had she bothered to glance towards the rear of the stand, she would have seen Adam Walker staring fixedly at her.

105

THE EXPLOSIONS WERE deafening.

The crowd cheered each fresh eruption, and applauded the multicoloured fragments that sprayed the heavens as each new salvo of fireworks was ignited.

Hailey was standing at the bottom of the steps leading down from the VIP stand, watching as car after car arrived to ferry guests from the gig venue to the Pavilion Hotel for the ensuing party. Most had already left, though she knew for a fact that the band themselves wouldn't be arriving there for another hour at least. Their partners had gone to join them backstage. So had James Marsh and countless members of the local and national press, as well as music journalists and other interested individuals.

The crowd was drifting away now.

The scene they left behind them was one of utter devastation. Empty bottles, scraps of paper, plastic cups, containers – even abandoned clothes and footwear. What had been one of the best outdoor concert venues in the country, just hours earlier, now resembled an enormous dustbin.

But that, mused Hailey, was one of the few things that *wasn't* her concern tonight.

Everything she'd needed to handle she'd done immaculately, and now – with virtually *all* the VIPs safely in their cars and on their way to the hotel – she could start thinking about the next stage of the proceedings.

It had been a great gig; that was all that mattered to the paying customers. All that mattered to the VIPs now was how much free food and drink they could stuff down their throats when they got to the party itself.

She felt a hand tugging at her skirt. Hailey looked down to see Becky smiling up at her.

'Did you enjoy that?' Hailey asked, bending down to kiss her little girl.

'It was great, Mum,' Becky said.

Even Rob was grinning. 'Maybe I was wrong,' he said. 'They're not *that* bad.'

Becky put her hands on her hips. 'Oh, Dad,' she said, 'they were awesome.'

'Awesome, eh?' Rob said and swept her up into his arms.

Hailey smiled as she saw him swing their daughter around, heard her giggles of delight.

'You two go on to the hotel,' Hailey said, touching her husband's cheek. 'I've got to make sure the last of this lot get into their cars safely. I won't be long.'

Rob nodded. 'What about the band?' he asked.

'Their record company is taking care of them. They'll be there, though.'

'So you're not the *only* one working tonight?' Rob mused.

Hailey smiled.

There was a car pulling up.

'You two go in this one,' Hailey told him. 'I'll see you soon.'

The driver stopped the Jag and climbed out to open the doors for Rob and Becky.

She kissed her daughter.

'Don't talk to any strange men,' said Rob cryptically.

He slid in beside Becky. The doors were slammed shut and the Jag pulled away.

Cars continued to arrive, picked up passengers, then left.

Hailey looked at her watch. Then at the next car heading towards her.

She frowned. This was no Jag or Mercedes.

It looked familiar.

The Scorpio halted next to her, and she saw that it was indeed Adam Walker's car.

Caroline Hacket was driving. Walker was sitting in the back.

What kind of joke was this?

He pushed open the front passenger door.

As Caroline looked across at her, Hailey saw that her eyes were red-rimmed, her cheeks tear-stained.

'Get in,' said Walker flatly.

'What's wrong?' Hailey asked. 'What are you doing?'

It was then that she saw the gun. The pistol was pressed against the back of the driving seat where Caroline sat.

'Get in, Hailey,' Walker murmured. 'Or I'll blow her in half.'

106

THE EXPLOSION OF white light was almost blinding.

Dozens of flashes went off simultaneously as each car's doors were opened.

Rob could see hordes of newsmen gathered around the entrance to the Pavilion Hotel. There were also several camera crews from local and national television, and the powerful lights used to illuminate the hotel forecourt added to the general brilliance.

Reporters fought to get close to each car as it pulled up, though only anxious to snatch a few words with the members of Waterhole should they be the ones to emerge.

Becky watched them jostling for position.

'What are those people doing, Dad?' she wanted to know.

'Their jobs.' Rob grinned as the procession of cars approaching the hotel continued.

He saw Nicholas Barber clamber from one of those ahead, pausing a moment on the steps to wave theatrically at the half a dozen newsmen who bothered to snap him.

Barber loitered a moment longer, as if determined that all the assembled hacks should get a good look at him. He saw James Marsh walking towards the main entrance and, smiling broadly, stepped towards the factory's owner to shake his hand.

A good photo opportunity?

More lights. More microphones shoved in his direction. Barber was keen to foster the new government's belief in its own popularity. It preached constantly of its awareness of public tastes. Prided itself on being comprised of men and women who considered themselves no different from those who had voted them into power.

Rob looked on at this charade with distaste. Watching Barber pose with his arm around Marsh's shoulder.

Hypocritical bastard!

Two stretch limos were approaching the hotel and the media, almost as one, swung to meet them.

The limos slowed to a crawl, then stopped to disgorge their passengers.

Waterhole and their various partners emerged into the glare of camera flashes and a volley of questions.

'There they are, Dad,' said Becky excitedly.

Rob nodded and watched as the band members made their way towards the main entrance.

'That's Craig and Simon,' Becky informed him. 'They're brothers.'

Rob watched impassively.

Craig Levine was wearing a battered leather jacket, jeans and a baseball cap. Close behind him, Jenny Kenton adjusted her dark glasses, ran a hand through her hair, and stared unsmilingly at the assembled photographers.

As the other band members made their way towards the entrance, two of them adopted a goose-stepping march.

Becky giggled. Rob shook his head.

'They're great, aren't they, Dad?' Becky said.

'If you say so, babe,' Rob murmured, grinning at her.

He saw Nicholas Barber posing for more photos, this time with both Marsh *and* the band.

Then they all made their way inside, the photographers still shouting for more pictures.

Rob looked around.

Where the hell was Hailey? Surely she should be here by now?

'Where's Mum?' Becky wanted to know, as if reading his mind.

'She'll be here soon.'

I hope.

He noticed that Walker hadn't arrived yet either.

Rob swung himself out of the car and helped Becky down. Thoughts were tumbling through his mind, some of which he didn't care for.

Were Hailey and Walker together now? Snatching a moment behind his back?

He tried to drive the thoughts away, but they remained.

'Mum won't be long,' he said, taking Becky's hand as they made their way towards the main hotel entrance.

As they were climbing the three steps that led into the foyer, one of the photographers called to them – obviously taking no chances. Among this sea of nobodies might be someone important, so best to get everything on film.

They turned round and he took Becky's photo.

The little girl giggled and pressed her head against Rob's thigh. He grinned and ruffled her hair.

'There you go, babe,' he said, chuckling. 'Now *you're* famous.'

Behind them the cars continued to arrive.

107

They drove in silence.

Hailey unwilling to speak. Caroline unable to.

In the back seat, Walker remained quiet: gaze fixed on the two women in front of him.

Every now and then, Hailey would glance into the wing-mirror on her side of the car, trying to catch a glimpse of his face, but it was shrouded in darkness.

She had no idea which of them the gun was pointing at.

Once or twice she had glanced across at Caroline and seen the terror on her face: her jaw clamped shut, a knot of muscles pulsing at the side.

Hailey had wanted to ask what was going on. But each time she had tried to speak, it seemed as if her mouth would not open.

All she could think about was the gun.

Gun?

No matter how many times she ran the word through her mind, it didn't seem to register. She and Caroline were being held at gunpoint.

Impossible?

If only it was. This seemed all too real.

Hailey tried to swallow, but her throat felt as if it was filled with chalk. Fear had dried her mouth more effectively than blotting paper. Her heart hammered against her ribs.

Caroline never took her eyes off the road.

It became apparent to Hailey, after the first few moments, that they were heading towards Walker's house.

Thoughts tumbled through her head with incredible speed.

Jump from the car?

They were moving at a steady forty. She would probably be killed in the fall, or hit by an oncoming car.

But her recurring thought was of Becky. She was convinced she was never going to see her daughter again.

Caroline swung the car into the street where Walker's house stood.

Now, when the car stops, run like hell?

In her fevered mind's-eye she could see him raising the pistol, shooting her in the back as she ran.

Again she tried to swallow. Still she couldn't.

Caroline parked the car and waited for further instructions.

'Get out,' Walker said. 'Walk to the front door, slowly.'

He was out first, the gun held low.

Caroline nearly stumbled as she made her way to the door. Her legs would barely support her.

Hailey walked behind her, not daring to glance round at him.

Run now. He won't fire the gun in the street – will he?

Walker unlocked the front door and ushered them inside, closing it behind him. He left the lights off.

Hailey heard the key turn once more. They were locked in.

In the semi-darkness she saw the glistening barrel of the pistol.

'Go through,' Walker instructed them, nodding towards the study.

They obeyed. What else could they do?

There were two chairs set in the middle of the room.

Both had pieces of nylon rope hanging over the back.

'Caroline, sit down,' Walker said evenly. 'Hailey, tie her up.'

For long seconds the women hesitated, looking helplessly at each other.

Hailey saw tears welling up in her friend's eyes. She felt as if she herself might lose control any minute.

'Do it,' Walker repeated softly, his voice almost a whisper.

With shaking hands, Hailey began her task.

*

Rob looked at his watch.

How much longer?

He sipped at his mineral water and looked around the dining room of the hotel.

It was bedlam: the noise, the constant ebb and flow from table to table, the clutch of people standing around the bar, the waiters and waitresses moving about so efficiently amidst the throng.

He saw James Marsh talking to the group.

Saw Craig Levine pointing towards his groin and laughing. The crowd around him laughed, too.

Nicholas Barber was speaking to a couple of local councillors.

David Easton – the bass player with Waterhole – was juggling with peanuts, to the obvious delight of the roadies watching him.

Beside him, his girlfriend, a stunning raven-haired woman wearing a red dress that looked as if it had been sprayed on, was chatting to Jenny Kenton, who was sipping her spritzer and looking regally around her. Occasionally she adjusted her dark glasses.

'Where's Mum?' said Becky.

'She'll be here soon, babe,' Rob replied, putting his arm around his daughter's shoulders.

I hope.

He continued to scan the heaving mass of people.

No sign of Walker or Caroline Hacket either.

Again Rob looked at his watch.

108

Hailey tried to twist her arms behind her back, to free them from the rope cutting into her flesh.

It was useless. Walker had tied her too tightly.

She could only sit helplessly opposite Caroline who was weeping silently, tears coursing down her cheeks.

'Why are you doing this?' Hailey finally asked. Each word seemed like an effort; her voice cracked as she spoke.

He flicked on the light in the study and walked to one end of it.

Towards the huge canvas covered by a sheet.

'Adam, please,' Hailey said imploringly, forced to fight back her own tears.

He paused for a second and looked first at Caroline, then at Hailey.

'You really *don't* understand, do you?' he murmured.

Hailey shook her head and sniffed.

Walker crossed to her and wiped away the single tear that trickled down her cheek.

For precious seconds Hailey found herself gazing deep into his eyes. He stepped back slightly.

'You don't realize that all this is for *you*,' he said, his eyes narrowing slightly.

'All what?' Hailey tried to control her breathing.

'The first time we ever met, I helped you. I found your daughter. I saved her. I brought her back to you.'

'And I appreciate that,' Hailey said, sniffing back more tears.

Walker smiled crookedly. 'You had a funny way of showing it.'

'I'm *sorry*,' Hailey blurted out.

'Sorry. I've heard that word so many times during my life,' he muttered. 'And it's never meant anything.'

Caroline was still crying softly. Hailey looked across, saw her body quivering.

'I don't want to hurt you,' Walker continued, his gaze never leaving Hailey.

'Then what *do* you want, Adam?' Hailey asked. 'Just tell me. If there's anything I can do to help, just . . .'

'Like showing my work to Waterhole?' he chided. 'You *were* going to help me, weren't you? But you didn't.' He moved towards the study door. Stood there a moment, then slipped out.

Hailey could hear his footsteps in the next room.

'Caroline,' she whispered, trying to control her breathing.

Her friend looked at her blankly.

'We've got to get out,' Hailey insisted.

As she spoke, she twisted frantically within the confines of the rope, wincing as it cut into her flesh.

'Help me,' she rasped.

Caroline could only shake her head.

Walker re-entered the room. Hailey could see the pistol jammed into his belt.

If only she could get her hands free. Could she reach it? And . . .

And what? Grab it? Wrestle it from his grip? Shoot him?

There was a large wooden chest close by. It looked antique. Expensive.

Walker crossed to it and lifted the lid.

'I tried to help you,' he said, reaching inside.

He turned to face her, arms outstretched.

'This was just for you,' snarled Walker.

Hailey's eyes bulged in their sockets.

Walker was holding up the severed heads of Sandra Bennett and David Layton.

Hailey finally found the breath to scream.

109

It was all Hailey could do not to vomit.

Her stomach contracted violently as Walker stepped towards her, holding each of the heads by its hair, pushing them towards her.

Caroline Hacket's entire body was shaking. If not for the nylon restraints, she would have fallen to the floor.

She stared in horror at the heads, tears pouring down her cheeks.

Hailey tried to look away, to tear her gaze from the monstrous sight before her.

The blood on the severed heads had congealed black in places – in the deep wounds on Sandy Bennett's face.

One of David Layton's eyes had been sliced in two by a particularly savage cut. Part of its eyelid was hanging like a tendril.

The other eye was wide open. It fixed her with a blank stare, the soft orb already close to liquescing.

God alone knew how long these heads had been decomposing in that antique trunk.

'This woman almost destroyed your marriage,' said Walker, holding up Sandy Bennett's head. 'She almost destroyed *you* – that's what you told me.'

Hailey screwed her eyes tight shut until stars danced behind the lids.

'And this man, her brother,' Walker continued, 'he was scum.'

'How did you know he was her brother?' Hailey blurted.

'I followed him for a couple of days. I watched him. I even spoke to him once. I saw him with her. With others he knew.' Walker shook his head. 'He wasn't a very nice man, Hailey.'

He dropped the heads onto the floor, where they landed with a thud.

'You didn't have to kill them,' Hailey whispered.

'You said *you* would have killed whoever it was who attacked Rob,' he reminded her.

He walked across to where Caroline sat motionless, her face drained of colour, her eyes riveted to the severed heads.

Hailey glanced at her friend and saw the glazed stare. She guessed that Caroline had gone into shock.

Walker began massaging her shoulders gently.

'And what now?' Hailey wanted to know, watching his fingers working tenderly on her friend's shoulders and neck.

He continued his gentle ministrations.

Caroline didn't move.

'I just want you to understand that I did this for you, Hailey,' Walker said, looking at her. 'I don't expect you to thank me, but I wanted you to know.'

He stroked Caroline's cheek with one index finger, brushed a tear away.

'They betrayed you,' he said. 'And so did your friend.'

He turned Caroline's head so that she was looking at him.

'She tried to tempt me away from you, when she should have known that *you* were the only one I ever wanted.'

Walker placed one hand on either side of her face, and kissed Caroline lightly on the lips. The expression on his face barely changed.

It was the power in his grip.

He suddenly clamped his hands hard around Caroline's head, one cupping her chin, the other gripping the back of her head. He twisted savagely to one side.

Her neck broke with an audible crack.

This time Hailey couldn't even scream. She merely began to sob uncontrollably.

Caroline's head lolled uselessly onto her chest. Walker pushed at it with one index finger, seemingly amazed at how easily it moved on the shattered vertebrae. Like that of a puppet with its strings cut.

Hailey was still crying when Walker crossed to her and began undoing the ropes that held her.

He pulled her to her feet, her hands still tied behind her back.

She knew she was going to die.

She stood motionless.

An image of Becky flashed through her mind.

'One more thing,' he said, smiling.

He crossed to the large canvas at the end of the room and pulled the sheet off.

Hailey looked at it.

It was all there. Like some obscene collage. But completed with consummate skill.

She recognized the figures.

Herself, Rob and Becky.

Walker, Sandy Bennett, David Layton, Caroline.

There were others too.

She didn't recognize the other faces. They had been painted with their features spattered by blood, mouths open in silent screams of agony.

'It's finished at last,' he said proudly. He held her by the shoulders, leaning close to her ear. 'Come on, we've got to go.'

'Go where?' she asked him.

Walker smiled.

110

'WHY?'

The question hung in the air like a bad smell.

Walker merely drove on, eyes alert. As he turned a corner, he could see Hailey staring at him from the passenger seat.

'I've already told you why,' he said flatly.

'You didn't have to kill them. You didn't have to kill Caroline. If you were trying to impress me, it didn't work.'

Walker grinned. 'It was nothing to do with impressing you, Hailey.' He chuckled. 'I was protecting you.'

'By killing my best friend?' She sniffed back tears.

'I told you, she betrayed you. I know all about betrayal. My mother betrayed me when she ran off with another man and my father did the same when he viciously abused me. Trust me: I know what I'm talking about.'

'So three people had to die because of that?'

'I thought so,' he offered.

'And how many more will die?' she wanted to know.

Walker didn't answer, merely kept his eyes on the road, easing his foot down a little harder on the accelerator.

Hailey allowed her head to flop back. She gazed out of the side window.

'You're going to kill *me*, aren't you?'

He didn't answer.

'You'll never get away with this, Adam.'

'I know,' Walker said flatly. 'But there's always a price to pay for fame, isn't there?' He looked at her and smiled. 'People are going to know my name after tonight, Hailey. Just like they know the names of people like Charles Manson, Denis Nilsen, Peter Sutcliffe, Michael Ryan, and Thomas Hamilton. And *they* all paid a price too. They paid with their freedom, or their lives, but people remember them. They will do for years to come. They'll be written about and talked about. They've become part of our culture, no matter how much people supposedly despise them – the media need them. TV and papers condemn them because they know they have to, but they're fascinated by them, and I'll tell you why. They know that those men did things that *everyone* is capable of. It's just that not everyone has the *courage* to do it.'

'They killed innocent people,' Hailey said, trying to control her breathing. 'What's so courageous about that?'

'It takes a lot of strength to take another life, Hailey. More than you'd think.'

'Was *that* the kind of fame you always wanted?' Hailey said slowly. It felt as if her entire body had been enveloped by a cold chill that had started at the back of her neck and spread outwards. As if someone had injected iced water into her veins.

'I always told you I wanted people to know that I'd been here. I wanted to make a mark.'

'Like Manson? Like Sutcliffe? Like the rest of those killers?'

'If necessary.'

'You admire them, don't you?'

'Yes. They only thought about themselves. They were single-minded. They didn't care what people thought of them. They didn't worry about things like conscience, remorse or morality. And, yes, I *do* admire that.'

'People will know your name, but they'll hate you for what you've done.'

'And you think I care?' he said sardonically. 'I'll be doing the world a favour.'

Hailey looked puzzled. 'But you said you killed Caroline and the others for *me*,' she said falteringly. 'What's that got to do with anyone else?'

'They were just the beginning,' he told her sharply. 'Did you think I expected to be remembered for killing some small-time criminal and a couple of slags? You underestimate me, Hailey. I've got more ambition than that.' He chuckled. 'But now you'll see.'

He looked at his watch. 'And we're nearly there,' Walker observed, smiling.

At last Hailey understood.

111

THERE WAS SOMETHING wrong. Rob was convinced of that.

There *had* to be.

He sat gazing intently towards the main entrance of the ballroom, hoping

(*praying?*)

that Hailey would walk in at any minute.

How long since she'd waved them off?

He rechecked his watch. An hour? Two hours?

Becky also seemed to have tired of the constant babble of conversation and music, and was now concerned only with seeing her mother again. She sat beside Rob, swinging her feet over the edge of the chair and looking up at her father.

He ruffled her hair a couple of times, sure that even his own daughter must realize how fake this gesture was.

Could the car carrying Hailey to the Pavilion Hotel have crashed?

Was she even now lying by some roadside in need of help?

And where the hell was Caroline Hacket?

Or Adam Walker?

Had they all decided to ride here in the same car?

No, she wouldn't do that. She wouldn't be that insensitive.

Would she?

He felt a hand on his shoulder and spun round.

James Marsh was standing there.

'I was looking for your good lady, Rob,' Marsh said, smiling.

'That makes two of us,' Rob told him.

'Where's my mum?' Becky added.

Marsh touched her cheek and winked. 'She should have been here by now,' he offered thoughtfully. 'We've got a presentation to make in twenty minutes. I want her here for that.'

Rob got to his feet, lowering his voice and turning his back on Becky, anxious she shouldn't hear him.

'Look, no offence, but I couldn't give a flying fuck about your presentation,' he rasped. 'I just want to know where Hailey is. And I'll tell you something, if she's not here in ten minutes, I'm going to call the police.'

'No need, Rob. I'll do it myself. You're right, she should have been here by now.'

'Are all the other guests here?' Rob wanted to know.

Marsh nodded, glancing around the crowded ballroom.

'Perhaps the car's broken down,' he mused.

'Then send someone to find her,' Rob said, glaring at the older man.

'All right, calm down,' said Marsh quietly.

'I'm telling you,' Rob persisted. 'Ten minutes and I'm calling the police.'

'I'm sure there's a perfectly simple explanation for why she's not here.'

'Then tell me what it is,' Rob hissed.

Somewhere behind them, there was a sound of breaking crockery, followed by a loud cheer.

Both men turned and saw two members of Waterhole gathered around a couple of broken plates lying on the parquet, each pointing an accusatory finger at the other. They were laughing, ignoring the food that had spilled onto the floor.

Rob looked at them with something akin to disgust, then returned his attention to Marsh.

'I'd better have a word with them,' said Marsh, moving away.

Rob didn't speak. Merely watched him make his way across the crowded ballroom towards the two band members, where he was joined by Ray Taylor. The band's manager was sipping a Bacardi and Coke, looking on silently and grinning.

Becky pulled at Rob's hand. 'Dad, I've got to go to the loo,' she told him. 'Will you come with me?'

He nodded. Together they threaded their way through the maze of party-goers, Rob occasionally nudging people aside in his annoyance.

The toilets were in the main foyer, through a set of white double-doors.

'I'll wait here, babe,' he said, standing outside the door marked LADIES.

Becky entered, almost knocked over by a tall young woman in her mid-twenties who was emerging.

Rob registered the dark make-up, the black-painted nails, the long skirt, slit to the thigh, the laced-up boots beneath.

Trudi, without the 'e', gazed blankly at him and wiped her nose with her thumb and forefinger, sniffing loudly.

'Great party,' she said, running appraising eyes over him.

He nodded.

A moment later Jenny Kenton appeared, pushing her dark glasses back on her nose. She too sniffed loudly.

'You missed some,' said Rob disdainfully, pointing to some fine grains of white powder around one of her nostrils.

The former actress wiped away the residue and strode off in the direction of the ballroom, Trudi in tow.

He could hear them laughing as the double-doors swung shut behind them.

Becky emerged, hurrying across to her father.

Rob put a protective arm around her shoulders and prepared to lead her back into the ballroom. Then he remembered that he'd seen a row of phones in the foyer as they'd entered.

He looked at his watch.

Six minutes, and he'd call the police.

Might as well wait.

'Shall we go for a walk before we go back in?' he said, taking Becky's hand.

'Perhaps we'll see Mum,' Becky offered.

'Perhaps we will,' murmured Rob.

112

THERE HAD TO be some way of warning them.

That was Hailey's only thought as she walked from the car with Adam Walker.

There *had* to be.

She glanced down once or twice at the small case he carried, shuddering each time she thought about its deadly cargo.

The well-lit façade of the Pavilion Hotel shone like a beacon in the darkness, and she also saw the lights glinting on the bodywork of dozens of cars parked outside. They belonged mostly to guests at the party going on inside. A party that was about to become a bloodbath.

Unless she could stop him.

But how?

He had one of the pistols jammed into his belt on his left hip, hidden from prying eyes by the folds of his jacket. He carried the case in his left hand, too.

They were close to the steps that led up to the main entrance now, and Hailey saw two burly security men standing there.

Tell them? Scream? Shout to them that this man is carrying a gun?

'If you open your mouth I'll kill you, *and* them,' Walker hissed under his breath, touching the butt of the automatic to reinforce the threat.

'You're going to do it anyway,' she rasped. 'Why wait?'

'Just keep walking,' he instructed.

The security men stepped aside as they saw Hailey and Walker, one of them even ushering the newcomers towards the ballroom.

Walker smiled graciously. They continued on through the foyer.

'Please don't do this, Adam,' Hailey said, her voice cracking.

He didn't answer.

There were two more security men on the doors that led into the ballroom: big-built men in dark suits.

Hailey showed them her VIP laminate. Walker did the same.

Beyond the doors, she could hear music, talking, laughter.

'Adam,' she said, looking straight into his eyes. 'I'm begging you: don't do this. My husband and daughter are in there – you *know* that. Please don't do this.'

She looked at the security men. Saw Walker's left hand move towards his left hip.

'No,' she gasped.

'Is something wrong?' one of the security men asked.

The taller of the two men took a step towards her.

'*No!*' Hailey screamed at the top of her voice.

Walker turned, pulling the Steyr from his belt.

To Hailey it was as if the entire world had slowed down. As if every movement was in slow motion.

She saw Walker pull the Steyr free . . . saw him shoot the taller security guard in the face . . . saw the bullet shatter bone, tear through his skull and explode from the back of his head, carrying away a flux of brain matter and blood.

The guard had barely hit the floor when Walker shot the other man, pumping two bullets into his chest. The first of them shattered his sternum, the second burst one lung and erupted from his back. A huge crimson slick of blood splashed across the wall as the second bullet exited. It looked as if someone had thrown red paint at the brickwork.

The guard slumped to the ground.

Hailey took her chance. She launched herself at Walker, but he saw her clumsy attack too soon.

He slammed the butt of the automatic against her forehead, throwing her backwards through the doors into the ballroom.

Hailey felt pain filling her skull. Unconsciousness began to envelop her.

Pushing open the doors, he stepped past her, opening the case with the guns inside.

Through a haze of pain, Hailey saw him pull the MP5 free. She saw him slam in one of the magazines.

The Steyr in one hand, the sub-machine-gun in the other, he stood gazing at the throng of people before him.

For what seemed like an eternity, no one moved.

Every pair of eyes in the place was fixed on Walker.

And on the weapons he held.

The silence was unearthly.

Then, as if a switch had been thrown, everything began moving again.

From somewhere inside the ballroom there came a scream.

Walker opened fire.

113

HE SWEPT THE sub-machine-gun back and forth, firing quick bursts. The muzzle flash left a searing white imprint on Hailey's retina. The sound of the weapon filled her ears as she tried to crawl away.

The noise was absolutely deafening, and Hailey feared for a second that her eardrums had been ruptured by the savage sound-blasts.

Spent cartridges rained down like brass confetti, some landing on the marble floor.

The stink of cordite stung her nostrils.

Through a haze of pain she saw the appalling results of those first few bursts of firing.

Bullets had thudded into wood, glass and flesh alike. Chunks were blasted from tables. Crystal was shattered by the heavy-grain slugs. Some of the windows at the rear of the ballroom were hit, holes punched through them as if by invisible fists.

Hailey saw two men being shot. One pitched backwards over a table, blood spouting from a wound in his throat. The other collapsed onto a pure white tablecloth, crimson spilling out around his upper body.

Screams began to fill the air.

Walker calmly slammed a fresh magazine into the MP5, and opened up again.

Apart from one exit door to the rear, there was only one way in and out of the ballroom – and he was blocking it. Standing there like some murderous sentinel, pouring fire into those before him.

His face was expressionless, only creased occasionally by the effort of changing magazines – something he did with chilling efficiency.

A woman in her forties took a bullet in the back. It smashed her right scapula and burst from her chest. As she tried to rise, to continue her escape, another slug tore off the left side of her face.

The man with her hesitated a moment, realized he could do nothing to help, and turned to flee. But two more shots cut through his spine, and sent him toppling over a table.

Walker muttered under his breath as the hammer slammed down on an empty chamber. He gently laid the sub-machine-gun down for a moment, and gripped the Steyr in both hands.

The slide flew back as each shot was squeezed off.

Very few missed a target.

Hailey was murmuring something under her breath, her lips moving silently as she crawled across the floor, touching one hand to her forehead. When she pulled it away, she saw blood.

She had to get out of here.

Get help.

Find Becky and Rob.

If they were still alive?

Walker put the Steyr aside, slammed a fresh magazine into the MP5, then pulled the Scorpion from the case, too.

Holding one in each hand, he advanced towards the other terrified people in the ballroom.

Above him, the chandelier that dominated the room looked like thousands of frozen tears.

He raked the ceiling with fire from the Scorpion, and stood watching as the massive crystal construction wavered, then came loose.

It struck the floor with a deafening crash, pieces of glass flying in all directions like gleaming shrapnel.

Those crammed into the one doorway, trying to get out, now redoubled their efforts – those at the back of the crush aware that Walker was no more than twenty yards from them.

He saw James Marsh. Looked directly into his eyes.

Walker shot him.

Dotted lines of death appeared across Marsh's chest and abdomen as the bullets hit him, a number of them exiting from his back, carrying pinkish-red lung tissue with them. It spattered those who stood behind him.

Walker stepped over the corpse and shot down three more people.

The room was not acoustically suited to such thunderous noise, and each fresh explosion of gunfire reverberated off the walls and ceiling, deafening those who were about to die.

Walker emptied a magazine into the terrified crowd that clogged the doorway.

Many of the bodies remained upright because of the crush. Others toppled backwards, or sideways, like bloodied mannequins.

More of the windows were blasted out by bullets, the sound of crashing glass now mingling with the staccato rattle of the submachine-guns and the shrieks of pain and fear.

Hailey managed to rise to her knees, tears streaming down her cheeks.

From her position behind an overturned table, she could see Walker spraying the rest of the terrified guests with bullets. Saw them falling in untidy heaps. Others were trying to escape through the broken windows. She saw one man even punching glass out of a smashed frame, trying to pull himself through to safety.

Walker shot him in the head and back.

She looked towards him, then at the door behind her.

Could she make it?

He fired off another burst.

Hailey saw him stop to reload.

Now, run! Go now, for God's sake!

She got to her feet and hurtled for the doors that led out into the foyer.

Walker chambered a round and prepared to fire again.

Hailey was inches from the door when he spotted her.

114

THE FIRST BURST of gunfire swept over her head, missing her by less than six inches.

Hailey threw herself down, feeling the air part above her, shredded by the high-velocity shells.

She saw holes blasted in the double-doors. Then, to her horror, she saw them open. Saw people standing there.

Security guards.

The second burst took out two men. Hailey screamed as she saw one reel backwards, his right eye socket drilled empty by a bullet.

The other man dropped to his knees, hands clasped to his stomach as if to hold the blood in. She noted, with horror, that part of his lower intestine was bulging out through the gaping hole in his belly, like a bloodied swollen worm. He fell forward.

Hailey made another dash for the door, and this time made it.

She threw herself to the floor, then rolled. Chanced a look over her shoulder to see if Walker was pursuing her.

He wasn't.

Find a phone. Get the police here now, while there's still someone left alive.

The foyer was deserted.

When the shooting had begun, she assumed that anyone else in the hotel had fled. Or perhaps, even now, some were cowering in their rooms.

The reception area was totally empty.

She looked around desperately, the rattle of gunfire still filling her ears.

Deafened by the continuing blasts, her face bloodied, her head reeling, she staggered towards the reception desk.

Towards the phone.

She lifted the receiver and jabbed out three nines.

Tears were coursing down her cheeks.

She waited for the phone to be answered.

Waited . . .

Were Becky and Rob already dead?

Waited . . .

Her daughter and her husband, both riddled with bullets?

She looked towards the open ballroom doors, expecting Walker to emerge at any minute – his weapons aimed at her.

The phone was still ringing.

Inside the ballroom the bursts of fire were replaced by an appalling silence, now broken only by screams of agony and moans of suffering.

He must be reloading yet again, she thought, her body racked by sobs.

Jesus, how much fucking ammunition did he have with him?

To Hailey it seemed as if this nightmare had been happening for hours.

Less than six minutes had actually passed since he'd fired the first shot.

'Emergency here. Which service do you require?' She heard the calm voice in her ear.

'Police and ambulance,' she said, trying to control her gasping. 'Please hurry.'

'Can you give me your name?' the voice asked.

'Help me,' Hailey shrieked.

'I need your name and . . .'

'The Pavilion Hotel. For God's sake, send someone to the Pavilion Hotel now, please,' she begged and dropped the phone.

Inside the ballroom the shooting had begun again.

115

THREE MEMBERS OF Waterhole were already dead.

Adam Walker could see them lying on the marble floor, each in a pool of his own blood.

Nearly everyone else inside the ballroom was either dead or wounded by now . . . Apart from a small group still trying to force their way through the emergency exit at the rear.

There were corpses piled up in front of them, and the stench of blood and excrement filled the air as densely as the more pungent odour of cordite.

Walker laid the MP5 on a table and pulled the Sig-Sauer P225 from his belt.

Nicholas Barber turned to face him, his features contorted with fear and splashed by blood.

'Please don't kill me,' whimpered the MP, dropping to his knees. He clasped his hands together before him in prayer. 'Please.' He lowered his head slightly, unable to look at the yawning barrel of the Sig.

Walker touched the automatic to his forehead, and he heard a soft rumbling sound. Barber had filled his pants.

'Please,' the MP sobbed.

Walker fired once.

The bullet punched in a portion of Barber's skull, ripped through his brain, and erupted from the back of his head.

He went down like a butchered calf in an abattoir, blood spouting from the hole in his forehead, his body quivering.

Jenny Kenton was lying close by. A bullet had punctured her left eye, blasting the lens of her dark glasses back into the riven socket. Pieces of glass had been forced into the blood-filled hole. Vitreous liquid was spilling down her cheek. Another bullet had punched in two of her front teeth, and ripped away most of her top lip.

Her blonde hair was matted crimson.

Beside her, Trudi was trying to crawl away on one arm, the other having been practically severed at the elbow by a 9mm round. The shattered bone protruded whitely amidst a bleeding pulp of flesh. Another bullet had torn off her right ear: just the lobe remained attached to her head, her earring still hanging from it grotesquely.

Walker shot her in the face, and moved on.

Something crunched beneath his feet and he noticed that several teeth lay on the floor. Blown from other dead mouths by his well-placed bullets.

'You fucking cunt!' screamed Craig Levine, turning to face him.

Walker raised the 225 and shot him twice. One bullet entered his mouth and exited through the back of his neck, severing his spine, killing him instantly.

Ray Taylor was slumped over a table nearby, eyes open accusingly. His body had been punctured by more than a dozen shots.

Others, either wounded or hiding, knew that all they could do was wait.

Walker moved swiftly around the room, overturning tables, looking for those who sought to evade him.

He shot in the head each one he found.

As he made his way back towards the main entrance of the ballroom, he realized how hard he was finding it to breathe. The smoke in the room was now choking him too, and he was sheathed in sweat. He took a glass of mineral water from one of the tables as he passed and drained its contents, wiping his mouth with the back of his hand.

Hot work.

Walker heard breathing. Low, guttural, close by. To his left.

He noticed that two tables had been pushed together on their sides, as if to form some kind of rampart. A bloodied tablecloth had been drawn over the top.

Walker could see bullet holes through both the tabletops and the cloth.

He stood still, ears alert for the sound.

He heard something else: a faint whimper.

He raised the Scorpion and aimed it at the two tables. Taking hold of the cloth, Walker pulled it away and looked down.

There were two of them hiding there.

The man had been hit in the shoulder, but it looked as if the bullet had gone right through.

His companion, whom he sheltered, was unharmed.

Walker smiled. 'I wondered where you were,' he said quietly. 'Hello, Becky.'

116

'GET IT OVER with.'

Rob Gibson looked up defiantly at Walker, one arm around his daughter, the other hand clamped firmly to his shoulder. Blood was seeping through his fingers.

Walker pulled the tables aside and offered his hand to Rob to help him up.

Becky was crying softly.

'If you're going to kill us, then do it, you insane fucker,' Rob snarled.

Walker lashed out with the butt of the automatic, and caught Rob across the face.

Becky grabbed at her father, clinging to his leg as he rose uncertainly, blood now running down his cheek from the new cut just below his eye.

'Watch your language in front of your daughter, Rob,' Walker said evenly, staring straight into his eyes.

'At least let Becky go,' Rob offered.

'You want to stay with your dad, don't you?' Walker said, smiling.

Becky looked up at him with swollen red eyes. She sniffed back tears.

'You bastard,' rasped Rob.

Walker struck him again. A blow that cracked two of Rob's front teeth and sent him reeling backwards.

'I warned you about your language,' Walker hissed, pointing the automatic.

Rob hauled himself tentatively upright, his head spinning.

He already felt sick from the wound in his arm. It felt as if his shoulder was on fire. A dreadful numbness had begun to envelop that arm as far down as his elbow. He could barely move his fingers. He ran his tongue over the edges of his teeth, then spat blood.

'Why are you doing this?' Rob asked.

Walker grinned. 'Hailey asked me the same thing,' he said.

'Where is she?'

'I don't know.'

'If you've hurt her, I'll . . .' Rob snapped.

Walker pushed the 225 towards his face.

'You'll what, Rob?' he said flatly. 'You're hardly in a position to threaten me, are you?'

'So tell me *why*?'

'You saw all the photographers out there when you arrived, didn't you? Local newspapers, nationals, television? Can you imagine what they'll make of this? It'll be all over the media tomorrow. You won't be able to pick up a paper or turn on a television without *this* being mentioned. And, the funny thing is, the media *made* it happen. They love things like this: Dunblane, Hungerford, now this. They won't let things rest, you see. They're always talking about how we mustn't forget these tragedies. But what never occurs to them is that by constantly dragging them up, by always reminding people who it was who carried out these atrocities, they're giving other people ideas. They offer us immortality, Rob: immortality to anyone who wants it. But they take no responsibility for what they encourage. It'll be like a feeding frenzy once they get here. And they'll all want to know the name of the person who did this.' He made an expansive gesture with his hand designed to encompass the dozens of bullet-riddled corpses scattered around the room. 'And we're talking about dead celebrities too? It's a media dream!'

Walker smiled.

Rob tried to swallow, but his throat was too dry.

'You did *this* just to get your name in the papers?' he croaked.

'You could say that,' Walker told him.

He pushed a chair towards Rob. 'Sit down,' he instructed. 'You too, Becky.'

They did as they were told.

'Drop the guns.'

The voice came from the bullet-riddled main doors.

All three of them turned.

Hailey stood at the top of the small flight of steps.

She was holding the Steyr in both hands, clumsily aiming it at Walker as best she could.

'The police will be here in a minute,' she said. 'It's over, Adam. Put down the guns.'

'Come in, Hailey,' Walker said, smiling. 'I've been expecting you.'

117

'Mum.'

Becky's mournful cry echoed around the devastated ballroom.

'It's all right, babe,' Hailey called back, taking a step forward. 'It's all right now.'

But it wasn't all right.

Far from it.

Hailey was shaking, the Steyr trembling unsteadily in her grasp. *Christ, it was heavy.*

She looked at the scene before her. The bodies, the blood.

She smelled the coppery odour and the stench of excrement. Her ears were still ringing from the savage fusillade of gunfire.

She saw Becky clinging to Rob's leg, her face glistening with tears. Saw the wound in Rob's arm, blood still trickling over his hand. He had blood on his face, too.

Behind them stood Walker.

No, this was anything but all right.

'What are you going to do, Hailey?' Walker demanded, watching as she moved a little closer, the automatic still pointed towards him.

'Let them go,' Hailey said. 'You've done what you came to do.' She almost stumbled over the outstretched leg of a corpse.

Hailey looked down and saw that it was a young woman, no more than thirty.

Eyes open and gazing blankly at the ceiling.

A bullet hole in her left breast, another in her hand.

There was an engagement ring on that shattered hand.

Hailey tore her gaze away – back to Walker and her family.

'Rob,' she called.

'Rob saved Becky,' Walker interjected. 'Wasn't that good of him? Just like *I* saved her that day in the shopping centre. Just think, if she'd never got lost, we'd never have met. That must have been fate.'

Hailey continued moving closer.

'Now put the gun down before you do something stupid, Hailey,' Walker ordered.

She shook her head.

'Are you going to shoot me? he asked scornfully. 'You've never fired a gun in your life. Do you know what kind of recoil you get on those automatics? And it's heavy, isn't it? Why don't you just put it down?'

Walker raised the Sig and pressed it to the back of Rob's head. He did the same with the Scorpion, resting the barrel lightly against Becky's skull.

'Even if you manage to shoot me,' Walker said softly, 'even if you kill me with the first shot, my muscles will spasm. My fingers will tighten on these triggers. And *that's* if you even manage to hit me. If your aim is off, you could hit Rob or Becky. If I were you, I'd put the gun down. For *all* our sakes.'

She hesitated, slowed her pace.

Stopped no more than ten feet away from him. Hailey glared at him with hatred in her eyes.

'If you kill *them*, then I *want* to die,' she said angrily. 'So then I can shoot and it doesn't matter, because I swear to God I'll get *you*.'

'Fighting talk,' Walker said mockingly.

Rob stood still, the metal of the gun barrel cold against his scalp.

He could feel Becky clinging to his leg, and he reached out with his free hand to touch her cheek.

She clung tighter.

Think! What the fuck do you do?

He closed his eyes so tightly that white stars danced behind their lids.

THINK!

The table close to him was relatively untouched. A half-drunk bottle of champagne still stood on it. So, too, did a plate of food . . . knives, forks, a broken glass.

He leant against it, steadying himself, as a wave of nausea swept over him.

Hailey looked at him in concern.

'He's losing blood,' Walker said. 'Put down the gun, Hailey.'

'You're going to kill us anyway,' she rasped. 'Why not just do it?'

'If I kill you, who's going to tell people what happened here tonight?' Walker grinned. 'No, someone has to survive.' His smile broadened. 'And I'm going to let *you* choose who that is.'

Hailey frowned, the Steyr wavering.

'Do you understand me?' Walker continued.

Hailey took a step closer, her heart hammering against her ribs.

'You decide,' Walker said evenly. 'Your daughter or your husband? Which one dies?'

118

'ADAM, PLEASE,' HAILEY said, the colour draining from her cheeks. 'For God's sake, don't make me choose. I'll do anything. but, please God, don't kill them.'

'God has very little to do with this, Hailey,' said Walker flatly. 'He's had very little to do with anything in my life. Now choose.'

'Shoot *me*, you mad fuck,' snarled Rob.

'Shut up,' Walker snapped, pushing the barrel hard against the back of his head.

'Come on, do it,' Rob insisted, raising his voice.

'Perhaps I should start with Becky,' Walker announced, trailing the barrel of the Scorpion over her silken hair.

'Please,' Hailey begged.

'Put the gun down,' Walker ordered.

'Come on, shoot me – or are you too gutless?' Rob persisted, half turning to look at his captor.

Hailey felt the Steyr wavering in her grip. Its weight seemed to increase by the second.

'Choose, Hailey,' Walker said again.

'I can't,' she said, her voice a whisper.

'Choose,' he said loudly. There was anger in his tone.

Becky was crying uncontrollably now, seeing the anguish on her mother's face.

'I need you as my witness, Hailey,' Walker told her. 'I need you to tell people what happened here tonight. I need you to tell them my name.'

Hailey felt faint. She looked from one face to another.

Her daughter?

Her husband?

The guns at their heads.

No, this wasn't right. No one should have to make a decision like this. Madness lay along that road.

Rob avoided her gaze.

Was he trying to make it easier for her?

Hailey could feel tears running down her cheeks as she continued looking from face to face.

Becky was crying. 'Mum,' she whined, that plaintive agonized call for help more devastating than all the furious blasts of fire that had gone before.

Again Hailey felt faint.

'Choose,' Walker told her.

She raised the Steyr so that it was pointing at his face.

Walker merely shook his head.

Hailey looked at Rob.

I love you!

He met her gaze. Nodded almost imperceptibly.

He wants Walker to shoot him. Save Becky. Save your daughter. Save our daughter.

There was an unearthly calmness in Rob's eyes. A resignation.

It said, '*I understand.*'

She studied his ravaged features. The cuts on his face. The blood on his jacket. The wound in his shoulder.

Some of his red fluid had splashed onto Becky's little party dress.

Becky?

The Scorpion machine-pistol pressed against her skull.

So much love.

'You know what?' Walker observed. 'You're right: no one should have to make a decision like that, should they? How *would* you choose?' He shook his head. 'Let *me* decide for you.'

He pulled both triggers simultaneously.

119

Gunfire.

Screams.

Sounds welded together to form one monstrous cacophony.

Hailey's eyes bulged madly in their sockets as she saw her child and her husband shot down.

She could hear screams, but she was barely aware they were hers. And yet they rose like the gunsmoke – screams torn raw from the base of her spine.

Screams of complete abject devastation.

She was still screaming as she pumped the trigger of the Steyr.

Once. Twice. Three times. More.

The recoil was massive.

The pistol slammed back against the heel of her hand. The muzzle-flash blinded her. Pieces of lead and fragments of carbon flew out. Some struck her cheeks. The spent cartridge cases spun into the air and bounced off the floor.

The first bullet missed.

The second caught Walker in the chest.

It tore through his lung, erupted from his back, and sent him toppling.

The third hit him in the left forearm, shattered bone, caused him to drop the Scorpion.

The fourth hit him in the thigh.

Severed the femoral artery.

Massive gouts of blood began to spurt high into the air as he hit the floor. Some of the crimson fluid struck Hailey in the face, but she continued to advance. Continued to pump the trigger.

From such close range it was difficult to miss.

Another hit him in the stomach.

Green bile mingled with the dark blood as his spleen and gall bladder were lacerated by a high-calibre slug travelling at over 1,500 feet a second.

He was lying on his back, the Sig still gripped in his right hand.

Hailey stopped firing.

She stood over him. Between the bodies of her husband and her child.

She knew there was no point checking to see if they were still alive.

Was there?

Do you believe in miracles?

Her hearing was practically gone. It felt as if she'd been struck repeatedly with a hammer.

Numbness.

Her throat was dry. Clogged, like her nostrils, with the stench of cordite and gunpowder.

And blood.

Her husband's blood.

Her daughter's blood.

Walker was smiling slightly, blood dribbling over his lips.

He was trying to speak, but the effort seemed too great.

Somewhere in the distance Hailey heard sirens. Drawing closer.

'Tell them,' Walker managed to gasp, and the effort caused him to vomit. Bloodied matter gushed from his mouth as he coughed. 'Tell them who did this.'

Hailey moved like an automaton, eyes blank, movements mechanical.

She picked up the Scorpion and wiped the butt and frame.

Then she did the same with the MP5.

Walker watched in bemusement.

She wrenched the Sig from his hand and did the same.

Then, as he watched, she gripped each of the weapons in her own hands.

She held each to her breast for fleeting seconds, as if it were some kind of suckling child. Then she dropped each on the table behind her.

The sirens were really loud now.

Hailey knelt close to him. Between the bodies of her husband and her daughter.

'My witness,' he gasped, the smile fading slightly. 'Tell . . . who . . . did this.'

Hailey spun the Steyr in her fist, pushed the barrel up under her chin.

Why live?

If Walker had possessed the strength, he would have tried to stop her.

She fired.

Blew the top of her own head off.

'No,' Walker gasped.

Hailey's body fell sideways, across that of Becky.

The sirens were even closer.

Walker heard urgent footsteps rumbling through the hotel, towards the dining room. Voices were raised. Shouts heard.

He saw uniformed men.

He raised a hand – but barely an inch.

Blood was still jetting madly from the wound in his thigh, but now even that was beginning to abate.

His heart was stopping.

He felt so cold.

And afraid.

He closed his eyes . . .

EXTRACT FROM THE *MIRROR*, 17 APRIL:

. . . All four members of the band Waterhole were killed in the massacre, which also claimed the lives of sixty-three other guests.

Police say that the attack seemed motiveless, and as yet they have no idea why it was carried out, or why Waterhole were singled out.

Fingerprints found on four weapons discovered at the scene of the massacre have been identified as belonging to Hailey Gibson, who, police believe, murdered her own husband and daughter as well as so many other party guests, before finally taking her own life.

All the casualties have been identified except one man in his early thirties, thought to have been the last of Gibson's victims. He was dead upon arrival in hospital, and his identity still remains a mystery . . .

Just when all seems fine and I'm pain-free,
You jab another pin, you jab another pin in me . . .
Metallica

He who despairs over an event is a coward,
but he who holds hope for the human condition is
a fool.

Albert Camus